Praise for Anna C

Murder by Misrule was selected as one of Kirkus Review's Best Indie Books of 2014.

"Castle's characters brim with zest and real feeling... Though the plot keeps the pages turning, the characters, major and minor, and the well-wrought historical details will make readers want to linger in the 16th century. A laugh-out loud mystery that will delight fans of the genre." — Kirkus, starred review

"*Murder by Misrule* is a delightful debut with characters that leap off the page, especially the brilliant if unwilling detective Francis Bacon and his street smart man Tom Clarady. Elizabeth Tudor rules, but Anna Castle triumphs." — Karen Harper, NY Times best-selling author of *The Queen's Governess*

"Well-researched... *Murder by Misrule* is also enormously entertaining; a mystery shot through with a series of misadventures, misunderstandings, and mendacity worthy of a Shakespearian comedy." — M. Louisa Locke, author of the Victorian San Francisco Mystery Series

"Castle's period research is thorough but unobtrusive, and her delight in the clashing personalities of her crime-fighting duo is palpable: this is the winning fictional odd couple of the year, with Bacon's near-omniscience being effectively grounded by Clarady's street smarts. The book builds effectively to its climax, and a last-minute revelation that is particularly well-handled, but readers will most appreciate the wry humor. An extremely promising debut." — Steve Donoghue, Historical Novel Society

"Historical mystery readers take note: *Murder by Misrule* is a wonderful example of Elizabethan times brought to life...a blend of Sherlock Holmes and history." — D. Donovan, eBook Reviewer, Midwest Book Review

"I love when I love a book! *Murder by Misrule* by Anna Castle was a fantastic read. Overall, I really liked this story and highly recommend it." — Book Nerds

Praise for *Death by Disputation*

Death by Disputation won the 2015 Chaucer Awards First In Category Award for the Elizabethan/Tudor period.

"Castle's style shines ... as she weaves a complex web of scenarios and firmly centers them in Elizabethan culture and times." — D. Donovan, eBook Reviewer, Midwest Book Review

" I would recommend *Death by Disputation* to any fan of historical mysteries, or to anyone interested in what went on in Elizabethan England outside the royal court." — E. Stephenson, Historical Novel Society

"Accurate historical details, page turning plot, bodacious, lovable and believable characters, gorgeous depictions and bewitching use of language will transfer you through time and space back to Elizabethan England." — Edi's Book Lighthouse

"This second book in the Francis Bacon mystery series is as strong as the first. At times bawdy and rowdy, at times thought-provoking … Castle weaves religious-political intrigue, murder mystery, and Tom's colorful friendships and love life into a tightly-paced plot." — Amber Foxx, Indies Who Publish Everywhere

Praise for *The Widows Guild*

The Widows Guild was longlisted for the 2017 Historical Novel Society's Indie Award.

"As in Castle's earlier book, *Murder by Misrule*, she brings the Elizabethan world wonderfully to life, and if Francis Bacon himself seems a bit overshadowed at times in this novel, it's because the great, fun creation of the Widow's Guild itself easily steals the spotlight. Strongly Recommended." — Editor's Choice, Historical Novel Society.

Praise for *Publish and Perish*

Won an Honorable Mention for Mysteries in Library Journal's 2017 Indie Ebook Awards.

"In this aptly titled fourth book in the Francis Bacon series, Castle combines her impressive knowledge of English religion and politics during the period with masterly creativity. The result is a lively, clever story that will leave mystery fans delighted.—**Emilie Hancock, Mount Pleasant Regional Lib., SC, for Library Journal.**

Also by Anna Castle

The Francis Bacon Mystery Series

Murder by Misrule
Death by Disputation
The Widow's Guild
Publish and Perish
Let Slip the Dogs
The Spymaster's Brother
Now and Then Stab

Bacon's Dozen: Thirteen Historical Fiction Short Stories

The Professor & Mrs. Moriarty Mystery Series

Moriarty Meets His Match
Moriarty Takes His Medicine
Moriarty Brings Down the House
Moriarty Lifts the Veil

The Cunning Woman Mystery Series

The Case of the Spotted Tailor
The Case of the Tangled Maypole
The Case of the Miscast Curse

LOCK UP HONESTY

A Francis Bacon Mystery — Book 8

ANNA CASTLE

Lock Up Honesty
A Francis Bacon Mystery — #8

Print Edition | January 2022
Discover more works by Anna Castle at www.annacastle.com

Cover design by Jennifer Quinlan
Editorial services by Jennifer Quinlan, Historical Editorial
Chapter ornaments created by Alvaro_cabrera at Freepik.com.

ISBN-13: 978-1-945382-58-1
Library of Congress Control Number: 9781945382581
Produced in the United States of America

ONE

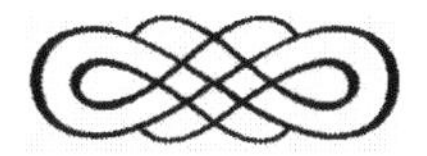

7 November 1594, Gray's Inn, Westminster

"Let us now raise our cups to welcome our newest barrister, *Master* Thomas Clarady!" The treasurer raised high his cup. The assembled members of Gray's Inn cheered as they echoed the gesture. "Mr. Clarady!" Their shouts rang from the hammerbeam roof.

Tom stood beside his bench as the roar washed over him. He bowed, first to the benchers on the dais, then to the men at the tables stretching the length of the hall. The society boasted over two hundred members, most of whom were in residence in the middle of Michaelmas term. Most had lingered after supper to mark the occasion — and enjoy a cup of the excellent hollock Tom had supplied.

He reveled in the cheers, though some men made only a show of lifting their cups. And he hadn't failed to notice the emphasis on the title *Mister* in the treasurer's toast, as if pointing out that the title might not be deserved. Some Graysians would always consider him the son of a tradesman, whatever he might achieve over the course of his life.

What did it matter? He'd passed the bar. He'd paid his dues, literally and figuratively. He'd met every requirement and risen to every challenge. He'd learned

Law French, the barbarous jargon used only by English lawyers. He'd made a special effort in the past year to participate in every moot court and legal exercise to demonstrate his knowledge of the law. Yesterday, he'd taken his oath of allegiance to the crown. He was a barrister-at-law in Her Majesty's courts and thus incontrovertibly a gentleman. Tonight, he would rejoice in this first giant step toward his destiny.

The second step, attaining his livery from the Court of Wards, came next. If all went according to plan, he'd win through in a matter of weeks. But that bitter battle could take one night off.

The cheering died down. He resumed his seat in the middle of one of the long tables. He turned to his companion, his first true friend at Gray's. "Less than I hoped for, but better than I feared."

"Nonsense," Benjamin Whitt replied. "They're all proud of you." He raised his cup again. "I know I am."

Tom's heart swelled with affection for the long-faced, long-limbed man folded onto the bench beside him. Ben hadn't changed much in the seven years since they'd met. A few faint lines at the corners of his eyes and a little fullness under the jaw, mostly hidden by a thick brown beard. He'd lost his melancholy air, that mournful hound-dog look. Tom had thought it part of his nature. Now the man radiated contentment like a brick-lined hearth. Family life suited him.

"Couldn't have done it without you, old chum." Tom punched him lightly on the shoulder. "I took your measure the day I moved into your chambers. I knew you were the man to follow. Less gallantry, more scholarship. I was green as grass, but even then I knew I couldn't charm my way past the bar. I'd have to do the actual work. Study hard. Learn things from books. You were the expert at that, and you shared it with me. For which I am eternally grateful." He raised his cup, then drained it.

He reached for the jug on the table. Enough left for one more round.

"I was a tiresome old lump back then, wasn't I?" Ben said. "I might never have ventured into the city if it weren't for you. We complemented one another. You were the sail; I was the anchor."

"Yet I'm the one who stayed put." Tom had changed far more than Ben. He'd lost the brashness of youth, shedding it along with the garish wardrobe he'd brought with him that first year. The memory made him laugh.

"What a spectacle I must have been! Strutting about in my yellow stockings and pink garters, making sure my robes flapped open so my fine clothes could be seen. It's no wonder this lot had their doubts about me."

"I never did." Ben smiled. "You had the style of a popinjay, but you were determined to make good, whatever it took. And not just because your father wanted it. You saw this society as a castle you had to conquer."

"Not conquer. I don't need to own the place. I just wanted them to let me in. Which they did, thanks to Mr. Bacon. He's helped me hang on by showing his acceptance."

Tom had come to Gray's at the age of nineteen, trailing in a lord's wake. He'd had nothing but a smattering of Latin, a ready smile, and his native wit. And a full purse, which smoothed a lot of rough patches. But he lacked the central requirement of gentility. His father had been captain of his own ship and had grown rich through privateering, but a captain was a tradesman nonetheless.

Captain Clarady had wanted his son to rise. He'd made a bargain to pay Francis Bacon's debts in exchange for tutelage, thus setting Tom on the long road to the bar.

Bacon's name had shielded Tom from the scowls of the senior members. Tom had learned to ignore the lesser slights of the junior ones. Ben's honest friendship had made it all tolerable.

"You've learned a lot from Mr. Bacon, I'll wager." Ben sounded envious. "Being in the same room when he chooses to speak about the law or philosophy. Or politics, ethics, gardening . . ."

"More like his aching head, Sunday's boring sermon, and how you kept him waiting for five whole minutes out of doors in a light drizzle."

They laughed at their old tutor's foibles. Bacon could be as fussy as an old man, though he was only thirty-three.

Ben asked, "Where is he anyway? I should think he'd be here tonight, of all nights. It's his achievement too, in a way."

"He's hiding out at his lodge in Twickenham. He's sick of the inn these days. Sick of Westminster. Sick of everything related to the law or politics." Tom leaned in to murmur, "It's the Attorney Generalship. They've been dangling it over his head for more than a year now. The strain is too much for him."

"Is he all alone out there?" Ben sounded ready to leap into a wherry and dash to the man's rescue.

Tom gave his friend a knowing grin. "Still a few smoldering embers, eh?"

Ben and Bacon had been lovers for a few terms. Ben idolized Bacon — not entirely without reason. But after he passed the bar, he had submitted meekly to the marriage his parents arranged. The couple had forged a solid partnership. Without passion, perhaps, but they'd produced three healthy children.

Ben blushed, one of his endearing traits. "I'm only concerned about his health. He's delicate, as you know. Easily overset."

"Delicate! He'll outlive us all. Trust me, I know everything about his little maladies. His apothecary and I are great friends. And never fear, Bacon has a gift for finding people to take care of him. His current *affaire de coeur*, or perhaps convenience, is Don Antonio Pérez. A *Spaniard*." Tom spat the word. "And sixty years old, if you can believe it." He shuddered.

Ben chuckled. "You give beauty too much importance. It's led you astray more than once. I imagine Señor Pérez is a fascinating individual. I wish I had time to meet him."

Tom grunted. He had no such desire. "I wish you could stay. I'd love to have you at my side in the next few weeks." He'd launched a suit for his livery from the Court of Wards at long last. He would win, eventually, thus freeing himself from his guardian and the court. But the ancient rituals of the suit were notoriously long, costly, and full of pitfalls. He had been a ward for seven years because his father died a few months before Tom's twenty-first birthday. Technically still a minor, the court had leapt at his rich estate. Certain lands owing feudal duty had thrown him into wardship, where he had been trapped by fines for obsolete infractions. He couldn't pay the fines until he was out of wardship, but he couldn't get out of wardship until they were paid.

Such was the logic of the Court of Wards.

"You'll be fine," Ben said. "You're ready. We've been over your list of charges. You have sufficient monies for the court fees, at least."

"And a plan for the rest." Tom owed his guardian three hundred pounds for refusing a marriage she'd proposed for him back in '89. Guardians had the right to arrange marriages for their charges — a holdover from the days when lords feared hostile alliances among their tenants. Never mind that Tom's mother still lived or that most educated gentlemen waited until they neared thirty before marrying.

Lady Russell had deliberately proposed a match she knew he would refuse, or so Tom believed. That had trapped him under her thumb until he paid the value of the marriage, which was based on the amount his bride would have brought to him. Since his guardian controlled his assets, he couldn't raise the funds from his rents. It was a legal paradox, a vicious circle that kept many a man in wardship well into his twenties.

A man at the next table over rose and stepped over his bench. He wobbled a little as he lifted his cup and cried for silence. "I lift my cup to Thomas Clarady. Today, he is made a barrister. Tomorrow, he'll buy a house, and then he'll want a wife to live in it. Watch out for your sisters, my brethren. Comely Tom Clarady is on the prowl!"

Everyone laughed, including Tom. He grinned broadly and raised his cup to the speaker. He didn't mind having a reputation as a gallant, though he wondered that it lingered on. He'd given up his wanton ways when his guardian cut short his allowance.

As the laughter died down, a man a few seats to his right spoke just loudly enough for Tom to hear. "Not *my* sister. My parents aim higher than a tradesman's son." A couple of his chums laughed.

Tom caught Ben's gaze with narrowed eyes. Ben sighed and shook his head. "There will always be a few. I'd chalk it up to envy if I were you and let it go."

"Hmph." Envy might play a role. That churl had a bulbous nose and poor taste. But he had given voice to an opinion many men held and would hold for as long as they lived. Tom couldn't change that for himself, but his son, if he ever had one he could claim, would surpass him, as a son should do.

Ben gave him a wry smile. "You should let Lady Russell arrange a match for you. If you won't borrow the money, I can't see another way out. She knows all sorts of people. How bad could it be?"

"Never." Tom pounded his fist on the table. "I'll be thrice damned if I let that woman choose my wife. She's a Calvinist, Ben. As rigid as a bar of iron. I'll do my own choosing in my own good time."

"Don't wait too long. You're pining for a home of your own. I can see it. You get a wistful look every time I mention my brood or my daily routine."

Tom couldn't argue with that. "I would love riding the bounds of my manor once a week, watching the grain grow and chatting with the tenants." He thought about such things more and more these days. It didn't help that his two best friends — Ben and Trumpet — talked endlessly about the trials of parenthood and estate management. Their words expressed complaints, but anyone could hear the love and pride behind them.

He shrugged it off. "It's more a matter of *if* for me, not *when*. You know why."

"She'll learn to accept it. Fair is fair, after all."

She was Lady Alice Trumpington, aka Trumpet. She was Tom's one true love, as he was hers. That had been the *status quo* for six years — more, as she told it. Nothing could change that central fact of their lives, not husbands or children or professional careers.

She'd married three years ago and had two children already. She'd had little choice in the matter and none in choosing her mate. Women of her rank weren't allowed to remain single or to marry their inferiors.

Tom didn't blame her for making the best of it. Even so, the situation rankled. He glanced at the other men seated at their table. They had broken into two groups. One set shouted insults across the table, while the other had started a round of "Heigh Ho, Nobody Home" complete with harmony. Tom and Ben might have been invisible.

He leaned a little closer just in case. "Her life has grown larger — husband, children, two great houses — while mine has been stuck in the mud. Sometimes I think she likes it that way. She wants to have her cake and eat it too."

"That's not quite fair. The houses and children are her purpose in this world, will she, nill she. Trumpet was never one to shirk her responsibilities. And she's not to blame for your wardship, which is what keeps you in that little room at Bacon House." Ben cocked his head. "She doesn't love him, you know."

"I know." Tom met his friend's eyes. "I do know. You've seen them together. They're less intimate than you and me."

Ben startled. "I never thought of you as —"

Tom held up his hand, laughing. "I didn't mean that. I mean they never stand around in week-old nightshirts scrubbing their teeth and bickering about whose turn it is to pay the laundress. They don't so much as pat each other on the shoulder. They're cordial and courteous, friendly and familiar. That is all. He has his lovers, and she has hers, meaning me. She has to be more discreet about it than he does, but it's not uncommon for persons of their rank."

"You could do that too, in a different way. In my observation, that's how most successful marriages work. Not the love affairs on the side, but the cordiality and cooperation."

"My lord and lady enjoy separate bedchambers in opposite wings. That's a big help."

"If your wife is truly a suitable match, you'll be able to afford all the space you need."

"I know. But I won't abide a devout woman. Church on Sunday and a prayer at bedtime — that's enough for me." He twitched his lips, giving Ben a measuring look. Then he decided to say what he could never tell anyone else. "Here's the truth of it, between you and me and this empty jug. Trumpet is Trumpet. An extraordinary person. She can juggle six balls at once without missing a one. She puts things in boxes — Stephen over there, me over here, the children in a pretty one tied with ribbons. I'm not like that. I'm all or nothing. What if liking my wife turns into loving her? What if she becomes the one who puts the spring in my steps and the whistle on my lips?" He lowered his voice. "If I lose my grand, hopeless passion for Lady Alice, who am I?"

Ben, the truest of friends, did not laugh. "That's a risk, I grant you. But, Tom, you were nineteen when you met her. Allow yourself to change as changes happen. I'm not saying you will. Your love for each other may burn as hot in twenty years, for all I know. Or it may grow into a deep, abiding friendship that leaves room for other loves."

Tom met his friend's wise gaze. "I do want children I can call my own." He blew out a breath. "Bah. Time enough for that trouble when my case is settled. I mean to negotiate a plan for quarterly payments to Lady Russell that won't gobble up all my rents every year. She can be reasonable when she wants to be."

Ben hummed a dubious note. "Let us hope. When will you stand before the court?"

"December second."

"Your birthday?" Ben twitched his lips. "Only two days before the end of term. Cutting it a bit fine, aren't you?"

"Long enough to cope with one setback, though I don't anticipate any. I have my list. I have the money for the court fees, with a margin for an extra bribe or two. I have time before that for a couple of bouts with Lady Russell to persuade her that my plan is good for both of us."

Ben flicked his dark eyebrows. "I'll pray for you."

Not quite the ringing endorsement Tom wanted, but no matter. His plan was sound. Trumpet thought so. Mr. Bacon had refused to render an opinion, but if it had been utter nonsense, he would have said so.

Tom raised his cup one more time. "The day I turn twenty-seven, I'll be a free man. A wealthy man, in point of fact. Also a barrister and a gentleman."

Ben raised his cup. "To freedom!"

Tom drank down the wine. He'd taken a great step this week, no question, even though he couldn't argue a case before the bar for five more years. Nothing happened in a hurry in the courts of Westminster. Passing the bar was more like buying passage on a ship than setting sail. He could start building a practice, though, finding clients to care for, guarding their wealth and their families from cradle to grave.

Everyone would expect him to marry now, as soon as might be. Ben, his mother, his guardian, the benchers at Gray's — even Bacon's apothecary had been asking him teasing questions already. He'd find a wife, one who wouldn't ask too much of him, and buy a house where she could raise their children. They'd want some dogs and a few more horses. He'd have to cultivate the worthies of the county to build a sound reputation as a worthy gentleman himself.

Freedom? Ha! He'd been so intent on the two hurdles in front of him he hadn't surveyed the rest of the course. Now he could see that shaking off the bonds of wardship would only free him to step into another yoke.

TWO

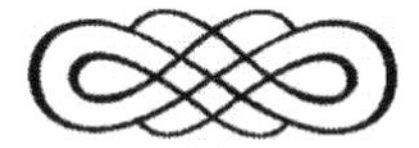

"God Almighty planted a garden." Francis Bacon spoke to the air, knowing his words would rise to heaven. He stood with his fists on his hips, admiring the garden he'd laid out at Twickenham last spring. As intended, it still offered delights to the eye in November.

The rosemary had flourished, growing up to his knees. He had intertwined it with lavender and germander for variety of height and color. These remained green, or grayish green, throughout the winter, delighting the eye even on the starkest days. Clusters of carnations bloomed in shades of pink and yellow, livening the evergreen herbs.

Francis drew in a deep breath redolent of rich earth and sun-warmed lavender. He let it out with a contented sigh. He could stay here in Twickenham forever, tending his gardens and writing his books. The hurly-burly of the royal court could run its fevered courses without him.

"So we compare ourself to God Almighty this morning." Antonio Pérez strolled up to stand beside him. "I'll allow it. You must be feeling as good as I do."

Francis laughed. He did feel good. There was nothing like a night of expert lovemaking to restore a man's bodily vigor and sense of mental well-being. "I'm trying out a first line for an essay. Gardens work wonders for the soul. They merit full recognition."

He'd been working on a set of essays for several years. Most of them dealt with aspects of court life with titles like "Of Cunning" and "Of Adversity." Those themes only wearied him these days. He wanted to write about something more uplifting. He plucked two sprigs of lemon balm and handed one to his friend. He crinkled the other and held it under his own nose, inhaling the wholesome fragrance.

"This garden must be beautiful in the spring." Antonio held his lemon balm under his straight nose as he studied a patch of yarrow, its yellow blossoms dry and stiff. "Now it is a bit sad, I think."

"I disagree. We have a few flowers still, here and there. We have an abundance of greens in the vegetable garden for the pot or a cool sallet. November is a time of preparation for winter. We plant fruit trees against sheltered walls and cover tender plants with straw. After a season of rest, the flowers burst forth fresh and ready for a new year."

Antonio, ever alert to nuance, must have heard the wistfulness in his tone. "A transformation you wish for yourself, eh? A season of rest, then back into the fray." He cupped the back of Francis's neck and laid a kiss on his cheek. "Though I find you lusty enough, *mi cariño*."

Francis accepted the affection — and the accolade — with a smile. Some might wonder at his choosing a lover twice his age. But the turmoils of the past year had worn him out, making him feel old. Antonio might be over sixty, but his wiry frame retained its strength. His short hair and thick beard held as many black strands as silver ones. His dark eyes snapped with intelligence and wry humor, though they were rimmed with sprays of wrinkles.

The wily Spaniard's history of danger and intrigue also threw Francis's troubles into perspective. His life story was worthy of a revenge play by Thomas Kyd, who had died recently from injuries sustained in Bridewell

Prison. While serving as a trusted secretary of King Philip, Antonio had conspired with the Princess of Éboli to assassinate a rival. He'd been held prisoner in various castles for a dozen years, escaping three times. The last time, two years ago, he'd crossed the Pyrenees in the depth of winter disguised as a shepherd.

He'd made his way to France, gaining King Henri's favor by selling tidbits from his store of secrets from the Spanish court. Anthony Bacon had invited him to bring his wares to England. He'd found a ready audience — and Francis — in the circle around Lord Essex. Whether his secrets were worth the hundred pounds' of lands Her Majesty had settled on him remained to be seen.

In the meantime, Francis enjoyed the old wolf's company. He liked spending time with an outsider who took an independent view of the machinations of the English court.

"If only I could stay here," Francis said. "I'm a better gardener than I am a courtier."

"How is that?"

Francis pointed to the nearest fruit tree. "I planted those medlars only five years ago, yet see how much fruit they bear."

"I look forward to sampling it. I hope it is very sweet."

"Tonight, perhaps," Francis said. "But attend, please. I am drawing an analogy."

Antonio stepped back into a bow, spreading his arms wide to signify his obedience.

Francis rewarded him with a kingly nod. "My garden bears fruit in abundance after only five years. Yet I planted myself in Her Majesty's service eighteen years ago — eighteen! — when she sent me to France with her ambassador to study Continental law. Since then, I have never refused a commission or evaded a command. On the contrary, I have laid my talents at her feet, ever seeking ways to further her goals. My roots are deep, but my branches are barren. That early planting has borne no fruit whatsoever."

Antonio offered him a sympathetic pout. "Monarchs have many trees, do they not? All striving to reach the rays of the sun. Your queen demands absolute loyalty, as do they all, but she is sparing with her rewards. What can be done? That is the way of the world. But you, *mi cariño*, you need an end to this wearisome game. You need rest, which is why you are here poking about in these fragrant weeds."

"They're not weeds. But I do need rest, and more than a few days." Francis sighed again, less bitterly this time. It helped simply to be understood. "Though even this refuge may be too close to court. Perhaps I should run away to another country. Denmark, perhaps. Won't you come with me? We could disguise ourselves as fishermen and hide among the barrels of herring."

"Denmark! What would you do in so cold a land? Worry and plot. The same as here."

"I would hide away in a high tower filled with books. I would lie on a bed covered with bearskins and read until spring came."

Antonio laughed, a rich, warm sound. "In that case, I will come with you. The bearskins will keep us warm."

A flash of color blazed through one of the oval openings in the hedge bordering the front of the garden. Francis trotted over to see a man in a mustard-yellow suit striding toward the front of the house.

A visitor? A messenger? Francis didn't want either one. "What now?"

"Quick, let us hide," Antonio said, not moving.

Francis let his shoulders slump. "They'd find me. They always do." He led the way through the geometry of garden paths and an oak-trimmed doorway set into the red-brick wall. This led them directly to the front of the simple three-story lodge.

The man turned toward them and bowed. He pulled a square of paper from the pouch at his waist. "Mr. Bacon?"

Francis held out a hand. "Pay him, won't you, Antonio?"

"Me?" The Spaniard treated the messenger to an apologetic shrug. "I do not bring money out to survey the weeds."

"It's all right, Mr. Bacon," the man said. "The sender paid me. But I'm to wait for a reply."

"Very well." Francis recognized Tom's hand on the outer square. He slit the seal with the point of his knife, replacing the blade in the scabbard at the small of his back. He read the note and blew out a disgusted breath. "Tell him he doesn't need me. If the clerk asks for more money, he must swallow his pride and pay it. There is no other option."

The messenger's lips moved as he repeated the message under his breath. Then he bowed again and left.

Francis spoke to Antonio. "Tom wants me to come back and review his list of payments again. His last large fee is due next week, and he's worried about not having enough. He wants me to tell him all will be well. I could do that from here, although I'd be lying. Who can predict the outcome of a case in the most corrupt court in England?"

"Roberto Diavolo, perhaps." Antonio had quickly learned that mocking Robert Cecil, effective master of the Court of Wards, would win him favor at Essex House. "Their corruption is like a contagion. Your young friend should take care not to catch it. Yes, he must pay, but he must also object. When the day comes that you accept bribery as natural and right, that is the day you lose your soul."

"Mine is long gone, then. It may not be natural, and it certainly isn't right, but if you don't pay, you can't move forward." He turned back to the garden, hoping to regain that sense of peace. "Let me show you the orchard." He held out a hand, which Antonio clasped.

"I am all eagerness to see these peaches of which you speak so proudly. Your lord uncle has given you that much fruit for your years of service, has he not?"

Francis had begged slips of Italian peach trees from his uncle, Lord Burghley. "I suppose he has." Small reward for years of advice papers and delicate translations.

They had scarcely strolled inside the walled orchard when hoofbeats sounded on the road leading south.

"What now?" Francis shook his hand free and ran over to climb up a ladder left leaning against the wall. He was showing off a little, exhibiting his still-youthful agility and his well-shaped legs. Peering over the wall, he saw a brown mare trotting up the lane bearing a man in green-and-white livery — Tudor colors.

He tilted his head to the sky with a cry of frustration. "Will they give me no peace?" He hopped down and beckoned for Antonio to come back to the house. "It's from Nonsuch, I assume."

This folded square bore the Lord Chamberlain's seal. Francis opened it and read the note aloud to his friend. Why not? He could see at a glance it was of no importance.

His Lordship's assistant desired to know if Mr. Bacon still required lodging at Nonsuch, given that Her Majesty would be removing to Somerset House within the week. The palace was crowded, as usual. If accommodations were to be provided, Mr. Bacon should advise them forthwith.

"Forthwith?" Antonio's dark eyebrows arched.

"Without delay." Francis spoke to the messenger. "Tell my Lord Chamberlain's assistant that Mr. Bacon will not be returning to Nonsuch either this week or the next."

The man waited, plainly expecting some gratuity. Francis treated him to a level gaze until the churl returned to his horse.

Francis watched him ride off. A waste of everyone's time and effort. "They should house me in the stables since I'm little more than a nag to be trotted between Her Majesty and my Lord of Essex, braying feebly."

"Never a nag, *precioso.*" Antonio laughed, patting Francis's shoulder. "Perhaps a fine pony, strutting across the field to show his excellent conformation and skill."

Francis rolled his eyes. "They stopped bickering about my qualifications sometime last spring. Now it is purely a battle of wills, which my lord refuses to admit he's lost."

He gazed toward the orchard walls. A powerful sense of loss overtook him for the beautiful morning laid waste by mundanities. "Let's go inside and find something to drink."

"Bueno," Antonio said. "You may show me your peaches later." He said it with a comical leer that coaxed a smile, if a wry one, from Francis.

They poured themselves cups of beer and settled in chairs in the large front room. Francis loved this "little hunting box," as he liked to call it. The whitewashed walls shone softly in the light admitted through the leaded windows set in both the front and side walls. A long table stood ready for feasts or experiments under the two square side windows. An assortment of chairs with cushions and footstools were arranged in clusters before the fireplace and along the kitchen wall. The room could accommodate a whole party of men gathered to debate philosophy between meals and walks in the garden.

Francis hadn't invited such a group here for some time. He couldn't bear questions about the status of his bid for the Attorney Generalship. At this point, the thought of debating political ethics made him physically ill.

His churlish humor made him cut down every effort to cheer him up. "The horse is long dead, my wise friend. Yet my lord keeps flogging it, and Her Majesty refuses to let it be dragged away."

She wouldn't give him the post, but she wouldn't let him withdraw from consideration either. She kept him dangling to teach her young favorite a lesson in power. Francis had nothing to do with it, nothing at all. It had taken a year of rising hopes and crushing dismissals to understand that truth.

He sat in his favorite chair and lifted his feet to a low stool. Antonio took a chair an arm's length away. They began a desultory conversation about the contents of the larder. Could they content themselves with a simple dinner and a simpler supper, or should they send the cook to town for more provisions? Antonio suggested they might venture downstream to Ham or Petersham to sample the local taverns.

Francis rejected that idea out of hand. He hated public places. "The food will be vile, and the air will reek of tobacco smoke. Noisy drunkards will stumble over our feet. Let's stay home. Let's put on comfortable old clothes and slippers. We'll snuggle by the fire with our bowls of pottage and talk about poetry." He raised his cup to Antonio. "To a peaceful life!"

The Spaniard raised his cup and drank. "Something neither of us is likely to enjoy."

No sooner had he spoken the words than a series of sharp raps sounded on the front door. Francis glared at his friend. "You had to say it, didn't you? You summoned a demon to add to my torment."

"Shall I grab a poker from the fire and chase him off?"

"Yes. I would like to see that." Francis grunted and got to his feet. "Which is it this time? Anthony or my Lord of Essex?"

"One from each. It is half past nine, after all. They have not heard from you since yesterday and will have a hundred new questions."

A man in orange-and-white livery — Essex's colors — handed Francis a single letter. He read it standing at the door with sinking spirits. This summons could not be ignored. "Tell His Lordship we are honored by his invitation and will be there by one o'clock."

He closed the door and leaned against it, waving the letter at Antonio. "Our lord wishes us to dine with him. He wants our opinions of the speeches he's devised for Accession Day."

"That is on the coming Sunday, is it not?"

Francis nodded. "We must be witty yet diplomatic. Trenchant and topical, but never tedious. We'll eat too much rich food and drink too much strong wine. You'll end up in your room at Essex House, sprawled across the bed with your shoes on, while I dodder up to Gray's to lay my throbbing head on my solitary pillow. The afternoon will be wasted."

Antonio chuckled, his deep voice rich with sympathy. *"Ay, mi pobre* Francisquito!" He drained his cup and rose to take Francis's arm. "Come along then. If we are to arrive in time for dinner, we must change our clothes at once. Let us dress the old nag in the gaudiest blanket with a harness lined with silver bells. We shall trot her out for one more demonstration."

THREE

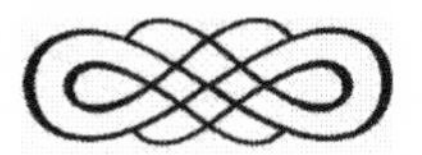

Tom surrendered to the tide surging past Charing Cross, letting the throng of odiferous Londoners push him onward. At least they were shoving him in the right direction. They had come to cheer the queen as she moved from Somerset Place on the Strand to Whitehall this Friday afternoon. He, contrarily, had an appointment with the Attorney of the Court of Wards in Westminster.

Why that had to happen today, of all days, he couldn't say. Either the attorney failed to keep up with news of the queen's movements or he considered his business more important. The latter, most likely. The progress would only take an hour. The business of collecting fees to fill the queen's coffers never ceased. Tom would add fifteen pounds to her purse this afternoon — his last major fee.

Every church bell from St. Clement's near the Temple Bar to Westminster Abbey clanged and bonged without pause. Every now and then a great cheer would rise from the crowd. Tom couldn't see the procession well enough to know why, nor did he care. Buffeted by heedless people and drowned in hellish noise, he had all he could do to stay on his feet.

Most of the crowd turned back at the Holbein Gate, leaving more room to breathe on the other side. Tom hurried down King's Street to a row of brick buildings opposite Westminster Hall. Court officials occupied the chambers on the lower floors year round, while retainers of courtiers crowded into the upper stories when the queen was in town.

Too bad there wasn't room for a maze. The yew trees would freshen the dusty air, and the labyrinth would put petitioners in the proper frame of mind for dealing with the court.

Tom made his way to the wide anteroom outside the attorney's chambers and took a seat on a bench. He merely breathed for a few minutes, waiting for the ringing in his ears to subside in the relative silence indoors. The dimmer light and cooler air helped restore his jangled senses.

Then he looked about at the other petitioners, half a dozen or so, seated on benches around the wide space. Some waited for clerks in another court, but most were fellow wards of the queen. He knew them from the many hours spent cooling their collective heels outside these chambers. He hoped he wouldn't have long to wait today.

He nodded at Dorothy Leynham, a young woman seated next to her uncle, Geoffrey Leynham. The only girl among the regulars, her comely features and colorful garb tended to draw the eye. She smiled back at him with a touch of special interest. They'd met — with her uncle, of course — once or twice at the Antelope or the White Bear after the offices closed for the day. They had found each other good company, the way people do when suffering under the tormenting lash.

The odd fellow with the carrot-orange hair sat in his usual corner. Sometimes he propped his head against the wall and took a short nap. He spoke a dialect so barbarous no one could understand him. If others were talking, he would watch them intently, as if hoping to catch a word or two. He wore the same brown wool doublet and brown velvet cap every day. He must be a ward, but why had he been sent here with neither guardian nor interpreter?

Another cruel trick of the Court of Wards, no doubt, remnant of a custom so old no one could remember its purpose. It would cost the poor fellow, though, one way or another. That part never changed.

Tom pulled his list of charges from his sleeve and unrolled it. Today he would pay the fee for passing the Great Seal. Fifteen pounds! The clerk of the liveries had only taken six for his signature. The oath of supremacy had been cheap at seven shillings. Never mind that he'd already taken the selfsame oath to pass the bar. He could have been seduced by scheming Jesuits from one day to the next.

He'd paid a pound and a half for drawing up this schedule, which he'd checked and double-checked. Ben and Mr. Bacon had reviewed it too. Thirteen shillings for enrolling the decree and another shilling for entering the rates. Three shillings four pence for "expedition," which must be someone's idea of a joke. This must be the least expeditious process in all of English law. He'd been at it for weeks already and was scarcely halfway through.

If he could go to one place and pay the whole sum in one swoop, it wouldn't be so bad. But no, each official had his own little fiefdom whose protocols must be observed. First, you went to a workshop stinking of ink and lambskins to get your roll of parchment. Then you walked a quarter mile through a maze of alleys with wet sheets strung on lines over your head, dripping on your hat and shoulders. You paid a shilling ten pence for a seal on your fresh parchment and staggered off to the next bend in the maze.

"Thomas Clarady?" A clerk stood in the doorway to the attorney's chamber.

"Here." Tom rose and let himself be waved inside. The clerk vanished through a rear door set into the oak paneling.

The attorney sat behind a large desk and had two backed chairs for visitors. A portrait of the queen hung over the attorney's head — a bad copy of one hanging in Whitehall. The artist had probably painted this one from another copy. Still, it brought Her Majesty's authority into the small chamber.

Tom pulled his purse from his deepest pocket and held it in his hand. "I'm ready to pay for the Great Seal today. Shall we mark it off on our respective lists?"

"Not so fast." Attorney Richard Strunk hadn't bothered to rise. Now he held up a flat palm and lifted his upper lip in a supercilious smirk. His brown hair had retreated from the rest of his small features, leaving a pale expanse down to his fleshy nose and his brushy moustache.

Tom's eyes narrowed. He hadn't expected a smirk. "That's why I'm here today, isn't it? To pay for passing the Great Seal?"

"There's the little matter of the king's fee first."

"King's fee? I've paid that." Tom stuffed his purse back into his pocket and unrolled his schedule of fees. He showed the scroll to the attorney, marking the relevant line with his finger. "See? Pricked and dated, eighth of November. Last Friday. I paid the clerk — ah, Boxer, I think it is. Perhaps he failed to register it properly."

"I doubt that. Mr. *Bowcer* is quite thorough. Diligent. He wouldn't be Clerk of the Court of Wards otherwise, now would he?" The smirk widened, revealing a row of tarnished teeth. They could use a good scrubbing with a salted cloth.

Tom would do it for him, and not gently. Or he could punch them right out of that sneering mouth. "I paid it, I tell you. The king's fee. Right here." He stabbed at the parchment, knowing it wouldn't help. All he had was his word, backed by the marks on his private list. There must be an official record somewhere in this office, but short of forcing his way into the rooms behind these front chambers and tearing through the hanging rows of files, he had no way of proving it.

Attorney Strunk held the upper hand, and he knew it. "Eleven pounds, eight shillings, eight pence. The precise amount, please. If you need to exchange some coins, the merchants on King's Street will likely oblige you."

Tom's teeth clenched as he repressed a growl. "I've paid it already, I tell you. I won't pay it again."

"In that case, I'm afraid we've reached an impasse." The attorney's voice took on a pedantic rhythm. "Fees must be paid on schedule or the special livery cannot be granted. You were informed of this when you began these proceedings."

"I've been paying my fees on schedule." Tom nearly shouted it. His hands curled into fists. He shook the one clutching his precious parchment at the villain seated before him. "This is extortion, plain and simple. You and that Bowcer will split those eleven pounds between you, won't you?"

"That is a serious accusation, Mr. Clarady, very serious indeed. And a groundless one, as I'm sure you must know. How would we maintain our positions if we treated the queen's wards in such a fashion?"

"It's the essence of your positions!" Tom loomed over the desk, planted his fists on the oak, and roared at the pusillanimous pile of shit. "I won't pay twice, do you hear me? No more bribes!"

The attorney pushed his chair back. "Now, now, Mr. —"

"You ought to be whipped, every last one of you! I'll do it myself. I should wring your neck right here and now, you thieving pirate. How dare you ask me for another bribe? I gave you a gift already. Two bottles of excellent Rhenish, which cost me a pretty penny. I didn't mind at the time. That's the way things are done. Everyone says it. It will smooth your path, they said. Was everyone wrong?"

Tom forced himself to step away from the desk. He took a deep breath, letting it out in a throaty growl. "You've made a mistake today, Mr. Strunk. You've tested the wrong man. I have friends in high places. They will hear about your little game."

The attorney gave a contemptuous snort. "Do you think they don't know? You'll pay what I ask or you'll remain a ward forever."

Tom wanted to drive his fist into that smug face. But he mastered his rage and opened the door. Then he turned back to stab a finger at the scoundrel. "You'll get what's coming to you one of these fine days. And I hope you choke on that wine!"

He strode through the door, promptly stepping on Mrs. Leynham's skirts. His foot caught in her farthingale, and he had to grip her shoulder to keep from falling. He caught a whiff of her flowery perfume as he righted himself and grinned a sheepish apology.

Her cheeks flared pink — not only from the brief touch of his hand on her tender frame. She and her uncle had moved closer to the door while Tom had been inside, practically pressing their ears to the oak. Well, he hoped they'd heard something to their advantage.

"He tried to extort a bribe from me." Tom addressed the Leynhams, but he spoke loudly enough for everyone to hear. "Keep your hands on your purses today, my friends."

"Soft, soft," the uncle said. "Better to keep these things under one's hat."

"Why?" Tom demanded. "If everyone spoke out, they couldn't keep getting away with it."

The uncle shook his head. His small round eyes were the color of hazelnuts. "Steady on, lad. Best to play the game the way it's laid. Cool down is my advice. Then come back and apologize on Monday."

"Never." Tom touched his hat to the young woman and turned toward the exit. He caught the eyes of the brown-capped man in the corner and nodded at him, tapping his nose. "A word to the wise, my friend. Watch out for false fees."

The man said, "Haddaway, mon!" Tom had no idea what it meant, but he nodded as if he agreed.

He wanted a drink, a strong one. Maybe more than one. He rolled up his list and tucked it back up his sleeve. Then he left that den of thieves and walked down to the White Bear, a large inn popular with folks suing one another in the courts of law. Some of the other wards had taken lodgings here.

Sure enough, he found Charles Midley, a ward from Kent, sitting at a table near the front window. His hand curled around a clay mug as he gazed at the traffic on the street. His relaxed posture suggested he'd been sitting there for hours, nursing the same mug of ale. Whatever was cheapest, no doubt. Charles was harder pressed for coin than Tom.

Tom asked a passing wench for a large cup of dragon's milk, an extra strong ale. "No, wait. Bring two cups to that table over there." He pointed with his head. He walked over and took a seat without asking. "Thought I might find you here."

"Where else would I be? Touring the wonders of London?" Charles sounded bitter. The sour humor didn't suit him. His round face and easy smile had been made for happier times. He kept his straight blond hair trimmed in a line above his clear blue eyes and his beard closely shaped to his jaw. His features were regular —

handsome, even — apart from a deepening line of worry crossing his brow.

"What brings you here?" Charles asked. "I thought you preferred the Antelope."

The wench brought their mugs, setting one in front of each man.

"Too far." Tom raised his cup. "Dragon's milk. Thought you could use one too."

"Thanks!" Charles raised his cup as well, then paused. "What are we celebrating?"

"Nothing. Taking the edge off, if that's possible." Tom took a deep swallow and sighed as the fiery drink coursed through his veins. "Ah. That helps."

Charles drank from his mug and let out a breathy "Hoo." He shook his head. "If only I could drink this stuff all day long. It smooths out the edges, all right."

Tom took another sip, then cocked his head toward his companion. If anyone could sympathize with this afternoon's wrangle, it was Charles. "Afraid I made a bit of noise at the attorney's office today."

"That place could use a little noise. Have you noticed how people don't talk while they're waiting on those benches? A nod here, a nod there, but scarcely a courteous word."

"There were words today. That whoreson knave tried to charge me twice for the king's fee. I refused. Forcefully, I might add." Tom grinned as he showed his fist.

"King's fee? That's more than eleven pounds!" Charles seemed more fearful than outraged. "Has he been asking everyone for that?"

"I don't know." Tom's grin faded. "Don't pay it if he does. We have to draw the line somewhere."

"Are you mad? There's no line. There's just an endless stack of coins moving from us to them."

"But it's wrong," Tom insisted. "It has to stop. Someone has to say, 'Hold! No more.'"

"Who do you think you are, King Canute? You can't stop the tide of corruption by yourself. You'll only succeed in remaining a ward for the rest of your life. They own us, man. Not just our guardians — the whole cursed court, from the lowliest clerk on up to Sir Robert Cecil and his father, Lord Burghley."

"That's the thing," Tom said. "Does the top know what the bottom is doing? If no one complains, how can they?"

Charles scoffed at him. "They know. Lord Burghley is the most corrupt man in England, and his son is a close second. His Lordship is the master of the court. If he wanted it honest, it would be. Some share of those eleven pounds will trickle up to him, never you fear. And there's not one cursed thing you can do about it."

Tom grumbled into his mug. Everyone said the same. He hated feeling so helpless. He took another sip of dragon's milk, but the drink had lost its magic. He stared out the window at the passing crowd. Some wore brightly colored silk and velvet, probably more than they could afford. No doubt they hoped to be mistaken for courtiers, though you wouldn't find anyone who mattered walking this far south of the gate. The majority wore the sober black robes of clerks and lawyers, the functionaries without whom no modern nation could exist.

A scurrying mix of fools and scoundrels. Which was which, he wondered? Did they even know themselves?

"Talking about me?" Dorothy Leynham appeared behind them, a flirtatious smile on her narrow lips. Her floral scent wafted in with her, dispelling for a moment the usual tavern stink of stale smoke and beer.

"Naturally." Tom jumped to his feet. He'd been a gallant once upon a time, and old habits died hard. She looked well today in her lace-trimmed attifet, poised to display her light brown hair. Her round hazel eyes shone as she beamed at Charles. She turned a lesser smile toward Tom, seemingly as an afterthought.

That pricked his pride. He must be getting old. He went to find another chair and set it opposite his.

Charles granted her a weak welcome but didn't trouble himself to rise. They'd known one another since childhood, according to Dorothy, growing up a mere fifteen miles apart. Geoffrey Leynham served as Charles's guardian as well, which often threw the young wards together.

"All done for the day?" Tom asked.

Dorothy made a small drama of spreading her dark pink skirts and settling in the chair. "We're getting close to the end, I think." She cast a critical eye on the two mugs in front of Charles, then spoke to Tom. "We have a point of conflict about one of my smaller manors. But Attorney Strunk is sorting things out for us."

"I find that hard to believe." Tom couldn't imagine that pasty poltroon being helpful.

"Ah, we knew we'd find you here!" Geoffrey Leynham walked up carrying two wooden cups. He set one in front of Dorothy, then looked about for another chair. No one got up to help him, so he set his cup down, walked a little distance to choose a backed chair, and sat between Tom and Dorothy.

"Have you been out at all today?" Leynham asked Charles. He cast a frown at those two cups as well.

"I walked around for a while. I'm becoming quite the expert on the alleys and byways of Westminster. Perhaps I can find work as a carter or a coachman once I've surrendered my lands to the court." He gave his guardian a look of loathing.

"Now, now," Leynham said. "It isn't that bad."

Charles snorted. "Clarady tells me that whore" — he shot a glance at Dorothy — "that attorney is getting bolder in his demands. Eleven pounds! I don't have it. I don't know where I could get it if he asks me."

"You could offer him that little ring." Tom nodded at the small gold ring Charles wore on his right hand. "He might decide something is better than nothing."

"Not much," Charles said. "This is more sentimental than valuable." He didn't elaborate on the source of the sentiment.

"I'll bet your mother can come up with something." Dorothy patted his arm, but Charles pulled it away. She clearly liked him as more than a mere neighbor. The feeling, alas, did not seem to be mutual.

"I've already written to her. She has a silver mirror with a matching comb. It can't be worth eleven pounds, but I was hoping it would help with the expediting."

That got a bitter laugh from Tom. "Expediting. Do they hear the irony when they use that term?"

Leynham gave them both quelling looks. "Honey catches more flies than vinegar, you know." He shook his finger at Tom. "Threats won't get you anywhere, my lad. The attorney can delay your case if he has a mind."

Tom had forgotten about that in the heat of the moment. Any delay at this late date would push his case off until Hilary term in January.

"You didn't tell me you threatened him." Charles grinned. "I would've liked to see that. A sound thrashing, was it? Or a solid punch on that porky nose?"

Tom chuckled, but his heart was no longer in it. "I offered to wring his neck."

"We didn't hear that part," Dorothy said. "We heard you wishing he would choke on the wine. But there wasn't any wine in his chamber that I could see."

"I gave him two bottles of Rhenish," Tom said. "A very good wine which cost me plenty, from that vintner near Temple Bar."

"Temple Bar, eh?" Leynham nodded as if making a mental note. "We Kentish folk don't know the city like you do. Wine is an excellent gift."

"Not worth eleven pounds, though, is it?" Charles said. "You should write to your mother, Tom. She must have some jewelry."

"It's too late for that. Term will be over before I could get a package from Dorset. Besides, my advisors recommend impersonal items like bottles of wine or pairs of gloves. Things the bribee can sell if they want. Jewelry is too easily recognized if it turns up at a pawnbroker's."

"That's a useful observation," Leynham said. "You want something neutral. Something anonymous. Of course, nothing beats hard coin for that."

"If you have enough of them," Tom muttered.

"Ah, Mr. Clarady, you have my sympathy. All our sympathies, eh, children?" Leynham encouraged his wards to chime in. Dorothy contributed another glowing smile, but Charles glared at his guardian from under his blond eyebrows.

Tom wondered how Charles had ended up in Leynham's clutches. He wasn't kin and had a mother still living. Hadn't she bid for her son's wardship? Charles counted his coins as often as Tom did and with the same worried frown. He had some four hundred and fifty pounds per annum, or he would when he attained his livery. Plenty of funds — if his guardian supported his suit. Leynham must be unwilling to let go of his ward.

Leynham tapped a finger on the table in front of Tom. "There's nothing for it, my lad. You'll have to give in and pay up. Make your peace with the attorney. A bottle of Rhenish won't do it this time. Borrow what you need to pay the piper. Go back with your hat in your hand and eat those hasty words. A hearty slice of humble pie can work wonders, you know. That and eleven pounds, eight shillings, and eight pence." He grinned as if he'd solved all of Tom's problems with his stale inanities.

Kneel to that pasty-faced toad? The unfairness of the attorney's demand — the sheer, brazen greed of it — chafed at Tom's soul.

And yet he'd heard the same advice from both Francis Bacon and Benjamin Whitt, the two men he respected most. Once you were caught by the Court of Wards, there was only one way out. You had to sacrifice your dignity to win your liberty and surrender your estate to gain it back.

FOUR

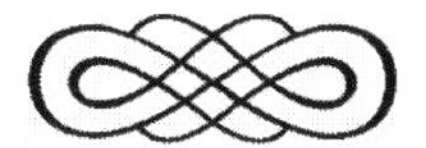

"That's one." Francis set the letter he'd just encoded aside. He blew on the writing to dry the ink, then set it on the opposite corner of his desk. These letters contained only mundane exchanges between his brother Anthony and his intelligencers abroad, but they held enough details to identify both spy and master. Therefore, they must be encrypted.

He laid out another letter, dipped his quill, and began counting off *a*'s and *b*'s. Francis enjoyed working with the scheme he had invented. Also, the rote work made no demands on his aching head. He would catch up on this neglected chore until dinner and then go back to Twickenham for a long nap.

Yesterday, Sunday, had been Accession Day. Having been banned from the queen's presence, he'd been obliged to stand in the late November sun with a sweaty group of Graysians. Lord Essex had won all his tourneys to resounding applause. His Lordship reveled in these events, but the noise, the dust, and the stink of warm bodies and fried food had exhausted Francis.

Afterward, he had gone to Bishopsgate for supper with Anthony in his new house. Antonio Pérez had met him there. They'd stayed up far too late and had drunk far too much wine. Francis had enjoyed a few golden hours in the company of the two men who best understood his plight. It had been a balm to his wounded spirits. Now his poor, abused body had to pay for it.

A knock on his door made him jump, shaking ink across his page. Before he had time to call, "Go away," Tom strode in and plopped himself in the chair on the other side of the desk.

"I heard movement up here, so I thought I'd poke my head in." He glanced out the window to judge the time. "It's nearly noon. You must have been up late last night."

Francis didn't deign to respond. He slid the ruined sheet of paper to the floor and laid out a fresh one. Then he dipped his quill and encoded the first word again.

Tom watched him write in silence, though his foot tapped incessantly on the rush matting. He plainly had something to say. More complaints about his suit, no doubt.

"I hope Strunk isn't at dinner today," he finally blurted out.

An unexpected beginning. Francis looked up from his work. "Richard Strunk? The Attorney for the Court of Wards?" Strunk was a long-standing member of Gray's Inn.

Tom nodded. "I had a bit of a" — he wagged his head from side to side — "an altercation, shall we say, with him Friday afternoon. I didn't see him around here on Saturday. He must've gone home directly from Westminster."

"Strunk lives in Hampshire. Too far for a two-day visit. But not seeing a man you are trying to avoid does not entail his absence." Francis consulted his table of correspondences and encoded another word.

"He wanted a bribe. In fact, he blatantly demanded it." Outrage put a growl under Tom's words. "Eleven pounds!"

"That's an enormous sum." The recipient of this letter in Saxony would only receive two pounds for a full year's work. "You could lease chambers here for a year for that amount. Not the best ones, but habitable."

"I know." Now the heel starting tapping, jittering Tom's knee up and down. "He claims I haven't paid the king's fee. Which I have, duly noted and dated on my schedule. I should've made him sign it. Why does the king — or queen, rather — need such a thumping great amount anyway? I suppose she gets the lion's share of the fifteen pounds for the Great Seal as well. That's what I went there to pay on Friday."

Francis set his quill in the holder and smiled at his erstwhile clerk. "That is the purpose of the Court of Wards, as you should know. Henry the Seventh established it to generate revenue for the crown. He revived the obsolete feudal duties of knight service and supervision of noble marriages as a pretext for a substantial tax on land."

Tom bared his teeth. At the floor, not at Francis, but the ferocity of the gesture was alarming. His humors had been severely unbalanced by this suit. Once it was over, Francis would recommend he spend a month in his mother's house, well away from the struggle and strife of the courts.

A month on the windswept coast of Dorset, with nothing to do but read and take long walks? Francis might go with him.

"I threatened to wring his neck." Tom blurted the words like a confession.

"That was rash."

"I didn't mean it."

"Of course not."

"I mean, I did mean it. At least, I felt it. I wanted to punch him." Tom raised clenched fists. Anger hardened his glare, emphasizing the dark circles beneath his eyes. "He was so smug. He knew I'd paid that fee already. And he knew that I knew that he knew. I wanted to smack that smirk right off his face."

"But you didn't, did you?" Francis spoke lightly, refusing to acknowledge the anger. Tom should request a cooling sallet at dinner today with cucumber, if it could be found. Those choleric humors must be reduced. Perhaps he should return to being bled once a week to draw off some of the heat. "The law, in its wisdom, draws a clear line between thinking and acting. If not, no one would escape the noose."

Tom grunted. His fists uncurled. Francis's shoulders released a tension he hadn't known they'd been holding.

"You'll have to apologize, you know," he said. "Strunk can delay your case well into spring if he chooses. It would somehow just keep falling off the docket."

"I know." The last of the fire went out. Tom hung his head, and his shoulders slumped. "I'll bring a gift this afternoon. It won't be worth eleven pounds. I don't have that much. But I could put a couple of pairs of scented gloves on my bill at the tailor's. Let Lady Russell make one last payment from my funds."

"Gloves are a good idea, as long as your apology is sincere."

Tom scratched his bearded jaw. "That will be the hard part. But a good lawyer knows how to lie, doesn't he? I'll consider it practice." The smile that stretched his lips held no humor.

"Strunk will accept the gloves." Francis would, in his position. "He'll know he overshot his mark. He'll pretend nothing happened and let you pay for the Great Seal. I would be more concerned about your debt to my aunt if I were you."

"I have a plan for that."

"Have you?" This was the first Francis had heard of it. "Will you borrow against your estate?"

"No. I'm going to propose a compromise. She agrees to release me from wardship and I agree to pay off a portion of my debt each quarter. We'll sign the contract before the whole court on December second. We can dicker about that quarterly payment. I'm prepared to add a reasonable rate of interest."

"Will you negotiate this contract yourself?"

"Of course. It isn't complicated." Tom managed a small chuckle. "I know how to persuade Her Ladyship by this time."

"Do you?" Francis folded his hands together. "This is the woman who requires everyone from the queen on down to refer to her as the Dowager Countess of Bedford, even though her husband died months before his father. The earldom went to a younger son. She had herself named the Keeper of Donnington Castle even though she is" — he raised one finger — "a woman" — another finger — "who resides most of the year in London, and" — a third finger — "is bedridden much of the time from the pain of a twisted back."

Tom laughed. "That's what I love about her. She reminds me of Trumpet — accept no limitations." His laughter faded as he recognized the import of his own words.

Francis shook his head in bemusement. The fact that Tom could express real affection for his chief adversary revealed his qualities like nothing else. "Your proposal sounds fair to me, for what it's worth."

"It's worth a lot."

The horn would sound for dinner soon. Francis scratched out a few more encoded words. Nearly done. Then he remembered another matter. "Do you still intend to take Anthony's chambers downstairs? I'll have to charge the usual amount, you know. We're both a bit short these days, thanks to my campaign for Attorney General."

"I'll have the money when it's due. Don't give them to anyone else." Tom heaved a weary sigh. "I'll sort it all out, one way or another. I always do, don't I?"

Not to Francis's knowledge, but perhaps battles had been won in his absence. He finished the letter and set it aside. He had time for one more before dinner. A short one.

A rhythm of light knocks sounded on the door, which swung open to reveal Pinnock, Francis's personal servant. He looked breathless, though he couldn't have come from much farther than one floor up or down.

"The sheriff's at the door! He wants to talk to Tom! They found a man dead this morning, in his chambers at Westminster. That attorney, what-d'ye-call-him, at that court. The one Tom's always so angry about."

"Dead?" Francis frowned. "Strunk?"

"The sheriff!" Tom jumped to his feet. "I won't go, I tell you. I won't set foot in another jail." He stared at the door, his comely features contorted with terror.

Francis knew he wasn't seeing the well-polished oak that guarded his well-appointed chambers or smelling the usual scents of ink and rosemary. His open eyes looked onto a monstrous vision of the battered door at Bridewell Prison, and his flaring nostrils were filled with the memory of fouled straw and his own sweaty fear.

"Calm down, Tom." He spoke in a soothing rhythm. "I'm sure it's only routine. We don't know what —"

"No!" Tom shouted. He rolled wild eyes at Francis and ran into the bedchamber, slamming the door behind him.

Francis blew out a breath. He hoped this didn't start the nightmares again. Apart from the toll they took on Tom, they tended to wake the whole house.

He put down his quill and rose from his desk. He set a hand in his lower back and stretched a little. He must learn to stop hunching his shoulders when he wrote. "I suppose I should speak to the sheriff myself. Bring him up."

As the lad turned to go down, Francis added, "But take your time. We're in no hurry."

Francis opened the door to his bedchamber. The room was empty, but the window hung wide open. He leaned out and saw a figure sprinting across the fields, arms and legs pumping. He looked down at the ground some fifteen feet below. Quite a jump. Although, if Tom hung by his hands at full length, he'd only have three or four feet to fall. And fear supplied a powerful impetus.

He wished Tom well and closed the window, latching it firmly.

Let the sheriff do his own work. After what Tom had been through last June, he could be forgiven for his panic. Even a short stint in jail — even one night — might undo all the healing work of the past year.

Francis put on a hat before returning to his desk. Hearing footsteps on the stairs, he remained standing. He composed himself in a receptive posture, then caught a glimpse of the confidential correspondence on his desk. He hastily pulled blank sheets of paper over anything with writing on it.

Another round of Pinnock's special knocks and the door opened again. Sheriff Peter Hanton walked to the center of the room and stopped with his hands on his hips. He looked from one side of the elegantly furnished chamber to the other, frowning deeply. He shot a baleful glance at the closed door to the bedchamber. "Where is he?"

"Of whom do you speak?" Francis adopted his haughtiest manner, the one he'd learned watching his mother deal with local authorities who underestimated her.

"Clarady." The sheriff strode across to fling the inner door open and step through it. He returned in a few seconds.

"I assume you mean *Mr.* Thomas Clarady. A barrister of the Inns of Court. He doesn't occupy my chambers."

"I'm told he lives in this house." The sheriff strode back to the desk. He was one of those long-legged, short-waisted men whose every step gobbled up three feet. "I'd like your permission to search the place from top to bottom."

"I do not grant it. You have my word that Mr. Clarady is not presently inside this house." He gestured at the chair where Tom had been only moments ago. "Sit down, Sheriff, and tell me what this about. Perhaps I can answer your questions."

Hanton huffed into his fluffy blond moustache but took the chair. Francis resumed his seat behind the desk and folded his hands in front of him. "I understand that Attorney Strunk is dead. What happened to him?"

"Poison, as far as we can tell. We're having the rest of the bottle tested."

"Bottle?" Francis prompted. "Perhaps you should begin at the beginning. When was the body found?"

"This morning, by his clerk. Nine o'clock, by the bells. The clerk swears he's never late." The sheriff blew another puff into his moustache and surrendered to the exigencies of the moment, leaning back in his chair. "Mr. Strunk was last seen alive by the same clerk late Saturday afternoon. He never met clients on Saturday, reserving the day to review deeds or some such legal documents."

"I know what they are."

The sheriff's pale eyebrows rose. "Then you know more than I do. I haven't looked into his work yet." He held up a hand to block any explanations. "Nor do I need to at this time. He was alone most of the day. The clerk says a boy in blue apprentice garb turned up around two to deliver a bottle of French brandy. Costly stuff. Mr. Strunk seemed pleased at the gift and set it on a side table. The clerk went home soon after that. Then this morning he found his master sprawled across the desk with his tongue hanging out. Dead as a —" He closed his mouth on some bit of gallows' humor. "Clearly dead. A little ripe. A fine sight to greet a man on a Monday morning. The bottle had been opened and one cup poured out. I assume the drink was poisoned."

"A logical conclusion." Francis tried to forget the word "ripe." "Do you know where the brandy came from?"

The sheriff nodded. "Vintner near the Temple Bar, name of Henry Belvoir. My undersheriff is there now."

Everyone in the Inns of Court bought wine from Belvoir's shop. "What leads you to believe my cler — my colleague, Mr. Clarady, had anything to do with it?"

"There are two witnesses to a dispute between Clarady and Strunk on Friday afternoon. A man named Leynham and his niece. They said Clarady shouted at Strunk as he left, threatening him. Their turn came next and was the last one for the day."

"Mmm." Francis offered a patronizing smile. "Suing for one's livery from the Court of Wards can be a trying experience, Sheriff. There is a constant demand for fees, both official and unofficial, if you understand me."

"They want bribes. I've heard that. I can see how that would anger a man enough to do some shouting. I only want to talk to this Clarady, same way I talked to the Leynham pair. How did Strunk respond? Did he mention any other sort of trouble? The usual questions."

"Then you don't intend to arrest him?"

The sheriff frowned, lifting one shoulder. "I might take him into custody for a short stint. A night in jail tends to focus the mind."

"I see. Well, Sheriff, I should think twice about apprehending a barrister of Gray's Inn if I were you. Especially when a bencher of this august body, by whom I mean myself, is prepared to vouch for his innocence. If that isn't enough for you, you might pay a visit to my cousin, Sir Robert Cecil, son of the master of the Court of Wards. He has a high opinion of Mr. Clarady and will doubtless expect him to be treated with every courtesy. Shall I send him a note to say you're on your way?" Francis picked up his quill.

The sheriff sprang to his feet. Red spots darkened his lean cheeks. "No need for that. No need at all." He bobbed a shallow bow. "If you could mention my visit to Mr. Clarady, I'd be grateful. You might ask if he could find a moment to assist us with our inquiries. At his convenience, of course. Here, if he wishes, with legal counsel at his side."

Francis smiled, swallowing the urge to laugh. Ah, the effects of a powerful name! Would that his could work such magic. "I'll do that." He rose, gesturing at the door.

Pinnock opened it, standing behind it to hide the grin splitting his freckled face.

"I'll let you know if we hear of anything useful," Francis said.

The sheriff nodded. "I'll trot along now, with your permission." And off he went.

"Well, that was exciting." Francis removed his hat. He dropped it on the empty chair and sat down to pen a swift note to Lady Dorchester. *He'll be tossing pebbles at your window in a few minutes, or whatever it is you do. Give him dinner and send him home. He won't be arrested, nor will he be brought anywhere for questioning. I have seen to that. They will speak to him here, in my presence, when he is ready.*

He signed it, thought again, and added, *This is all I know.* He jotted a quick summary of the meager information the sheriff had supplied. Then he folded the note, sealed it, and handed it to Pinnock. "Dorchester House. Quick as you can, my boy."

Pinnock thundered down the stairs. The horn sounded for dinner. "A busy morning," Francis remarked to no one. He rose and put on his hat, then paused to listen to footsteps coming up again. Too heavy for Pinnock. "Now what?"

Sir Avery Fogg, Treasurer of Gray's, heaved himself onto the landing. He'd grown stouter over the years but held on to a full head of curls, as much gray now as black. His moustache had gone nearly silver.

He panted for a minute, fist on hip, then turned to speak through the still-open door. "Ah, there you are, Mr. Bacon. If I could have a quick word? I know the horn's gone."

"Of course." Francis gestured him inside, but Fogg shook his heavy head.

"Really only a minute. Sheriff Hanton was just here, I believe?"

Francis nodded.

"It appears Strunk's gotten himself murdered. Can't say I'm surprised. Never met a greedier man, and I live among lawyers. Nevertheless, he was one of ours. Can't leave such things to the sheriff's office. They'll make a hash of it. The benchers and I want you to take charge. Do what you do. Ask questions, poke around. Sort it out. Catch the villain." He turned his lips up in a smile.

"Ah, Sir Avery. I'm not sure —"

"We'll pay you. Whatever's fair." He held up a finger. "Don't go too far."

"Certainly not." Francis took a minute to think about it, though he knew the answer. Why not? Investigating murders was what he did, or one of the things. It would distract him from the Attorney General hubble-shubble. He'd earn a mark or two from the benchers, rare enough to be a reason on its own.

Furthermore, it would put Tom in his debt. Tom, the main suspect. Tom, a man who would soon be freed from wardship and take control of a large estate — a very large estate. A man with a moral obligation to lend his faithful old tutor a few hundred pounds.

He would do what he could to defend Tom anyway. They'd been through a lot together over the years and were friends beyond the bounds of master and student. But Francis did need money badly, and Tom would have quite a lot of it if things went the right way. A man could have multiple reasons for performing the same deeds.

He returned the treasurer's smile and stepped out to the landing. He had a good appetite today, after all. "I'll do it." They negotiated his fee on the way down to the hall.

FIVE

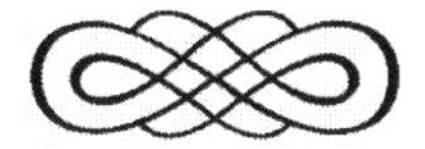

"It's from Mr. Bacon." Trumpet gave her maidservant a mock frown. "What can he want, I wonder?" The back of her neck prickled. Could it be something fun? Something intriguing? Bacon didn't often write to her since they each saw Tom at least every week and had little reason to correspond.

She was sitting at her desk in the library, writing a letter to her mother-in-law. The dowager countess expected daily reports on her grandsons' doings. Trumpet didn't mind the chore in the least. She loved talking about her offspring. They changed a little every day, and each change deserved commentary. William, now two years old, had discovered running. Fortunately, his little legs couldn't carry him very fast or very far. Trumpet had assigned a youthful usher to shadow his steps.

Baby Stephen, six months old, had taken on a clear resemblance to his father. Unlike his papa, he possessed a cheerful, open disposition, laughing at the slightest provocation. He found his own toes a source of infinite delight and loved to be tickled.

Trumpet adored her children and intended to have more of them, but lately she'd found herself growing restless. She'd hired excellent nursemaids who knew their jobs and needed little supervision. She'd sorted out the kitchen at Dorchester House early on. The steward, a

Dorset gentleman also skilled at his job, kept an eye on the rest. The large household thus required only a portion of her attention, and most decisions tended toward the mundane. She understood why so many of her peers turned to religious devotion. It gave them something to do.

She picked up her silver penknife and slit the seal on the letter. "Let's hope he doesn't want to borrow money from us." She unfolded the sheet of paper and read it through. "God's mercy! Tom is coming."

"Now, my lady? It is almost the hour of dinner." Her handmaiden, confidante, and accessory to mischief, Catalina Luna, knew well the proper times for dalliance. She'd abetted many a discreet meeting between the two lovers.

"A man's been murdered, and Tom's a suspect. I'm guessing he ran when the sheriff knocked on Mr. Bacon's door. Bacon assumes he's coming here. Where else would he go?" Trumpet tapped a finger on her desk, thinking fast. "Broad daylight. He can't climb the wall. He'll have to seek admittance at one of the gates. Front or back, do you think?"

"Back. If he is hiding, he will not want to stand in the street."

"Agreed." Trumpet rose, folding the letter and tucking it into her sleeve. She'd burn it later. "He'll run down Strand Lane to our wharf. He could be there by now. We'd best go down to meet him."

"What will we tell the guard, my lady?" They took great pains to conceal Tom's visits from the servants or, if pressed, to connect them to some legitimate cause.

Trumpet couldn't think of anything. She was the mistress of this house, however. "We'll tell him nothing. It's only natural that Mr. Clarady should seek shelter from his most powerful friend in time of need." She strode to the door, then took a moment to grin happily at her companion. "Another murder! Just what we've been wanting!"

"Shall we investigate, my lady?"

"We most certainly shall."

They found Tom panting at the river gate, bent over, hands on knees, under the curious eye of the guard. He must have run the whole way at full speed. Trumpet bade the guard admit him and led him up to the green parlor. Here the windows overlooked the corner of the Strand and the narrow lane that separated Dorchester House from Somerset Palace. Most of the view consisted of the tops of fruit trees in the palace orchard, but they might catch a glimpse of the sheriff if he came up from the west.

Tom shrank from the windows, backing himself into a corner. "Don't let them take me." His terror was palpable. He paced back and forth across a self-set boundary, too agitated to stand still. Trumpet knew the pacing spanned the limits of a cell in Bridewell. "I can't go to jail again, Trumpet. Not ever."

Her heart broke at the sight of him. Tom had always been the first to leap in, whatever was doing, with a grin on his lips and a gleam in his eye. They'd hurt more than his body in Bridewell last June. She'd thought the worst of that had passed, but that loathsome sheriff seemed to stirred things up again.

"I won't let anyone touch you." She took his hands and led him to a chair, well away from the windows. "They won't look for you here. And Mr. Bacon says you're safe. He sent me a note. I'll bet he mentioned some important relative's name. Lord Burghley, probably. You've worked for him, remember? He likes you, and he's protected you before."

"That's true." Tom blinked rapidly and blew out a loud breath. "That's true." The panic faded from his eyes. "Thank you."

Trumpet dropped a kiss on his forehead. "Stay here as long as you want."

An usher appeared at the door. "Dinner is ready, my lady."

"We'll have it here. The three of us." Stephen had decided to dine with the court since they were just across the lane. Trumpet accompanied him some days but more often made the excuse of having young children to manage. Her Majesty always dined in her private chambers anyway.

She stood by the window, watching people, horses, carts, and wagons pass by on the short stretch of the Strand visible from these windows. She could look directly across into an upper chamber of the palace, which appeared to be a corner of the library. Every now and then someone would spend an hour at the large table reading. No one glanced her way, as far as she knew.

The lane below had no traffic apart from the occasional idle wanderer strolling down to look at the river. Or the odd barrister fleeing from the law. People and goods entered the palace from the Strand or the river.

The sheriff would most likely come from the other direction — if he were somehow inspired to seek Tom at random among the mansions on the Strand. It would be a last resort. A man didn't reach the high office of Sheriff of Middlesex County by irritating the great.

Ushers appeared with a trestle table. They set it up with three chairs, laying a white cloth over its smooth surface. Others followed with trays of plates, cups, spoons, and dishes of food. Savory aromas rose from the silver bowls — lemon, thyme, vinegar, and nutmeg. Trumpet's stomach growled.

The last usher filled three cups with wine, leaving two bottles on the sideboard. He left with a short bow.

Trumpet had to persuade Tom to join her and Catalina at the table by waving forkfuls of sturgeon in a nutmeg-and-onion sauce under his nose. "If you want wine, you must sit at the table and eat some food."

"Yes, my lady." He took the seat facing the door, then shot a sheepish look at Catalina. "You must think I'm being foolish."

"No one thinks it." She moved the best dishes closer to Tom's hand, then sat down herself. "Me, I would be on a ship already."

Trumpet let him drink a little wine and eat a few bites, but she burned with curiosity. "What happened? Mr. Bacon didn't say much. Only that someone named Strunk had been found dead this morning, poisoned with brandy from a bottle delivered on Saturday. What does that have to do with you?"

"Nothing," Tom snapped. "Why should it?"

"There must be something or the sheriff wouldn't want to talk to you."

He tore up a piece of manchet bread and sopped it in the sauce. His stony expression betrayed some sort of guilt. Trumpet leveled an impatient gaze at him. He refused to look her way, but she knew he could feel it.

After polishing off his sturgeon, Tom served himself some stewed greens and the largest of the apple fritters. Trumpet took a drink of wine without shifting her gaze one inch. At last, Tom dropped his spoon and groaned in resignation, as if she'd been nagging him without cease for an hour.

"I may have threatened him on Friday afternoon. Just a little, though, I swear."

"Oh, Tom!"

"He tried to squeeze another king's fee out of me. That's eleven pounds."

"Even so." She clucked her tongue. "He's an official of the court in which you have a suit pending. You won't win many cases by provoking the staff, you know."

"I wouldn't do it if it were someone else's case. I wouldn't care enough." He lifted his cup and took a gulp. "The man's a thief, I tell you. An extortionist. He's as brazen as a pirate on the high seas."

Trumpet quirked her lips. "His character is not at issue."

"It should be. He should've been hanged after a lengthy and humiliating trial. Poisoning is too easy for the likes of him."

"Tom!"

He lifted his chin, refusing to apologize. He would never truly wish a man's death merely for trying to extract a bribe. Bribery had its uses, after all. It made the wheels of government run more smoothly, for one. Everyone knew that.

"Did you kill him?"

He answered that with a loud lip fart. "I wanted to, for a minute — or three. But no, Your Ladyship, I did not murder the pug-faced, pusillanimous Attorney of the Court of Wards."

"Good. Because that would be a lot more trouble for me and Mr. Bacon." Trumpet took an apple fritter and cut off a slice. Fresh apples, a touch of honey, lightly fried on a well-seasoned pan in the merest hint of butter. Perfection. "Did anyone hear you threaten him?"

"Everyone, I should think. I was pretty loud there, at the end."

"Who is everyone?" Trumpet let her tone carry her impatience. He knew what she wanted — a full report, the kind he would give Bacon. Why did she have to drag each detail out of him one by one?

Tom swallowed a chunk of fritter and held up a pacifying hand. "I know, I know. Give me a minute." He drank more wine, tapping two fingers of his left hand in a mindless rhythm on the table. Then his set his cup down.

"The first thing you should know is that Richard Strunk, the dead man, was a member of Gray's."

"Is that significant?"

Tom shrugged. "I don't know. I doubt it."

"What happened after you lost your temper and barged out of the building boiling with righteous fury?"

"Now that's not quite fair."

"I said righteous."

He poked a tongue in his cheek. The friendship, the security, and the wine had soothed his roiling humors.

"I went down to the White Bear for a strong cup of ale. I found Charles Midley there, as I expected, and bought him a drink. The Leynhams turned up soon after."

"Who are the Leynhams?" He hadn't mentioned them before, though she hadn't seen much of him since his suit began. She still knew him better than anyone else in the world, however. One of those Leynhams was a pretty young woman. She'd bet these silver serving dishes on it.

"Dorothy and her uncle. Geoffrey. He's her guardian. Charles's too, as it happens. They're all from Kent."

Trumpet pursed her lips at the stream of fresh facts. She stuck to the one with the girl in it. "Were they looking for you, these Leynhams?"

"At the inn? So they said. They were concerned, they said, because they heard me shouting at the attorney. They were sitting right outside the door, as close as they could get without standing up and blocking the way." He laughed shortly. "I shouted something like 'I hope you choke on that wine' with the door wide open. Anyone on the ground floor could have heard me. I was angry, and thus I was loud."

Trumpet offered him a smile, batting her lashes just a little. "Tell me more about this Dorothy."

Tom gave her a wise look. "She's nothing. Don't think about her. Comely enough, I suppose, if you're not fussy. Too thin for my tastes, especially the lips. Beady little eyes. And she strikes me as empty-headed, apart from anything concerning Charles."

Trumpet accepted that with a skeptical grunt. "Are they lodging at the Bear?"

"They're at the Antelope. Charles is at the Bear." His eyes narrowed as he pointed a finger at her. "You're investigating already, using me as your first witness. Admit it, Trumplekin."

"You're all I have at the moment." She loved it when he called her by that youthful nickname. It made the years fall away. She loved her present life, even the frustrating parts, but nothing compared to sitting with Tom in a smoky alehouse arguing about some thorny legal conundrum. She would never wish for a man to die just to give them something to debate, but there was no reason not to enjoy it when it happened.

She expected him to jump right in. He used to love their arguments as much as she did. But he leaned back and crossed his arms. "Well, I won't help you. Strunk was the worst of the worst, preying on the helpless. I don't care who killed him. I'm not sure I even want the poor knave caught."

"Knave or femme. Women can poison bottles of brandy as easily as men."

"Granted. And yet I repeat that I have no interest here."

"No interest! You're the principal suspect. Mr. Bacon may have sent the sheriff away with a flea in his ear today, but that won't be the end of it. The Attorney of the Court of Wards is a person of importance. If you're all they've got, you're the one they're going to arrest."

Tom glowered at her, though she could tell by the shadow in his eyes that he knew she was right. "They'll never catch me. I could jump in a wherry outside your gate and take it up to Twickenham. I could borrow a horse from Mr. Bacon and be in Portsmouth in three days. It'd take that long to get through whatever screens you and he throw up behind me."

"And then what? Abandon your livery suit after all you've been through? You could never come back, you know. Not to Gray's. Not to Westminster. Not to London. You couldn't even practice law in the outer reaches of Dorset. What good is passing the bar if you can't set foot in a court?"

He scratched his bearded jaw, scowling at her for a long moment, then gave in. "I will tell you what I know, but I won't go around asking questions. I'd attract too much attention. It'd be like waving a red flag under the sheriff's nose."

Trumpet nodded somberly, though she wanted to hop up and give him a kiss. A juicy one. "Will Mr. Bacon help us, do you think?"

"Why should he?"

"Because Strunk was a Graysian. I'll bet you an angel the benchers ask him to look into it."

"I don't have an angel to spare. And I'm not sure he cares what the benchers want or don't want these days. He's almost as crazed with frustration as I am."

Trumpet clucked her tongue. Had she asked him to go around asking questions? Anyone could see how stupid that would be. She didn't need him or Francis Bacon. She could do this one on her own. And she knew exactly where to start.

She shot a wink at Catalina, then pushed her plate aside to lean her elbows on the table. Resting her chin on her folded hands, she met Tom's beautiful blue eyes. "Dorothy Leynham is living at the Antelope, you say. Is she the friendly sort?"

SIX

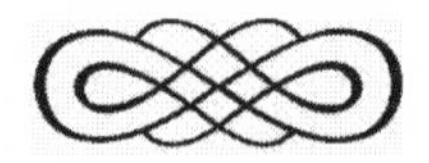

After dinner, Francis conducted a lively epistolary debate with Anthony. He used up his whole store of farthings tipping the boy who ran the letters from Gray's Inn Road to Bishopsgate and back.

In the end, Francis conceded the necessity of informing their Lord of Essex of the recent murder. His Lordship expected to be kept apprised of his counselors' doings, especially while their bid for Attorney General remained in play. The courtesies must be observed, though Francis doubted His Lordship would be much interested in the death of a minor official.

Francis missed having Anthony living in his house. He missed long talks by the fire in his slippers, sipping Jacques's delicious hot drinks. He missed having his best counselor on the spot, ready to discuss anything that perplexed him. He did not miss the pounding feet of secretaries, translators, and messengers on the stairs or the scowls and scoldings of the benchers, who disapproved of Anthony's large, active resident staff.

Anthony was happier in his own house near the theaters, though he himself never visited them. One avoided the unwashed masses as a rule. But he enjoyed the vitality of the city and the freedom to host noisy supper parties and the privacy of a busy street. No one noticed individual men coming and going in the general throng. At Gray's Inn, most people entered through the gatehouse under the watchful eye of the gatekeeper, and several hundred men with briefs to write spent many collective hours staring out of the windows.

The earl replied with an invitation for Francis to come at once if he didn't mind a bit of clatter. Francis speculated on the meaning of that warning on the short walk down to the Strand.

An usher led him into the hall, whose ceiling rose forty feet above the black-and-white-chequered floor. High windows admitted the afternoon light, but torches had also been placed along the interior walls. His Lordship stood in the center, dressed from head to toe in shining armor. Cool daylight and warm torchlight reflected from opposite sides of his steel suit. He looked magnificent, like a mighty warrior stepped straight out of a painting.

"My lord!" Francis swept off his hat and bowed, his forehead touching his extended leg.

Essex laughed merrily. He was in an excellent humor today. "Rise, my good man, rise." Then he held out his arms and turned in a full circle. "What do you think?" His voice echoed oddly from inside the crested helmet.

"I think I have never seen anything so wondrous in my life, my lord." Francis had no need to feign admiration. He took a few steps closer to peer at the engravings. "The artistry is extraordinary."

Essex nodded. "Jacob Halder. Never fails to satisfy."

Halder of Greenwich was the premier armorer in England. He doubtless earned his whole year's wages devising these costumes for the Accession Day tilts.

The armor was made of highly polished steel and fit His Lordship to perfection. Some true master of the art had decorated the front with a smiling sun centered across the midsection. Its golden rays extended up the cuirass, across both arms, and down both legs.

Essex turned again to show off the back, on which the artist had depicted the moon in silver and black. The full moon frowned. A gleaming crystal tear glinted beneath one eye. A silvery web of orbs descending up and down shone bright near the edges, where they presumably received light from the sun.

"Do you apprehend the conceit?" the earl asked, turning around again. His tone held a teasing note. He plainly longed to explain it.

"I'm not certain, my lord." Francis could readily guess, but why spoil the fun?

"Ha! Well, as you can see, I have the sun on the front and the moon on the back. When I'm riding toward Her Majesty, who will be seated in the gallery with her ladies, the sun blazons her glory. When I ride away, the sorrowful moon appears. She is the sun to me, you see, the source of all light and happiness. When I am forced to turn away from her, all is sorrow and darkness."

"Artful." Francis nodded his approval. "Yet sincere. And beautifully executed. I'm sure she'll be impressed."

"She'd better be. It's costing the earth. To be safe, I'll have a man dressed as a Roman senator explain it to her in verse. Her Majesty will grasp the concept at once, but we mustn't leave her ladies in the dark."

"I like the Roman element, my lord. It gives the whole conceit a classical grounding."

"Dorchester came up with the idea, if you can believe it. The man has parts." The earl took another slow turn, flexing his wrists and elbows this time. "It feels good." He raised each leg in turn, testing the knee and ankle joints. He caught the eye of two men in craftsman's blue livery. "You may take it off now."

He bent stiffly so they could remove the helmet. Once clear, the earl shook his head. "Ah! Better. It gets stuffy inside those things."

"I can only imagine." Francis would never allow himself to be encased in metal, much less invite another metal-clad man to try to push him off a horse with a long stick. But Essex loved jousting, and so did the queen. And so did the crowd that gathered whenever the event was offered.

Accession Day had been such a roaring success Essex had scheduled another tournament to take place on the morrow. He had vowed to tilt against all comers. Every lord with a suit of armor had added his name, including the Earl of Sussex, the Earl of Southampton, and the Earl of Bedford. Dorchester loved armor and pageantry but was evidently less keen on the actual jousting. He would judge instead; truly a better use of his talents.

Francis admired Stephen's ability to stand his ground, if well to one side. It showed both good judgment and a strong sense of self. His lady wife had doubtless influenced both qualities.

Francis would attend the tournament, but only because it would be noticed if he didn't. He hated crowds, dust, noise, and violence. But he liked pageantry if it was well themed, so the day would not be wholly without appeal.

Essex said, "I'll be out of this in a minute. We'll move somewhere a bit more private to talk. You didn't come here just to see me in my armor."

"I'm glad for the opportunity, my lord. I won't be able to admire the detail from the stands." Francis clasped his hands before him in a patient posture and turned his attention to the musicians occupying the far end of the hall. Pipes, drums, and a variety of horns produced music suitable for riding around a tiltyard. They would presumably play with greater gusto at the event.

"All done." The earl gave himself a shake. He wore a short, stiff doublet of a simple design and narrow slops — the sort of thing workmen wore when handling dangerous machinery, only of finer quality. He gestured toward the huge fireplace, where a low fire glowed. Two chairs had been placed beside a small table. Here His Lordship could converse with a guest while remaining accessible to the men preparing for the pageant.

Francis followed him, waiting until His Lordship sat before taking the other chair.

"So," Essex said, "another murder at Gray's Inn. Your life is more exciting than mine, Mr. Bacon."

"Heaven forfend, my lord." Francis pretended to be horrified. Nothing could induce him to participate in any sort of martial action. That was not his role in the world, thank God. "But, though the victim was a member of our society, the murder did not take place at Gray's. Mr. Strunk was the Attorney for the Court of Wards. He was found dead at his desk in Westminster this morning, apparently poisoned."

"Court of Wards, eh?" The earl let out a short laugh. "From what I hear, it's a wonder more of its officials aren't found dead at their desks."

"Indeed, my lord. It does seem that Attorney Strunk pushed some of the wards too far." Francis summarized the facts, few as they were, ending with the sheriff's early focus on Tom.

"Ah, that explains your interest. You can't have your own clerk arrested on such a charge, now can you?" Essex smiled, still in good humor. Though he lolled in his wide chair with his long legs extended before him, a light tension in his pose suggested he might leap up at any moment to stride across the room, issuing orders and taking up arms.

"Strictly speaking, my lord, Thomas Clarady is no longer my clerk. He passed the bar this month."

"A barrister and still a ward?" Essex whistled. "That is embarrassing. I feel for him." His Lordship had been thrown into wardship after his father died. As master of the court, Lord Burghley had granted the highest-ranking wards to his own care. Essex had dined every day for many years in that well-ordered household alongside the Earl of Southampton, the Earl of Surrey, the Earl of Rutland — and bent-backed Robert Cecil. That rivalry ran deep.

Francis smiled. "It partly explains his losing his temper on Friday afternoon. But as you observed, my lord, there must be many men — and women — with grudges against the Court of Wards."

"Hundreds would be my guess. All sorts. But I have every confidence in your ability to find the right one." His tone revealed his loss of interest in the topic. His gaze shifted toward the armorers, now wrapping each component in linen cloth to prevent scratching before placing it into a box.

He watched them for a moment, then a smile spread across his handsome features. He snapped his fingers in the air. "What about that vacant position? How would you like to be the next Attorney for the Court of Wards?"

Francis startled, so surprised by the suggestion he couldn't stop blinking for a moment. "My lord, I — I don't know what to say."

Essex laughed, not unkindly. "Merely a thought. I can't pull you from the Attorney General contention until Her Majesty makes her decision."

"It's not a bad thought," Francis said as he worked his mind around the idea. "My father was the attorney for Wards, you know."

"I did not know. When was this?"

"Oh, long before I was born. Not many years after the court was established in 1540. King Henry wanted a full accounting of his tenants and lands after dissolving relations with the Catholic Church. Vast tracts of lands were released by that act. The crown wanted to ensure it exercised its full feudal rights when those properties changed hands."

"I don't doubt it." Essex smiled wryly. "Monarchs are always hungry for money."

"They do carry the burdens of the state, my lord."

"Mmm. Was your father appointed by William Cecil?"

"No, my lord. There was another master back then. Let me think." Francis cast his mind over the lists of officials of important institutions. "My lord uncle attained that post in 1561, I believe. My father had already been named Lord Keeper by that time."

"Had he?" The earl's eyes moved as he calculated something in his mind. "We seem to have skipped right past Edward and Mary." He waved his hand to signal an end to that brief digression. "Your father was our queen's first Lord Keeper, then."

"He had that honor, my lord."

Essex gave him a thoughtful look. "So there is a precedent. A man might rise from the Court of Wards into the highest legal seat in the land. If we fail to get the Attorney Generalship for you, or even Solicitor General, we could do worse than aim for this other post."

Francis struggled to return his patron's cheerful smile. He had never aspired to a place within that institution. He muttered, "I may not be corrupt enough for an office in the Court of Wards."

Essex laughed out loud, tilting his head back. "We would not be sitting here together if you were, Mr. Bacon. I have higher standards than the Cecils. In fact, I believe I'd make a better master of that court than Robert."

"I had no idea you were interested, my lord."

"Why shouldn't I be? True, Robert has taken on the day-to-day responsibilities from his father. Lord Burghley has grown too feeble for his multiplicity of offices. But I have as much right to be considered for some of them as Robert does. More."

"That is true, my lord." In principle, at any rate. Her Majesty would do what she always did: maintain the existing state of affairs until something demanded a decision.

A happier thought struck Francis. "If you were master and I were the attorney, perhaps I could remedy the faults of that court. Perhaps I could restore it to the level of integrity it enjoyed under my father's watch."

Essex frowned, nodding as if considering that proposal. Then he winked. "Perhaps not *quite* that level, Mr. Bacon. I hold up my share of the burdens of the state, as you know."

"All England is grateful to you for it." Francis swallowed his disappointment.

The earl nodded, accepting the flattery as simple fact. "I wouldn't be as greedy as the Cecils. But I wouldn't mind having the Court of Wards filling my purse." His gaze shifted toward the fire, which exhaled a faint scent of burning ash wood. Then he turned again toward Francis. "But do I truly want it? Is it worth as much as they say?"

Francis puffed out a breath. "More, I should think. I believe my lord uncle built Theobalds with the gifts of hopeful guardians." That was Lord Burghley's palace in Hertfordshire, built to accommodate the queen in splendor.

"Did he now? That sounds promising." Essex nodded at Francis. "You could do me a favor, Mr. Bacon, if you're so inclined."

"Always, my lord." He could hardly refuse. He owed the earl a few hundred pounds and had no hope of repaying it in the foreseeable future.

Essex knew that. "While you're poking about among the officials of that court, see if you can find out how much they actually take in — on the side, I mean. Not the official fees. It could help me decide how hard to fight for the mastership when it comes up." He tapped a finger on the arm of Francis's chair, eyes sparkling. "Sounding the depths of their avarice could supply me with ammunition as well. Evidence of the Cecils' gross abuses, I mean. She wouldn't like hearing about it, but once heard, she would be obliged to consider it when choosing the next master."

"So she might." The words came out almost in a whisper. Francis's breath had frozen in his chest. Had His Lordship instructed him to expose the corruption in the Court of Wards, his uncle's most reliable source of revenue?

Neither Burghley nor the queen would thank him for that intrusion. He had a simple choice to make. He could please Essex and heap more coals on Her Majesty's indignation or protect his uncle's notorious court and come back empty-handed to his only reliable patron.

SEVEN

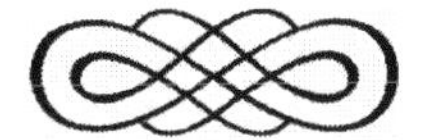

It started with the squeak. A tiny sound, like a mouse behind a wall, only it wasn't a mouse. The pulley high over his head needed a drop of oil, though it wasn't likely to get it. His torturers were probably half-deaf from the screaming their work induced.

Tom groaned, hearing that squeak, and tried to curl himself into a ball even as his arms were slowly hauled up over his head. He buried his face in the piss-mottled straw, mumbling, "No more. No more."

This moment of dread — this brief moment before the torment began again — was the worst. They gave him a few moments of rest now and then for reasons of their own. He lay in a heap, panting, grateful for the absence of agony. His wits came back to him, and he knew who he was again. Then he heard that squeak and knew what was coming — and that he was helpless to make it stop.

He rolled over, begging for mercy, thrashing his head against the pillow and releasing the scent of . . . roses? Here? How?

His eyes fluttered open. His gaze rested on a polished bedpost flanked by red velvet curtains. The room was silent, empty but for him. He didn't know where he was, but it certainly wasn't Bridewell.

A deep sigh of mingled relief and disgust escaped him. He hadn't had that dream for months. He hated it. It left him sweat-soaked and shaky. He hoped he hadn't screamed out loud. It scared people, if anyone was near enough to hear.

His arms had worked their way under the lofty pillows to press against a carved wooden headboard. He lowered them gingerly, bracing for that old ache, but his shoulders had long since healed. He pulled himself up to a sitting position and looked around in absolute confusion.

Where was he?

This room was much bigger than his closet at Bacon House and far better furnished. Painted cloths covered the walls with a soothing green decorated with yellow-and-white fleurs-de-lis. A small table held an ewer and basin along with a folded towel and an ivory comb. A round mirror hung above it. One high-backed chair rested against a wall, its rails and styles carved to match the bedposts.

He swung his legs over the side of the high bed and looked out the diamond-paned window. He couldn't see much beyond the top of a tree backed by a soft gray sky. He must be on an upper story.

He rose and went to the window, releasing the wholesome smell of dried tansy with each step. This room was well-kept. But who kept it?

He looked out and down and gave a soft laugh. Carts and wagons jostled one another on a wide street while well-dressed men and women on fine horses wove around them. That could only be the Strand. He must be in Dorchester House. And that recognition brought the rest of the day back.

He breathed in a cool sense of peace along with the wholesome smells. He'd had a fright with the sheriff coming to Bacon House and then run half a mile at top speed in a blind panic. Top that off with a heavy dinner and it was no wonder he'd had the nightmare again.

After dinner, Trumpet had charged an usher with showing him to this chamber on Stephen's side of the house. He'd toed off his shoes, unhooked his doublet, and fallen into a sound sleep the minute his head had landed on the thick down pillow.

Tom wished he could linger in this quiet retreat, but his life was at Gray's. He couldn't hide forever. He had to put himself back together and go home.

He washed his hands and face in the basin, then combed his hair and beard and restored his doublet and shoes. He paused in the corridor, looking left and right, trying to remember how to get downstairs. He heard a child shriek with laughter toward the right.

The nursery? He decided to risk a peek.

The door hung wide open, revealing a large room comfortably furnished for the education and care of small children. A bed stood beside the far wall, draped with red woolen cloth. A tall stand held a basin and pitcher with a shelf above it for folded towels. A family of wooden dolls dressed for court reclined atop a large chest. A row of curtained windows sat about two and a half feet from the floor, which was covered in thick rush matting. Every hazard or moveable object had been stowed well out of the reach of a toddler, apart from a set of leather balls strewn across the floor.

A nurse sat rocking a richly carved cradle containing a baby swaddled up to his chin. That must be Stephen the Younger. Stephen the Elder knelt on all fours, waggling his backside while pretending to snarl at Tom. He shouted, "The monster has awoken! Defend us, my lord!"

Two-year-old William squealed and charged at Tom, pummeling his knees with his little fists. Tom's heart turned a somersault at the touch of his much loved, but rarely seen, son. The boy had green eyes and no dimple, but the shape of his cheeks and nose betrayed his true father — for those who knew to look. Tom and Trumpet had agreed that he should avoid being seen with the child.

He understood it, but he hated that rule more than anything, even more than his wardship. He'd give up everything he ever hoped to possess to live with William and Trumpet as a family. He usually managed to turn his mind away from such thoughts, but the ban made a hole in his heart that ached constantly. Necessity was a harsh mistress.

He blinked away a film of tears and tilted his head back in mock dismay. "Mercy, mercy, my lord, I beg you!" He bent to turn the boy around, stealing a single stroke of the silky sun-yellow hair. "That's the real monster. See how he glares? Attack him!" He gave the boy a shove, and William toddled gleefully across the room to pound Stephen on the back.

Stephen wagged and roared for another minute, then stood up, lifting the boy into his arms. He gave him a sound kiss on the cheek before handing him to the young usher who had been waiting nearby. "It must be close to suppertime for this bold warrior."

Tom smiled at his old chum, bemused by the changes time and independence had wrought. He envied him, though he didn't resent him — a graceful state achieved after many months of wrestling with his baser nature. Stephen had done both Tom and Trumpet a favor by accepting the marriage his parents had arranged. Tom had been eaten up with jealousy at first but came to understand that things could have been much worse — especially for Trumpet.

"You're a good father, my lord."

Stephen's sidelong glance showed he'd caught the slight note of surprise. "My father was such a bad one that I'm determined to do better. I ask myself, 'What would that hard-hearted old whoreson have done?' Then I do the opposite." He clapped Tom on the shoulder. "Your father played with you all the time, I'll wager. You were so good at thinking up games when we were boys."

Tom smiled, casting his mind back. "I don't remember being this young, but I do remember building forts in the sand when I wasn't too many years older. Dad said we had to keep a sharp eye out for pirates." He chuckled at the bittersweet memory. "We would splash through the waves, shaking our wooden swords and shouting into the wind."

"My lady wife has a castle near the sea in Suffolk. Perhaps we'll go there next summer." Stephen tilted his head to lead Tom out of the nursery. "You couldn't find your way out, could you? This house is a maze."

"I could use a guide, my lord."

"I'm on my way down anyway."

They turned back the other way, walking side by side down the long corridor. This area bore little decoration apart from the fine oak paneling and a few clouded portraits.

"Thank you for letting me sleep here for a while," Tom said. "And for an excellent dinner."

"My lady wife is an attentive hostess." Stephen shot him a curious look. "She told me about your predicament. You're welcome to stay as long as you like. You did have a powerful motive to murder that churl, from what my lady says. Although she thinks you should go back to Gray's, and she's usually right about these things."

"I'm on my way. It just roused my old fear of being trapped in a jail." He'd spent a month in this house after the incident at Bridewell. Stephen had been in Dorset, but Trumpet had written to him from the start and told him all about it later. When one lived in a state of extended deception as she and Tom did, it was best to tell the truth as much as possible.

Stephen clapped him on the back. "I fully understand. You're always welcome here, Tom. I never had any real fun until you came to live with us. That was a gift for me back then."

They reached a staircase and started down. They descended two flights to reach the ground floor. Stephen led him unerringly to the great hall and on through the screens to the anteroom. He pointed toward the front door, then paused. "Or would you rather go out the back? I could have a wherry drop you at Temple Wharf."

"Thank you, my lord, but I can walk a few yards up the Strand. I'll go straight home and seek Mr. Bacon's counsel."

"Good plan. He'll need you anyway."

"How's that, my lord?"

"To investigate. That's what you two do, isn't it? You run about town asking questions, then he works out what it all means. I'd get right on it if I were you. You won't be truly safe until you catch the knave who did your murder for you."

* * *

Tom walked into the hall at Gray's for supper. He wanted a simple, peaceful meal, with no pointed questions about brandy bottles or dead attorneys. He would eat, he would listen to his messmate whine about his ever-nagging wife, and then he would go back to his room and read himself to sleep. He had an English translation of *Orlando Furioso* waiting for him. Adventure and chivalry would take his mind off his own troubles. The Court of Wards had no dragons to fight, for a mercy.

Roger Maycott was in fine form tonight. "Why must every domestic crisis happen during court terms? I ask you! We're only here twelve weeks out of the fifty-two. Can't things fall apart when I'm at home?"

"Evening." Tom slid onto the bench across from the beleaguered barrister. He nodded at the man on his left, Philip Littlebury.

Littlebury returned the nod, adding a knowing grin. "Decided to come home, eh?"

Tom tucked his chin in surprise. "How's that?"

"You were seen racing across the field toward Holborn as if a pack of wild dogs was nipping at your heels. That might not be so odd in itself, but the sheriff had just turned up."

Tom scoffed. "Can't abide the man. His breath stinks."

"His jails too, I reckon." Littlebury nodded as if he knew all about Tom's situation, which he most assuredly did not. "And here's another funny thing. Richard Strunk — did you know him?" He pointed a finger across the table at Maycott.

"Not well." Maycott shrugged. "But if you're trying to surprise me with the news that he's been murdered, you're too late. Everyone already knows."

"Hunh." Littlebury grunted. "But has everyone considered that Strunk was Attorney for the Court of Wards and that Clarady here is suing for his livery in the said court?"

"Pure coincidence," Tom said. What was he getting at?

Servers arrived with bowls of pottage and loaves of bread. Others followed to fill cups with ale. The food might be simple at Gray's, especially in the evening, but it was always well prepared, and there was plenty of it. They fed two hundred hungry young men twice a day. You couldn't expect boar's heads and marzipan at every meal.

Littlebury dipped his spoon into the fragrant mutton stew, but he had more to say about Strunk. "I hear he was poisoned. A bottle of brandy, they say. Seems like a waste. And a point in your favor, Tom. You wouldn't spend that much money on a drink meant to be spoiled."

"I certainly wouldn't," Maycott said. "You can poison a man just as well with a mediocre tinto." He tore a loaf into three parts, tossing one to each of the others. Their fourth tablemate was probably supping at the Antelope.

He'd fallen in love with one of the wenches and spent every free hour mooning at her like a lovesick calf.

Tom grinned into his own loaded spoon. He hadn't wanted to talk about Strunk, but he liked the trend of Maycott's thinking. These two had turned the tragic news into yet another source of supper-table raillery. That wouldn't hurt him; in fact, it might help.

Littlebury chewed down a wad of bread. "I'd've struck the knave on the back of the head. Quick, quiet, and cost-free."

Maycott shook his head. "You'd be seen coming and going."

"I'm not so sure." Tom decided to join in. "That place is a tomb on Saturday. Nobody but old Strunk sitting there in his dim little chamber, scouring the property records for more victims."

"Sounds like the Strunk I know," Maycott said. "Or knew, rather. I borrowed money from him once. He heard me bemoaning some debt my wife had incurred and offered to help. He was too eager. I should've known. As the weeks ticked by, he kept adding new charges. Asking for this little gift and that little favor. He threatened to tell the benchers how much I owed him if I didn't pay."

"Why would that matter?" Tom asked. Everyone owed money to someone around here. Obligation knitted societies together. That sounded like an aphorism, though he couldn't think who had said it. Some Roman, no doubt.

"I don't know. The original purchase wasn't entirely . . ." Maycott wagged his hand from side to side. "Not entirely what you'd call proper."

Tom drank some ale to hide his frown. What did that mean? Had Maycott's wife borrowed money to buy stolen goods? Something smuggled, most likely. Lace or brandy

— or Catholic impedimenta. Maycott wouldn't want the benchers to hear about that sort of thing.

"How did Strunk know?" Tom asked.

"Sharp questions, shrewd guesses. You're probably doing some of that guessing right now, but I don't have to answer you. I was so grateful for the loan at the time, I didn't realize I was helping him set his hooks in my flesh."

Tom shot at glance at their neighbors, who were arguing about something in Latin. Then he leaned in and lowered his voice. "He tried to charge me twice for the same fee. Eleven pounds!"

Littlebury let out a low whistle. "Who has that much money lying around? A bottle of brandy's cheap by comparison."

"True." Tom sat back up and dipped his spoon in his pottage. He extended his nose over the spoon to appreciate the aroma. Rich meat broth laden with garlic and thyme, balanced by the earthy savor of barley. "I wouldn't spend that much to poison a rat."

His messmates spluttered out laughs.

Tom hadn't meant it as a joke. "Besides, I'd already given him two bottles of good Rhenish. A gift to expedite matters, as Strunk put it. Ha!"

"Expedite his personal matters," Littlebury said. "I hear he has a mistress near Aldgate who is *very* demanding. Had a mistress. I wonder if she knows he's dead."

There was a cruel thought. But Tom refused to feel sorry for anyone connected to that greedy churl. She'd find out one way or another and move on to another patron.

"He always had the best of everything," Maycott said. "He has engraved silver bowls and Venetian glass goblets in his chambers."

So did Mr. Bacon, but he got his the honest way, by inheriting them from his father. Sir Nicholas might well have received them as gifts during his time in the Court of Wards, come to think of it. That silver wheel kept on turning, generation after generation.

"I wonder how many Graysians he lured into his debt?" Tom asked. A short list of alternative suspects could get him off the sheriff's hook. How could he get those names? Mr. Bacon might know a way.

"More than a few," Littlebury said. "Have you noticed that no one's grieving? Sir Avery said a few words at dinner, but nobody stood up to tell a fond tale or say how much he would be missed. I mean, take a look at that table over there. Those are his peers, barristers in their fifties. He sat at that table every day for dinner and supper when the courts were in session."

Raucous laughter ebbed and flowed from that side of the hall, the sound of men trading bawdy jokes. Not the hushed voices of men who had lost a friend. They seemed as merry as usual this evening, calling for ale and leaning across the table to jab a finger to emphasize some crucial point.

"I wonder if anyone's gone to tell his wife." Tom used the last of his bread to sop up the dregs of his pottage. He hoped the servers would bring out something sweet. He wouldn't mind one of those apple fritters Trumpet had given him at dinner.

"She may not miss him either," Littlebury said. "He spent more time here than most men with fine manors to call home. More time with those property records, one supposes."

Tom barked a bitter laugh. "The Court of Wards is ever vigilant."

"It's a dirty business." Maycott drained his cup and signaled to a server to bring another round. Then his dour face brightened. "But a lucrative one. I wonder who'll get Strunk's post. It's in the queen's gift, isn't it? I hope it's another Graysian. If there must be someone to exploit the wards of England, may it be one of ours."

The usher brought a jug and filled their cups. All three barristers raised them to cry, "To one of ours!"

"Your master should make a bid for it," Littlebury said. "He's qualified, if anyone is."

"Former master," Tom said. "I'm not a clerk anymore."

"No offense intended." Littlebury smiled. "If I could claim a connection with one of the Bacons, I'd leap at it. He kept the sheriff from your door, they say."

"No doubt he feared they'd make a mess. But he can't ask for the Wards position, I shouldn't think. Not while his suit for Attorney General is still pending."

Maycott grunted in sympathy. "I'm glad my ambitions don't reach that high. Rich widows and squabbling merchants are good enough for me."

"Rich widows!" Littlebury raised his cup again. The others echoed the toast.

Maycott said, "I hear the benchers are placing bets on the next attorney. They're the only ones close enough to make a reasonable guess. I'd bet on whoever has a few thousand pounds to add to Lord Burghley's treasure chest."

"It'll go to the highest bidder," Littlebury said. "That much is certain."

"Well, that rules out Francis Bacon," Tom said with a laugh. "Besides, he's not venal enough. Or sly enough. I can't see him sitting there angling for a bribe with a smarmy smirk on his face. And he loathes corruption in the courts. He thinks it makes them inefficient and damages the public trust."

"Trust!" Maycott made a rude noise. "That's not a word relating to the Court of Wards. Everyone hates them."

"Whoever wins the bidding," Littlebury said, "they should give Tom a nice gratuity. After all, you cleared the way for them, didn't you, you old rascal?" He chuckled as he dug an elbow into Tom's side.

EIGHT

Tuesday morning, shortly after breakfast, Francis knocked on Tom's door. It opened almost immediately. He'd been waiting.

"Are you ready?" Francis asked. "Sir Avery will meet us there."

"Ready enough, since it has to be done." Tom closed his door. He'd dressed for the occasion, wearing his second-best suit. It displayed no slashings or pricks, and the buttons were glossy black, not brass or silver. But the fabric had the gleam and drape of fine cloth, and he'd chosen a ruff with a quarter inch of imported lace. The distinctive velvet welts on the sleeves of his barrister's gown displayed his status.

Francis wore his bencher's gown with its tufts of silk and velvet, as well as a tall hat with a lavender ribbon. Sir Avery would be wearing his serjeant's red robes with the coif and furred cloak of that office. Sheriff Hanton would see at a glance that Gray's Inn did not take threats — however mild, however implicit — to its members lightly.

Francis noted the hollows under Tom's eyes. "Did you sleep?"

Tom shook his head.

"I'll send Pinnock for another bottle of laudanum."

"Thanks."

They crossed the corner of the yard to the great hall and went upstairs to the treasurer's chamber. Though paneled in well-tended oak, this room was meant for work, not ostentation. Although portraits of famous Graysians did adorn the walls here and there. Francis sat beneath the painting of his father, though the sheriff might not see a resemblance.

Sir Avery, seated at the head of the table, put aside the document he'd been reading and gave Tom a narrow-eyed inspection. "You look exhausted. That isn't good. An innocent man sleeps a dreamless sleep."

"Unless he has reason to fear a groundless arrest," Francis said. "He can't help how he sleeps."

"True, true." Sir Avery smiled. "I merely note that his appearance works against us to some degree."

"I'll endeavor to keep my chin up," Tom said. He sat next to Sir Avery, opposite Francis. A goodly expanse of polished bench ran from them to the small chair at the foot. But the sheriff would most likely remain standing.

They barely had time to compose their expressions when the door swung open to reveal Sheriff Hanton. He had to duck his head a bit to clear the lintel. When he straightened again, he stopped still, his gaze taking in the evidence of legal prowess presented before him. Doubt clouded his features for a moment, and his shoulders sank. But he rallied, squaring his short-bearded jaw and his shoulders together.

He bowed to the seated men as a group. "Sir Avery, I appreciate your taking the time to allow me to question this man."

"Only a little time, I hope." Sir Avery granted the intruder a thin smile. "I am too busy for a goose chase this morning."

The sheriff's eyes flashed. "Mr. Clarady was heard to threaten a man who was murdered soon after. I think we can all agree that he should at least be questioned."

"For the record," Tom said, enunciating each word, "I did not threaten Attorney Strunk. Either your witnesses are exaggerating or you are." That struck its mark. The sheriff's nostrils flared. Tom smiled for the first time. "What I said was, 'I hope you choke on that wine.' Wine I had given Mr. Strunk as a token of my appreciation for his work."

Francis raised a finger before adding the clarification. "A hope is merely a wish, not a threat or a promise. It cannot be construed as an act. The law does not apply to our fancies, Sheriff. You therefore have no sound reason to suspect our colleague."

The sheriff's lip curled. He brought up the card reading 'From a gentleman of Gray's." Francis made short work of that as a viable piece of evidence.

Hanton managed a few more questions about when Tom had arrived, when he had left, and who else had been present at both times. Tom answered each question as succinctly as possible, letting his disdain for their triviality color his tone. Hanton's gaze made the rounds from Tom to Francis to Sir Avery after each one, lingering longest on the treasurer.

Sir Avery, master of intimidation, allowed his increasing boredom to show on his heavy features. "I believe we've given you all you need, Sheriff."

Hanton pressed his lips together, but in truth there was little to be asked or answered. He turned to give Tom his full attention. "I'll be keeping an eye on you, Mr. Clarady."

"Toward what end?" Francis snapped.

Hanton's eyes shifted to acknowledge the questioner but then returned to hold Tom's gaze. "I want to make sure I can lay my hands on you when the time comes."

The master key turned smoothly in the lock, and the door opened with nary a squeak. Either his servant had been more diligent than the average or Strunk had been a keen-eyed task master.

Francis suspected the latter. He'd borrowed the key from Gray's steward to perform a search of the late attorney's chambers. No record of unofficial payments had been found in his office in Westminster, according to Sir Avery, who received daily reports from the sheriff.

But a man like Strunk would keep records. Francis wanted a look at them. He also wanted a look at another hypothetical list, this one of loans made to Graysians. There must be one here somewhere. Tom had told him about Roger Maycott's complaints. Strunk's money-lending seemed to have shaded into extortion, at least in Maycott's case — a good motive for murder. They only needed a few names to provide alternatives to Tom.

A man like Richard Strunk, who spent most of his days searching old records for vulnerable properties, would keep track of his sources of income. Illicit or not, he would want to know how much he received from whom on what date. Indeed, an affinity for records and account books would have been a requirement for attaining his position.

That, and a large bribe to the master of the court.

Some government positions cost thousands of pounds, paid to whomever held the prize in his gift. The queen appointed the Attorney of the Court of Wards, but she would follow Lord Burghley's recommendation. She might receive some share of each bribe, but more likely she would regard them as payment for an otherwise unfunded post. So the bulk of those "gifts" would go straight into His Lordship's purse. Or rather, his houses.

The salary for the office had been ninety pounds per annum in Sir Nicholas Bacon's day. A goodly sum back then. It probably hadn't risen much, though costs had shot up. Still, ninety pounds was considerable — about what a prosperous merchant might earn. A man could keep a wife and children in a comfortable house in Holborn on that salary. He could dress according to his station and entertain friends at holidays.

He couldn't raise horses on a large estate in Surrey or send his sons on tours of the Continent. He couldn't drink wine from Venetian glassware or pick nutmeats from a silver salver. Strunk had made a moral choice — the wrong one — when he decided to turn himself into a major landowner.

His father had been a gentleman and his mother the daughter of a knight. Strunk Senior had served his turn as justice of the peace and other county offices. He'd been a worthy member of the Surrey gentry, but not a wealthy man. Francis had learned that much from Sir Avery. Whether the Court of Wards had corrupted its official or Strunk had sought a seat known for such venality could now never be known.

The original bribe that bought him the post had been raised somehow. Had he paid it off over the years? Or had pressure from his creditor provoked greater pressure on the wards? Corruption bred corruption, after all.

Francis sighed, then breathed in the well-loved smell of ink and paper. Francis no longer noticed that underlayer in his own chambers, but it struck him afresh here. No one had opened that door since the servant had left on Saturday afternoon. Two days and three nights. The place had an abandoned air, though whether that came from some specific source, like dust or from Francis's imagination, he could not judge.

As he walked toward the desk, he crushed the lavender strewn across the wood floor to ward off fleas. The wholesome fragrance relieved the fustiness. Francis stood in the center of the room and turned full circle to survey the whole. Strunk had a fine taste in furnishings, almost as fine as Francis had himself. An ornately carved cupboard displayed a collection of silver cups and plates.

Not a matched set, however. Some plates bore engravings around the rim, some cups had decorative feet, while others had plain stems.

Gifts from petitioners, most likely. The sort any official might expect to receive. Strunk wouldn't have had to ask for those; they were routine in court cases.

He also owned a set of goblets made of Venetian glass. One sat on the desk next to an unopened bottle of wine, ready for the master to refresh himself after a hard day in Westminster. A silk tapestry hung over the mantelpiece. It portrayed a hunting scene, though Francis doubted Strunk had ever chased a deer. Two large sets of shelves leaned against opposite walls, each holding many books. Some looked costly, with leather bindings and gilt titles. One shelf displayed a row of bottles in different shapes and sizes, presumably wine and spirits from different vintners. More gifts, no doubt. Tom's Rhenish must be among them.

Francis opened the door to the bedchamber and found a similar level of opulence. A coverlet of squirrel fur lay across the bed, whose posts and headboard boasted elaborate carvings. The hangings were of supple scarlet wool. Two large chests stood against the walls, doubtless filled with tailored garments of best cloth. Silver candlesticks stood on walnut tables on either side of the bed.

The ledgers might be buried under layers of cloth inside those chests, but Francis guessed not. If they were his, he would keep them somewhere more accessible. He closed the door and went to sit at the desk.

He plucked a quill from the silver stand and fiddled with it as he contemplated the quiet splendor of the room. He lived in a similar style, although none of it had come from bribes, at least not to him. Who would offer him a bribe? He had less power than Tom, who was gifted with a comely face and figure and an abundance of natural charm.

The costly goods that soothed the turmoil of his life had been acquired by his father and his elder stepbrothers during their turns in Bacon House. The three brothers had inherited large estates in Norfolk and Suffolk. They also owned houses in London for the rare occasions when they came to town. Sir Nicholas had died before he'd been able to arrange similar support for his youngest son. A few pieces of plate and a goblet or two were scant compensation for that lack.

It occurred to Francis for the first time that some of his finer pieces might have been gifts to his father during his tenure as Lord Keeper. In fact, some of them must be. His Venetian glass vase, for example. It was a work of art, not something pragmatic Sir Nicholas would purchase for himself.

But the Attorney of the Court of Wards sat far below the Lord Keeper of the Great Seal. One wouldn't expect so much finery at this level without some additional pressure. Strunk couldn't even have afforded these chambers on his salary, not without skimping on something else. Chambers on the first floor of Stanhope's Building cost more than any others at the inn. They offered privacy, being set behind the Middle Gallery. The windows overlooked the leafy, tree-lined inner court instead of the busy, graveled Chapel Court. No one came back here who didn't have good reason to.

Francis could observe the comings and goings through the gate from the window behind his desk, which he often liked. He could see men queuing up for dinner or coaches delivering notables to some festivity. He was impervious to distractions when working, but not all men enjoyed that facility.

He tapped the quill on the polished desktop. Now that Anthony had moved out and taken his army of clerks with him, Francis could lease the chambers on his second floor to another Graysian. He couldn't charge as much as this set in Stanhope's building, but it would be worth noticing how much these went for. The benchers wouldn't waste any time finding another lessee for this desirable property. If Tom achieved his livery, Francis might even be able to raise the rate for his ground floor chambers as well.

But he hadn't come here to assess Strunk's goods. He'd come to find out how he'd paid for them. Where would the man keep his private account books?

Where would Francis keep such things if he had them? He acknowledged a twisted kinship with the attorney after studying his precious objects. In some ways, they were two sides of the same coin.

He wouldn't hide anything he wanted to retrieve on a regular basis anywhere the least bit troublesome. So not in that low chest covered with a figured carpet, for example. A tall bronze candelabra stood atop the carpet. One would have to lift that down and then pull off the heavy carpet in order to raise the lid of the chest. Far too much effort.

His gaze lit on a stack of thick books lying on a bottom shelf within easy reach of the desk. He bent to peer at the title on the spine of the topmost volume: *Littleton's Treatise on Tenures. Hmm.* Strunk doubtless kept another copy in his chamber at Westminster to consult when reviewing a questionable deed. He wouldn't have much need for it here.

Francis scooted his chair toward the shelf and lifted the book from the stack. He set it on the desk, opened the stiffened front cover, and laughed. A ledger about half the size of its host lay inside a neatly cut hole. A classic hiding place for a man of letters.

Most convenient! He took out the ledger, then closed up *Littleton* and put it back on the shelf. He centered his chair at the desk again to examine his find. The small book was bound in thin, flexible gray leather. It would fit snugly in the deep pocket of a pair of round hose in case its owner wished to carry it back and forth from work.

Strunk hadn't bothered with a title page. Perhaps the book's color was sufficient identification because this book clearly held notes about his loans to fellow Graysians. Each entry included the name of a borrower, most of whom Francis recognized, and an original loan amount. The interest to be paid came next inside parentheses. The date and amount of each monthly payment were duly recorded as well.

Many loans contained no other information. They were ordinary loans, in other words, such as the ones Francis had received from one or two — or perhaps three — Graysians over the past year. He'd had to send gifts to Privy Council members and other courtiers, encouraging them to support his bid. His cheeks burned at the thought of his name jotted down in similar ledgers elsewhere around the inn.

Such loans might engender mild embarrassment, but they were hardly enough to rouse a man to murder. Tom's messmate, Roger Maycott, had hinted at something much worse. Tom had said he'd borrowed money to cover a debt for a purchase his wife had made, something he didn't want anyone here to know about. Tom had guessed it was some sort of contraband, probably religious in nature, like Catholic impedimenta. No one here would worry much about buying Belgian lace without paying the import tax.

Francis flipped to the end of the book and worked backward until he found Maycott's entry. He'd borrowed seventy-five pounds to be repaid in monthly increments of seven and a half pounds. An enormous sum! That purchase hadn't been lace or ivory rosaries. A whole

Jesuit priest, perhaps, with a shipful of men to be bribed into silence.

Strunk would have made the same calculation. Poor Mr. Maycott! Lucky for him, Francis had no obligation to report his guesses to anyone, especially about such tangential matters. His task was to identify a murderer, not scour around for crimes in general.

This entry had an additional line noting a ten-pound fine for "consideration." Francis snorted. A euphemism for "silence," one assumed. This was clear evidence of extortion. Not completely explicit, but anyone with any understanding of the world would recognize it.

He paged backward, looking for that extra line. He found several more recording similar sums. Some men had paid for consideration again and again, tithing ten pounds a month to their rapacious master.

The secrets had not been written down, but some of the names were prominent ones in Graysian society. Francis would commit this notebook to the fire once he'd gleaned everything relevant to the murder. He would have to show it to Sir Avery, but he was confident the treasurer would agree that the details should be restricted.

Francis closed the small ledger and leaned back in the well-proportioned chair. Strunk had extracted hundreds of pounds from his victims over the years. He had died a wealthy man. Respected, if not much liked. No one here seemed to miss him in the least.

Strunk might have been the single most corrupt man Francis had ever known, now that the depths of his extortions had been plumbed. Yet he had participated in events at Gray's on a congenial footing, contributing generously to the Christmas revels and maintenance of the grounds. His beneficence had been made possible by his avarice, however. Perhaps that stink had clung invisibly to his offerings. They would be accepted out of need, but the donor would not be appreciated.

Francis had come here looking for possible enemies. He'd found them, well enough. He had a list of names of men he'd lived among for fifteen years, rubbing elbows as they crowded into the hall for dinner or a lecture. Men he had respected for their demeanor, their learning, and their achievements. Now he knew some of them possessed a secret dark enough to pay a monthly tribute to a grasping villain. Could he look at them this evening at supper without wondering what each one kept hidden?

He gazed at the treasures collected in the ornate chamber and felt sick to his stomach. He must get away, get back to the clean air at Twickenham. He'd meant to have supper in the hall, but he couldn't face Strunk's victims this evening.

He jumped up, stuffed the book into his pocket, and fled. He hastened down to Temple Wharf and flung himself into the first wherry headed upriver. It wasn't until they had rowed past Westminster Hall that he remembered he still had the steward's master key.

NINE

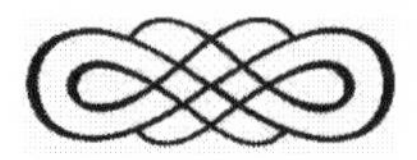

"I probably won't need it for more than a week, but I'll pay rent for two weeks to be on the safe side." Trumpet sat in the private parlor behind the common rooms at the Antelope Inn on Holborn Road. She'd come to negotiate terms for a room with special support from the staff.

Her plan was to pretend to be a middling sort of woman — gentle, but not rich — with a suit in the Court of Requests. She would live at the Antelope while her case ground on, as did so many of her kind. She and Catalina would take meals in the public room and linger in that sociable milieu. Many guests used the public rooms as parlors, especially if their bedchambers were small. Sooner or later — sooner, if Tom had it right — Dorothy Leynham would appear. Then Trumpet would pounce. She would befriend the woman and learn everything she could about the other wards. Some detail, some slip induced by too much wine on a dull afternoon, would lead to the killer.

If her plan succeeded, and there was no reason why it shouldn't, Trumpet would solve the case before Mr. Bacon and be the one to save Tom from the sheriff's grasp.

Besides, she and Catalina loved playacting and costumery. They hadn't had much chance to exercise their skills lately. Many goals would be satisfied by this simple stratagem.

"If you don't mind my asking, my lady, what would you be wanting this room for?" Mrs. Sprye, proprietress of the popular inn, sounded a trifle wary. "You've been changing costumes in my private chambers these past few years without complaint."

"And the favor is much appreciated." Also paid for, but money couldn't buy the level of discretion Mrs. Sprye provided. Only friendship could do that, and Trumpet had no intention of testing that bond.

Their relationship had begun many years ago, when Trumpet discovered that her favorite uncle, a barrister of Gray's Inn, had been counterfeiting coins at her castle in Suffolk. She had also learned that he spent those coins smuggling Catholic literature into England.

Such intriguing secrets! So full of possibilities! He would do anything to protect them, and Trumpet knew exactly what she wanted — a year of study at Gray's. An unusual price, perhaps, but then she had never been an ordinary girl.

He complied in full. Indeed, he enjoyed the deception as much as she did. She'd filled a trunk with boy's clothes and moved into his chambers. That very day, he'd brought her to meet Mrs. Sprye, knowing she'd prove a useful ally. The late Mr. Sprye had been a barrister and had encouraged his wife to follow his cases and learn the law. She was writing a book about the law's regard — or lack of same — for women. Trumpet had agreed to help her with that monumental task in exchange for laundry services and general support.

Thus the bond was formed. Trumpet still helped with the book, looking up references in the law books she'd installed in the library at Dorchester House. She and Catalina still dressed as tradeswomen now and then to meet Tom for supper. Supper only — they had never taken advantage of Mrs. Sprye's generosity by using her house for dalliance.

Trumpet suspected that was the matter of present concern. She'd intended to confide in the innkeeper anyway. Mrs. Sprye had keen eyes, sharp ears, and a ready wit. She might well have noticed something useful about the Leynhams.

"Please sit," Trumpet said, gesturing at a well-worn armchair. This room had neither window nor hearth, but a large cloth painted with a blue-and-red floral design cheered the small space. A desk piled high with papers stood against one wall. An unlit brazier had been pushed into a corner. Two chairs faced one another in the center of the room, ready for conversation. "My request comes with a story."

"I like stories." Mrs. Sprye took her chair and folded her hands in her lap.

Trumpet told her everything she knew about the murder of Richard Strunk. It didn't take long.

Mrs. Sprye shook her head, though a smile brought out the crinkles around her blue eyes. "I shouldn't smile, though I doubt he'll be much mourned. He didn't come here often, but the Court of Wards has its reputation, doesn't it?"

"A foul one. Strunk must have had many enemies, which works in Tom's favor. But the sheriff will want names. That's why I need a room here for one or two weeks. Two of your guests, Dorothy Leynham and her uncle, were the last persons to see Mr. Strunk alive."

"Apart from his clerk." Mrs. Sprye thought for a moment. "And his servant at Gray's, one assumes."

Trumpet clucked her tongue. "I forgot about the servants. A gross oversight."

"Not in this case, my lady. Not in my estimation. They couldn't afford a bottle of brandy, either of them. And both would have had simpler means to hand. It isn't difficult for a servant to murder his master. It's a wonder it doesn't happen more often."

"Thanks for that. Fewer to worry about." She heard the contradiction in her words and laughed. "We want more than one, because that one is Tom, but not so many that we can't look into them all."

"It's a balance, isn't it?" Mrs. Sprye cocked her head. "Then you'll only be pretending to spend nights here, my lady. Is that correct?"

"Yes. And though you're too delicate to ask, Tom will not visit me in my room. I'll go home every evening. My husband is in town, though he spends most of each day at the palace. And I don't intend to miss my sons' supper if I can help it."

"You know I don't like to pry, my lady."

"I appreciate that. My plan is to play the role of a widow who has come to Westminster to pursue her rights in the Court of Requests. She has a stepson almost her age, you see, who is attempting to seize a manor she inherited from her mother before her marriage."

Mrs. Sprye laughed with delight, slapping her hands on her thighs. "You are the very soul of wit, my lady! I'm proud of the way you've held on to the knowledge you gained during your year of study. And what better use for it than to keep our Tom out of jail?"

"None that I can think of." Trumpet's cheeks burned with pleasure at the praise. She valued the source more highly than any other, apart from Mr. Bacon. Though he seldom troubled himself to offer such encouragements.

"You've thought of every detail." Mrs. Sprye joined eagerly into the game. She loved to see women taking charge of their own lives. "The Court of Wards is next door to the Court of Requests, isn't it? I've listened to cases in Requests many a morning. It's the best bargain for a woman of modest means, in my opinion, and much cleaner than the theater."

"I'll move into my room today, if possible, and spend an hour or two lurking about both courts. There must be a common waiting area."

"There is, my lady. A wide corridor with long benches. Always people in there, as far as I've seen. I know Mrs. Leynham has spent time there because she's complained about it. I believe the Clerk of Requests sits down the hall from the Attorney of Wards. The Clerk of the Court of Wards is in that building too, somewhere. You could probably find Mrs. Leynham there as well, though I couldn't tell you when, precisely."

"That is useful information." Trumpet beamed at the older woman. "But I only need to see her in passing or to be able to claim that I did. I mean to strike up a friendship here in your public room." She set a finger under her chin, tilting her head in a pose. She spoke in a tone of girlish surprise. "Do forgive the intrusion, but haven't I seen you at the Court of Requests?"

"Just like that, my lady. She'll correct you and invite you to join her. Your charm will do the rest."

"Thank you." Trumpet thought of the one thing that would sink her little ship before she left the harbor. "She does visit the public room from time to time, doesn't she?"

"Every day. They dine here, naturally. The uncle usually takes a nap afterward, but Mrs. Leynham and her maidservant often go out for a stroll. Then they sit near the windows gazing about as if wishing someone would pop up and introduce themselves. She's longing for a friend, in my opinion."

"Perfect." Trumpet rubbed her hands together. "Now about that room."

Here she met a minor obstacle. Rooms within a short walk of Westminster were hard to come by during court terms. The best the Antelope could offer her was the worst room in the house — the top floor at the front, where she'd have stairs to climb and noise from the street. On the other hand, a small chamber troublesome to reach justified spending time in the ground-floor public room.

Better still, the stair to that level could be reached without walking through the tavern. The central yard was always busy during the day, with horses being mounted, dismounted, or loaded with bags. People milled about welcoming or bidding farewell to their friends. Trumpet and Catalina could whisk unnoticed up to their retreat and descend in clothing suitable to their pretended stations.

They settled on the terms and shook hands. "Remember," Trumpet said, "I'm Alice Truman until further notice. Catalina is my companion, Mrs. Catherine Smith."

"Understood." Mrs. Sprye tapped her nose. "And, my lady, if I may be so bold. If you do end up having one of my guests arrested, would you kindly not do it under my roof?"

* * *

Trumpet and Catalina went home and had dinner. They then spent an hour in Trumpet's private chambers sorting clothes. They'd accumulated quite a collection of costume pieces, both male and female. Although, now that she'd borne two children, Trumpet found her men's clothes less comfortable. They would all have to be let out.

Their favorite garb was that of the lesser tradesman's wife. Comfortable, durable, and easy to care for. Such women commonly roamed the city on their own without the least reproach. If you hung a basket over your arm and walked with a sense of purpose, no one thought twice about the propriety of your behavior.

This campaign, however, required a better cut and cloth. Trumpet had decided that Alice Truman would be worth some twenty-three pounds a year, even without the disputed manor. That would add an additional seventeen. She liked odd numbers. They seemed more plausible somehow. Dorothy Leynham must be worth at least that much, or she wouldn't be a ward of the queen. Trumpet wanted to place herself in a similar class, but a bit lower, so Dorothy could have the pleasure of gracious condescension. She would spill more confidences to an inferior than a superior.

Trumpet and Catalina had made a study of women's and men's garb. They loved nothing more than leaning out the first-floor windows at Aunt Blanche's house on Bishopsgate, watching the passersby below. Or sitting at a table in the King's Head on Cheapside, where they could get a street-level view. They evaluated every detail, from feathers in hats to bows on shoes, guessing at the wearer's worth. They had no way to test the truth of their appraisals, but they reckoned they came close most of the time.

Trumpet had decided to wear a wig for this deception to cover her black hair. Catalina had found one in a nondescript light brown that fit well and didn't itch. Topped with an embroidered coif or lace-trimmed attifet, it looked quite natural.

They couldn't hide her distinctive green eyes or Catalina's Spanish complexion, but they did their best to mask and deflect. Trumpet stuck a large brown mole on her chin to draw the gaze from her eyes. Catalina wore bodices and skirts of a light tawny and dusted her face with powder.

Mrs. Sprye sent a servant from the Antelope to collect the large trunk from Dorchester House. Trumpet and Catalina dressed for shopping and let the wherryman take them down to the bridge. They waited a few minutes, then took another wherry back upriver to Temple Wharf. A short walk and they were climbing the stairs at the Antelope to transform themselves into two gentlewomen from Suffolk.

They went downstairs prepared to wait some time for their prey to appear. But Dolly, the barmaid who abetted Trumpet's disguises, pointed at two women seated near the front windows. "The tall one is Mrs. Leynham," she whispered. "The other one's her companion, Mrs. Fleming."

Trumpet thanked her. She and Catalina began a slow stroll through the tavern as if considering the choice of tables. She passed Dorothy, then stopped and turned full around. "Do forgive the intrusion, Mistress. But haven't I seen you at the Court of Requests?"

"Wards," Dorothy replied. Her smile showed her eagerness for an intrusion.

Her companion smiled too, giving the newcomers a welcoming nod. She appeared to be five years older than her mistress. Well-dressed but without the adornments her mistress enjoyed.

"Wards?" Trumpet took a step closer, feigning confusion.

"The Court of Wards," Dorothy said. "It's next door to Requests." She gestured at the two empty stools at their table. "Won't you join us? We're just sitting here watching the world go by — what we can see of it."

"We'd be delighted." Trumpet sat next to Dorothy, leaving the other stool for Catalina. "There isn't much to do in the afternoon, is there? Apart from waiting for court officials. One's feet can only bear so much shopping, and the city is so noisy."

"Isn't it, though? In a way, I love it. So different from the endless chirping of birds at home in Kent. But it is exhausting."

"Exhausting!" Trumpet wouldn't trade the traffic on the Strand for the most musical birds in all England. "I'm Alice Truman, and this is my friend Catherine Smith. We're from Suffolk."

"Dorothy Leynham. My companion, Martha Fleming." The four women beamed at one another. "We're having a little treat to hold us til supper. Pear tarts and white wine. I highly recommend them."

"Sounds lovely." Trumpet wiggled her fingers at Dolly, who came to take their order. She folded her hands on the table and batted her lashes at Dorothy. "What is this Court of Wards of which you speak? I've never heard of it."

"Consider yourself lucky." Dorothy proceeded to deliver a cogent summary of the history and function of the court. This woman was no dunderhead. She'd done some reading and asked some probing questions. Tom had her completely wrong. How typical of a man! They always start out thinking comely women must be stupid. But Tom, of all people, ought to know better.

Dorothy was also prettier than Tom had implied. True, her eyes were as round and brown as hazelnuts and a smidge too close together, but they were ringed with thick, dark lashes. He hadn't mentioned those, nor the gleam of intelligence shining in their depths. He'd noted the thinness of her lips, but not the playful smiles that often passed across them.

And yes, her face was longer than average, as was her neck, but she wore a ruff four inches deep to hide that slight flaw. A four-inch ruff would cover Trumpet's chin. Dorothy was thin with a shallow bosom, but that made it possible for her to wear a nearly transparent partlet that would make a bustier woman look like a bawd.

"I'm here to sue for my livery," Dorothy finished. She laughed at Trumpet's wide-eyed response. "That's less dire than it sounds. Perfectly routine, for the most part. My twenty-first birthday is next Monday."

"Felicitations!" Trumpet said, clapping her hands.

"Thank you. My uncle — whom you're bound to meet if you're staying here — has been my guardian. We have fees to pay and seals to collect, that sort of thing. And then I'll be a free woman."

Her eyes flashed at that prospect. Trumpet understood. She would never wish her father's death, but she had often imagined how her life would be if she'd been able to inherit before she married. She could live where she pleased, when she pleased, for one thing. But she couldn't dally with Tom. How would she explain a baby? She could marry him and shock the world — and spend some time in the Tower. The queen had the right of approval when the daughters of earls sought to marry, and she punished violators rigorously.

"Your turn," Dorothy said. "What is the Court of Requests? I've heard the name but haven't the least notion what it's about."

"Well," Trumpet said, "it's a woman of property's best friend. It's an equity court, which means the judge considers all sorts of things to make his ruling. Promises made and personal circumstances, the history of the disputed property — that sort of thing. They say the common law looks to the cause, while equity looks to the person. The Master of Requests is free to decide for himself if your case has merit, even if you can't pass every test of the common law. Are you missing a deed? Has your principal witness died? Then the King's Bench won't help you, nor will the Court of Common Pleas. Off you go, with nothing to show for your trouble and expense."

"That sounds so unfair." Dorothy's gaze shifted as if she were reviewing something in her mind.

"It is harsh. And expensive! You can pursue your whole case in Requests for as little as ten pounds."

"Ten pounds! We've paid that much for a single fee in Wards."

The women shook their heads in expressions of mutual disgust. Trumpet inwardly reveled in the lucky chance. Finding a common enemy was the best way to make a friend.

Trumpet smiled up at Dolly as a small plate and a footed wooden cup were placed before her. She took a sip of wine and hummed with pleasure. "This is a lovely inn, isn't it?"

"We've been pleased so far, though it is dreadfully crowded." Dorothy gave Trumpet time to sample the pear tart, then asked, "I'm intrigued by this Court of Requests. I may have a cause of my own to bring in the coming year. What is your suit, if you don't mind my asking?"

"Not at all." Trumpet wondered about that cause. It must be property — lawsuits were almost always about property. People also sued over unpaid wages and chattels removed without permission, but those losses had to be quite large to justify the cost of a suit. The vast majority of cases she had heard involved disputes over land ownership.

Dorothy's case must be related to her wardship. She hadn't had time to complicate her life enough for other causes. Perhaps she meant to sue her guardian for mismanagement, if that was possible. Mr. Bacon would know. Though how that would provide a motive for murdering a court official, Trumpet couldn't begin to guess.

"I lost my husband last year." Trumpet accepted the conventional response with a sad smile. "In accordance with his will and local custom, I retain all rights to the manor in which we lived during our marriage. It was brief, sadly, but legally registered in our parish church. I'm only twenty-four. We were married when I was twenty."

She drank a sip of wine. "That part is all very well. I have my house and the lands around it. I won't go hungry. But my mother left me another manor worth almost as much. She died when I was sixteen. It fell under my husband's control, of course, when we married, but now it ought to revert to me."

"That sounds fair." Dorothy frowned. "Isn't it?"

"Well, yes. It is fair. That's where the Court of Requests comes in. My husband's will was badly written, as it turns out. He left his residual estate, as they call it, to his son from his previous marriage. Simon is twenty-two and very greedy. He moved new tenants into my manor and refuses to pay me the rents I'm due."

"That's difficult," Dorothy said. "I hadn't thought about tenants. Whose side are they on?"

Ah, her problem involved tenants, did it? The outline of Dorothy's future cause began to take shape in Trumpet's mind. She'd focused on property law during her year at Gray's for this very reason — to protect her lands from her husband and his issue. That knowledge had been worth a year of gluing a moustache to her upper lip every morning and ripping it off every night. Meeting Tom had been an unexpected gift.

"It doesn't matter whose side they're on," Trumpet said. "They can stay, for all I care. They seem to be good people. But I should be the one receiving their quarterly payments."

"Do you have any chance of winning?"

"A very good chance. I have my mother's will. She died a widow, so it's legal. And I have testimony from her sister and her sister's husband. There is no question about my mother's intentions. My husband's will was written by a pettifogger from Furnival's Inn. I have testimony from friends in Ipswich about other mistakes he's made, proven against him in court. That residual estate should have been limited to the other two manors in my husband's disposition. I'll prevail, never fear." Trumpet raised her cup.

Dorothy echoed the gesture, taking a large swallow. "And all you must suffer is a few weeks in the capital, dining out and shopping."

"It is a great burden," Trumpet agreed. She tapped her hand on Dorothy's arm. "We must go exploring together one of these afternoons."

They traded notes on shops they'd already visited. Both agreed that the shops on the bridge were far too dear, but those in the Royal Exchange were worth another look. A lively discussion followed among the four women about the merits of London wares. All agreed they were superior to anything found in either Suffolk or Kent. Someone mentioned the comeliness of London clerks, and everyone laughed.

"Speaking of superior looks," Trumpet said. "Do you happen to know that handsome fellow who turns up nearly every day outside the courts?"

"Charles Midley?" Dorothy raised an eyebrow at Trumpet, as if assessing a competitor. "He's another of my uncle's wards, as it happens."

Trumpet had meant Tom, but she liked this answer better. She would enjoy reporting how he'd been skipped over, for one thing. It didn't hurt to poke a hole in one's lover's pride now and then. Besides, she wanted to hear more about Charles Midley. He'd been at the White Bear after Tom lost his temper. He'd heard about the threat to choke on the wine. That put him as high on the list of suspects as Dorothy and her uncle.

"Is he your cousin?" Trumpet asked.

"No, no relation." Dorothy wagged a finger to make that clear. "He's a neighbor. His house is only fifteen miles from mine. We've known each other all our lives. We're the very best of friends." She smiled with a touch of smugness — or possessive satisfaction.

Trumpet got the message. Charles belonged to her. "Is he suing for his livery too? Your uncle must feel a bit put upon."

"It's the natural course of things. Charles is a little short of funds though. He's having trouble meeting the fees, to say nothing of the extra fine."

"Extra fine?"

"He refused a match my uncle offered him a few years ago."

Trumpet waved her hand. "Oh, I remember. You said guardians had the right to propose marriages for their wards. And if the wards refuse, they must pay a fine. That doesn't sound right to me."

Dorothy rolled her eyes. "It's meant to mirror the queen's right to approve marriages among the nobility, I suppose. It's a trap, if you ask me. They can propose a match they know you'll refuse. Then they get to hold on to your lands for however long it takes you to pay the fine. That can be an enormous sum for people like me and Charles. The fine is usually the value of the marriage, which usually means the value of the lands the betrothed would bring to the ward. In Charles's case, the court agreed on six hundred pounds."

"God's breath!" Trumpet gaped at her. "That's a fantastic sum! Who did your uncle propose? Some old baroness with black teeth and a widow's hump?"

Dorothy gave her a sly look, with one of those smiles playing on her lips. "Charles's proposed match was me."

"Oops." Trumpet clapped a hand over her mouth.

Dorothy laughed. "The timing was all wrong. I was willing — I still am — but he had developed an infatuation for an iron merchant's daughter. Wealthy, but not good enough for the grandson of a baron."

"Oh, I see." Status was everything when it came to marriage — especially first marriages. Widows had more latitude.

"My father was a knight," Dorothy said, "the same as his. They both served as justices of the peace. Our estates are similar in value and close enough together to be easily managed by the same steward. It's an excellent match for both of us."

"I suppose the merchant and his daughter lived in a town house?"

"However well appointed, it isn't the same as a country house with a park, is it? And it's the only house they own."

Trumpet shook her head. There could be no comparison.

"In fact," Dorothy said, "if my uncle had proposed *that* match, Charles could have sued him for disparagement."

"Just as well your uncle nipped that romance in the bud, then, isn't it?"

"Charles doesn't see it that way yet. But he will. The faithless wench married someone else a few months later. Another ironmonger. Now Charles has to pay my uncle those six hundred pounds before he attains his livery." Dorothy shook her head. "He got off lightly, if you ask me. Better to pay now than spend a lifetime with the wrong wife."

"Mmm." Trumpet would wager a few pounds that the ironmonger's daughter had been pushed into her hasty marriage to thwart any attempt to elope with Charles. Tom had described him as alternating between gloom and sullen anger. Small wonder!

Dorothy took a large drink and licked her lips. Then she leaned toward Trumpet, losing her balance and coming in a little too close. She'd become a trifle tipsy. Trumpet signaled for more wine all around. *In vino veritas*, or so it was said. Wouldn't it be lucky to learn what she needed to know on her first try?

Dorothy giggled and braced herself on one elbow. She lowered her voice to a near-whisper, "We're going to try again. I'm willing to void the fine from the first refusal if he agrees this time around."

"That sounds generous. Do you think he will?"

"He loves me, underneath it all. And it's the only way he'll ever get free of Uncle Geoffrey."

"He'll do it, then. You have so much in common. That's the best foundation for a happy marriage. You'll both be free of wardship and all its obstructions. You can build a fruitful life together."

"That is all that I want." Dorothy sighed as if her dreams were those of a simple woman of the middling sort, like Alice Truman. But if her marriage was worth six hundred pounds and Charles's estate was similar, they would be as rich as lords once they married. Trumpet could have reached much higher for her disguise and saved some bother changing clothes.

She should've dragged more details out of Tom. Ah, well. Too late now.

Trumpet sipped her cool, sweet wine, wondering what else to ask. Her quarry seemed willing to answer anything. Then she remembered a contradiction in Dorothy's story. "Wait. Didn't you tell me that a female ward can sue for her livery in two years? If your parents died when you were fourteen, wouldn't you have been out of wardship when you turned sixteen?"

Dorothy sat up straight again. She traded a brief look with her companion, then she cocked her head to look sideways at Trumpet. "I didn't know about that at the time. I was as ignorant as most girls that age, as you can imagine. My uncle presented me with an unacceptable match while I was still fifteen. That changed the rules."

"That sounds terribly unfair. How could you be expected to know your rights? I'd never heard of the Court of Wards until today, and I'm a grown woman."

"Your guardian should tell you as he guides you through the different stages. Uncle Geoffrey says he was too shattered by his brother's death to remember such legal trifles. He also claims I refused to listen, but I'm certain he never brought it up until it was too late."

"What happened? How did the rules change?" Trumpet let her real anger at the injustice color her words. "I haven't met your uncle. I'm sure he's an honest man, but he let you down on that score."

Dorothy shrugged, making a little humming sound as if it had been a small matter. "He claims he thought a good husband would be the best thing for me."

"At age fifteen?" Not even Trumpet's father, chronically short of money, had tried to sell her off that young. The nobility often contracted marriages for their children at that age, or even younger, to preserve bloodlines and entailed estates. But even they were more likely to wait until the girl was sixteen to perform the actual ceremony. The practice was nearly unheard of among the gentry and middling classes.

Dorothy gazed out the window, distaste twisting her mobile lips. "He chose a baron with lands in Surrey. Debt-free, my uncle said, as if that mattered to a girl my age. The man was forty years old if he was a day and had two sons already — older than me. His breath was sour, and he belched for a full minute after every meal. I counted." Dorothy turned flashing eyes toward Trumpet. "Can you imagine listening to that every day for the rest of your life?"

Trumpet shuddered. Things could have gone that way for her if Stephen's father hadn't made her father a decent offer in the nick of time. She'd been lucky, though she hadn't felt that way at the time.

"You refused, I take it."

"What else could I do? But the contract had been signed by the baron and my uncle. Then — and only then

— Uncle Geoffrey explained the consequences. Since I had refused the match, he would retain control of my estates until I turned twenty-one. Usually, the suitor offers the guardian a bribe to make the proposal. In this case, I wonder if it didn't go the other way around."

She tried to turn that into a joke, but it didn't work. Her eyes shone as hard as stones. And though her lips curved upward, her jaw had tightened under clenched teeth. Anger flowed from her like heat.

Trumpet sat back, blinking. Six years of buried wrath made an excellent motive for murder in her book. But if so, the wrong man had died.

TEN

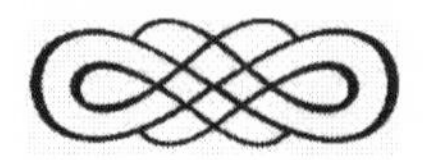

"What are you expecting to find here, Mr. Bacon?"

Proof that someone other than Tom poisoned Attorney Strunk, although that was more a hope than an expectation. "I want to get a few basic facts about wards with active cases. My premise is that someone with a reason to be angry or resentful about the progress of their suit was responsible for your colleague's death."

Ralph Bowcer frowned. The gesture emphasized the fleshy folds behind his square blond beard. "Now that's an ugly thought. We must have a hundred wards come through our doors each year. We can't please them all. It's not our job to try." He sniffed loudly, and not from disdain. He'd been snuffling back a drippy phlegm since Francis walked in. He must be afflicted with a cold and lacking a handkerchief.

Francis said, "A man driven to murder would be more than merely displeased."

Bowcer cleared his rheumy throat. "More likely to be someone unrelated to the court, I should think. Some domestic difficulty, most like. We never know what goes on inside another man's home, now do we?"

Francis considered the possibility that Strunk's wife had ridden up from Surrey to purchase and poison a bottle of brandy to send to him at his office. He dismissed it at once. Wives had many options for murdering their husbands without provoking suspicion. Accidents on the stairs, fractious horses, the wrong mushroom stirred into the gravy. She would know his weaknesses better than anyone.

He hadn't come to the Clerk of the Court of Wards for more theories. He wanted figures — values of estates, fees paid, and fees still owing. He also wanted to know if Mr. Bowcer knew about Strunk's demands for bribes, though he didn't want to ask directly. An innocent man would be shocked, but a guilty one would be put on his guard.

"I saw a number of young men waiting in the anteroom," Francis said. "Are they all waiting to see you?"

"No, thanks be to God." Bowcer grimaced. "No, most of these today are here for Requests. We're in a bit of a hotchpotch at Wards with no attorney. I'm sure you understand. I can't take on his work as well as mine. I don't study the deeds, for one thing. I manage the calendar. I record the writs sent to instigate inquisitions after the death of the landowner. I keep a schedule of wards and fees, as well as the dates of their court appearances. It's quite enough, I assure you." He cleared his throat again — a repulsive sound.

Francis edged his chair back a little. He knew that much already. He'd refreshed his knowledge of the court and its officials before coming here this morning. "Are none of the men out there wards, then?"

Bowcer heaved a sigh as if accepting a monstrous burden. "If you must know, open the door. I'll take a look."

Francis did as he was asked. He caught the eyes of a young man sitting on the nearest bench. Francis smiled politely, receiving a scowl in reply. The man's turn had been delayed when Francis presented himself as the commissioner of the benchers of Gray's Inn. His name had added weight, and he'd been ushered straight in.

"Ah," Bowcer said. "Those two at the front are Arthur Goodman and his guardian. They came up yesterday from Essex. They haven't even paid for the drawing of their schedule yet. Lucky they don't have far to travel. They might as well go home and wait until a new attorney can be appointed."

How long would that take? If Francis's experience gave any indication, it would be years before the Court of Wards resumed its normal functions. He bit back a bitter laugh. He doubted any of the candidates, whoever they might be, had infuriated the queen as thoroughly as he had done. Besides, Lord Burghley had ongoing construction at Theobalds, with masons to pay and marble to buy. He couldn't wait for the bribes to start flowing again.

"See that fellow in the corner?" Bowcer pointed with his beard at a rangy man with ginger hair snoring softly against the wall. "He's from the north. We've managed to gather that much. No one can understand a word he says. Best guess is he's Gordon Shaftoe from Northumberland, here two weeks early. We're waiting for his guardian to arrive with an interpreter."

"Why does he sleep here?"

Bowcer motioned for Francis to close the door again. "Who knows? Short of coin is my guess. And where would he go if he can't so much as ask directions?"

"That's sad."

Bowcer shrugged. He clearly had no concern about the well-being of the queen's wards. "Will that be all?"

"Not yet." Francis resumed his seat. "I'm interested in two other wards. They heard my colleague shouting at the attorney —"

"All of Westminster heard your colleague threatening Mr. Strunk." Bowcer's blue eyes hardened. Tom would find no mercy here.

"Idle threats, made in anger." Francis smiled. "One of the wards is Dorothy Leynham. She was here with her guardian, who is also her uncle."

"That's right."

"What is her standing? Is her case a difficult one? Is she having trouble paying her fees?"

"Standing, good. Difficulty, minor. Fees, paid on schedule."

"Mr. Bowcer." Francis gave him a reproving look. "I am doing a job, as you are. I wouldn't like to go back to Gray's and report that you were uncooperative."

Bowcer pressed his lips together in a stubborn line. But he opened up a ledger and flipped through the pages. He used a stubby finger to find and mark an entry. "Leynham, Dorothy. Lands in Kent worth some six hundred pounds per annum. Quite a wealthy young woman, isn't she? Entered into wardship at age fourteen. Refused a marriage at age fifteen. No details there, but it isn't uncommon. She'll turn twenty-one next week. She may be done by then, although there is a small dispute about one manor which the attorney was helping to resolve."

"What sort of dispute?"

Bowcer shrugged — his habitual response. "You'd want the record of the inquisition for that. Usually, it's about the feudal status of one of the properties."

The feudal status of a single small farm could throw a vast, multi-county estate under the jurisdiction of the Court of Wards. If it had been misidentified, the ward might have grounds to invalidate the wardship and sue her guardian for any profits he might have extracted from the estate. Such a suit would put Dorothy at odds with her uncle.

Six hundred pounds per annum was a lot of money. How much would Mr. Leynham be obliged to pay if such a dispute went against him? The figure might be impossible to calculate, depending on Leynham's record-keeping.

Francis said, "I'd like to have a look at that inquisition's report."

"That information is not usually available to the public." Bowcer smiled as if he might say more given sufficient motivation. His coy expression irritated Francis until he realized the man was fishing for a bribe.

He was hinting at the wrong man. Even if Francis had any notion of a suitable amount, he had no money. He had enough for the wherry home and not a farthing more. Besides, Sir Avery could probably lay his hands on that report without charge.

Francis returned to the main topic. "Dorothy Leynham has paid all her fees, you say? Including the king's fee?"

Bowcer gave Francis a sharp look. As good as a confession, for present purposes. "Fees paid on schedule, as I said. She lacks only enrollment in the Exchequer and related charges. That's about forty shillings. She's good for it, from what I've seen."

"No grounds for contention there, then."

Bowcer shrugged. "I don't know what she contends. You'll have to ask her."

"I will, never fear."

A smirk and a snuffle showed the clerk's lack of concern for that mild threat.

Francis moved on. "What about Charles Midley? He wasn't here Friday afternoon, but I understand he heard about the incident shortly afterward."

"Midley." Bowcer returned to his ledger, moving his finger half an inch down the page. "That's a different story. His estate was valued at four hundred and fifty pounds per annum at the time of his father's death, which was, let's see . . . three years ago. The infant was twenty years old at that time. No questions about feudal duties here, I can assure you. The ward is the grandson of Baron Terston. Some of the properties have been in the family for generations."

"Is his guardian also a relative?"

"The Midley guardian is Geoffrey Leynham."

"Dorothy's uncle? How did that come about?" Leynham must have won the bidding, which meant he had the ear of a courtier. Or he had a friend in the Court of Wards. These days, Sir Robert selected guardians only at the recommendation of someone worth cultivating — and only for a substantial fee.

"I'm not privy to such matters," Bowcer said. "Though I understand the estates are not far apart and the families are friendly. The mother is still living, I see, though mothers are rarely granted guardianship when the estate is of any size."

They rarely had the political connections to reach past better-placed contenders. That had happened to Tom as well. His mother might have been able to ask someone like Thomas Ayers, a deputy at Corfe Castle, for support, but the contest would have been over before her letters could reach Westminster. Francis had known this when he secured the most responsible party likely to prevail — his aunt, Lady Elizabeth Russell, sister to Lord Burghley's late wife.

Bowcer leaned back in his chair and folded his hands over his gray doublet. He smiled as if remembering an enjoyable event. "As I recall, Lady Midley made a feeble attempt to conceal two manors owing feudal duty. A waste of time. She signed them over to the tenants, hoping the properties would be overlooked. Fortunately for the queen, Leonard Hughes had been keeping his eye on the Midley estate. Sir Charles — the father — had been ill for years. It was only a question of when."

That was always the question, in the end. "Who is Leonard Hughes?"

"Was," Bowcer corrected. "He died, oh, about three weeks ago. He was the feodary of Kent. He knew his county, Hughes did. That's another one who'll be hard to replace."

Two Court of Wards officials dead in a matter of weeks? Francis wondered if he hadn't cast his net too narrowly. How could he find out more about this feodary without alarming anyone?

Feodaries were the ones who kept the wheels turning at the Court of Wards. They knew their counties and were always on the watch for fresh wards. The master of the court appointed each county's feodary with advice from the attorney. Kent was covered with old convents and abbeys, every parcel of which owed feudal duties. The Cecils wouldn't leave that post unfilled for long.

A gleam shone in Bowcer's blue eyes. "Where are you from, Mr. Bacon, if you don't mind my asking?"

"I grew up in Hertfordshire, not far from St. Albans."

"Ah." Bowcer patted his hands together. "We have an excellent feodary in that county at present. Even so, we estimate that many wards slip through our fingers on an annual basis. We can always use another intelligencer, you might say, who knows his way around a deed. Those who do a good turn for the court are well compensated, I can assure you."

How should he respond to this? Francis had no intention of prying into his neighbors' deeds — or rather, his mother's neighbors. But he didn't want to offend this clerk with a blunt refusal. He managed a weak, "Hmm, yes. That's something to think about."

That seemed to be enough. Bowcer produced a satisfied smile, marred by another loud sniff.

Francis seized the mood of the moment. "It must make things easier for the court to have an experienced guardian managing both estates. Taking both wards through their livery suits at the same time makes sense as well. Is Mr. Midley equally up to date with his fees and court appearances?"

"I'm sorry to say he is not. He is a very angry young man. Very angry indeed, though he is treated with every courtesy, I can assure you. He balks at every charge. He claims not to have the money, but at four hundred and fifty per annum, he ought to have more than enough for whatever we want —" The clerk caught himself. "Whatever the court deems necessary. These are long-established procedures. Deeply rooted in tradition. I happen to know that Mr. Leynham counseled Mr. Midley in advance on the steps to be taken and the fees to be paid. The lad has no grounds for complaint."

Tom had mentioned Mr. Midley's poverty. He had a good nose for such things, so Francis believed it. Perhaps Midley had scraped together enough money to pay the official fees, as Tom had, but not enough for the unofficial ones. Had Leynham known about them and failed to prepare his ward?

It was time to go. Francis had learned what he could here. More than he'd expected, though new questions had been raised. He'd have to seek those answers elsewhere, however.

He rose and offered a nod of his head to the clerk. "I thank you for your time, Mr. Bowcer. And you have my sympathies for your loss."

Bowcer had taken out a large handkerchief to dig into his wide nostrils. He wiped his nose and blinked up at Francis. "What loss is that?"

Francis gaped at him. "Your colleague, Mr. Strunk."

"Oh yes. Yes, yes, yes. A terrible thing. He won't be easy to replace, will he?"

He'd said that before. It seemed to be his only concern. He and Strunk had worked on the same floor of the same house for the same employer for more than ten years. They had likely colluded in the extortion of bribes from the wards whom they were meant to serve. Surely that created some sort of collegial bond. Could Bowcer really be so callous?

More pertinently, could he be so oblivious to the implications of Strunk's murder? Especially considering the recent death of another court official, the feodary of Kent. Coincidences happened, but the timing suggested Hughes might have been murdered as well. If so, who would be next?

ELEVEN

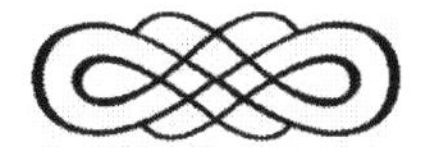

Trumpet speared a blackberry tart on the point of her knife and shook it at Francis. "What earthly motive could the clerk have for poisoning the attorney? Aren't we thinking they were co-conspirators?"

She and the Bacon brothers had gathered around Anthony's dining table in the sumptuous room on the first floor of his house on Bishopsgate. He'd laid out an assortment of delicacies to stimulate conversation. If they hoped to save Tom from spending a night in jail — or worse — they must present the sheriff with a better suspect.

The French servant Jacques kept their glasses full of a light red wine sweetened with honey. He was a bit too attentive to his task. Trumpet had spent three hours drinking with Dorothy Leynham at the Antelope yesterday, and her head had not yet recovered.

Anthony answered her. "There may be personal reasons we know nothing about."

"That's always true," Francis said. He'd drawn a plate of sugared almonds out of the others' reach to work his way through them.

Let him have them. Trumpet didn't have the strength to chew on a hard nut. But she could never resist a plump, ripe berry.

"Or," Anthony said, "the clerk had grown tired of sharing the booty. He has primary responsibility for drawing up the schedule of fees, doesn't he? He could solicit bribes without the attorney's help if he so desired."

"He can do as he pleases," Francis said. "These officials have no supervision, apart from one another. To whom would a ward complain? Sir Robert?"

They all laughed at that. The average ward would never get near the queen's right-hand man. His secretary wouldn't even forward a letter unless it came from someone Robert knew or offered something Robert wanted.

"One more motive, if I may." Anthony raised a finger, displaying the wealth of lace at his wrists. "Perhaps, after hearing Tom's tirade on Friday afternoon, the clerk feared the attorney had pushed things as he threw down that challenge."

"Pish, tush," Francis said. "It would be a poor strategy. He would risk greater exposure with a far weightier penalty. No one seems to care about bribery in the Court of Wards." He popped another almond into his mouth.

Trumpet nibbled on her blackberry tart. She loved listening to these two brilliant men debate one another. It seemed to be a brotherly habit of long standing and one they both enjoyed. Furthermore, the game could be played without rising from one's chair.

Anthony's gout kept him at home, where Jacques could carry him up and down the stairs and tend to his every need. He held court at this table several evenings a week, inviting the brightest wits from among London's writers, Inns of Court men, and members of Parliament. He collected fine objects with the same astute taste. This dining room glittered with glass vessels and sliver plates. Silk tapestries adorned the walls, and sweet herbs refreshed the matting on the floor.

Trumpet would love to spend an evening here, garbed as a young gentleman who could participate in the lively arguments without constant deference to her sex. She could envision it with candles blazing and voices rising as everyone tried to make his point at once. Someday, perhaps, she'd give it a try. Anthony would enjoy the joke.

The brothers were skilled at constructing arguments, but once they'd concluded their debate, they considered the job to be finished. Tom should be here. He had the knack of prodding them into action by asking the right stupid question at the right moment.

"Bowcer has no motivation," Francis said. "In fact, he has a motive to keep the attorney alive and working. He can't be certain the new appointee will be willing to play the same games. He could lose a substantial portion of his income."

"Who appoints the new attorney?" Trumpet asked.

"The queen, ostensibly," Francis said. "In practice, Lord Burghley, who is master of the court."

"Cousin Robert, then." Anthony's lip curled in disgust. "Our lord uncle is no longer up to explicit acts of bribery. Another fat fly dropped into his web."

"Fat indeed." Francis's lip curled as if smelling the same sour odor. "And there's another juicy one. The feodary of Kent died two weeks ago."

"Feodary," Trumpet echoed. "Such an awful word. It sounds like you're trying to spit a bit of grape skin off your lip."

Anthony laughed, but Francis frowned. "It's an excellent word because it reminds us that the Court of Wards is fundamentally a feudal institution. Why should the queen be allowed to arrange marriages of untitled landowners? Through the medium of the court-appointed guardians, I mean."

"Why indeed." Trumpet plucked up another tart, but it lacked the sweetness of the first one.

"Do you think the feodary's death is related?" Anthony selected a candied marigold as if choosing a jeweled pin from a tray in a shop on London Bridge.

"I don't know enough to form a thought," Francis said. "Although it is suggestive." He petted his moustache for a moment, staring at nothing "Maidstone isn't too far away. I'll write to the clerk at the guildhall there. He'll know something and can easily lay his hands on the notice of Hughes's death." He glanced at Trumpet. "That was the man's name."

She nodded, regretting the motion. Her head throbbed. But she had not been bred to give in to minor infirmities. "Why would the deaths be linked? What has the feodary to do with the attorney?"

"Everything," Francis said. "Especially in the early stages after the father's death. The attorney, if he's been doing his job, will know or suspect that the estate includes lands owing feudal duties. Most feodaries keep an eye on such things as well. They are responsible for every action and transaction that takes place within the county. They collect fees and conduct the *inquisition post mortem* to appraise the estate. In between official duties, they solicit information from high and low about the health of landowners and the status of their lands."

"Some may be honest men." Anthony spoke as if recounting a fable. "But I've heard that some pay servants in great households to pass along gossip pertaining to lands, marriage contracts, and the master's health. Your alert feodary doesn't want to be caught off guard when a great one dies."

"He sets spies in people's houses?" Trumpet recoiled at that idea. "I wonder if we have any."

The Bacon brothers offered her sympathetic frowns, but no advice — nor reassurance. How could she find out? She could not afford to have spies of any kind in her household. Things were complicated enough. Happily, Stephen was young and in the best of health.

"Do you know," Francis said, "that scoundrel Bowcer tried to recruit me to spy on our mother's neighbors in Hertfordshire?"

Anthony laughed, forming an O with his pink lips. "She must know everything about everyone in the county. She's probably its oldest resident." He flicked his dark eyebrows at his brother. "What did you say? We are desperately short of funds."

"I said I'd think about it. I didn't want to offend him there on the spot. He seemed to take it as agreement."

"Thieves assume everyone is in the same game," Trumpet said. "He can't imagine anyone turning down a chance to earn ten pounds by throwing a neighbor to the wolves."

"That is his world," Anthony agreed. He ate the chosen marigold, glossy with sugar, in two delicate bites. Then he flicked an invisible crumb from his pointed black beard.

"It's a despicable practice," Francis said. "I could never stoop so low. Besides, twenty pounds is only a drop in the bucket for us."

"So true." Anthony ate another marigold with less consideration. "If only we had a noble orphan to sell. That might be worth a few hundred."

Francis clapped a hand to his chest. "I completely forgot, speaking of noble orphans. Our Lord of Essex asked me to tease out how much these officials take home in bribes on an annual basis." He gave the others a bleak look. "To be honest, I have no idea how to go about it."

Trumpet understood at once. "It's not your job, that's why. Tom would take a lesser clerk out to a tavern and get him drunk. He'd pretend he wanted a similar post in another court and was wondering if it was worth the gifts he'd have to spread about to win the post."

"That might work." Anthony gave his brother an impish look. "Why don't you try it, Frank?"

Francis leveled a sour look at his elder sibling.

"Gifts shouldn't count," Trumpet said. "They're different from bribes, aren't they?" She wouldn't miss this chance to learn these fine distinctions from masters of the art. "Stephen and I are finding our way toward becoming persons of influence. We're often uncertain how to respond to offerings sent with a request for some favor."

"Thank them and pass them on to someone else when it's your turn." Francis lifted his cup. "Or say nothing. That's common too. They're not bribes since you have no official positions in your gift, apart from your own household."

"It can be a fine line," Anthony said, "though it's usually a clear one. Money, for example, is always a bribe."

"Bottles of brandy and other comestibles are always gifts," Francis added. "As a general rule, the more personal the item, the more readily it may be construed as a gift."

"What about jewelry?" Trumpet asked.

"Those lie on the border," Anthony said.

Almost simultaneously, Francis said, "Jewels are gifts."

The brothers glared at one another. Francis won the staring contest. "I offered Her Majesty a fine ruby cabochon as a *gift*" — he laid strong emphasis on that word — "to thank her for considering me a candidate for the position of Attorney General."

"Which she promptly returned," Anthony said, "because it looked too much like a bribe. It lay upon the border. Or" — up came that finger again — "she had already made up her mind, and some shred of honesty deep within her breast prevented her from accepting a gift she knew you could not afford to give for a position she did not intend to bestow."

Francis scowled at him and buried his nose in his silver cup.

Trumpet offered him a smile but doubted he saw it. To Anthony, she said, "That's very helpful. Thank you."

A storm of shouted curses rose up from the street below the window-fronted room. Francis startled, accustomed to the quiet surroundings of bucolic Gray's Inn. Trumpet and Anthony, seasoned city dwellers, chuckled at the creative use of language. But the subsequent squealing of some wheel on some cart lanced through her head.

She rubbed her brow, wincing. "I spent most of the afternoon with Dorothy Leynham yesterday. God's teeth, that woman can drink! She kept me till nearly five o'clock. I had to pretend to be overflown to escape from her. It wasn't far from the truth. Then Catalina and I had to sneak upstairs, change clothes, sneak down again, and scurry home. I told Stephen I'd been visiting my aunt, which is my excuse again today." She heaved a grievous sigh. "I need more friends. Someone along the Strand would be ideal."

"Are we not friends?" Francis pretended to be offended.

She clucked her tongue. "Ones I can claim outside this circle."

"My poor lady." Anthony wiggled his fingers to summon Jacques and asked him to bring a cup of mint-and-chamomile tea for the afflicted guest.

"Did you learn anything from Dorothy?" Francis asked.

"Mainly that she hates her uncle with an icy rage. She always smiled when she spoke of him, but her teeth were clenched behind her lips. Catalina could feel her wrath from across the table."

"What has he done?" Anthony asked.

Francis sat back and stroked his moustache with a knowing smile. He'd learned something about it from the clerk.

Trumpet gave him a curious tilt of the head. "I think she's planning to sue him once she attains her livery, which should be in a week or so. There's a dispute about some small manor. She refused to give me any details in spite of all the wine. But she peppered me with questions about the Court of Requests. I had a hard time staying within the bounds of what Mrs. Truman might know." She shook a finger at Francis. "Do not underestimate that woman, however much she may giggle and bat her lashes. She's as sharp as a needle and every bit as probing. She's crafty too. All I could learn was that the dispute had something to do with the purchase date of a property owing feudal duties."

Anthony and Francis gaped at one another. Anthony asked, "Is that possible?"

Francis shrugged. "It depends on how long it takes for the court to set its wheels to grinding."

"Grinding what?" Trumpet demanded. "Don't speak in riddles."

"Our apologies, my lady." Anthony offered her a bow of the head. "If the only property owing feudal duties was purchased after the father's death —"

"— the whole edifice of wardship crumbles to the ground." Francis shook his head with wonder. "The court would have had no reason to intrude. Dorothy would simply have inherited in accordance with her father's will."

"She could sue her guardian for everything he took during her wardship," Anthony said. "Depending on the value of the estate, it could be hundreds of pounds."

"She has six hundred per annum," Francis said. "He would be allowed sixty each year for her maintenance and education. Since she does not attend the court, she would only need a fraction of that. He could be pocketing fifty a year from her allowance alone."

Trumpet did a few quick sums in her head. "Ten percent of Tom's estate would be sixty pounds too. It costs more than that to attend an Inn of court, doesn't it?"

Francis chuckled. "Not if you leave out the gambling, the velvet doublets, and the courting of gentlewomen. But it would be tight. My lady aunt received an increase in consideration of her ward's requirements." He surveyed the treats laid out on the table and reached for a plate of mushroom tarts. He picked one out, then paused. "But guardians make most of their profits from the marriages."

"Marriages!" Trumpet snapped her fingers. "Dorothy had one of those too. A match she could be expected to refuse, I mean. Like Tom's. That's why she's still in wardship at the age of twenty."

"How does that work?" Anthony asked.

Trumpet explained how a guardian could trap a girl between the ages of fourteen and sixteen by the simple method of offering her an undesirable husband.

"That's a dirty trick," Anthony said.

"Isn't it?" Trumpet took another sip of her tea. The minty fragrance alone had done wonders for her head. She might try some of those tiny cheese pies in a minute. "The ward then owes the guardian the value of the match. I don't know how much that would be in this case, but the prospective suitor was a baron with some lands. Much older, with grown sons." She shuddered at the thought. "I refused a match like that, though mine was a viscount. I didn't have to pay a fine for it, thanks be to God."

Anthony held up a finger. "I thought the match she refused was to Charles, the neighbor lad."

"That came later," Trumpet said, "and it was Charles who refused. So he owes a great walloping sum as well."

"We've missed our calling, Brother!" Anthony slapped a hand on the table. "We should have put everything we had into wardships. I always supposed the advantage lay in skimming off your ward's profits, but these marriages. God's mercy! They're like plucking golden apples from a low-hanging branch."

Francis gave him a sour look. "And we wonder why the people have so little respect for the government. Tom owes Aunt Elizabeth three hundred pounds for refusing the goldsmith's daughter. He says he has a plan for payments spread out over several years."

"She'll never agree to that," Anthony said. "She likes to keep the reins in her own hands as long as possible."

"That's what I told him. But he's stopped listening to me."

Trumpet's thoughts had gone in another direction. She tapped her finger on the table. "We're missing the central feature of the Leynham conflict, gentlemen. That potential lawsuit gives the uncle a motive to murder his niece, not the other way around. And the attorney has nothing to do with it."

"He might have," Francis said. "It would take some finesse to locate and purchase the right property at precisely the right time."

"I should think it would take months," Anthony said.

Trumpet agreed. She had two clerks, one in Dorset and one in Westminster, scouring the combined estates of Orford and Dorchester to identify lands with feudal sources. They had found several already. She intended to sell them and buy unencumbered properties, but that could take years. She simply must keep Stephen alive until

William turned twenty-one. She would never surrender a child of hers to the Court of Wards.

"Weeks, at a minimum," Francis said, "unless you happened to be friends with the Attorney of the Court of Wards. It's his business to identify and keep track of such properties. How did the parents die?"

Trumpet said, "They caught the plague in Brandenburg while touring the Continent. Dorothy blames them for being reckless. She's lucky she wasn't with them. Uncle Geoffrey was lucky too. The will left everything to the sole child, Dorothy. If she'd been a little older, he'd have had no excuse to poke his nose into her affairs."

Anthony grunted. "He must resent being left out of that will. Perhaps he felt entitled to make the most of what he could grasp."

Francis had been consuming mushroom tarts as if they provided essential fuel for his mighty wits. Now he shook one at them. "Leynham might be one of those casual informants the Court of Wards relies on so heavily."

Trumpet frowned. "How would he know anything about other men's estates?"

Anthony chuckled. "If he's the sociable sort, he could dine out twice a month. People love to gossip, and in the country there's nothing to talk about but one's lands, one's children, and one's health."

"Ugh." Trumpet grimaced. "Don't remind me. I avoid those dinners as much as I can when we're at Badbury House. When I can't get out of it, I play the ninny. That worked so well for me at court."

Anthony gave her a considering look. "Actors say it's easiest to play a role that is opposite to their own natures."

Francis rapped his knuckles on the table to regain their attention. "As I was saying, Leynham might have known about that disputed property well ahead of need. Then, when his brother died abroad, he could have moved quickly to purchase the place. His expectations would be high enough to offer an inflated price. It would be a bold move, not knowing how the attorney would react."

"If he knew the feodary," Trumpet said, spitting the word, "he might know something about the attorney's qualities."

"Given the reputation of the court," Anthony said, "it would be a fairly safe bet."

Francis nodded. "Strunk would then have done the rest. He could have bribed the clerk in Maidstone to enter the wrong date on the deed. Fifty pounds per annum leaves plenty to go around. They could even have had someone else discover the property during the inquisition to obscure their involvement."

"Someone like Feodary Hughes," Trumpet suggested, "who is now conveniently unable to testify about the timing of those events."

Anthony steepled his fingers, smiling with delight. He loved intrigue of all kinds. "That is devious. Ingenious. But plausible, quite plausible. They would have had plenty of time, wouldn't they, waiting for the parents' bodies to be returned to Kent. At least four weeks, I should reckon. It would have been less risky if Leynham and Strunk were already friends. Has anyone looked into that?"

Francis and Trumpet traded frowns. "I should have asked," she said. "But Dorothy wore me out."

"Another reason we need Tom," Francis said. "He has a way of prying without seeming intrusive. People don't mind answering his questions."

"It's the dimple," Trumpet said. They traded rueful smiles across the table. How many riddles had been solved by the employment of Tom's dimple in the right direction at the right time?

"I could try again," Trumpet said, "although Dorothy might not know. I don't know all of my uncle's friends."

Francis choked on a mouthful of wine. Patting himself on the chest, he said, "I should be horrified if you did. Your uncle has, shall we say, a most diverse acquaintance."

Trumpet grinned. Uncle Nat was a barrister of Gray's Inn in good standing. He also had a profitable line of by-work smuggling Catholic propaganda and gewgaws to and from France. He had given up counterfeiting, as far as she knew. Smelly work, apparently, and not something he could do on his own.

"If she does know," Anthony said, "we have a motive for her to kill the attorney. Not a good one, in my view. She'd be better off waiting until after she wins her lawsuit. She might need the attorney as a witness, assuming he would turn on his friend."

"A safe assumption." Francis sounded bitter. "Strunk seems to have been a man wholly without scruples. If Dorothy paid him enough, he would indict whomever she chose."

"And this man helped determined the fate of our orphaned children." Trumpet felt a bitter taste in her mouth as well. She washed it away with the last of her tea. "But Dorothy would rather bankrupt her uncle than murder him. Or first bankrupt him and then murder him. Then why bother at that point?"

Anthony grinned at her. "Why indeed? So much more satisfying to watch him struggle. She could offer him a few pounds here and there, pretending to be bountiful. Naturally, she would make it clear such assistance put him in her debt. She could draw his punishment out for a lifetime."

He signaled Jacques to refill his and Francis's wine cups and to bring Trumpet another cup of tea. They sat nibbling tidbits for a few moments in silence — indoors, at any rate. Once they stopped talking, the rattle and hum of the busy thoroughfare outside filled the room.

Trumpet spoke first. "Charles owes a fair sum to Geoffrey Leynham for refusing a marriage as well." She told the others about Leynham offering his niece as a match and Charles's alleged infatuation with another woman.

"It would be quite a good match, I think," she said. "So does Dorothy. She loves him. She made that clear, to make sure I had no designs on him. Their estates almost march together, and they have a great deal in common. She wants to try again. Charles owes her uncle six hundred pounds for refusing her. Her plan is to forgive his fines if he agrees this time around."

"Difficult." Anthony shook his head. "His pride will be an obstacle. Though he was wrong to refuse it in the first place. He has a duty to his family, after all."

Francis coolly agreed. "They would never have accepted the ironmonger's daughter. Her life would not have been pleasant among the Midleys on that account."

Such wisdom in the ways of matrimony from two confirmed bachelors. Although Trumpet had to agree. "It's another motive to murder Leynham instead of the attorney. Strunk had no role in that proposal."

"True," Francis said. "The clerk described Midley as an angry young man. Further, his mother tried to hide two manors owing feudal duties. The feodary caught her at it."

"The late and unlamented Feodary Hughes," Anthony said. "Without whom neither of these young people would now be suing for their livery."

Francis held his brother's gaze for a long moment, then shook his head. "It's purest speculation until we know how the man died. He might have been seventy years old with a weak heart."

"Tom's an angry young man too," Trumpet said. "I'm worried about him, to be honest. I know he didn't poison that attorney, but only because I know he wouldn't choose that method. If Strunk had been found stabbed in the chest by a rapier or pushed out of a boat, I wouldn't be so certain."

Anthony frowned, clearly taken aback. "Are things as bad as that?"

"He's been avoiding me," Francis said. "But he seems to be his usual self at meals in the hall, talking with his messmates and so forth."

"He's the same on the outside, usually," Trumpet said. "I've seen a lot of him. He considers our house a safe haven. He plays cards and fences with Stephen. He reads in the garden. He's courteous and friendly and respects the household routine. The servants love him. But I can feel it, that simmering fear below the surface. I'll catch him staring at nothing with a wild look in his eyes. Then he'll shake himself and offer me an awkward laugh. His humors change every hour. The nightmares have come back, I'm sure of it."

"That's what I feared," Francis said. "I don't know what we can do for him other than identify Strunk's murderer as swiftly as we can. Tom is still the only suspect, and from the sheriff's point of view, he's an excellent one. Why bother to look farther afield?"

Trumpet sighed. "Tom says every ward in England, past and present, has the same motive. He says the old villain got what he deserved, only his words are less polite. He shifts from fear of imminent arrest to confidence that someone else will pop up any minute to take the blame. Now and then he expresses regret that he can't help more, but he's convinced that he'll cross paths with an undersheriff if he goes out to question anyone who might be relevant. We'll have to get along without him this time."

Anthony pulled the plate of mushroom tarts away from his brother and ate the last one. "Tom's absence does seem to hamper your efforts. You function best as a team, the three of you. Lady Dorchester befriends your female suspects and teases secrets from them with wine and gossip. Francis can gain access to any clerk or official in the realm and expect answers. Tom gets in everywhere through his unique combination of charm and audacity."

"I can't get out in men's garb as much as I used to." Trumpet patted her bosom with a frown, drawing a sympathetic pout from Anthony.

"I would like to know who bought that bottle of brandy." Francis heaved a great sigh. "I suppose I could inquire at the vintner's."

"Do that," Trumpet said. "I'll see if I can persuade Tom to question Charles. He spends almost as much time at the White Bear as he does at my house. And I'll contrive another afternoon with Dorothy — once I recover from the last one."

Anthony hummed a note that sounded half-encouraging and half-doubtful. "I wish I could do more. I so enjoy being a party to these reviews. But we haven't done terribly well today, have we? We were looking for a better suspect, and all we've found is a better victim — Mr. Leynham. Sadly for our theories, he is still very much alive. We also have two wards with motives to murder their guardian, and a guardian with a motive to murder his ward. But none of that does Mr. Clarady much good, does it?"

TWELVE

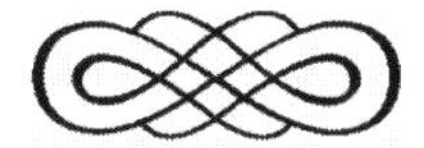

Tom surveyed the arrangements in the private dining room at the Antelope and found them satisfactory. The room was on the ground floor, as requested. A man never knew when he'd have to make a quick exit. Two tables had been laid with white cloths — a large square one for the four principals and a small rectangular one for Dorothy's companion. It seemed a little lonely, but Mrs. Sprye had assured him it was quite correct.

Jugs of beer and bottles of claret stood amid an array of footed cups and clay mugs on the sideboard. Candles had been lit there and on both tables, though a faint evening light still showed outside the tall window.

That window was wide enough for Tom's shoulders if he turned sideways. He'd tested it to be sure.

It was unlikely — highly unlikely — that he would need it. No one knew he was here, apart from Mrs. Sprye, the staff at the Antelope, and his guests. And Trumpet, of course. He had to tell someone he trusted where he had gone in case he disappeared.

He felt safe enough in the short circuit between Gray's Inn, Dorchester House, and the Antelope. They lay almost in a line from Gray's to the river, and he knew all the shortcuts and alleyways. Another yard down the Strand, however, and beads of sweat would form on his brow. He would start glancing over his shoulder like a man afflicted with St. Vitus dance and be forced to hie himself back to the safety of Dorchester House.

But nothing untoward would happen tonight. Tonight, he would celebrate. He had good cause. He intended to enjoy the company of good friends with good food and good wine. If he managed to tease out answers to some of the questions on Mr. Bacon's list, so much the better. He could assist in his own defense, if in a limited fashion.

He shifted the small candelabra on the main table half an inch. Then the door swung open to reveal a gaggle of lovely ladies.

"Here we are!" Dorothy Leynham sang out. She entered the room, skirts swinging. She looked the very portrait of a prosperous young gentlewoman in a rose-pink gown with dark pink velvet trim. A long strand of pearls drew the eye along her slender torso. Another strand adorned the shining brown braids atop her head.

"I hope you don't mind." She placed her palms together in supplication and made a little bow. "I invited my friend Mrs. Truman. She's staying here while pursuing a suit in the Court of Requests, which is practically next door to the Court of Wards. So she's twice times a neighbor." Dorothy bent toward Tom to display her flat bosom and dropped her voice to a loud whisper. "And she has nothing else to do, poor lamb."

"By all means!" Tom raised his voice to be heard out in the corridor. "The more, the merrier! I'd love to meet your friend." As Trumpet and Catalina made their way into the chamber, he bowed from the waist. Rising, he said, "Mrs. Truman, was it?"

She beamed at him, the toothy smile she used when playing a featherbrain. That wasn't right, though, was it? Mrs. Truman was meant to be a shrewd advocate for her widow's rights. But that didn't matter. Tom knew why she was here.

"And you must be the famous Mr. Clarady I've heard so much about."

He returned the insincere showing of teeth.

The two maids offered him shallow courtesies and moved on to their private table beneath the window. By the comfortable tone of their low conversation, they had already become friends, in the way of confidential servants who are thrust together by their mistresses' affairs.

Tom held out a chair for Dorothy. "Do sit, Mistress." She obliged him with an unnecessary, but not unappealing, amount of wiggling.

So they were playing that game tonight, eh? He would have tamped things down right away if it had been just the Leynhams, Charles, and him. Charles and Dorothy had some sort of connection with which Tom had no desire to interfere. She could find another way to tweak her lover's nose.

But Trumpet's presence shifted the balance. Indeed, it shifted the whole tenor of the evening. She could only be here to pursue the identification of Strunk's murderer. She was here to do his job without hint or warning. She'd told him about the meeting at Anthony's house. Had they decided he was incapable of asking a few questions on his own? He knew these people better than she did.

Ah, well. She was here. No doubt she'd stay all evening since Stephen had gone to Essex House to plot the overthrow of Ireland or some such. Tom happened to know that Stephen would go on to spend a few hours with his current paramour, Lady Edith Courtenay. Her much-older husband preferred hounds to courtiers and thus stayed in the country while his wife did her duty attending upon the queen.

He held out a chair for her in turn. "Mrs. Truman."

She thanked him and sat without fuss.

Tom gave her the neutral smile of a courteous stranger while he took in her costume for the evening. He loved the way she looked in simple garb. Her lace-trimmed attifet emphasized the sweetness of her heart-shaped face. She had the same green eyes and the same cupid's-bow lips, but that light brown hair distracted him. It was confusing and intriguing at the same time.

He turned his attention to Dorothy, showing her the dimple. "I have cool beer, if you're thirsty, or a delicious claret from Gascony."

Dorothy's mobile lips formed a narrow O. "Wine for me, please."

"I'll have beer," Trumpet said, being contrary. She usually preferred wine.

He filled cups and served them, then served the companions the wine they asked for. He poured wine for himself as well and had barely landed his buttocks in his chair when the door opened again.

"Sorry to be late." Charles strolled in. He removed his hat to bow to the ladies, then tossed it on an empty chair by the wall. He took the remaining seat on the side between Tom and Trumpet, then leaned toward Tom to whisper, "A problem with my bill at the Bear. I told them to ask Mr. Leynham for the money."

"As you should." Tom firmly believed that guardians should pay all the costs associated with a livery suit. They'd had their way with their wards' estates for some number of years. Time to pay the piper and dance away. Unfortunately, the ones he knew did not agree.

"Would you like beer?" Tom asked. "Or wine?"

"Beer for me. I'm always thirsty these days."

"It's warm for the season, isn't it?" Trumpet said. "Forgive me. Have we been introduced?"

"Haven't we?" Charles jumped to his feet, making a face at Dorothy.

She laughed. "Not properly. My fault, my fault." She performed the introductions with waves of her graceful hands. Long white hands with neat pink nails — very much the hands of a gentlewoman.

Trumpet's hands tended toward calluses and were always a shade too brown. She forgot her gloves half the time. Worse, she loved to ride out to unwatched fields to practice throwing knives with Catalina. She rejected the usual habits of a well-bred lady to follow her own angels.

Tom smiled at the thought. He wouldn't have it any other way.

Charles seated himself again.

Tom asked Dorothy, "Isn't your uncle coming? I'm sure I invited him."

"You did, yes. And he thanks you but asked me to make his apologies. He's a little tired and wanted a quiet evening."

"He wouldn't get that here. Not if I have my way — which I fully intend to do." Tom picked up his cup and held it high. "I've invited you to this merry feast to help me celebrate a victory only you can appreciate."

"What victory?" Dorothy asked, eyes bright.

"They affixed the Great Seal to my livery decree this afternoon. A mere fifteen pounds, but —"

A chorus of "Hoorah!" and "Well done!" drowned out the rest. Trumpet met his eyes for a moment. Just a moment, but he knew she was glad for him.

"How did you manage it?" Charles asked. "I thought the attorney had to do that part."

"I took the bit between my teeth," Tom said. "Who knows how long it will take to appoint a new pettifogger to that post? I know where the seal is kept as well as anyone — in York House with the Lord Keeper. I went there first thing this morning. I brought a flask of ale and some bread and cheese, determined to wait all day if necessary."

"And was it?" Dorothy asked, as breathless as if listening to him tell of stalking a tiger in the wilds of Zanzibar.

"Almost." Tom shook his head. "The underclerk who managed the queue kept glancing my way and sniffing loudly, as if I stank of pig dung."

Dorothy and Trumpet gave girlish cries of mock disgust. Charles laughed out loud. The story was going well, very well indeed.

Tom puffed out his chest. "I stuck it out though. Finally, he had no one left to serve but me. He beckoned me forward with his great, fat finger. 'The Attorney of the Court of Wards should be delivering this fee,' he said, as if I were a green schoolboy."

Tom paused, then backed up a step. "He had asked me what my matter was about when I first turned up. Now I had the perfect answer for him. 'He's dead. Haven't you heard?' He blinked at me like an owl with a sore head. I reached into my pocket and drew out an angel — the last of my store — and slid it across his desk. 'Can't we move this fee a little closer to the queen and cross it off my list?'"

"Did he take the coin?" Trumpet asked.

The others guffawed at her innocence. "Of course he took it," Charles said. "That's why the whore — the scoundrels seek those posts."

Tom gave them a knowing smile, then delivered the powerful finish. "I made him sign next to the entry on my schedule and write the date too, so I can prove I paid it." He pulled the tattered roll from his sleeve. He smoothed out the worst of the wrinkles, then turned it so the others could see. He pointed at the relevant entry. "Signed and dated. All correct."

"Good man!" Charles punched his shoulder.

"You are so wise." Dorothy's eyes shone.

Even Trumpet frowned and nodded to show she'd been impressed as well.

Tom enjoyed the praise until the door opened and two servers entered with the first course. He'd chosen the menu himself with guidance from Mrs. Sprye. The feast began with salmon in galantine sauce, accompanied by rice with currants and silvered almonds. Smaller dishes were placed on the maidservants' table.

Dorothy lifted her longish nose to sniff the air. "Smells heavenly."

"It does, doesn't it?" Trumpet agreed. "Such an excellent inn. I'm fortunate to have discovered it."

"May I offer you some fish, Mistress?" Tom sliced a portion from the salmon, balancing it on his knife with his spoon to place it on Dorothy's plate. He spooned sauce liberally over the fish. "It's as pink as your rosy cheeks."

Dorothy gaped at him. "Mr. Clarady! I hope you don't compare me to a fish."

"Of course not! No, never. I only noticed— I only meant —" Tom abandoned the attempt. What had happened to him? He'd once been the most graceful of gallants.

He caught Trumpet's amused smirk out of the corner of his eye. That gaffe was her fault. She was throwing him off his game with that distracting brown wig. She should be helping him, but no. That woman turned everything into a challenge.

Now she fluttered her black lashes at the Kentishman. If she batted them any harder, she'd blow out the candles. "I appear to be your responsibility, Mr. Midley. I feel I'm in very good hands."

A chair leg squeaked as Trumpet edged herself an inch closer to Charles. He spooned rice onto her plate and traded dishes. He served her some salmon, then looked directly into her face for the first time. And there he lost himself. Tom could see it in the sudden slackness of his jaw.

True, she had an exceptionally beautiful face — in certain humors. At the moment, the color of her peach-like cheeks and the tender curves of her strawberry lips struck him as purest playacting. Paints applied by the artist chatting softly by the window. He'd seen that matchless face covered with mud or runnels of sweat, scowling like a gargoyle. And he still loved it.

Trumpet smiled a winsome smile, recognizing the look on poor Charles's face. Then she shot a sparkling glance at Tom. He surrendered with a roll of his eyes. It all worked toward the same goal — worming their way into the confidence of these two potential suspects.

Silence fell while everyone eased the first pangs of hunger. Then Charles tilted his head toward Tom. "Great Seal is the largest fee. Fifteen pounds in one blow! I'm surprised you can afford this feast, if you'll forgive my noticing. Not that I object to it, mind you."

"Ah. This feast comes courtesy of my guardian, though she doesn't know it."

"How's that?" Trumpet's eyes narrowed. He hadn't told her about this during their short stroll around the orchard before the children had their supper. She'd been too busy filling his ears about the theories developed and discarded at Anthony Bacon's house.

"I sold the cloak pin she gave me. To celebrate our new partnership, as she put it. Two nested silver roses. Very pretty, but I never liked it, owing to the cause."

Charles understood. "It was a symbol of your imprisonment." He pointed at Tom's ear with his chin. "That pearl you're wearing would be worth a shilling or two, I'd wager."

"I'll never part with it." Tom fingered the large yellow oval hanging from his left ear. "It was a gift from my father." He supposed its twin, which the captain had always worn, lay at the bottom of the harbor at Rouen, along with his father's bones.

The others fell silent, showing respect for his loss. They'd all lost fathers, hadn't they? Except for Trumpet. She'd lost her mother at the age of ten. A sorrowful thing, no question, but it didn't throw you into wardship.

"Her Ladyship didn't like it." Tom touched the pearl again. "But I'll be my own man in a few weeks. I'll dangle whatever I like from wherever I please." He winked at Dorothy, who gasped in a show of mock dismay. Trumpet's lips twitched at his daring.

Bat your lashes at that, my lady.

Charles boomed a rich laugh. "Haha! Dangle, is it? That's a good one."

Tom grinned at him, but his eyes shifted toward his schedule, which still lay open on the cloth. "It's all smooth sailing from here out. I'm past the big fees. I only have another" — he turned the schedule his way and added numbers in his head — "another fifty-one shillings twelve pence. Fifty shillings, more or less. That's not bad. Not even three pounds. I have it, never fear, in the chest under my —"

Charles reached out a gentle hand and curled the top of the schedule inward. He leaned in to catch Tom's gaze. "Let's put the fees aside for a while, shall we?"

Tom stared at him blankly for a moment. Put it aside? The schedule was everything.

Charles patted the arm that held the bottom of the paper down. Tom shook it out of his head. "You're right. You're right. Let's forget about this loathsome business. Tonight, we shall be merry."

Charles slid the schedule from under Tom's hand and rolled it up, handing it to him to tuck back into his sleeve.

Tom raised his cup again and cried, "To our livery!"

Charles responded first. "Our livery!"

Dorothy giggled but lifted her cup to shoulder height. "Our livery!"

Trumpet raised her cup and drank with the others but said nothing. She could never fully understand the constraints and humiliations of wardship. She had tried, in all fairness, but she didn't feel it as they did.

The servers returned to replace the soiled plates with clean ones. They laid out dishes of chicken stuffed with spiced apples and oats, roast brawn with mustard, and cabbages stewed with carrots in a sweet vinegar sauce. The men served the women with less byplay.

The conversation turned to ordinary topics like the relative qualities of the Antelope and the White Bear. The congenial, undemanding talk smoothed Tom's ruffled spirits.

Then he remembered the missing guest. His gut told him Uncle Geoffrey was not the genial guardian he pretended to be. He had a cold, calculating eye, Tom had noticed, as if always sizing up men for their usefulness and goods for their value.

"I hope your uncle isn't ill," he said to Dorothy.

"No, not at all. A little melancholy, perhaps. He's not up to a jolly supper. He and Mr. Strunk were friends, you see, as well as colleagues of a sort."

"Friends?" Trumpet asked. "Had they met before?"

That was one of the questions Mr. Bacon wanted answered. Tom shot a quelling glance at Trumpet to signal that he had this well in hand. Then he remembered he wasn't supposed to know her and gave Dorothy an encouraging smile. "Friends, were they?"

She nodded. "Old ones, he said. They met here, in fact, long before I was born." She gave a feminine shrug. "It's one of those stories about how funny life can be."

Trumpet opened her mouth, but Tom beat her to it. "I love those stories. Do tell us."

"Well," Dorothy said, putting down her spoon, "Uncle Geoffrey spent a few years in London — or rather, Westminster, I should say." She glanced at Tom.

He nodded. "Did he study the law?" A safe enough guess. Many gentlemen did.

"Mmm. He became a member of Staple Inn. He said he wanted to know enough about the law to keep from being cheated. That's a wise precaution, in my view."

"Mine too," Trumpet said. She'd gone to great lengths to learn the law to protect her trust and her future dowry. Tom admired her for it. He never would have met her if she hadn't had the courage to do it.

That thought clenched his heart. A world without Trumpet? Inconceivable. Unbearable.

Dorothy took a sip of wine. "He said one of the things they do at the Staple Inn is listen to lectures given by barristers from Gray's Inn." She batted her thick lashes at Tom.

Surprised in the midst of thoughts about young Trumpet, he batted his back at her.

Dorothy gave him a puzzled smile and continued her tale. "One day, the lecturer was Mr. Strunk. He had already been named Attorney of the Court of Wards, so he lectured about wardship. Everything, my uncle said, from start to finish. Well, Uncle Geoffrey found that utterly fascinating. He knew several gentlemen in Kent, you see, with lands that once belonged to the church. He waited until the end of the lecture, then introduced himself to Mr. Strunk. They had so much to talk about, so they went out to supper." She paused to gaze around the room in wonder. "Here at this very inn, I believe. Isn't that a coincidence?"

Not much of one since Staple Inn stood only a few steps down Holborn Road from the Antelope and was popular among legal men of every stripe.

"And they've been friends ever since," Trumpet finished the tale. No doubt she'd grown bored in the middle, as Charles evidently had. His upper lip had curled at the start and remained that way throughout. He made no secret of his disdain for both Mr. Leynham and Mr. Strunk.

Now he said, "I'll wager Uncle Geoffrey wrote to his great friend Strunk the day he learned about your parents' deaths."

Dorothy bit her lower lip. She didn't answer, but the wariness in her eyes betrayed her knowledge of that pertinent fact.

Trumpet said, "I'm sure he only wanted to be prepared, knowing what might happen. He wouldn't want his beloved niece to be placed in the care of a stranger."

"Indeed not!" Dorothy rallied quickly. "He and Mr. Strunk made sure that wouldn't happen. He even came down to visit us during the first sad month. Uncle lost a good friend this week."

"He seems to be the only mourner," Charles said. "The clerk — that Bowcer — didn't seem to care a fig. I offered him condolences, and he just sneezed at me."

"Such a terrible thing," Trumpet said.

Charles scoffed. "A terrible waste of brandy, you mean. That bottle must have cost a penny or two."

Trumpet pretended to suppress a laugh, placing her fingers over her lips. Dorothy made a swatting motion at Charles. "You are *too* bad, Charles Midley."

He shrugged, grinning, pleased with their responses.

"Does anyone have any idea who did it?" Trumpet asked. She sounded merely curious, as if it were something she'd read in some sensational pamphlet.

A good question, and Tom couldn't have asked it, not so directly. He nodded at her to show his approval.

Dorothy and Charles traded knowing glances. Then Charles said, "Well, Tom here is the obvious choice." He shot Tom a wink to take the bite out of his words.

Tom could only blink at him. How could a man respond to that?"

Dorothy clucked a reproving tongue at Charles and patted Tom's hand. "We don't blame you, Mr. Clarady. Not one little bit. You were pressed too hard. And we'll gladly testify on your behalf, won't we, Charles?"

"Anytime, my friend. I am at your service."

A furrow formed between Trumpet's eyebrows, but Tom chuckled. True, he'd had a momentary shock, but he wasn't offended. In a backward sort of way, their easy assumption flattered him. They believed he'd stood up for himself — and for them.

He grinned and pointed from one to the other. "I assumed it was the two of you working together."

Dorothy laughed. "As if we could."

Charles shot her a sour look. "What good would it do me? I'm not far enough along to finish on my own. They sent those Essex folk back, did you notice? We're next, I'll wager. We'll have to wait until Hilary term or later. And what will you bet me they make us start from the beginning again?"

Tom shook his head. "I won't take that bet. But I intend to be done."

"We're nearly done too," Dorothy said. "Which is lucky because I doubt things would go as smoothly with a different attorney."

Now there was an admission of — of something. Collusion between Leynham and Strunk? But what sort of collusion?

Trumpet caught his gaze, then tilted her head toward Charles. Tom couldn't think why for a minute, but then he saw it. If Leynham benefited from Strunk's help, why was Charles so far behind? Couldn't he manage both his wards at once?

Or did he have a reason to keep Charles in thrall? There must be a hundred ways to exploit a large estate for short-term profit. Maybe Leynham needed time to put something in order before Charles took his lands back.

More questions for Mr. Bacon. Tom had studied the laws concerning wardship in great detail, but Bacon had knowledge of past cases and the gossip surrounding them stored up in his oversized brain. He might have some ideas about what sorts of tricks Leynham could have been playing. Although how they would find proof of any such thing, Tom had no idea.

He got up to refresh everyone's cups. The servers came in to remove the second course. They set out several small dishes of sweetmeats and ginger biscuits. Everyone leaned back in their chairs with a sigh. Glad faces turned toward Tom to thank him for his hospitality.

Trumpet selected a piece of marzipan, as he'd known she would. She loved it almost as much as she loved raspberries. She took a tiny bite and savored it. Then she turned her head toward Dorothy, letting it loll a little as if she'd had a touch too much to drink. Although she had been sipping so slowly at her beer that Tom had only added a few drops for show.

"I'm glad you're so close to finishing," Trumpet said. "These suits in the Court of Wards seem like truly horrible ordeals. Requests is far more straightforward. You present your evidence. Your opponent presents his. The judge considers everything. He might ask for more, but it would never occur to him to meddle in your marriage prospects. That seems the worst part of wardship, from what you've told me."

The others let out groans. "Not the marriages, I beg you," Tom said. "We're enjoying ourselves."

Dorothy's gaze lingered on Charles, who found something of great interest in the bottom of his cup. She moved on to Tom, giving him a simpering smile. "It is the most important question in a young woman's life."

"It is, isn't it?" Trumpet said. "We must choose wisely or pay for our mistake for the rest of our lives."

"Better to pay a fine than accept a bad match. That's what I did."

"You mean Leynham paid himself from your revenues." Charles's lip curled again. He couldn't utter his guardian's name without a sneer. "You could pay mine the same way, if you wanted to be friendly."

Dorothy took his bitterness in stride, giving him a tender look. "Since you mention it, we have had a few thoughts on that matter. It's no good getting through the schedule of fees in Westminster if your biggest burden is still hanging over your head."

"A few thoughts?" Charles snapped. "Do any of them include paying my mother's fine?"

"Your mother owes a fine?" Trumpet tucked her chin. "How did that come about?"

Tom could guess. "She married without a license, didn't she?"

"She didn't know any better." Charles's eyes smoldered.

"That's wrong." Tom frowned at Dorothy. "Your uncle should have told her."

"He didn't tell me anything either." She shrugged one slender shoulder, but her eyes had gone hard. She twisted her napkin into a tight coil, then gave a small laugh, shook it out, and used it to dab at her lips.

For one brief moment, Tom had felt that buried rage. Up to that point, Dorothy had spoken about her uncle as an ally. *We this, we that,* as if all their decisions were jointly made. Had he bribed her, promising her his support for something? Something like herding Charles into marriage, perhaps? She clearly wanted him. He equally clearly did not want her. Perhaps Uncle Geoffrey could shift the balance.

"How does the mother come into all this?" Trumpet asked, looking from one ward to the other.

Tom answered. "The court has the right to approve or disapprove the widow's marriage as well, if she chooses that path."

"Why, that's barbarous!" Trumpet exclaimed. "They're reaching too far. I can't believe anyone is willing to obey such an outrageous rule."

"It's a tradition," Dorothy said. "It isn't difficult to get around it. The widow has to get a license from the court, and then all is well."

"A license costing a third of her annual dowry," Charles pointed out. "That's fifty pounds in my mother's case."

"Without that license," Tom said, "she has to pay a whole year's income. The husband is slapped with a twenty-pound fine for good measure." He shook his head in disgust. "Your Uncle Geoffrey should have sat you all down around the table and explained all this on the first day. We know he knew, thanks to that lecture at Staple Inn."

The Kentish wards merely shrugged again. What else could they do?

Trumpet said, "That must add up to an impossible sum. Who could ever pay it?"

"Not us." Charles sounded angry — justifiably so. "Between us, my mother and I owe dear Uncle Geoffrey more than my estate earns in a year. I'll have to borrow to pay, but who will lend to me? I don't know anyone who isn't better friends with my guardian than they were with my father. I'm caught in a trap. I'll be a ward for the rest of my life."

Dorothy gave him a reassuring smile. "Don't give up hope yet, Charles. One never knows what waits around the corner."

"One never knows." Tom gave Charles a light punch in the arm. "Perhaps someone will send Uncle Geoffrey a bottle of brandy."

Charles laughed, but the women frowned.

"I don't like to be critical after such a lovely supper," Trumpet said, "but I fear that was in poor taste. I understand how frustrated you all are with your guardians, but I'm sure you don't wish them any real harm."

"Of course not," Dorothy said. "You know how men joke with one another. It doesn't mean anything." She leaned toward Tom, wrapping a hand over his arm. "But what about you, Mr. Clarady? Didn't you tell us you owed your guardian several hundred pounds for refusing a — what was she? A goldsmith's daughter?"

"That sounds like a good match," Trumpet said.

"Not for Mr. Clarady," Dorothy said. "He's a barrister. She's a tradesman's daughter. Money isn't the only consideration. It isn't even the most important one."

"I hadn't passed the bar yet," Tom said. "In truth, at that time nobody thought I ever would."

Charles said, "If she tried that now, you could sue her for disparagement."

That perked Tom up for a moment, but then his shoulders sank. "She's too wise an old bird for that. I don't think she'll try again so close to the end."

"Do you still have to pay her, even though it would be a bad match under present conditions?" Trumpet asked.

Tom blew out a weary breath. He'd been over this with both Ben and Mr. Bacon. "Most likely. First, because it was a good match at the time. I refused it because I didn't want to marry anyone, which doesn't count as a reasonable objection. Second, because Sir Robert Cecil is her nephew." He gave Charles a twisted smile. "Perhaps you didn't know. Any dispute is liable to be decided in her favor."

Charles grunted to show his sympathy and lifted his cup for a long draught.

Those looming, impossible three hundred pounds sank Tom's spirits again. He tried to revive them by draining his cup and forcing a smile.

He winked at Dorothy. "Then again, I might not have to pay. If they get me for giving old Strunk what he deserved, I'll hang before the money is due."

Trumpet's cry of distress jolted him. He shouldn't joke about it. Any day now, the sheriff would find a way past Sir Avery and Mr. Bacon to arrest him. He tried for another laugh, but it came out more like a whimper. All they seemed to do was uncover more ways guardians could cheat their wards. Nothing they'd learned tonight led back to Strunk.

Charles patted him on the shoulder. "You're always welcome at my house, Tom. I could hide you for a while. I also have a manor near the coast with decent people in it. They could put you on a boat to Jersey, where you'd be safe. Just say the word."

Tom nodded but couldn't hide his alarm at the well-meant offer. If his friends believed he killed Strunk, what jury in the world would acquit him?

THIRTEEN

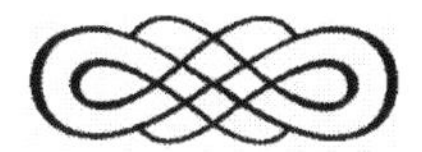

Francis donned his hat and left his chambers. If Tom refused to go so far as a shop on the Strand to follow up on an important clue, then Francis would have to step in. They could not hide under the bed and hope all would be well. Questions must be asked. Other suspects — better ones — must be found.

He had gone back to Strunk's chamber yesterday, after visiting the phlegmatic Mr. Bowcer, to search for a list of wards who had paid bribes. He'd leafed through every book and found nothing. However, such a list must exist. Why keep track of one type of crime and not the other? The sheriff might have found it in Strunk's office in Westminster and withheld that detail from Sir Avery. More likely, it had been so well hidden in that small chamber it had eluded his search. It might be there still.

Francis sighed. He would have to go and look, if he could think of an excuse.

But not today. This morning, he meant to walk down to the Temple Bar to ask that vintner about the brandy. For all they knew, the murderer had ordered the bottle himself, signing his name boldly in the register. Or her name, he reminded himself — poison was traditionally a woman's method.

He skipped down the stairs. In truth, he didn't so much mind a visit to the oldest and most respectable vintner in Westminster. He would treat Antonio to a bottle of something rare this evening, sending the bill to his brother to be added to the stack.

He pulled open his heavy front door and collided with the solid frame of Nathaniel Welbeck. Francis hopped back into his entryway. "What do you want?"

"Courteous as ever, I see." Welbeck followed him inside.

Francis puffed that away. "Why are you lurking on my doorstep?"

"Not lurking. On the brink of entering. I want a book. You do still keep our library here in your house?"

"Oh. Yes. Hmph." The fright evaporated from Francis's body. He took a restorative breath and turned toward the stairs. "You've never wanted a book before."

"Haven't I?" Welbeck gave him one of his taunting looks. Infuriating, because they never had any grounding in the current exchange. He pulled them out of the aether solely to be exasperating. "Surely I have. We've been here a goodly number of years, you and I."

True enough. "Let's go up, then." Francis led the way.

Welbeck stopped on the second floor and reached for the door handle on the left.

"It isn't there anymore." Francis beckoned him upward. "We shuffled things around when Anthony moved in. I haven't put them back in order yet." They continued their climb. "I've been waiting for Tom to settle in. He's taking the ground-floor rooms that used to be Anthony's."

Welbeck barked a laugh. "Keeping him under your thumb, eh?"

"More the other way around," Francis muttered. Tom had long ago decided it was his job to make sure his master dressed, combed his hair, and went out at least twice a week, whatever the weather, whatever recent affronts he might have endured.

At least he hadn't become a conduit for Lady Bacon's meddlings.

They reached the third floor. Francis paused for a moment to catch his breath, then opened a door that led onto a short passageway. Another door let them into a small, stuffy room crowded with shelves and chests. One dusty window admitted a weak band of daylight, the room's sole illumination.

"Sorry about the gloom." Francis turned sideways to allow Welbeck to enter. "We don't allow candles in here, for obvious reasons."

Welbeck looked aghast at the jumble of books and pamphlets. "God's jowls, Bacon! How do you find anything in here?" He started pawing through the stacks of volumes on the nearest shelf. He blew away a layer of dust and sneezed loudly.

"Ugh!" He drew a handkerchief from his sleeve and dabbed at the bulbous end of his long nose. There were women who found the Devonshire barrister attractive, or so one had heard. His dark eyes glittered with intelligence, and he retained a full head of dark hair. His beard and moustache had a silken quality even Francis found appealing on men whose personalities offended him less.

He and Welbeck had disliked one another from the day they'd met. They'd been messmates as junior barristers, which had fostered a minimal collegial tolerance. They were thrust into one another's company now and then thanks to Welbeck's niece, Lady Dorchester. And criminal investigations had on occasion led Francis to Welbeck's door.

This one had too, come to think of it. Welbeck's name appeared in Strunk's little book of blackmail.

Francis perched on the single stool provided for visitors and watched his guest flounder. No doubt Welbeck would prefer to keep his choice a secret. But why lose the opportunity for an uninterrupted chat?

"It's lucky we ran into each other. I have a question for you, as it happens. More than one, in fact. You may be aware that I've been asked to look into Richard Strunk's murder —"

"And you want to know if Strunk ever loaned me money." Welbeck turned around to show Francis a mocking sneer. "Really, Bacon, you're as subtle as an ox in a tailor's shop. Everyone knows you're looking into Strunk's murder. Many people know he loaned money to fellow Graysians on sometimes ruinous terms. You know that I have sometimes availed myself of, shall we say, less reputable sources of assistance. It wasn't much of a leap to guess you'd come to me for insights into Strunk's predatory practices."

The heated response took Francis aback. He had failed to make that deduction, though he should have done, even without the notebook. "Very well, then. I know he made you a loan for a questionable debt. I know he asked you for 'consideration,' which usually meant ten pounds a month. You paid once and then stopped."

Welbeck regarded him coolly for a long moment. "You do your job, Bacon. I'll give you that."

Francis waited for elaboration. None came. "Well? Are you going to answer me?"

"Have you asked a question?" Welbeck grinned, enjoying himself. He turned back to the bookshelf.

"What happened? How did you get off the hook, as I believe the expression goes?"

"If I tell you, will you help me find my book?"

"Of course." He would have anyway. Francis was the closest thing Gray's had to a librarian.

Welbeck turned full around and leaned against one side of the sturdy shelves. "This all happened many years ago. Taught me a lesson, I don't mind telling you. I had just launched my, ah, irregular endeavors." He paused to lick his lips.

"I don't need to hear about that."

"Good, because it's none of your business. At any rate, I found myself caught short between income and expenses. I needed funds to cover the gap. I'd heard about Strunk's by-work from someone else. Doesn't matter who."

Francis waved a hand. He didn't need names from Welbeck. He already had them. He wanted to know how it worked.

"He lent me the money," Welbeck continued. "Gave me what I needed when I needed it. I was grateful enough not to mind the exorbitant usage fee he charged. His assistance made it possible for me to make a sound profit."

"But it didn't stop there, did it?"

"You've learned quite a bit about this already." Welbeck cocked his head with a curious gleam in his eyes. "Where from, I wonder?"

"I have my methods."

Welbeck shrugged. "Well, you're right. It didn't stop there. A week or so later, he asked me for another ten pounds. 'To preserve confidentiality,' as he put it."

"Did you pay?"

"Once." Welbeck grinned. "Then I realized where that would lead and took him out for a drink on Holborn Road. I stopped in what used be an alley behind Purefoy's Building."

"I remember it." A warren of tawdry houses had been pulled down to build Fuller's Rents some years ago.

"I blacked his eye and bloodied his nose. And promised more if he ever asked me for money again." Welbeck shrugged a trifle sheepishly. "I was younger in those days."

"So were we all. How did he know whom he could exploit in that manner?"

"You went to him first, thanks to the quiet reputation he'd cultivated. He would ask why you needed the money. He sounded as if he wanted to be sure he wouldn't be abetting something untoward." Welbeck barked a laugh. "As it turned out, that's precisely what he was fishing for. But if you said something like, 'I need money to persuade men like the Lord Keeper to support my bid for the Attorney Generalship,' he would lend to you without the additional considerations." He gave Francis a knowing grin.

"Fortunately, I have better friends."

"I hope they can count on you in turn." Welbeck flicked his dark eyebrows. "At any rate, as you make your monthly payments, you develop a relationship of sorts. Strunk kept asking questions. He had a nose for dealings on the wrong side of the law. Useful for a lawyer, when you think about it."

"Some lawyers." Not Francis's kind. "So he dug until he uncovered your secrets."

Welbeck nodded. "You must understand the frame of mind a man is in when he's desperate for a large sum of money. Oh, but of course you do."

Francis sighed. His own financial straits were not the matter of interest here. "Can you think of any of Strunk's victims who might still be carrying a grudge?"

"All of them, I should reckon. He treated us shabbily." Welbeck stroked his beard for a moment of thought. "I can think of three who were especially ill-used, but I'd rather not name names. Not until it's absolutely necessary."

"I understand." Francis might be able to guess from the notes in Strunk's book, but confirmation would be important, if it came to that. "But tell me this — is one of them Roger Maycott?"

Welbeck tucked his chin. "I was thinking of men my age. Maycott, eh? Interesting." He chuckled a bit. "Here's hoping he hadn't paid yet."

Francis winced at the lack of sympathy for the dead man. "Strunk had a gift for pushing men too hard, even so long ago. He finally pushed someone over the edge."

Welbeck frowned. "Are you telling me Clarady actually poisoned that whoreson knave?"

"No! Not at all." Francis held up both hands. "He did lose his temper in front of witnesses. That's why the sheriff has fixed upon him. But never fear. I'll find the real villain — somehow." He muttered the last word.

"That's what I like about you, Bacon. That buoyant optimism." Welbeck chuckled. "Now what about my book?" He wanted a copy of *The Mirror for Magistrates.*

"Don't you already possess one?" It contained stories about famous historical figures written for busy justices of the peace. Most lawyers had a copy, though it was an expensive volume.

"I want the latest edition: 1587."

Francis hopped off the stool and burrowed into a row of shelves, sneezing as the dust rose. "We really must get these moved back downstairs," he grumbled to himself. "And dusted on the way." He emerged with the prize in his hands and handed it over.

Welbeck checked the title page. "Do you want to know why I need this particular edition?" He looked as if he wouldn't mind being asked.

"No." Francis couldn't care less. It was doubtless some sort of primitive cipher. "Don't take it out of the inn."

They walked back down the stairs, parting with minimal courtesy. Francis watched him go with a sense of time wasted. There were so many things he wanted to know in this world full of wonders. Whether the starry plane above had depth. Where tadpoles came from.

Alas, he had little time for those questions. Instead, his hours were eaten up with the sordid minutiae of other men's lives.

* * *

A bell rang when Francis opened the door under the sign of the grapes. Once he saw the sign, he recognized the place. Belvoir Wine and Spirits had occupied a narrow shop across from St. Clement Danes for as long as he could remember. He didn't buy wine in shops, as a rule. He wrote for deliveries and usually preferred a less expensive vendor.

The smell of fermented fruit struck him forcefully as he walked inside. It made his stomach rumble, longing for dinner. They wouldn't have wine of this caliber at Gray's, however, not even at the benchers' table. Belvoir catered to the wealthy houses along the Strand. He also supplied gifts for lesser men seeking favors from greater ones.

Or lesser officials who stood before a gate through which one wished to pass.

"What d'ye lack, Master?" the blue-clad clerk behind the counter asked with a practiced smile.

"Oh." Francis hadn't expected to meet a clerk. Silly of him. The owner wouldn't waste his days behind the counter. Why couldn't Tom have taken on this one small chore? "I wondered if I might have a word with your master, Belvoir. Is he here?"

The clerk frowned as if Francis had violated some sacred rule. "Is there some complaint? I assure you, Belvoir's is the most —"

"No, no. No complaint. I only want to ask him a few questions."

The clerk's eyes narrowed. He leaned across the counter and whispered, "It's about that brandy, isn't it?"

"Well, yes." Francis supposed he ought to be grateful for the power of rumor to obviate the need for preambles. "I'm here on behalf of Gray's Inn."

"Ah." The clerk nodded as if that meant something to him. What, Francis couldn't imagine.

Nevertheless, the clerk vanished through a rear door. Moments later, a man of middle age with a comfortable build and a neatly pointed black-and-gray beard came through the door. He held a wide ledger in one hand. "I am Henry Belvoir. How may I serve you, Mr., ah . . ."

"Bacon. Francis Bacon. I have a few questions about the bottle of brandy your shop delivered to Attorney Strunk's chambers in Westminster last Saturday."

"Yes, so my clerk said. I provided what little information I have to the undersheriff on Monday morning."

Francis gave him a tight smile. "Unfortunately, Sheriff Hanton did not share what his subordinate learned with Gray's Inn."

"I don't suppose he would, all things considered." Belvoir set his ledger on the counter and opened it to a page he must have marked in advance. The entry he pointed at lay close to the top of a well-filled page, evidence of a thriving business. "You'll want to know when it was ordered, I assume. Saturday morning around eleven o'clock. Ten shillings paid in full. That should be clear enough."

"Did you deliver it?"

Belvoir shook his head. "The gentleman took it with him. He wrapped the bottle in sackcloth and tucked it inside a leather satchel."

That meant some stray boy in blue livery had carried it into Strunk's chambers later that day. Many young apprentices took their time running their master's errands so they could pick up a farthing or two on someone else's.

Francis cast his mind back to the previous Saturday. Westminster would have been mobbed with messengers and carters delivering goods to the courtiers moving into Whitehall in Her Majesty's train. Chaos would have prevailed on the major thoroughfares.

He couldn't expect himself to search for that messenger. No one would remember one apprentice among dozens. He smiled at the thought of an onerous task avoided.

"Do you remember anything about the gentleman?" he asked.

"I fear not." Belvoir shrugged, raising both hands in the French manner. "We had three or four customers in the shop at that time. That's not unusual for a Saturday morning."

This small space would be tightly packed by four gentlemen with two men serving them. "Can't you remember anything distinctive about him? A hat? Something about his clothes?"

Belvoir shook his head. He seemed a trifle bored. "Nothing stands out. I suppose he was the average sort. You know, about your height and coloring."

Francis let that pass. "Did his voice have any peculiarities? Higher than usual? Lower?" He couldn't quite bring himself to ask if the voice had sounded feminine.

"His *voice*?" Belvoir frowned at the unusual question. "Not that I can recall."

Francis tried another line. "A bottle of French brandy is quite a costly gift."

"Handsome, I would say. It makes an impression, especially on men of discriminating tastes."

"Just so. You'd think the giver would wish to be acknowledged, wouldn't you?"

"Indeed you would." Belvoir chuckled. "Especially in this case. One can hardly expect — what do you lawyers call it, expedition? — if the official you're nudging along doesn't know whom to thank."

Francis gave a small chuckle. It sounded false to his ears. Better to leave the chuckling to Tom. "Full credit would be essential, I should think. And yet there was no note, or none that I heard of."

"There was a note. They found it in the office when they examined the —" Belvoir cleared his throat. "The undersheriff brought it with him on Monday. He asked the same questions, I might point out."

"Some repetition is inevitable." Francis managed a tight smile. "I suppose Sheriff Hanton forgot to mention it to me. What did the note say?"

"You can read it for yourself." Belvoir pulled a slip of stiff yellow paper from the back of his ledger. "The undersheriff left it behind. I thought someone would come for it at some point, so I tucked it in here for safekeeping."

"A wise thought." Bacon took the small card. It had a neat hole punched in one corner through which a loop of string must once have passed. He surmised that the card had been tied around the neck of the bottle.

He read the brief message. "From a gentleman of Gray's." He shook his head at the vintner. "I don't recognize the hand, and I've lived at Gray's Inn for fifteen years."

"There's no reason why you should know it, Mr. Bacon, since you're not one of my regular gentlemen. I wrote it myself at the gentleman's request."

"I see." Clever, very clever. Did that imply that the purchaser feared someone familiar with his writing might see the note? Who would see it? Strunk's clerk, for a start. Then the sheriff and a constable or two. The wards were unlikely to recognize each other's hands.

But Graysians traded letters and legal documents around as a matter of routine. How many hands could a man reliably identify? A dozen, certainly. There were that many men on the bench. One's own clerk, one's students, if one had any. Colleagues on cases. Judges and their clerks. Two dozen, all told? The steward could probably match even a message this brief with his records.

The method of writing that note favored the Graysian theory. Francis would keep it to himself for a while. He tucked the card into his pocket. Belvoir watched him do it and said nothing.

"How was the bottle sealed?" Francis asked.

"With a bit of linen soaked in rapeseed oil. It has the mildest flavor, you see."

Francis nodded. He had opened many a bottle of wine. "Do you keep bottles of brandy ready to sell?"

"Indeed not. We don't sell many of them. Not at ten shillings apiece." Belvoir smiled. "I drew it from the cask in back. I gave the gentleman a small taste, as I always do. We aim to give satisfaction at Belvoir's. He approved it, as I knew he would. It's a particularly fine cask, if I may say so. Then I plugged it good and tight. It could be carried in a saddlebag without losing a drop."

"Mmm." Francis smoothed his moustache, trying to think of something else to ask. "Did anything else occur? Anything out of the ordinary?"

Belvoir gave his head another weary shake. "No. He took the bottle and packed it into his case, as I told you. He paid his ten shillings, bade me a good morning, and left. I turned directly to the next gentleman. I forgot all about the first one until the undersheriff turned up Monday morning."

Turned up, asked questions, and left behind a major clue. No wonder the sheriff had been so reticent about the details.

Francis had no more questions, but he still wanted a treat for this evening. The vintner recommended a fragrant red hollock from Spain. Francis told him to send the bill to Mr. Anthony Bacon on Bishopsgate Street and accepted the dark green bottle. The belled-out bottom fitted nicely in the crook of his elbow.

He thanked the vintner for his time and left. He walked slowly back up Chancery Lane, trying to imagine the steps undergone by the unknown gentleman. Or lady, he reminded himself. Trumpet's maidservant Mrs. Luna was about his height. Dorothy Leynham was taller than the average woman, Tom had said, but not so much as to be remarkable. She could easily have assumed men's garb to make this brief foray.

Whoever it was had probably gone straight home. To his inn, if he or she was one of the wards. Or to Gray's. He could easily have extracted the oily rag and introduced some poison in liquid form. He might have to drink a little first to make room. Replace the rag, clean the neck of the bottle, and affix the card. A matter of minutes, assuming one had the poison ready. He had only to toss a penny to the first idle boy he saw and the deed would be done.

Francis would get nowhere attempting to find the delivery boy or trace the poison. Previous efforts had taught him that poisons of every variety were easy to acquire. Besides, asking for them tended to arouse the suspicions of respectable apothecaries.

The note had been worth the walk. Alas, it weighed on the wrong side of the balance.

If the bottle had been sent by a gentleman of Gray's, why draw attention to that society? Attorney Strunk had died in his chambers near the Court of Wards. Why not allow the authorities to reach the obvious conclusion that someone entangled in that court had sent the poisoned gift? Also, one would think most members of Gray's would have the bottle delivered to Strunk's chambers.

The murderer had chosen that phrase deliberately. He'd chosen Gray's, for a start, rather than one of the other Inns of Court. That suggested the villain intended to throw suspicion on that particular society. But only one Graysian had anything to do with the Court of Wards at present — Thomas Clarady.

A chill ran down Francis's spine, though his body had warmed from walking. He'd found the first sign of active malice working behind the attorney's death. Anger and revenge were unruly passions. They worked swiftly, hotly, and then spent themselves. They could be understood and usually revealed themselves in unguarded words.

This note betrayed a colder mind. More vindictive, more callous. The note had brought the sheriff to Bacon House on Monday morning, even though he'd lost it. The note pointed the finger of blame at Tom more than any other bit of evidence.

The killer knew him. He or she either hated him or considered him a convenient blind. And that cast a different light on the whole matter.

FOURTEEN

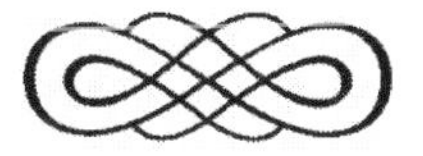

"I've worked it all out," Tom said. "You can examine my figures, if you like." He drew a roll of paper from the front of his doublet and attempted to hand it to his guardian.

Lady Elizabeth Russell waved it off. "I'm sure your plan would make sense if we were discussing the leasing of a farm. Your marriage is a far weightier matter."

She lay in her bed, propped up on a mound of pillows. Her back ached too much to get up today. Her spine curved instead of running straight, and sometimes the pain got the better of her, physically. Nothing and no one could best this woman mentally. She was impervious to reason, emotional appeals, or even dimples.

Tom had come to Blackfriars to negotiate terms for the repayment of the three hundred pounds he owed her. Never mind that the debt itself was outrageous; it had been legally incurred in accordance with the rules of the Court of Wards, obsolete as they were. He had to pay.

He could never save up such a sum, not when Her Ladyship controlled his income. He didn't want to borrow that much, assuming he could find a lender. He'd only be trading one master for another.

But he could pay fifty pounds a year for the next six years once he had the full use of his six hundred per annum. That sum would allow him to grant himself and his mother substantial increases while continuing to improve his properties. And to purchase that little manor south of the Thames he'd been dreaming about for years.

"You can't hold me as your ward forever, my lady." Tom held out both hands in supplication. "I'm twenty-seven years old. Need I remind you that I have passed the bar? I'm no longer a feckless youth in need of guidance."

"I am so proud of you, Thomas. You've exceeded all our expectations. I flatter myself that I played some part in that achievement." She dabbed at her nose with a lace-trimmed handkerchief.

Tom had never visited a woman in her bedchamber, apart from his mother — and Trumpet, but that was different. He'd rarely set foot in this chamber over the six long years of wardship. Until today, his visits could always be postponed when Her Ladyship felt ill. He'd expected to find an elderly dame in a state of discomfort. He'd modified his proposal in his head as he climbed the stairs, not wanting to be too abrupt or demanding.

He needn't have worried. Lady Russell could rule from her bed as rigorously as from her library. The bed itself inspired respect. Wide enough for three dowagers, the walnut headboard and posts were thickly decorated with carvings. Both the tester and the tasseled curtains were made of red wool embroidered with golden thread. The snowy linen covering the pillows and mattresses was thick enough to lie smoothly but thin enough to feel soft against the skin. Red flannel lining gleamed under a coverlet of rabbit fur.

Her Ladyship wore a dressing gown of finest scarlet with white velvet trim around the wrists and neck. A crisp white coif covered most of her red hair, now streaked with gray. Her dark eyes sparked with the keen intelligence and unshakeable confidence she brought to everything she did.

Tom's own confidence slowly drained away, as if leaking through a crack in his soul. How had he ever imagined that this proud, unyielding woman would grant his sensible proposal so much as a minute of genuine consideration?

He swallowed the last morsels of his pride and began to beg. "There must be some way to reach an agreement, my lady. The alternative is for me to borrow the money from a goldsmith or some such. I know you wouldn't want me to do that."

She gave him a coy look, tilting her chin down to catch his gaze with twinkling eyes. That look never boded well. Lady Russell's idea of a delightful surprise was seldom delightful and rarely surprising. Her sense of humor attested to her Calvinist convictions.

Tom's heart sank further.

"I am prepared to expunge your debt to me in its entirety." She waited for some response. Eagerness? Joy? She shrugged when it failed to appear. "All I ask is that you allow me to assist you in finding a suitable wife."

Tom couldn't stop the groan that emerged from his throat. "My lady, I beg you. Not this again."

She raised an imperious finger. "Hear me out. I agree that my earlier proposal may have been a trifle premature. And, given subsequent events, not appropriate. A goldsmith's daughter is not a suitable match for a barrister. However, that attempt did have the worthy result of ensuring that this important matter should be placed in my experienced hands."

Tom could feel himself shrinking, going backward in time. Soon he'd be hanging his head and scuffing his feet, whimpering, *Nay, my lady, I beg you. I don't like that girl. Her hair is dull, and she has spots on her chin.*

He turned his face toward the windows. They opened onto a gallery overlooking another set of elegant rooms carved out of the old Blackfriars monastery. Creamy linen curtains softened the light and obscured the view, depriving him of the wished-for distraction.

"I know it upsets you, Thomas. I know you like to imagine that one day you will fall in love with a woman who loves you equally. You dream of an elopement with no fussy contract negotiations or stuffy elders poking their crooked noses into your star-kissed romance."

Tom's brow creased. He had grown out of those youthful illusions long ago. "You underestimate me, my lady. I'm well aware that marriage involves negotiations. I prefer to conduct them myself with a woman of my own choosing. I'm twenty-seven years old and a barrister of Gray's Inn. I am fully capable of both choosing wisely and negotiating a mutually beneficial contract."

She waved a graceful hand. "The differences are merely a matter of degree. No one of your station — the station which you have attained through persistence and hard work — makes his own match. Not without the guidance and counsel of his parents. Your mother, who I'm sure is a fine woman in other ways, lacks experience in the circles which you now inhabit. As your guardian, I stand in the place your father would have occupied. And may I say, you're the better for the exchange in this context."

"You leave my father out of it." Anger heated Tom's words, but he didn't apologize for it. She'd insulted both him and his mother with her sneering words about hard work and lack of experience. No, he had not been born a gentleman, but by God, he'd become one. And his mother had arranged successful matches for all three of his sisters, one of whom had married the son of a knight.

Her Ladyship met his glower with a slow blink. "You are obviously in need of my assistance, Thomas. In my observation, you have made no effort whatsoever to meet suitable young women. You cling to the confines of Gray's Inn, a wholly masculine preserve. You limit yourself to the chapel at Gray's when you ought to have been attending my church, in my company, where you could see and be seen by a variety of suitable women. You should be cultivating friendships with fellow Graysians who have sisters near your age. You should be spending at least part of your vacations in their homes getting to know those sisters. And yet you have done none of these things."

She paused, giving him time to defend himself. He couldn't. He hadn't thought of it until this moment, but that was how many a Graysian met his mate. If he hadn't surrendered his heart to Trumpet, he would doubtless be doing the same already. Ben, the dearest of friends, would be delighted to introduce him to every eligible maiden in Suffolk.

Lady Russell granted herself a victorious smile, knowing she'd struck her mark. "I fear your blatant disinclination, which must have been remarked upon by some of your fellows, has been encouraged by the lamentable disposition of my nephews. They eschew the company of women. Sadly, I have no control over them. Nor, it would seem, does my sister. But when you refuse every opportunity to mingle with attractive and appropriate young women, you become subject to speculations of a nature you may not intend."

God's bollocks! Was that what people thought? He'd been so intent on learning the law and proving it to the senior members at Gray's he'd lost sight of the sociable youth he once had been. Although, in fairness, Her Ladyship kept him on a tight leash. He hadn't the coin to keep up with the other gentlemen's leisure pursuits.

His shoulders had slumped during her admonition. Now he drew himself up again, lifting his chin. "I shall refrain from taking offense at your implication."

She puffed out her opinion of that weak response. "You're angry now, but you'll thank me later. I consider it my solemn duty to ensure you are settled in a productive marriage that does credit to both parties before releasing you from my care. When — you will notice that I don't bother with the hypothetical — *when* we arrive at a mutually acceptable arrangement, I will expunge your debt to me in full."

Her eyes twinkled as if she'd granted him his most cherished desire. In truth, she had, but at an exorbitant price. "The debt will inspire your cooperation. If you truly desire to attain your livery by your birthday, we mustn't dally."

Borrow the money from a stranger and risk falling into the clutches of someone like Strunk? Or accept whatever match Her Ladyship proposed? A devil's choice.

Tom sighed. "Who do you have in mind this time?"

Lady Russell clapped her hands together in girlish glee. "A lovely woman, only a few years younger than you. You have a great deal in common since she is also presently a ward of the queen. She's quite wealthy, with lands mostly in Kent. She even has a pleasant manor right on the Thames a few miles east of Greenwich. Just what you've been wanting, I believe. Her name is —"

"Dorothy Leynham. We've met."

Lady Russell studied him with her keen eyes. That coy smile returned. "You like her, I perceive. That's more than enough for a start."

Tom smiled through clenched teeth. "You doubtless have it all worked out. Very well, my lady. Set up a meeting. I'll talk to Mrs. Leynham and her uncle. No promises, however."

Her Ladyship acknowledged his caveat with a nod. She had him in her power, and she knew it.

He bowed himself out of her chamber and let the housekeeper usher him back onto the street. He walked down to the wharf and stood waiting for a wherry going upriver.

He cursed himself for a blind fool. He should have known money would never be the central issue for Lady Russell. She founded her every thought and deed on moral principle. She believed God had given her the responsibility for securing a successful domestic future for her ward. Her conviction was worse than corruption, from his point of view. An honest woman could not be bribed to change her mind.

He would never love anyone but Trumpet. This he knew in his bones. But Ben hadn't loved Sarah when they married, and Trumpet didn't love Stephen — at least not in the romantic sense. He knew other flourishing couples who'd made the same compromise. Why should he be the exception?

A Calvinist argument occurred to him — too late to present today, but perhaps he could use it later. Wouldn't it be a cynical act to marry a woman he didn't love and knew he never could? Calvinists considered cynicism a sinful attitude. Therefore, Her Ladyship's incorruptibility would force him into a sinful act. Let her answer that one, if she could.

He could hear her laughter echoing in his mind.

* * *

Tom strode into the anteroom outside the clerk's chambers intending to pay his remaining fees and be done with this ordeal once and for all. He'd worn a cap with a wide brim pulled low to shadow his face and kept a wary eye for constables in the short walk up from the wharf. The sheriff might guess that he'd have to return to this house, but he couldn't know when. With luck, Tom would be in and out before an informant, if there were any, could send a message.

He'd also shored up his pride somewhat on the trip upriver. He would meet with the Leynhams. No harm in a little conversation. However, he would also seek out a reputable lender of large sums. A goldsmith, most like. That thought raised a chuckle. Perhaps he should ask the father of the girl he'd refused five years ago.

One way or another, he'd find a way out of Her Ladyship's trap.

His eyes lit on the other two females who plucked and tore at him like devils sent direct from hell. Beautiful, perhaps, but demons nonetheless. Women always had a list of demands, obscure and obvious, which neither time nor reason could diminish.

Trumpet and Dorothy Leynham sat on a bench as close together as their skirts would allow, leaning toward one another in low-voiced talk. When he came into view, they turned their charming faces toward him with welcoming smiles.

He stopped several feet short of their bench. He gazed at them but found himself unable to muster a friendly look. He didn't have it in him. A sympathetic shadow crossed Trumpet's face. She knew where he'd been and why. In fact, she'd warned him not to get his hopes up.

She'd been right. His hopes, never very high, had been dashed to pieces against Lady Russell's adamantine will.

Dorothy cocked her head. "Good afternoon, Mr. Clarady. I trust you are well?"

"Well," Tom echoed. "I suppose I'm well enough." A rude answer, but he couldn't do better at the moment. He didn't want to see these women — these two out of all the women in the world. He didn't want to talk to them. He had an errand to complete as quickly as he could. He felt exposed out of his narrow circuit and wanted to get home again.

The door to the clerk's office opened, and the northman came out. He looked at the wards waiting on their benches and said, "What fettle?" It sounded friendly, whatever it meant. He loped over to his usual corner and settled himself for a nap.

Odd fellow. Tom's heart went out to him. At least he was safe from unwanted marriage partners lying in wait here in Satan's anteroom.

Another young man rose, but Tom forestalled him. "I'll only be a minute." He blocked the man's way as he reached for the door handle.

"Mr. Clarady." Clerk Bowcer's initial frown shifted to a calculating smile. Maybe that was the only sort of smile the man had. His job consisted of endless calculations, after all. His schedules and figures were the stuff of every ward's nightmares. "Was I expecting you this afternoon?"

"How would I know?" Tom heard the discourtesy and found it pleasing. Why be polite to his tormentors? He dropped into the chair in front of the desk, which tilted sharply to the right. He had to shift himself portside to regain his balance.

Never mind the cursed chair. "I've come to pay the last of my fees. There's no reason to drag this out any longer." He pulled his much-creased schedule from his sleeve and unrolled it. "You can see that I've paid for affixing the Great Seal."

He showed it to the clerk, who nodded but said nothing.

Tom gave him a moment, then sailed along. "Nothing left but a pound here and a shilling there for enrolling in the Exchequer. A docket for the barons of the Exchequer and, oh yes, another shilling for polishing the baron of the Exchequer's shiny white arse."

"Mr. Clarady!" Bowcer's head rocked back as if he'd been struck.

That had been a trifle too strong. Tom held out a placating hand. "I apologize. I'm a little overwrought today. Bad news on another front." He forced his lips to curve upward. "But there's no reason we can't settle up here, is there?" He fished out his purse, which made the chair list starboard again. He gripped the seat with both hands and raised his weight to rebalance it. That didn't work. It had one short leg.

"Did you choose this cursed thing on purpose?" He glared at the clerk.

"It's only a chair, Mr. Clarady."

Tom narrowed his eyes. Part of the torment, no doubt. Put the wards at an even greater disadvantage. He refused to be distracted so easily. He opened his purse and began counting coins onto the desktop. "The total is fifty-one shillings twelve pence. No doubt you'll want to add that up for yourself."

Bowcer set his hand on the desk to form a barrier against Tom's coins. "Wait one minute now. We're not quite at the end of the course yet."

Tom stopped, leaning forward with his hand inside his leather pouch. "How's that?"

"There's the little matter of the king's fee." Bowcer's smile held a challenge. He knew what he was asking.

Tom willed himself to calmness. "I've paid the king's fee. You can see where I checked it off right here." He exhibited his well-marked schedule.

"I see a mark in dark ink. You could have placed that there at any time, whether you paid or not. The entry for the Great Seal is affirmed by the Lord Keeper's underclerk's signature, which of course I recognize." He flicked his fingers against Tom's paper. "You should have done the same with the king's fee."

"Should have done the same," Tom muttered under his breath. Then his voice began to rise along with his temper. "It hadn't yet occurred to me that I might be pestered for the same fee twice. Or thrice, counting today. I hadn't yet fathomed the depths to which you villains are willing to sink."

"Now, now." Bowcer faced his client's anger coolly, almost with amusement. "Don't distress yourself. If it's a question of ready money, I might be able to bridge the gap."

"Bridge the gap?" Tom's wits stuttered. What could he — *Oh, say not so!* This evil cozener wanted to lend him the money to pay his own bribe. Was there no bottom to the man's perfidy?

"I won't pay that fee again, do you hear me?" Tom scooped his coins back into his pouch and restored it to his inner pocket. He rolled up his schedule and stuffed it back into his sleeve. The infernal chair rocked back and forth with each movement, making him look like a drunken fool. No doubt that was its purpose.

His voice rose. "I wouldn't borrow money from you if I was naked and starving on the street." He pounded a fist on the desk, making the slimy turd jump.

He liked that jump. He wanted to see it again. He shouted, "Naked and starving, do you hear me?" The chair wobbled, throwing him off his balance. He had to push out a leg and raise his arms to center himself again.

"Now, now, Mr. Clarady." Bowcer pushed away from his desk, getting his back against the wall.

"Don't 'now, now' me! I won't be placated." Tom roared, "I know your tricks. And I'm done with them, do you hear me?" The cursed chair wobbled again.

Enough was enough. He jumped up and grabbed the thing. He raised it high and smashed it against the floor. It fell to pieces, leaving one leg in his hand. The short one, no doubt.

He shook it at the thief cowering against the wall. "No more false fees, do you hear me? I'm done with it."

"Help! Help!" Bowcer cried. He climbed out of his chair and edged along the wall. He squeezed past Tom, his face distorted with apparent fear.

What a coward! And what a dolt. You'd think he'd keep a weapon in his desk, like any sensible pirate. Tom made a mock bow, gesturing with the chair leg that the villain might pass freely.

Bowcer reached the door and flung it open. "Fetch a constable! He's gone mad!"

Constable? God save him!

He felt strong hands gripping his arms to march him into the dungeon at Bridewell. He heard the door bang shut as clearly as if it were happening right here, right now.

Never again!

Tom pushed past the clerk, dropping the chair leg on the way. He jogged past the ladies on the bench and ran smack into Charles Midley. Charles grabbed him by the shoulders to keep them both from falling.

"God's teeth, Tom! Slow down."

"Stall him! Stop them!" Tom shouted, then ran on. He hesitated at the juncture of two corridors, head turning right and left, seeking the shortest route outside. He spotted a shimmer of light and ran toward it. He crashed into the sturdy leaded panes of glass before remembering that windows could be opened. He fumbled at the latch, glancing fearfully over his shoulder, then leapt onto the sill and out into the air.

Fortunately, the Court of Wards kept its offices on the ground floor.

He raced through an alley, then burst across King's Street, ignoring the startled cries rising behind him. He sprinted past Westminster Hall, dodging clients and barristers alike, and flung himself into a wherry. He grabbed the end of an oar and thrust it at the boatman.

"Row, man, row! My life depends on it!"

FIFTEEN

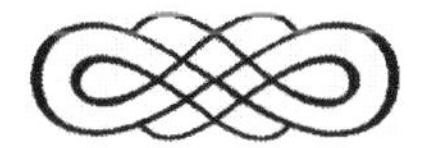

Trumpet watched Tom stagger off down the corridor and out of sight. He had truly gone mad this time — stark, raving mad. She must catch him, bring him home, and calm him down. The first parts shouldn't be too hard. He was most likely heading for her house.

She caught Dorothy's eyes. "If a constable comes, stall him. Keep him here as long as you can." She jumped up to join Catalina, who was already waiting in the corridor.

"But why —"

The general uproar drowned the rest of Dorothy's objection. Everyone leapt to their feet and started yammering. Charles Midley had appeared out of nowhere and pressed the clerk back toward his office.

Let chaos reign! The confusion would give Tom time to escape.

The corridor Tom had chosen led to the back door, so they went that way. Best to follow as closely as possible in case he turned aside. He might go to Twickenham, even though that Spaniard might be there. Tom hated the Spanish almost as much as he feared the sheriff's men.

Trumpet and Catalina didn't run. That would only attract attention. They walked as swiftly as they could. In a few yards, they entered a shadowy alley, too narrow for the sun to penetrate. Trumpet slowed, looking up to check the windows. No one seemed to be watching. No reason why they should be. All the shouting had been done indoors.

"Stop a minute." Trumpet plucked at her maidservant's sleeve. "Get me out of this wig." She couldn't turn up at her postern gate in disguise. The guard would be alarmed by Tom's wild humor and thus be doubly suspicious of anything strange.

She pulled long pins out of her hat, holding them between her lips. She caught the hat while Catalina tugged off the wig, stuffing it into a deep pocket. A farthingale could hide a dozen wigs — one of the benefits of women's garb. Catalina smoothed Trumpet's hair a little. Then Trumpet replaced the hat, pinning it in place, while Catalina moistened a corner of her handkerchief with spit and scrubbed vigorously at her mistress's eyebrows.

She gave Trumpet's face a quick review, then nodded. "It will do. We must not tarry."

"Ready to run?"

They picked up their pace and fairly flew across the wide square in front of Westminster Hall. They pounded onto the wharf, pushing past the people waiting for wherries.

Trumpet turned to one, a young man with an alert look about him. "Did you see a man run up and jump into a boat? Tall, fair, comely. A bit frantic, perhaps?"

The man pointed an arm in a pinked sleeve downriver. "That way." He gave Trumpet a measuring gaze, smiling to show he liked what he saw. "Let him go, Mistress. I would never run from you." He gave her a broad wink.

She turned her back on him, though she didn't entirely mind the flattery. She spoke to the wherryman in the nearest boat. "A shilling to take me first and row as fast as you can."

He rose to help the two women into his boat. Then he held up both hands to stop anyone else from boarding. "There's always another one, good people. No need to crowd."

He sat on his narrow bench and pushed off, steering skillfully into the flow before asking, "Where to?"

"Dorchester House." No details were necessary. Every wherryman knew the great houses that lined the north bank from Westminster to the Inner Temple. They pointed them out to visitors who came to the capital to gawk.

As they rounded the bend in the river and passed Durham Place, Trumpet leaned forward. Yes, there was Tom, standing on her wharf with his hands on his hips, staring upriver. He stood erect in spite of his panic and made a striking figure in his black suit with his barrister's robe flapping behind him.

He must have been denied entrance by the guard, who wouldn't have liked his distraught manner. He would guess — no, he would know — that she wouldn't be far behind.

"You're a fool," she shouted as her wherry pulled alongside the wharf.

Tom blew out a lip fart. He reached down a hand to help her out, then did the same for Catalina. To the maidservant, he said, "You wouldn't stand there waiting for them to take you in, would you?"

"I would run very fast. Find the safe place, hide, and watch."

"My plan exactly."

Trumpet rolled her eyes. She had benefited greatly from Catalina's unconventional past, but she wished the woman would take her side now and then as a matter of principle.

She bade the guard allow admittance to Mr. Clarady whenever he should arrive. She led her group inside and up to the green parlor. This had become their favorite haunt when rain kept them out of the garden or they wanted complete privacy. It was on Trumpet's side of the house and contained a trestle table large enough for four to dine. They left the door open, both as a show of innocence and so they could hear servants approaching.

The room overlooked tiny Strand Lane and part of Somerset Palace. Half the view consisted of treetops in the palace orchard, peaceful and calming, which Tom sorely needed.

Trumpet called for a mirror and a basin of water to repair her face. She would prefer to go to her bedchamber to change clothes, but she didn't dare leave Tom alone. He paced back and forth, twitching his fingers, as fretful as a trapped animal. His wide eyes seemed to be looking at another place in another time. Every now and then he sidled up to place his back against the wall beside the windows, peering into the orchard as if expecting archers with bows aimed upward to appear beneath the autumn leaves.

"Would you please sit down?" Trumpet said. "You're making me seasick."

He plunked his arse into the nearest chair. "They can't get me in here, can they?"

"They," Trumpet said, emphasizing the word to underscore its absurdity, "don't even know you're here. How could they, whoever they are?"

"You know who they are. The sheriff. The constables. The gaolers. All of them."

"Why would they look for you here? They'll try Gray's, possibly the Antelope, perhaps even Twickenham if they want to waste money on wherries. But your friendship with Stephen isn't widely known, and your friendship with me is a deep, dark secret."

"Hmph." Tom's shoulders relaxed a fraction of an inch. "Lucky thing, that. We never knew we might need another reason for discretion, did we? Now our friendship might very well save my life."

"Your life is not in danger." Though they both knew that wasn't quite true. If they failed to find Strunk's real murderer, Tom could hang — or be forced to flee the country. She'd have to go with him to keep their hearts from breaking. She'd be forced to abandon her children — an unthinkable thought.

She couldn't go; therefore he couldn't go. They must find the real killer without delay.

"What happened anyway?" she asked.

"Didn't you hear? I think I was shouting."

"Only at the end. You shouted, 'Do you hear me?' several times. Then we heard smashing sounds. I think you broke up a chair."

"That chair!" Tom bounded to his feet again, crossing the room in three long strides. "He chose that chair on purpose. It wobbles, you see. It's part of their plan to drive you insane." He loomed over her, his face dark with rage.

"Stop that at once." Trumpet faced him calmly. She knew he would knock himself unconscious before laying a hand on her in anger. "Sit down and behave yourself, or I'll have my strongest ushers hold your arms while I pour poppy juice down your throat."

He blinked at her as if he didn't know where he was, then shook himself like a dog. "Sorry. Sorry." He went back to his chair and folded his hands in his lap. "I don't know who I am anymore." His eyes pleaded with her. He dropped his voice almost to a whisper. "I'm so afraid of going to jail I can't see straight. It's like a gunpowder charge goes off in my skull and blows my wits apart."

The naked fear in his blue eyes broke Trumpet's heart. "I will always take care of you, my beloved. You know that. If worst comes to worst, Stephen will have some of his retainers smuggle you to Jersey. You can live there safely until Mr. Bacon and I sort this out."

Tom nodded, pressing his lips together. He drew in a slow breath through his nose, blowing it out through his mouth. Some of his terror went with it.

"So," Trumpet said, "what was wrong with the chair?"

"Oh, that cursed chair!" He gave a short chuckle — a good sign. "It wobbles. One leg must be shorter than the rest. I know he knows it. He must watch people rocking from side to side all day long. I'm sure he chose it to put us at a disadvantage. I couldn't take it anymore, so I smashed it to pieces." He grinned, and the old Tom returned for a moment. "That felt good, I can tell you."

"Why were you shouting at him? I thought you went in to pay the last of your fees."

"There's no end to them. Not ever. I learned that today. He told me I still owed eleven pounds for the king's fee. The same trick Strunk tried on me. Only this grasping, snot-nosed knave took it a step farther. He offered to lend me the money to pay his false fee."

She gaped at him. "I can't have heard that right. It sounds like the clerk offered to lend you the money to pay him a bribe."

Catalina sputtered, then covered her mouth with her hand. Trumpet glanced at her and had to bite her lip to keep from laughing. Tom looked from one woman to the other, a smile gradually forming on his lips. "That's exactly what he did. I told you they were pirates. Although after today, I owe pirates an apology. That whoreson clerk is far worse."

"Did he mention any terms?" Trumpet sputtered the words between giggles.

"He didn't have a chance." Tom grinned at her, a real grin this time. "That's when I started shouting."

Catalina collapsed in laughter, taking Trumpet down with her. Tom followed, laughing so hard he nearly fell off his chair. Trumpet clutched her stomach and managed to get hold of herself. She sighed loudly, patting herself on the chest. "The man has no shame. not one particle of it."

"None of them do." Tom's tone was bitter but sane again.

Trumpet looked at Catalina. "Perhaps we should have dinner in here."

The gypsy nodded and went out to set that in motion.

Trumpet told Tom, "You'll stay here until this is over. We'll send someone to fetch clothes from Bacon House. We have lots of books and a lute you can borrow. You can enjoy the gardens freely since they have high walls. Today, we'll have dinner in here and then go down to the music room. There's a small bed. You can rest while I practice on the virginals."

"I'll do whatever you want. Just don't make me go out there."

"Never." She thanked her merciful God that Tom and Stephen had been boyhood companions. Without that old bond, this would have been impossible. The old mansion might be huge and labyrinthine, but she could never hide a lover inside it for days on end without someone catching on.

Tom stared toward the window. The tension in his body told her he still feared imminent capture. She studied his beloved features, noting the hollows under his eyes and the lines drawn from nose to chin. Seven years ago, when they'd first met, nothing had daunted him. He'd been bold, impudent, eager for challenges. He should be striding on clouds of achievement these days, chin held high, a barrister at last.

Instead, he shifted from delusionary plans to wild rages in the space of a heartbeat. The Court of Wards was destroying him. Even after they caught Strunk's murderer, Tom faced obstacles too great to bear alone.

Somehow she would find those three hundred pounds and force Lady Russell to accept them. She could sell something — something Stephen wouldn't miss. There must be a valuable book or two in the library. The former owner of this rambling house had been a collector with a large purse and excellent taste.

Dinner was served, but no one had much of an appetite. They'd have a small repast later in the afternoon to tide them over till supper. Trumpet slipped a few drops of poppy juice into Tom's wine, which smoothed the creases from his brow.

After the sweet course, they went downstairs to the music room. Tom lay on the bed against the far wall, groaning with relief as his head landed on the goose-down pillow. Trumpet sat at her virginals and began to play a gentle tune. She'd barely gotten through the first verse when she heard a soft snore rising from Tom's corner. She beckoned to Catalina and asked her to slip out and fetch a writing desk from the library.

Trumpet stopped playing long enough to dash off a letter to Mr. Bacon, telling him Tom had shouted at another Court of Wards official and would be spending a few more days at Dorchester House. She asked him to have Pinnock pack some linens and other necessities and send them to her as discreetly as he could. She urged Bacon to redouble his efforts to solve Strunk's murder, promising to do the same.

Although she had no fresh ideas to bring to the task.

She returned to her music, glancing now and then at Tom's sleeping form. In another world, she would snuggle into that broad chest and let that breathy snore send her to sleep beside him. It was scarcely one o'clock. Stephen wouldn't be home for hours. She and Tom could easily meet in her bedchamber at the back of the house and chase away his fears with some tender lovemaking.

She gazed at that face, thinking that thought, and yet no spark ignited. She could no more press her attentions on that careworn man than she could leap from the green parlor into Somerset Place. His thoughts weren't turning in that direction either. Last week, he'd spent most of his time reading romances or playing games with Stephen. They fenced, they batted tennis balls around the hall, and they practiced cheating one another at primero.

She and Tom had formed an unspoken accord — no bed games while he was under her husband's protection. It would be dishonorable in a way their usual dalliance was not. It was one thing for Tom to climb through her window while Stephen was bedding Lady Edith. It was quite another to use Stephen's title as a shield and then cuckold him behind it.

Besides, Tom didn't have the heart for it. He needed rest more than anything. So she would restrain herself and not slide in beside him in the wee hours of the night.

Not only that, she would be sure to post a guard at his door. She couldn't have him wandering into the nursery in one of his wild moods.

* * *

She played. He slept. The day wore on. Servants came in to light the candles. Their bustle woke Tom up. He leaned against the wall, blinking and rubbing the back of his head.

Then the lord returned to his castle. Stephen strode into the room, dressed in an elegant court suit of tawny velvet and tan silk. His vitality brightened the room more than the candles. He nodded warmly at his wife, then wagged a finger at Tom.

"Ha! I knew I'd find you here."

Trumpet blanched inwardly. Could he suspect them? They hadn't done anything untoward in weeks. She struggled to sound merely curious. "How so, my lord?"

"There's been another murder in the Court of Wards. Our Tom was heard shouting and breaking up the furniture." Stephen winked at her. "It's all anyone can talk about. Everyone is shocked. Do you know, an expression of some sort almost crossed Sir Robert's face. Southampton and I watched him closely for a while, but it didn't happen again. One would think he'd be concerned though, wouldn't one? Being the master of the said court."

He plopped into an armed chair and stretched out his legs, crossing them at the ankle. He sighed loudly. "Ah. It feels good to sit down. Is there any wine?"

Trumpet signaled to an usher, but another one had anticipated his lord's needs. A tray was brought in and cups of sweet canary handed around. "Who was it? The murdered man. What happened to him?"

"The clerk, they say." Stephen shrugged. "You'd think they'd have more than one, but apparently this one was special. Someone broke his head in an alley between his chambers and the wharf. Around five o'clock, they say. The next man through that alley, which seems to be a favorite shortcut, found him lying there in a pool of blood." Stephen took a long draught of wine and let out another sigh. "It's work, attending upon Her Majesty all day. Don't let anyone tell you otherwise."

"Did they find the weapon, my lord?" Tom asked.

"The leg of a chair, of all things. They found it beside the body with blood all over it. Nasty business."

"Dreadful." Trumpet shot a quick glance at Tom, who had buried his nose in his cup. "A chair leg does seem like an odd choice. It's not something you find everywhere you look."

Stephen grinned at her. "That's one of the things I love about you, my lady. You're unshockable. They say the leg came from the chair that Tom broke apart in the clerk's chambers. That's when I knew I'd find you here. Not that you're not welcome."

"Thank you, my lord." Tom summoned a sheepish smile. "I fear I did lose my temper a bit this afternoon. That chair had the most aggravating wobble —"

"It's no good, Tom." Stephen shook his head. "You must stop ranting at these clerks. They don't like it, you know, and they have ways of getting their own back. A wise man is always polite to the staff. My mother taught me that. Besides, those churls at the Court of Wards seem to drop dead the minute you raise your voice."

"I didn't do it, my lord. I promise you I didn't."

"I know that, and my lady wife knows it. It isn't your style, for a start. I'm sure Mr. Bacon knows it too. But other people don't know you the way we do, do they, my lady?"

"I fear not, my lord." Not the way she knew him, at any rate. She hadn't looked directly at him once since Stephen came in, but she knew exactly how he was sitting and what expression he wore. She could feel every shift in his humors from across the room.

Stephen smiled. "You can't blame them, really. It's only natural to assume the one shouting threats is the one bashing clerks with bits of chair. You must get a grip on yourself."

"No more shouting, my lord. This is — this is much worse than I expected. I don't know what I expected, to be honest, but not this. I'm in serious trouble this time, I fear." Tom folded his hands around his cup, holding it as if in supplication. "Would you grant me shelter for another day or two, my lord? Until Mr. Bacon can work out what happened?"

"I only hope he can. If this goes on much longer, we'll have to find something for you to do." He winked at Trumpet again. "Perhaps we're feeding him too well."

"You are generosity itself, my lord." Tom blew out a breath. It sounded like he'd been holding it in for a while. "Any service I can perform I will gladly do. I make beautiful copies of legal documents. I used to do it for Mr. Bacon." He paused, then asked, "I am safe here, aren't I? The sheriff can't pester an earl, can he?"

"Indeed not." Stephen scoffed. "I can expel the varlet at my pleasure. But you know, these murders have been committed within the verge — scarce half a mile from Her Majesty's person. Everyone is talking about that too. Sir Walter Ralegh will take charge sooner or later. Sooner is my guess. Her Majesty made him Captain of the Yeoman of the Guard again now that she's more or less forgiven him for marrying without permission."

"God's breath," Trumpet said. "Sir Walter. I forgot about him. We can't turn him away so easily."

"Not at all, I should say." Stephen rolled his eyes. "Not without a great deal of fuss. And how would that look? He would win in the end. I can't stand against the queen. Besides, you should be out there helping Mr. Bacon solve this mystery. Isn't that what you do? Trot about asking questions while he sits in his chambers and thinks?"

Tom groaned. "You're right, my lord. But to my shame, I'm terrified of being thrown back into jail."

Stephen waved a lordly hand. "Perfectly understandable. But what are the odds? The sheriff can't be everywhere. You can use our coach to go out, if you like."

Trumpet nodded as if that made sense, which it didn't. Nothing drew the common eye like a nobleman's gilded carriage.

"It'd be good for you to have a task," Stephen went on. "A man can't skulk in the dark and still look himself in the mirror every day, now can he?"

Trumpet couldn't agree more. The looming threat of Sir Walter changed everything. She glanced at Tom. He sat in a slump, a crooked frown on his face, plainly thinking about hows and whens.

Stephen drained his cup and held it out A servant hurried up to replace it with a fresh one. "You're a friend of Mr. Bacon, which counts for something. And of mine, which counts for something too. We can slow things down, but not by much. Her Majesty can't have people murdering her court officials with impunity. She'll put Sir Walter on it tomorrow, I'll wager. That gives you a week — at most — before he comes knocking on my door. That's plenty of time for you and Mr. Bacon to catch your man. Best get hopping!"

Stephen raised his cup to cheer Tom on. "And this time it's your own neck you'll be saving. There's a spur for you!"

SIXTEEN

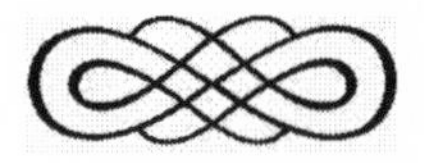

"*Dios mio, es* Roberto Diavolo*!"* Antonio Pérez pointed out the window facing the river. He looked like a man who had just rolled out of bed to take a piss, which happened to be the case. His commodious nightshirt billowed about his wiry frame, falling below his knobby knees. He wore one of Francis's densely embroidered nightcaps on his graying head and a pair of scuffed leather slippers on his bare feet.

"Cousin Robert?" Francis struggled to free himself from the tangled covers. "Here? At this hour?"

"What is the hour?" Antonio asked.

"How should I know?" The nearest church was over a mile away. Francis had a clock in the front parlor downstairs, but that didn't do him much good at the moment.

He broke free of the blankets and swung his legs down, shivering as his bare feet touched the cold floor. Where were his slippers?

Never mind the cursed slippers! He bounded to the window, shooing Antonio out of the way. He flattened himself against the wall on one side and peered out cautiously.

God's mercy, it *was* Robert. His men were poling his private barge into place alongside the wharf at that very moment. The so-called barge was nothing more than a wider-than-usual wherry. He'd made sure it could be recognized at a distance by having his coat of arms painted on both sides of the boat as well as on the canvas canopy stretched over the cushioned couch at the back.

Sheer excitement set Francis dancing on his bare toes. He turned to Antonio, who had started searching out pieces of clothing. "There can only be one reason for this visit, my friend. Her Majesty must have made up her mind at last. Not Attorney, I don't expect that. I stopped hoping for that months ago. But Solicitor — that was always the reasonable choice. It must be some such message. Why else would her busy little dwarf come all the way out to Twickenham so early on a Saturday morning?"

"There can be many reasons, Francisquito. I can think of three without trying."

"Well, don't tell me." Francis risked one more peek out the window. Robert stood in the boat waiting for his servant to hand him out. "Help me dress!"

He pulled his nightshirt over his head and clawed another one out of the linen chest. Never mind scrubbing his torso. A splash of cold water on his face would have to suffice. He pulled up the round hose he'd worn yesterday and stuffed his arms into the matching doublet. They both scrambled for stockings — two of the same color, please — and sleeves. Francis combed his hair and beard in front of the round mirror while Antonio laced everything together in back.

Francis turned from the mirror to let Antonio give him a quick inspection. The Spaniard nodded. "You look like you have been up for at least a quarter of an hour."

Francis clucked his tongue at the impudent old man. He snatched the first hat he saw and started to dash out the door. Then he turned and caught his lover's eyes with a stern look. "Stay upstairs and be quiet, I beg you. He mustn't know you're here."

Antonio gave him an impish smile. "I am certain El Diavolo knows everything already."

"But he'll ignore it if we let him. So let us let him."

Francis flew down the stairs, stopping three steps from the bottom to catch his breath. He recovered his dignity and walked the rest of the way down at a sedate pace. He found his cousin in the large front room, gazing out the side window with his hands behind his back.

"Robert. What brings you here so early in the morning?" Having known one another since early childhood, they rarely bothered with the social niceties.

"It's past nine o'clock. Not early by most people's standards." He paused, no doubt to let his cousin sputter excuses for his self-indulgence.

Francis had no desire to quibble. "It's still hours out of your way, assuming you are on your way to court."

"I love the river in the morning." Robert sounded wistful. "So quiet, with only birdsong and the gentle plashing of the oars. And the air is so fresh. I'm sure you remember what palaces smell like when the court is in residence."

A pointed reminder that Francis had been banned from that odiferous court. But why ramble on about the river? News should be delivered swiftly, especially good news.

Robert eyed him for a moment, his expression unreadable, as usual. Then his pink tongue darted over his bottom lip. "It's bad news, I'm afraid."

Francis's shoulders sank. "Not the — not the news I've been hoping for?"

"No." Robert's lip twitched in amusement. "That wouldn't come from me, in any event. My Lord of Essex will surely deliver it himself, whichever way it goes."

Francis gestured at a chair, then dropped himself into another one. "I suppose you'll get around to telling me this bad news before the day gets much older." He heard the peevish note in his voice and didn't care.

"I'm surprised you haven't heard already," Robert said. "You are living the quiet life out here! It was all over the court yesterday before supper."

Francis gave him a weary look.

Robert took the seat he'd been offered. He always seated himself with precision, lowering himself by bending his knees instead of thrusting his backside out. "The clerk of the Court of Wards was murdered yesterday around five o'clock."

"Oh dear." Francis knew where this was headed.

Robert nodded. "Your clerk —"

"Former clerk."

"Your former clerk is once again the most obvious suspect. He was heard shouting at Mr. Bowcer in his chambers. More threats, according to the witnesses. This time he broke up a chair and shook the leg at the man as he left. He ran out when Bowcer called for a constable."

Francis fell back in his chair. "He didn't do it, I'm certain of that. But he's been under so much strain with this livery suit. It really is the most appalling process, Robert. Wardship is a scourge upon the state. It's obsolete. Barbaric, even. The practice should be terminated. Tom has been caught in a trap, and it has sorely affected his temper."

Robert eyes narrowed slightly. He could hardly fail to hear the criticism directed at him as *de facto* master of the court. "Nevertheless, the law does not allow us to express our frustrations by killing those who obstruct us."

A thump sounded upstairs. Antonio must have dropped a shoe or struck a banister while sneaking into a position from which he could hear.

Francis held his breath. Fortunately, Robert leapt to the wrong conclusion. "You can't hide him forever, Frank. You may be able to put off the sheriff, but you can't stop Sir Walter. Not when he's acting on the queen's behalf as Captain of the Guard."

"I don't control Mr. Clarady. Nor am I hiding him, here or elsewhere." Francis enjoyed telling the truth when he knew it would be construed as a lie. It allowed him to maintain the moral high ground while misleading his interlocutor.

Robert tilted his long head as if listening for more sounds from the fugitive lurking upstairs. "I understand you have been looking into Attorney Strunk's death."

"On behalf of the benchers at Gray's, yes."

"And what have you learned?"

"I never discuss my early findings." Francis gave his cousin a smug smile. "People are so quick to make up their minds before all the facts have been uncovered."

"This is a matter of special interest to me as well."

Francis shrugged. He enjoyed using that gesture around Robert, who avoided anything that drew attention to his twisted back.

"I have yet to learn anything conclusive. But I can tell you in strictest confidence that it's a miracle Strunk survived as long as he did. He was a thoroughly greedy and corrupt man who used his office in the shameless pursuit of money. I believe Bowcer was cut from the same cloth. Indeed, it seems to be the livery of the Court of Wards." Francis grinned at the apt metaphor, which had sprung readily to his mind.

"I'm sorry you find a man's death so amusing," Robert said. "Didn't I mention that Clerk Bowcer was bludgeoned to death with the leg of a chair? A chair which Mr. Clarady reportedly broke apart in his fit of passion."

That sobered Francis. "I am sorry. Those men should have been expelled from office and prosecuted for extortion, not killed. The murderer is undoubtedly the same man in both cases. I will increase my efforts to bring him to justice. I consider it a moral duty."

Robert poked a tongue into his cheek. "It will get you out of the house, at any rate. You needn't pretend that helping your former clerk attain his livery — and escape hanging — won't benefit you. I understand he'll have quite a handsome income. He could cover all your present debts and have something left over to lend you afresh."

Francis glared at his cousin, loathing him for his hypocrisy. How many offices had he been granted already? A seat on the Privy Council must be worth hundreds of pounds a year in gifts alone, from men and women hoping for a favorable decision or a recommendation. It was easy to support the courtier's life when you had influence to barter.

Francis had to buy clothes to play the part and gifts to curry favor. He had to pay expenses at court — when he was allowed to attend. But he lacked the personal power to keep his own clerk out of jail. Friends had loaned him money — vast sums of money — on his expectations alone. If he failed — when he failed — all he would have to show for his efforts was debt.

The scolding was unfair. Cruel, even for Robert. Francis curled his lip at the twisted little man puffing himself up at everyone else's expense. "One thing I have learned is that nobody cared about Strunk's death. No one, though he'd been a member of Gray's for twenty years. His position is desirable, and many will contend for it, but not from respect for the man or the position. I've no doubt I'll find the same loathing and relief when I start questioning Bowcer's victims."

Robert opened his small mouth to speak, but Francis cut him off with a raised palm. "You should be careful, Coz. Everyone hates the Court of Wards. And you are its master, for all intents and purposes. You could be the next victim."

SEVENTEEN

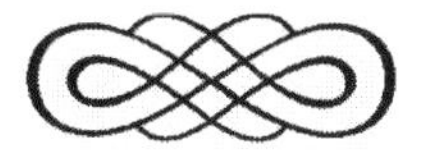

Trumpet sat at the library table on Sunday afternoon, struggling to pay attention to *The Histories* by Tacitus. She brightened when a liveried usher appeared at the door. "Mr. Francis Bacon to see you, my lady."

"Show him in. And bring us some wine and small cakes."

The usher bowed and left, then Mr. Bacon entered and bowed. "Good afternoon, my lady." His gaze shifted toward Tom, who had been restlessly prowling the bookshelves for the past quarter of an hour. Bacon nodded at him. "Tom, you look well."

A blatant lie. Tom looked like a madman who'd been cleaned up by a pair of determined servants for this meeting.

"Do I?" Tom gave his former master an up-and-down look. "You're looking a little frayed around the edges yourself."

Bacon ignored the rude response and took a seat at the long table opposite Trumpet. He removed his hat and set it on the board, where a servant whisked it away. "Frayed is the perfect word. I feel like a tennis ball that's been played beyond its time, batted back and forth between Her Majesty and my Lord of Essex until the felt has worn out and the strings beneath come unwound."

Trumpet gave him a sympathetic grimace. "Still no decision?"

He shook his head. "And like the ball, I have no say in when I am to be bounced across the court again. I offered to withdraw. I'm longing to withdraw at this point. But she won't allow it."

"She's using you to make an example of Essex." Trumpet admired the queen in so many ways, but Her Majesty had a cruel streak and could hold a grudge like nobody else. She abruptly turned her head. "Tom, please put the books back where you found them. There is an order to those shelves, you know."

"I can't imagine you know what it is." Tom snapped the book in his hands shut with a clap and stuffed it on a shelf, most certainly not in the slot from which it had come. He'd been doing that for the past quarter of an hour, pulling books out of their places, leafing through them too fast to read a single sentence, then dropping them on the nearest chair or table.

"There's an inventory. Lord Surdeval took great pride in his library."

"I'd love to explore that one day," Bacon said.

"*You* would be most welcome." She shot a glower at Tom. She wished he would sit down. He knew the purpose of this meeting as well as she did — to share notes and figure out where they stood on the Strunk matter. Strunk and Bowcer, she ought to say. Tom ought to sit down and take his usual part. They were doing this for him, after all.

Which he knew full well and approved of. He wanted to help, most days, within the bounds of his fear. But the very topic made him fitful.

He slid the book he was holding carefully into its place. "Sorry. I'm feeling fidgety." He gave her a placating grin. "I miss being able to get out and stride around the city."

"Now you know how I feel." Stride around the city! He had no idea what she would give for a fraction of his customary freedom. She would have elaborated on that theme, if they were going to trade causes for disgruntlement, but the usher returned with a tray. He served cups of wine and plates of small cakes and left. The refreshments would sweeten Tom's temper for a while.

She pointed at the cup placed ready for him, and he brought himself over to sit down. He took a drink, then sighed and folded his hands on the table, ready to cooperate. Fine lines marred his once smooth brow, and he carried a tightness around his eyes. She knew he was deeply worried and did her best to make allowances, but his fears made him selfish, and he had nearly stretched her patience to the limit.

She loved him as much as ever, deep within her heart. Every other part of her would be glad to see him back at Gray's. The only way to achieve that goal was to identify the Court of Wards killer and present the sheriff with solid proof.

She spoke to Bacon. "Have we learned anything useful about Strunk's murder? I assume we have nothing beyond the bare facts for Bowcer."

"If we ignore the limitless prospects of all past, present, and future wards," Bacon said, shooting a wry glance at Tom, "we can narrow the field to four, with a handful of outliers."

Tom frowned. "Four? Are you including me?"

"Ah. Five, including you."

Trumpet counted names in her head. "Who's the fourth?"

"Roger Maycott," Bacon said. "A member of Gray's Inn who was sorely abused by Richard Strunk after borrowing a sum of money from him."

"That's right," Tom said. "I forgot about the Graysians. Strunk liked to spread himself out, didn't he? Lending the money he stole from us wards."

"This is the first I've heard of it." Trumpet felt sorely abused herself. She narrowed her eyes at Bacon. "Did you know about this when we met at your brother's house?"

"I don't remember what I knew when."

That was most unlikely. Bacon's orderly mind was fully inventoried, like the late Lord Surdeval's library. These two men, whom she counted as her closest friends, had simply forgotten to include her.

"Forgive me, my lady." Bacon looked somewhat abashed. "My situation may not be as precarious as Tom's, but I too am hard-pressed these days."

True enough. He did look strained, like a man suffering from lack of sleep. "I forgive you. But you could write a letter, you know. Stephen pays no attention to messages not addressed to him."

"I shall endeavor to do so in the future." Bacon proceeded to recount his search of Strunk's opulent chambers and his discovery of the small notebook. The entries in it tracked loans made to Graysians involved in activities they would prefer to remain secret.

Trumpet gaped at Tom. "Did he belong to any other groups? Because I predict we would find another set of suspects there."

"Where would he find the time?" Tom grinned, and well he might. The list of men with motives greater than his had expanded tenfold.

"Why focus on Maycott?" Trumpet asked. "You say there were half a dozen men or more on that list."

"His entry is the most recent, my lady," Bacon answered. "The next closest one ended his payments last year. Strunk had the wisdom to bring his demands to an end, eventually. I see little value in murdering a blackmailer whose demands you have met."

Trumpet nodded. "Strunk must have seen trouble brewing and known when to stop pushing. Except with Tom. But isn't it a striking coincidence that Maycott should send Strunk a bottle of brandy two days after Tom made his threat?"

"More of a wish than a threat," Tom grumbled. "I said 'I hope you choke on it,' not 'I will choke you' or whatever they think I meant. I've been over it a hundred times. I'm fairly certain I didn't start shouting until after I mentioned the wine."

"The witnesses remember it differently," Bacon said. "Though they may be embellishing based on your subsequent conversation at the White Bear. Memories alter over time. And let us remember that coincidences do occur. However, I don't believe it was a Graysian. The note tends to argue against that conclusion."

Tom and Trumpet traded puzzled looks. "What note?" Trumpet asked.

"Didn't I tell you about the note?"

Trumpet blinked at him. Neither of her allies was performing to his usual standards. She was hindered as well, by home and family. Things had been easier when their lives had been less fraught. "Do tell us about this note, if isn't too much bother."

Bacon shrugged an apology and described the piece of stiff paper with the inscription, "From a gentleman at Gray's" written by the vintner.

"Clever not to write it himself," Tom said. "But that points to a Graysian, I think. He would fear you or me recognizing his hand. Between the two of us, we must have seen dozens. Think of all the wills I've copied for my colleagues. Also, it would be a simple matter for the sheriff to go from chamber to chamber asking for samples."

"I disagree," Trumpet said. "Why send the bottle to Westminster and then draw attention back to Gray's? I think it rules out your Roger Maycott."

"Maybe he meant it as a collective rebuke," Tom said. "We, the men of Gray's whom you have cozened and cheated, will now exact our revenge. Something like that."

"I hadn't thought of that interpretation," Bacon said.

This was more like it — the three of them throwing out ideas and tearing them apart. Trumpet loved this part.

"There is one irrefutable objection," Bacon went on. "I see no reason for any Graysian to murder the clerk."

"That whoreson Bowcer!" Tom growled. "He was worse than Strunk, and now he's spoiling our best theories."

"Not at all." Trumpet pushed the wine jug toward him, then set a plate of cheese tarts within reach of his hand. She'd learned to blunt the worst of his melancholy and manic fits with timely applications of food and drink. "I think the murderer is one of the wards. I still favor Dorothy. She wants to ruin her uncle, but she hates everyone who had a hand in her subjugation. She hasn't the power to remove Strunk or Bowcer from office. Killing them is her only recourse."

Bacon had started shaking his head somewhere in the middle of her speech. "I'm sorry, my lady, but Mrs. Leynham must be ruled out. She isn't strong enough to kill a man with a chair leg."

"Nonsense," Trumpet retorted. "It can't be that hard."

Tom laughed, a cheerful sound. The treats were working their magic. She took the laugh as encouragement. She drummed her fingers on the table, thinking it through. What could she use to serve as the head? Ah! She had it. She gave the table a final pat and grinned at Mr. Bacon. "I'll prove it to you."

"Surely not, my lady!" He pretended to be alarmed, but his hazel eyes twinkled. He used to hate these demonstrations, finding them jarring and too specific. But they'd proved their value time and again.

Trumpet went to the door to summon the usher. She told him what she wanted and sent him off to implement her plan.

She strolled back to the table and placed both hands on its polished surface, leaning forward like a marshal explaining a map. "Dorothy's taller than average. Healthy and well-muscled. You men might not notice that under her clothes, but Catalina has a good eye for such things. Much can be deduced from an arm or a glimpse of leg."

"I have never seen the woman," Bacon said, as if defending his ignorance. But he wouldn't necessarily notice a woman's shape if she stood naked in front of him.

"I have a good eye as well," Tom said. "Quite possibly better than Catalina's."

She stuck her tongue out at him, though she rejoiced at the sign that the old Tom still lived. "She's also very strong-minded," she went on. "I've never had such trouble maintaining a role as I did with her. Probing, pressing, questioning. She doesn't let up, even when she's almost cup-shot."

"Nevertheless, my lady," Bacon began.

He didn't get to finish. The usher appeared to announce that all was ready. He led them outside to the orchard, the last of the walled gardens behind the house. The apples had been picked, and the leaves were turning yellow. A few raspberry canes trained against the bricks still bore a smattering of red fruit. They were the lady's favorite, after all. They received special attention.

The gardener and his boy had erected a small platform about Trumpet's height from bricks and boards. On it sat a large orange gourd. It didn't look like a human head, being more pear-shaped than round, but it would serve.

"Don't stand too close," Trumpet warned as the usher tied a large cloth around her neck to protect her gown. Catalina was at the tailor's today, pointing out every last mistake he'd made in his last effort. She would be sorry to have missed this demonstration.

Tom and Bacon traded doubtful frowns. They must have guessed what she intended and didn't believe she could pull it off. *Fools!* They should know her better by now. She seldom boasted. She didn't have to.

She accepted a round piece of wood about fifteen inches long from the gardener. She passed it to Tom. "Do you allow that this is much the same as the leg employed in the incident at issue?"

"Very much the same, my lady." Tom passed it to Bacon, who hastily handed it back to Trumpet.

"In that case, gentlemen, observe."

Trumpet walked a few yards away from the makeshift platform. She turned around and hefted the stick in her right hand. Then she took three swift steps, raising the stick and rising onto her toes. She swung the stick down onto the gourd with all her might. It broke apart with a satisfying smash, sending seeds and bits of orange flesh flying.

"I rest my case." She thrust one leg back to make a full curtsy, spreading both arms wide.

Tom clapped his hands loudly, to her immense gratification.

Bacon laughed, shaking his head. "I could quibble about the relative density of a skull and a gourd, but I'll refrain. Your demonstration is convincing, my lady. Well done."

That was gratifying too. Trumpet hadn't lost her touch, in spite of the increased domesticity.

Tom picked up a large piece of broken gourd and tested it, snapping it with his fingers. He rapped his own skull with his knuckles, cocking his head as if listening for an echo. "A skull is harder, being made of bone. None of Stephen's rumors mention this degree of splatter. But otherwise, it fits, I think."

"Agreed," Bacon said. "The skull was cracked, not shattered, hence the pool of blood described in the rumors. Perhaps he bled to death."

"Likely," Tom said. "I think Dorothy is an inch or two taller than Bowcer. That would give her blow more force. He was the short and stocky type. She's tall and lithesome —" He broke off with a wry smile. "Or I should say, lanky. And I agree about the strong-mindedness. Dorothy is no bashful maiden. Far from it. She giggles and wriggles, but for reasons. You can feel it."

"Very well," Bacon said. "I will rule her back in. I still consider the uncle the most likely suspect, however. He has the greatest scope in terms of planning and freedom of movement."

"On to the uncle." Trumpet pulled off the gourd-spattered wrapper and dropped it on the ground for the servants to collect. "Shall we sit under the arbor?" She gestured toward a vine-covered structure with a bench under it.

They took separate paths. Tom strayed aside to pluck a ripe raspberry, which he presented to Trumpet with a bow. "Your prize for the least speculative contribution to this afternoon's inquiry."

She made a small curtsy, setting her farthingale swaying. "Why, thank you, kind sir."

Bacon had already planted himself on the sunny side of the bench. Trumpet took the other. Tom jogged back to fetch one of the half barrels from the gourd platform and used it as a stool.

Trumpet looked from one man to the other, collecting their attention. "Uncle Geoffrey wasn't there on Friday afternoon. He couldn't have picked up that chair leg."

Bacon turned a penetrating gaze on Tom. "Are you quite certain you dropped it outside Bowcer's chamber?"

Tom scratched his bearded jaw while he tried to remember. "I'm not certain of anything. Though I must have dropped it somewhere. I didn't have it in the wherry."

"We should've followed you out the window," Trumpet said. "It seemed faster to use the rear door, given our skirts. I can't remember seeing it in the anteroom either. Everyone jumped to their feet and started shouting when Tom came out shaking that club, which is what it looked like." Her gaze roved across the symmetrical branches of a pear tree trained against a wall. "Except for that odd northman. He sat there staring as if watching a play in a foreign language, which I suppose it was for him."

"Did he?" Bacon stroked his moustache, nodding to himself. "I shall make an attempt to question him as soon as may be."

"Good luck," Tom said. "He doesn't speak a word of proper English."

Trumpet asked, "Why would Uncle Geoffrey murder the clerk?"

"Why would Dorothy?" Bacon countered.

They each had their favorite suspect. Perhaps they should place bets. They'd have to be small ones if Trumpet was to have any hope of collecting.

Tom answered. "I see two motives here. Either the murderer is silencing accomplices, in which case Uncle Geoffrey is the most likely, or he or she is acting out of revenge. In that case, Dorothy, Charles, the northman, and any other ward that might have been lurking about on Friday is equally good." He screwed up his face, then once again shook his head. "I might have pushed that window open with the chair leg and not dropped it till I reached the alley. It's all a blur. Panic tends to narrow one's view."

"The location of the leg is crucial," Bacon said tartly. "If you dropped it in the alley, anyone could have picked it up. I can easily see Uncle Geoff — Mr. Leynham coming in that way to have words with Mr. Bowcer. A plot gone awry, perhaps. Or perhaps Bowcer knew about the illegal land purchase and tried to extort money. They meet and tempers flare. Perhaps Bowcer took the first swing. Perhaps Leynham stumbled over that round chair leg and stooped to pick it up."

"I can see it," Tom said. "Although it couldn't have taken long. Other people use that alley."

"We had time to remove my wig, replace my hat, and scrub my eyebrows. It's shadowed by an overhanging second story and looks unsafe. We would have gone another way if we hadn't needed those few minutes of privacy." Trumpet crossed her arms, hugging herself. It was too chilly to sit outside in the shade, but if she suggested going back inside, the men might take the opportunity to leave. They'd decided nothing yet.

"It doesn't look unsafe to me," Tom said.

Trumpet bristled at his tone. Why would it? He was a young man, an inch over six feet tall, and composed entirely of well-trained muscle. A woman or an older man would choose a less shadowy route. Although Bowcer, a fleshy clerk, had obviously used that path. Perhaps familiarity had made it seem safer.

Trumpet pressed her suit. "We should be able to determine when Dorothy left the anteroom. She and I, with our servants, were the only women." A horrible thought struck her. "God's breath! I'm as good a suspect as Tom. Catalina and I ran out right after him. We could have lurked in the area until Bowcer left."

Tom laughed, then stopped. "That's not a joke, is it? Dorothy knows who you are, or she thinks she does. And you've been seen by dozens of people at the Antelope."

"In disguise, fortunately. We should probably avoid the place until this is resolved." Although then she could contribute nothing. "I'll write to Mrs. Sprye. She'll know if anyone's been asking about me."

"Good thought," Tom said, his mind obviously elsewhere. Then he abruptly changed the subject, as if her peril were a mere side note. "I've been on the fence, but I'm coming over to Uncle Geoffrey's side. Revenge is a time-honored motive. I don't disparage it. But silencing accomplices is a better one to my mind. Forward-looking rather than backward, if you follow me."

"Some people are doomed to live in the past." Bacon had that tutorish look that warned of impending philosophy. "One might expect —"

Tom cut him off. "Leynham also has everyone's favorite motive — greed. With Bowcer's death, he's indebted to no one. If he murders Dorothy next, who has no siblings or other heirs, he'll inherit the whole estate. Six hundred pounds per annum could easily inspire a man to spend half an hour hiding in a dark alley."

"But how could he guess you would come through and drop a club at his feet?" Trumpet said.

"He couldn't." Tom shook a finger at her. "He would've planned to use his knife and then switched to the leg when it turned up. Swifter and less dangerous for him."

Plausible, quite plausible. Trumpet clucked her tongue. "Do we know that he inherits if Dorothy dies?"

"It seems likely," Bacon answered. "Unless he has an older brother of whom we have heard nothing. Dorothy can't legally write a will until she turns twenty-one."

Trumpet hugged herself harder, scowling at the neatly raked gravel path before her feet. Then she heaved a sigh of defeat. "You've convinced me. I'm coming over to Uncle Geoff's side. Six hundred pounds is a powerful motive."

Bacon smiled. He liked to win. But he was nothing if not thorough. "We have yet to discuss Charles Midley. We considered him a viable suspect for Strunk's murder. Could he have killed Bowcer?"

"He wasn't there on Friday either," Trumpet said.

"No, he was." Tom sounded surprised. "I nearly knocked him down on the way out. He missed the main event though." He watched Trumpet rubbing her arms and frowned in sympathy. He tilted his head toward the house, offering to go in. She shook hers. She could tolerate a few more minutes.

"I didn't notice him," she said. "It's astounding, the things we miss when we're excited."

"I find it fascinating," Bacon said. "I must devise a way of studying it that can be measured and reproduced."

Tom gave him a stern look. "I will not break up any more chairs. It's too hard on the hands."

Bacon chuckled. Trumpet enjoyed the brief exchange. She had few opportunities to see them together anymore. A strong friendship had grown up between them while they were bickering. She was happy to be a part of it.

"So," Bacon said, "Charles was there. I believe we can assume Dorothy would have told him about the cause of the to-do. He might have heard Bowcer declare his intention of leaving early. He could have picked up the chair leg wherever it fell along Tom's route and hidden in the alley to await his victim."

"He wouldn't gain much by it," Trumpet said. "Other than revenge, our second favorite motive. It seems less good to me now that we've discussed it. It's backward-looking, as Tom says. You're no better off than you were before."

Bacon smiled at her fondly. "That speaks volumes for your character, my lady."

She waved that off. Why praise the obvious? "If Charles is the murderer, his next target should be Uncle Geoffrey. He's treated the Midleys shamefully."

"Dorothy too," Tom said. "I see no grounds for choosing between them."

"Except for one thing," Bacon said. "From what you've told me, Charles has the most to lose from the delay caused by these murders."

Tom snapped his fingers. "That's right. He says he's way behind in paying his fees. He'll probably be sent home with no resolution to his case. I'm not sure why he's still here, to be honest. If he can't pay the fees, he can't collect his seals and signatures."

"Perhaps he's waiting for money from a source we don't know about," Trumpet said.

Tom shrugged that off. "Or working up the courage for a spot of burglary."

"If he's as poor as all that," Bacon said, "he has no hope of attaining his livery this year. With Bowcer gone, he can expect to start over again next year anyway."

"That is monstrously unfair," Tom said, scowling.

"Nevertheless."

"I do wonder," Tom said, "about something Charles told me one evening when we were drowning our sorrows at the Bear. At the time, I thought he was being ironic, but perhaps he meant it. He said there were some advantages to remaining an infant in the eyes of the law. You could defraud a tenant or two, for example, and escape responsibility."

"At his age? Most unlikely." Bacon smoothed his moustache. "Did you get the sense he had such a scheme in mind?"

"Would it work?" Trumpet asked.

Bacon shook his head. "Doubtful, as I said. Though not impossible, depending on the court and the tenant. He couldn't count on it. The law makes a most uncertain accomplice."

"What about murder?" Trumpet asked. This felt like something solid. Something that might tip the balance. "If he was caught, would he be tried as a child? He could escape punishment entirely."

"No, he couldn't." Tom and Bacon spoke together. Bacon inclined his head to allow his former pupil to answer.

"He can't sign contracts or write a will," Tom said. "Can't buy or sell property, which involves contracts. But the threshold of responsibility for criminal cases is fourteen. He could be tried, no doubt about that. And the jury would know his true age. If the testimony convinced them, they'd sentence him to hang twice for his effrontery."

"Once would be sufficient." Bacon pursed his lips in a pious expression. That usually indicated that he was making a joke, but his jokes were never funny.

"Does he know that?" Trumpet asked. "If he doesn't, it's still a factor."

Tom shrugged. "I don't know what he knows. Not much is my guess. He spent two years at Oxford, but that's all. He should have come to an Inn of Court or Chancery. Whether that was his decision or Leynham's, I couldn't say."

"Delay works in Leynham's favor also." Bacon had plucked a yellow leaf from a twining vine and was spinning it between finger and thumb as if studying its veins or assessing its color. "It gives him time to rectify whatever he's done before his wards can confront him in court. Dorothy may know that he's sold this or failed to sell that, but if the properties are in good order at the time of her suit, she'll have trouble proving harm done."

"The longer, the better for that old cozener."

Tom clapped his hands on his thighs and grinned. "I'm the only one who doesn't benefit from delay."

"Dorothy," Trumpet reminded him. He grunted.

"You also benefit," Bacon said to Tom. "Postponing your case until Hilary term gives you time to come up with the three hundred pounds you owe my aunt."

Tom groaned. "Those cursed three hundred pounds! Your lady aunt will accept nothing less than my marrying a woman she approves. Marry or remain an infant. Those are my choices."

Trumpet glanced at Bacon. He twirled his leaf, refusing to look at anyone.

Tom shook his finger at them, each in turn. "You insult me, you two. You truly do. After all these years of solving crimes together, you treat me like the greenest apprentice. If I wanted to murder those contemptible minions of greed, do you honestly think I would go to so much trouble to make sure I was everyone's favorite suspect?"

EIGHTEEN

Tom swooped in to strike the ball with an upward swing, driving it high over the makeshift net. It struck the side wall with a *plock* that echoed from the thirty-foot ceiling of the vast hall, barely missing the head of some long-dead stag. It rebounded into the service court, where Stephen caught it at precisely the right moment, smashing it back a scant yard from Tom's feet. He couldn't shift his body fast enough to reach the cursed thing — not at that low angle.

"God's great blue bollocks!" Tom threw down his racquet. "Point to you again. And that's game to you — again." He snarled at his opponent, but only in jest. Stephen was far the superior player, thanks to many hours of practice on Her Majesty's courts.

Tom did not begrudge his defeat, however crushing. Winning made Stephen happy, and Tom had a huge favor to ask this afternoon.

Stephen ducked under the long rope that hung across the hall to serve as a net. He stood beneath the stag's head, studying the plaster. "That's left a mark. My lady wife won't be best pleased." But he grinned as he waved Tom over to the table in the corner where refreshments awaited them.

Tom pretended to be dismayed. "Will she mind a great deal?" He knew she wouldn't care a fig.

"She'll cluck her tongue, but there's nothing for it. We don't have a proper court or room to build one. Besides, my father would hate it, which is encouragement enough for me."

"Indeed he would, my lord." Tom laughed at the thought of Stephen's sour-humored father catching his heir in such a frivolous activity. "And not just the spot or the net or the abuse of an ancient hall." He roughened his voice in imitation of the old earl. "The waste of valuable time! The disrespect! The wanton frivolity!"

Stephen laughed happily, tilting his head back, shaking his dark blond, collar-length curls. Laughter brightened his tawny eyes and softened the angles of his sharp features.

Tom smiled to see his old chum in such good humor. He'd never been free to laugh like that while his father lived. The old man had disapproved of everything that smacked of looseness or lightness. They'd spent far too many hours sitting in the chapel reciting lessons from the Bible in the days of their youth.

Stephen had had no defenses, having suffered under that tyranny since infancy. Then Tom had arrived to serve as the young heir's companion. That arrangement had been achieved by Tom's father, who meant to hoist his son up the social ladder as high as he could reach. He'd scouted around for a gentleman with debts and chanced on Lord Dorchester, whose religion had not prevented him from making some poor investments. Captain Clarady had covered the shortfall in exchange for having his son reared in a nobleman's household.

Tom had left his noisy, irregular, loving family to live with the stiff and silent Delaberes. He'd made the best of it. As soon as they were released from chapel every day, he'd led Stephen out of doors and into mischief. They'd stolen peaches, fought mock battles on the downs, and wheedled their first kisses from the dairy maids. They'd forged a friendship that had outlived a seemingly irreparable breach at the end of their first term at Gray's. The years between had given each man room to grow up in his own way.

Stephen had flourished once the old earl's heavy boot had been lifted from his neck. He'd gained confidence, discovered interests, and made friends among the other young noblemen at court. Trumpet had nurtured that growth like a skilled gardener training herbs into a knot garden. Cultivate this, snip away that. She used praise more than anything, along with advice gained from her stints as a lady of the Privy Chamber.

Tom grabbed a pair of towels from the stack on the table and tossed one to Stephen. They stood panting and wiping the sweat from their faces and necks. "Good game, my lord." Tom took a deep breath and let it out with a sigh of satisfaction. "There's nothing like a little hard exercise to restore a man's balance."

"Tennis is good for that. And you can play it on a rainy day."

Tom studied his old chum as he rubbed the back of his neck. They both wore loose galligaskins down to the knee with thin stockings tied under the hem. They'd shed their ruffs and doublets after the first round to play in shirtsleeves with open collars. The manly disarray suited Stephen. Keeping up with the other earls in hunting and boxing had hardened his body and straightened his back.

He'd developed a hint of belly though, only visible without a doublet. Doubtless caused by the plates of tarts and small pies that appeared every time he sat down. Tom resolved to advise Trumpet to limit the snacks. Stephen was too young to start emulating old King Harry.

Tom tossed the towel on the floor and poured cool wine into cups, handing one to his old friend and present protector. "You're an excellent player, my lord. I could scarce return half your shots, and I promise you I was giving it all I had."

Stephen preened at the praise. "I can beat Southampton, and he's a year younger. And he grew up with it."

"You've always had a natural grace. Tennis requires agility more than strength."

"Don't forget strategy. It also helps to know the court — and your opponent." Stephen shot Tom a wink. "You can't turn to your left, not at speed. Neither can Southampton. He'll trip over his own feet if you land the ball right."

"What about my Lord of Essex? I'll bet he's a good player." Time to nudge the conversation in the desired direction.

"Nobody beats Essex." Stephen took a sip of his wine. "Talk about natural grace! But in truth, he simply can't bear to lose. I've seen him smack himself witless running into a wall or launch himself full length into the air to get his racquet under a ball. That's partly gallantry — the ladies love it — but mainly a burning desire to win at all costs."

Tom took a big drink. Then he cleared his throat and jumped in. "Speaking of Lord Essex, my lord, I've heard he found a clever way out of wardship."

"Did he?" Stephen turned to survey the tidbits arrayed upon the table, choosing a cheese tart with a dried raspberry pressed into the top.

"His uncle, Lord Leicester, knighted him. According to tradition, a knight is able to perform knight service and thus cannot be considered a child. Hence, not a ward." Tom set his cup down and lowered himself to one knee. "My lord, I beg from you a boon."

"A boon!" Stephen gaped at him. "What in the name of — oh, Tom! You can't honestly expect me to knight you."

"Why not? It's the fastest, surest path. No fees, no approval from the cursed court. If I'm a knight, I'm formally available for knight service, and that's the end of it."

"The end of it! The start, more like. I can only imagine what Her Majesty would do to me if I even pretended to knight you. Throw me in the Tower for a month, most like." He looked down at Tom and burst into laughter. "Get up, man! You look like you're about to propose marriage. It's flattering, truly, but I'm already taken."

Tom got to his feet. "But what about Leicester? He was an earl, like you."

"Not like me." Stephen held up both hands. "Not even close. First, Leicester was the love of Her Majesty's life. Everyone knows it. Second, Essex is like the son she never had. She loves him dearly. Everyone knows that too. Third, Leicester was Essex's stepfather, and Essex was already an earl. Fourth, and most importantly, they were on a battlefield. Somewhere in the Low Countries. Essex fights like he plays tennis. He means to win. I'm sure he showed conspicuous bravery doing something or other." He raised his arms in a wide shrug. "What would I knight you for? Being a middling sort of tennis player? Passing the bar?"

Tom frowned and hung his head. "No, you're right. I'm just desperate to get out of these chains."

"I thought you were nearly there." Stephen put down his wine cup and picked up a ball and his racquet. He stepped a few feet away and began taking practice shots at the wall. Every strike of the hard felt-and-cork ball against the plaster echoed with a dull *thock*.

"Didn't you say you'd paid all your fees? What's left?"

"I've paid the big ones, but I couldn't do the last ones. That whoreson clerk — the one who died Friday evening — wouldn't let me. He wanted his bribe first."

Tom watched the racquet catch the ball squarely in the center every time. "It's a trap, my lord. They keep demanding bribes so you can never reach the end."

"Some people do. Most people. I'll bet you can get those fees paid, clerk or no clerk. But what about Lady Russell? It doesn't sound like you'll ever get around her."

"I don't know what to do about her. I honestly don't know which is worse. To remain her ward for the rest of my life — or her life, given her age — or to marry some woman I've never met and don't care about and live with *her* for the rest of my life."

"That's an easy one." Stephen turned to face him. "Marry the wench and take your lands back. I'm surprised you have to think twice."

Tom gave him a bitter look. "But isn't it dishonest to marry a woman you don't love? Isn't marriage supposed to be a sacred bond of mutual love and support, or something like that?"

Stephen laughed again, his triangular face creasing in long lines. "God's breath, Tom! You sound like a Calvinist. Who would have thought my father's preaching would stick to you instead of me?" He sighed, shaking his head. "Yes, marriage is a sacred bond of mutual everything. But you don't have to know each other beforehand for that to come about. Look at me and Alice. We both thought we were settling for the best of a bad set of choices. But once yoked, we learned to pull together. I wouldn't say we were like Tristan and Isolde, but we're fond of one another and make good partners. You'll do the same."

"How can you be so sure?" Tom eyed the plates of delicacies as if they were heaped with worms and ashes.

"How do you know you and Isolde won't come to despise one another once the passion burns out? You don't. Life is a gamble, old friend. You play the cards you're dealt."

"When did you get so wise?"

"It's common knowledge, Tom. You're kicking at lines that were drawn a thousand years ago."

Tom pursed his lips, then snatched a cheese tart and chewed it down. God's teeth, this house had a good cook.

Stephen held his racquet level and bounced the ball on it, catching it squarely every time. "Your Lady Russell has a good reputation among the people at court, though she doesn't turn up very often."

"She has a bad back." Tom knew all about her stainless reputation.

"She's Cecil's aunt, isn't she? She'll make you a good bargain, never fear." Stephen stepped farther from the table to toss his ball into the air, smashing it against the far wall. It struck to the right of his coat of arms. "I should put a portrait of the old earl in here to aim at. We have one at Badbury House I doubt anyone would miss."

He let the ball bounce away and strolled back to the table. He put down his racquet and picked up his cup. After several swallows, he pointed it at Tom. "Here's another reason for you to marry, or at least find the funds to go a-wenching again. I could introduce you to some lively lasses who know how to have fun."

"Lively lasses?" Tom frowned at the abrupt change of topic.

Stephen let out a whistle. "That's precisely what I'm talking about. You don't even remember what it's like to tickle a willing barmaid, do you? You used to be quite the round dog. Worse than me. What happened to that man?"

Tom's brow furrowed. He scratched his beard, at a loss for an answer. He couldn't tell the truth — that he'd lost interest in other women when Trumpet claimed his heart. "My guardian keeps me on a pretty short leash."

"Well, you should break free, at least in this regard. I've heard rumors that you've gone the way of the Bacon brothers. You know what that means. It wouldn't surprise anyone, living in that house among that lot and never going out. If I didn't know you so well, I'd believe it too."

"Who's saying those things?" Tom's fist curled.

Stephen scoffed at the fist. "One here, another there. You're not a major topic, but people run out of gossip when they spend their days doing nothing else. You don't want that kind of rumor running around. It'll ruin your chances of making a good match."

"I can't make a good match, my lord. I can only take what Lady Russell offers me — tomorrow, as it happens — or not." He grumbled into his cup. "I'm a man without choices."

"I thought self-pity was my specialty." Stephen shook his head. "I'll tell you what. My lady wife is taking the children home for Christmas. She leaves for Dorset in a couple of weeks. I'm staying with the court through the new year. One fine night, let's you and me sneak out to that bawdy house we used to like. What was the name?"

"The Two Bells." Tom hadn't been there in years. They'd had fun in those days though. Singing, drinking, wenching. Nights of freedom from study and judgment. Maybe that was what he needed. He didn't want people thinking he was a man who preferred men. That could only lead to trouble. "We could invite a few lads from Gray's to get the right sort of gossip started."

"That's the spirit!" Stephen ran the back of his hand under his short tawny beard. "You know, I don't give advice very often. People don't tend to want it. But no one else seems willing to tell you what you need to hear. Marry the woman, Tom, whoever she is. She'll be fair enough and rich, which is all that matters. Marry her and set her up in a nice house somewhere in the country. Put a child in her belly to keep her busy, then come back to town and do as you please."

Tom's shoulders slumped. "I don't even remember what I please."

Stephen laughed heartily and slapped him on the back. "God's teeth, man, you do need help! You're a barrister now, aren't you? Don't you have clients to cultivate? Whatever happened to that old plan of specializing in young widows? They shouldn't be too hard to find, with a war that never ends and plague running rampant every odd summer. And don't worry about losing your touch. You've still got that dimple."

Tom rolled his eyes. Oh, for the days when a dimple was enough!

NINETEEN

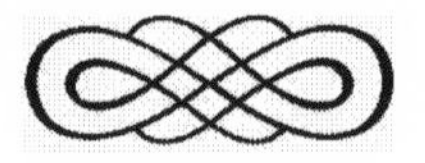

Francis went back to Attorney Strunk's office in Westminster on Monday morning. He planned to invite the underclerk out for a drink in a local tavern, where he would ply him with strong ale and elicit evidence of prosecutable crimes. That should have been Tom's job, but he just couldn't face the exposure. Still, it ought to be done. One never knew what a person might confess under the influence of strong drink. Tom and Antonio had agreed on that.

Also, Francis's every instinct told him Strunk had kept a record of the bribes he'd extracted from wards over the years. There must be a small notebook hidden in his office that the sheriff had failed to find or even thought to seek.

No one waited in the anteroom, not even the silent northman. Too early, perhaps. Besides, who could they expect to see?

Francis let himself into Strunk's unlocked chamber, finding it empty, as expected. A pale patch on one wall suggested a painting had been removed. The desktop gleamed with fresh wax, and its faint lemon scent freshened the small space. Two chairs had been positioned with precision on opposite sides of the desk. A short bookcase bearing a few large volumes leaned in the corner behind the desk.

Francis tilted each chair up to inspect the underside of the seat. Not a likely hiding place, but a possible one. He then opened every book on the shelf, finding nothing but pages securely bound between leather covers. Here was a well-used copy of Littleton's *Tenures*, as he'd predicted. The shelf itself concealed no secret drawers or oddly deep layers. It had no back to which a small notebook might be affixed.

He paced carefully around the room, pressing on the boards with the ball of his foot in search of a loose one. This house had been too well-built for secret caches beneath the floor.

Francis sat behind the desk and placed his palms on the surface to survey the chamber. If he were appointed Attorney to the Court of Wards — an unlikely prospect — he would spend most of his working days right here at this desk. He gazed at the door, imagining it opening to admit a ward. Someone like Tom — a young man, tall, well-dressed, and irritable.

Many of them would be ill-humored, one supposed, even without the bribes. The Court of Wards outraged everyone it touched. Others would be worried or despondent. Few would enter that door with a smile on their lips, ready for a few moments of pleasant chat.

He would hate this job. If Essex should be appointed master — an even more unlikely prospect — Francis would have to find a diplomatic way to beg him not to reward him with this undesirable position.

Enough of that. He leaned back to consider the design of the desk. The four legs were carved in a simple style, as were the cross-pieces that stretched between them. It was a solid piece of work, meant to last for generations. Two shallow drawers hung under the top. The one on the right held writing tools: quills, both sharpened and not, a penknife, a pouch of sand, a sifter, a ruler, and several small bottles of ink. The left one held sheets of paper of varying size and quality. Francis shuffled through them and found a small bound commonplace book. He pulled it out and opened it on the desktop, excitement raising the gooseflesh underneath his ruff.

But no, it was only a diary meant for the Master of the Court of Wards or whoever might wish to know which ward visited on what day. Each entry recorded the date, time, name of ward, purpose of visit, and fees collected — legitimate fees from the official schedule. Anyone could have predicted this book would be here, where the entries must have been written each day. The record of bribes would be less easy to discover.

But not too far away, surely. Francis pulled each drawer out as far as he could, feeling along the underside of the desk for a secret panel. Personal writing desks often had panels that slid aside at a touch or tiny drawers at the back of larger drawers. Skilled woodworkers vied with one another to create ever more ingenious hiding places.

This desk did not seem to boast any such artistry. Francis sighed and set his hat on the desk. Then he rose and sank to his knees. He grunted as he crawled under and turned awkwardly upside down, supporting himself on one straining elbow. He examined the underside of the drawers with both eyes and fingers, then rapped along the underside of the desktop as far as he could reach.

"What in God's name are you doing?" a reedy voice demanded.

"Huh?" Francis shifted too quickly and hit his head smartly on the underside of a drawer. "Ouch!" He managed to get himself onto all fours and crawled out from under the desk. He used the chair to haul himself to his feet. He dusted the knees of his black stockings and faced his inquisitor.

A small, pale man with a spade-shaped beard stood scowling at him. "What are you doing?"

"Ah!" Francis scrambled for an excuse. "Ha. Yes. I have an interest in classical furniture, you see. Some of these old desks in Westminster were made in Italy, you know. I was looking for a maker's mark." He smiled brightly. That sounded plausible to him.

The pale blue eyes narrowed. "Is that why you came in here? To look at Italian woodwork?"

"No. Haha." Francis shook his head, vowing to attempt no more chuckles. That had sounded more guilty than genial. He fell back on his original plan: to pretend he wanted the position and had come fishing for an insider view. "No, of course not. I came in hoping to find someone who knows what's happening here these days. Have they begun to search for a new attorney yet?"

A knowing look replaced the surprise on the clerk's face. "I imagine they have, though I don't expect a decision to be taken soon."

"These things take time."

First, the news must spread across the country. Then petitioners must rally their patrons to offer bids to Lord Burghley. Christmas was close upon them, and January brought rain and muddy roads. If the appointment was made before Easter, Francis would be astonished. "You doubtless have ways of staying abreast, Mr. ah . . ."

"Dickson. Tobias Dickson." The clerk bowed his head. "And you are?"

"Francis, ah —" He coughed, realizing his name might be recognized. "Francis Welbeck. I'm a barrister at Gray's Inn. There's been some discussion about the empty post, and I thought I'd stop in on my way to court."

"Won't you step into my office, Mr. Welbeck?" The clerk gestured through the door.

Francis followed him into an even smaller, plainer room. The clerk pointed at a chair in the corner stacked with papers. "Just put those on the desk, if you don't mind." He walked around to his customary seat.

Francis moved the documents — contracts, judging by the enumerated sections — and perched on the seat. "I'm sorry to interrupt your work."

"Never ends, does it?" Dickson cast an eye on the mound of papers at his left elbow, then turned a thin smile toward his visitor. "Mr. Strunk was a member of Gray's too. I imagine there's a great deal of interest among his former colleagues."

"Indeed there is." This couldn't be right, this ritual exchange of commonplaces. Such empty chatter could go on forever, in his observation. One would mention a noteworthy case before one of the courts; the other would agree that neither lawyer had presented a sound argument. They might descend into the weather or the traffic on the Thames for a span of wasted minutes. Then Francis would be ushered out no wiser than when he'd come in.

He could never worm confidences from this man in this setting. The clerk sat behind his own desk, fully sober, wearing his professional demeanor. He would be polite but guarded, in full possession of his small domain. Francis had to shift them to a neutral ground.

Tom had advised him to invite the man out for a drink. Francis had scoffed. Who would accept such an invitation from a stranger? Besides, the man might loathe taverns as much as Francis did and be offended by the suggestion. Tom had chuckled — a rich, natural sound — and insisted that most clerks, being sorely underpaid, would leap at the chance of a free drink.

Francis mentally rehearsed the words Tom had taught him. Then he painted a smile on his face and patted a stack of paper on his end of the desk. "I can see how busy you are, Mr. Dickson. You must have twice the work with the attorney gone. I would hate to add length to your day. And in truth, I would prefer a more informal conversation, if you understand me."

"Oh?" Dickson's eyebrows rose — a man awaiting an invitation. Curse the man. Tom had been right.

"Perhaps you would allow me to buy you a drink this evening when you're through for the day. Say, around six o'clock?"

A gleam flashed in Dickson's eyes. Had he misconstrued the nature of the invitation? But no, neither of them was young enough for a flirtation to develop so quickly with so little provocation. His interest could only be political. "I could manage that. The Lamb and Flag has a worthy ale and is right around the corner."

"I'll see you there." Francis rose and touched his hat. He let himself out. That hadn't been so bad, though he would never admit it to Tom.

* * *

"Let him think he's asking you the questions." Antonio had taken it upon himself that afternoon to tutor Francis in the art of subtle interrogation. Francis had questioned many prisoners in the Tower over the years, but there he had a list of questions and an assistant writing down the answers.

Antonio, in contrast, had spent many years in the cutthroat corridors of El Escorial, King Philip's great palace in Madrid. He had learned to tease out confidences without seeming to care about their content. Later on, he had used his skills to persuade his prison guards to look the other way at a critical moment. He had lived on his wits and had survived to reach this haven in England.

Francis granted that questioning informants in a tavern required a different approach. "What makes you think this clerk has questions?"

"That gleam you mentioned. He wants something from you. He does not know you, nor could he have known you would walk into his chambers this morning. He must see it as a stroke of luck. I suspect he may have been watching out for such a chance."

"A chance to do what?"

Antonio performed a full Spanish shrug. "That is what you must find out."

"What I must find out is how Strunk helped Leynham sneak those properties onto the rolls before the official survey."

"No, Francisquito. That is not the proper approach for a spy. You must be alive to anything of interest, whether it relates directly to your original quest or not."

Francis groaned. "I could be there all night."

Antonio patted him on the back. "I will wait up for you." He cocked his head to give Francis an inspection. He nodded at the plain black suit with black thread buttons, the one Francis wore to ride to and from his mother's house in Gorhambury. Neat but unremarkable.

"Keep refilling his cup," Antonio said. "And ask for a dish of salted nutmeats. The salt will make him drink more. Be sure he thinks you are seeking some advantage for yourself. You want to be the next Attorney for the Court of Wards. *Muy bien*, why not? You have the qualifications. Hint that he can expect a handsome gift when you attain the post and a share of the unrecorded profits as well."

"Unrecorded profits." This clerk must know something about those, surely. Or did he first learn of them when he heard Tom shouting that he wouldn't pay? "He could be innocent, this Dickson."

"He is not innocent. He would not trouble himself to meet you if he had nothing to sell or to buy."

"Perhaps he always goes to this place after work and jumped at the chance to get his drink for free."

Antonio raised his dark eyes to heaven. "Do not labor so hard, my friend. Go, talk. Learn what you can and come home."

"I'll try." Francis held out little hope. This sort of thing came naturally to rogues like Antonio and charmers like Tom. He, in contrast, had formed the lamentable habit of telling the simple truth as he understood it.

Antonio heard that thought. "Tell the truth when it is possible. It is easier to remember and will make the lies sound more convincing."

Francis opened the front door and stepped outside. The wherryman should be waiting for him at the wharf by now. "I wish you could come with me." But one couldn't trail about the taverns of Westminster with a Spaniard in tow. They'd be dragged out to an alley and beaten before they could ask a single question.

"I will be with you in spirit. And remember — you will make him drunk, but you must not drink too much yourself."

"I know that."

Tom had found it necessary to emphasize that point as well. Did they suppose he was a helpless sot? Bah. He was far more abstemious than either of his advisors.

* * *

The Lamb and Flag smelled every bit as foul as he expected, even on a Monday night. Stale tobacco smoke and spilled ale dominated, but he could detect greasy meat and garlic as well. The noise exceeded his memories, almost forcing him right back out the door. How could anyone carry on a conversation in such a cacophony?

His shoes stuck to the floor with each step. He refused to think about the nature of the glue. A woman in a kirtle with no partlet covering her bobbing bosom pointed him toward the end of a long table. Two men in clerk's somber garb leaned their heads together at the other end.

Francis lowered himself gingerly to the bench. He told the wench, "I'm expecting a man named Dickson."

"Good for you." She waddled off.

The clamor seemed to decrease a trifle at table level. More likely, he'd already grown used to it. He felt conspicuous sitting here alone and kept his gaze on the battered table. He tried not to think about the dark blotches gleaming wetly here and there.

The sun had lighted his way into the narrow street where this tavern stood, but its rays had sunk too low to penetrate indoors. Candles burned in round wheels overhead. Torches flared around the walls. The relentless blackness of the patrons' garb absorbed much of the yellow light. The Lamb and Flag was evidently a favorite among the lesser clerks of Westminster, whose numbers were legion.

He hadn't long to wait. Dickson suddenly appeared across the table. He was too short to spot from across the room, even if Francis had been watching the door.

They greeted one another. The wench returned. "A pitcher of your best ale," Francis said. "My treat."

"Make it Huffcap, bonny." Dickson winked at the woman, who shrugged one nearly naked shoulder. Then off she went again.

Francis had never heard of huffcap. He didn't like to ask, for fear of seeming ignorant. Tonight, he was an ordinary man. A tavern-going man, wise in the ways of public-house offerings. Nathaniel Welbeck had probably sampled every brew and fermentation from here to Bordeaux.

"A quiet day for you, I hope?" he offered, to start the conversation.

"Quiet as the tomb. Amazing how much a man can get done without a crowd of sniveling youngsters in the anteroom."

That remark betrayed an oppositional attitude — clerks versus wards. Not uncommon within institutions, unfortunately. One rarely met men in these lesser posts who displayed any degree of public spirit. It made it easier to fleece your charges if you thought of them as a flock of demanding sheep.

The wench brought them a large jug and two clay cups, plunking them onto the table. Francis remembered one of his instructions. "Could we have some salted nutmeats, please? Perhaps some slivered almonds?"

"Almonds!" The wench snorted. "Hazelnuts'll have to do."

"Hazelnuts are quite acceptable."

She laughed at him, not unkindly. He found that response baffling. He'd accepted her lesser nutmeats with courtesy. But then, this milieu was as foreign to him as another country. He could expect a few minor misunderstandings.

He reached for the jug, but Dickson had beaten him to it. The clerk filled both cups to the brim. Setting down the jug, he raised his cup. "To prosperity!"

"Prosperity," Francis echoed. A promising start. His plan depended on the man's greed, after all. He took a tentative sip of the huffcap. It tingled on his tongue, a pleasant sensation. The tingle carried all the way down to his stomach, then rose again up his spine and into his skull. There it seemed to wheel around his brains like a world-encircling ocean. He'd tasted aqua vitae, of course, but only in small doses. He hoped this huffcap had a milder effect.

The initial stimulation subsided. He ventured another swallow. That one went more smoothly, so he drank a little more.

Dickson took a drink and smacked his lips. "So, Mr. Welbeck. What did you want to talk about?"

Francis gave him what he hoped was a sly look. The twitch of the man's lip suggested he had succeeded. "You may have guessed that I'm interested in that position — Attorney to the Court of Wards. It's a good post in and of itself and can lead to greater things, I've heard."

"I've heard that too, though I haven't seen it. I've only been with Wards for seven years. It's a lot of work, mind you, studying deeds and contracts from every shire and town."

"I like studying old records." There was the foundation of truth — another instruction obeyed. So far, this adventure was proceeding as planned. Francis wetted his throat, enjoying the bite of the strong ale as it went down.

He took a step toward his main goal. "How closely does the attorney work with guardians — or rather, prospective guardians? Does he guide them along the path toward guardianship? Does he make recommendations to the master of the court?"

"Both, from what I've seen."

The wench came back to slide a bowl of cracked-and-salted hazelnuts onto the table. Dickson pushed them toward Francis, who took one to sample. Delicious. He ate another one, washing down the salt with a gulp of ale. A perfect combination of flavors and textures.

Dickson kept his hand wrapped around his cup. "Most guardians are grateful for the guidance. If the prospector is a close friend, the attorney can help him understand the subtleties, one might say, of the estate in question."

Francis wagged his finger at the man. "I believe I understand you. Not everyone knows when they possess a parcel subject to feudal duties. And many landowners fail to understand the implications."

"It is a specialized form of knowledge, isn't it? You'll want to be on the watch for those parcels. That is the most important part of the attorney's job — searching out properties of interest to the court."

"And then nudging things along in the right direction." Francis nibbled another nut or two, sipping thoughtfully at his ale. How would he know when Dickson was ripe for more direct questioning? He could produce conjecture and speculation on his own.

He leaned forward, peering at the clerk, trying to judge his level of sobriety. The man wobbled a little and offered him an amiable smile.

Francis took that as a good sign. "Speaking of nudging, the attorney could help the guardian make last-minute adjustments to the inventory, couldn't he? If it would help secure the ward."

"It can take weeks to arrange the initial survey." Dickson refilled Francis's cup. "The attorney has a variety of quills in his satchel, if you catch my meaning."

"Oh yes." Francis nodded several times. "I believe I do." He had no idea what the man was hinting at. Worse, he'd just realized he couldn't mention the specific case of interest without exposing himself. How would Francis Welbeck know anything about Geoffrey Leynham's swindle? Best to shift to his other prong of attack: how much the attorney took home in bribes.

He'd thought of a story for this one on the long trip downriver. He'd present himself as a man wishing to rise up the legal ladder. Another truth, considered from a different perspective. Climbing cost money, starting with the bribe for consideration for the post. Naturally, he would want some sense of how quickly that expense could be recovered.

He fortified himself with another drink. This stuff was wonderfully heartening. He leaned forward to rest his elbows on the dirty table and his chin on his folded hands. "If I may confide in you, Mr. Dockster."

"Dickson." The clerk mirrored his posture.

"I have aspirations beyond the career of a mere barrister. I wish to rise. But rising costs money — more than I possess. I'd have to borrow to gain any position worth the trouble. I've heard rumors about the Attorney of the Court of Wards. I wonder how much of what I've heard is true?"

That gleam reappeared in Dickson's eyes. "Most of it, I should think. I never passed the bar, nor am I ever like to do so, but a gentleman like yourself can seek higher if he has the means. You're wondering if this position will be worth the investment."

"Precisely."

Dickson lowered his voice. "The salary is only ninety per annum, you know."

Francis made a dismissive sound. It didn't sound quite right, so he tried again. That one felt better. "Hardly enough to live on with today's prices."

"I agree with you there."

"Strunk seemed better off than that. Much better. His garb, for one. He dressed well. He had a big house somewhere too. Surrey?" He couldn't remember anything compelling to bring forth as evidence.

"Mr. Strunk lived very comfortably." Dickson cocked his head. "I think you may be the man I've been waiting for, Mr. Welbeck." He lifted his chin and lowered his hands to glance first to the right, then to the left.

Francis glanced in both directions as well — twice for good measure. The movement made his head spin. What were they looking for?

Dickson reached into the front of his doublet and drew out a commonplace book, about six inches by eight. He put it down and laid his hand over it. "I found this behind the portrait of the queen in Strunk's chamber yesterday. It can't trouble him anymore, so I feel no qualms about sharing it. It could be helpful to man with aspirations." He slid it across the table.

Francis opened the front cover to find a blank page. He flipped that over and read a few rows of brief entries. He grunted, flicking a glance at Dickson, who nodded back, licking his lips as if sharing something tasty.

Francis picked up the small book and tilted it toward the light. He recognized the hand from Strunk's other record book. These entries were similar in nature — monies received with names and dates. Some included notes like "king's fee" or "entry fine."

He blinked, having a little trouble focusing. Holding the book closer to his nose, he added up a few rows of figures. Thirty pounds in a single week? Could that be typical?

He closed the book and gaped at Dickson. "The sums are staggering. Are you suggesting this is what I could expect if I were to win this position?"

"I am, Mr. Welbeck." Dickson reached across to pluck the book from Francis's slack grasp. "I would consider it a cooperative venture, if you comprehend me."

"We share. Not evenly, I assume. Most of the risk would be mine."

"I'm a modest man. Twenty percent would be sufficient for my needs."

"That sounds fair." Francis raised his cup in affirmation and took a deep draught. "Especially if you put in a good word for me for the post. I'll want to study that more closely." He reached for the book.

Dickson leaned away, holding the book to his chest. "I can't just give it away, now can I? You see my situation, Mr. Welbeck. I found this thing, this interesting thing. I knew at once the next attorney might be pleased to take charge of it. If he was the right sort of man, that is. No guarantee of that. I could lose my job if I showed it to the wrong sort."

"An honest man in the Court of Wards?" Francis blew out a long lip fart, then clapped a surprised hand over his mouth. He took a sip of ale to cover his embarrassment.

Dickson chuckled. "Stranger things have happened. Stranger things indeed. What I wanted was a fellow like yourself, Mr. Welbeck. A man looking to rise, with an eye on the main chance. A man not too proud to take advantage of a golden opportunity and a helpful partner when he comes across them."

"Like me." Francis tapped himself on the chest. His performance had been a rousing success, although his head seemed to have grown larger and less weighty. His hat still fit though. Perhaps that had expanded as well in some sort of sympathetic action.

"Like you." Dickson refilled both cups. "But as I said, I can't just give this little volume away. It's all I have."

"Ah." Francis nodded sagely. "How much?"

"Twenty pounds is a nice round number."

"Sold!" Francis slapped his hand on the table. Heads turned their way, and he shrugged at them in apology. "Too loud, too loud," he admonished himself.

Only then did he remember that he ought to have bargained for a lower price. Not that it mattered. He had less than a pound in small coins on his person. But the minute money had entered the conversation, he'd known exactly what he wanted to do with that book.

"I don't have that much with me."

"I'll accept a note with your signature. You said you were gentleman of Gray's Inn. I know where to find you." Dickson grinned, showing more teeth than he had before.

"Do you have paper? A quill? Ink?" Francis looked about, wiggling the fingers of both hands. Vitality coursed through his veins, filling him with the desire to complete this exercise and go home. This notebook was a gold mine. He couldn't wait to dig into it.

Dickson had the necessary tools brought to the table, including a taper in a short holder. Francis took a quill and tested it with his fingertip. A little dull, but it would do. He could write with anything, anywhere, no matter how much his head wobbled.

The first letter said merely, *On presentation of this note, please tender the sum of twenty pounds to Mr.* — He looked up. "What was your full name again?" Given the answer, he continued. *Mr. Tobias Dickson, a clerk in the Court of Wards, in payment for a document to be delivered to Sir Robert personally by the undersigned as soon as possible. The bearer of this note did not create or approve the document in question. He merely found it. He has acted responsibly in bringing it to me.*

Francis Bacon at the Lamb and Flag, this twenty-fifth of November 1594.

He looked up at Dickson. "Is it still the twenty-fifth?"

Dickson nodded.

"That's all right, then." Francis set that aside to dry and took another sheet. *Dear Cousin, you will think this an absurd amount, but pay it anyway. You'll consider it a bargain when you see what I've bought on your behalf. It pertains to the Attorney of Wards; indeed, to the workings of the whole court. I shall write no more here. We may discuss it at your leisure. Your devoted servant, Frank.*

He blew on the second page, then folded both together into a square with a blank outer face. He dripped a bit of wax from the candle onto the seam and pressed his small seal ring into it. "Ouch!" He should have removed it from his finger first.

He turned the square over and wrote, *Sir Robert Cecil, care of Michael Hickes, Burghley House.* He held the letter in the air. "My book now, if you please?"

They made the exchange. Dickson read the direction on the front and studied the seal on the back. "Looks like a pig."

"It's a boar."

Dickson's eyes narrowed. "How do I know Mr. Hickes will pay my money?"

"He'll pay. Sir Robert will be very interested in your discovery."

"He'll blame me for these entries, most like." Dickson's thin face creased with worry.

Fair enough. Francis hadn't expected this turn of events either. "I explained your part in the note." His head had grown heavier. He drank some more of the wonderful huffcap to lighten it again.

Dickson weighed the letter in one hand. "What makes you think Sir Robert will look at this?"

"He's my cousin. And now I must apologize for my earlier deception. I am Francis Bacon." He drained his cup and pushed himself onto his feet. He stuffed the notebook well into the deep pocket in his round hose. "I fear I must bid you good night, Mr. Dickson. Thank you for your cooperation." He attempted a short bow and had to place both hands on the sticky table to keep from falling on his face.

He found his way to the front door, making occasional use of a shoulder or a strong back to keep himself upright.

The fresh air from the river blew some of the fog from his wits. Stars shone overhead, sparkling more brightly than any earthly jewels. They dazzled him for a moment. He shook his head and trained his eyes on the street. He navigated down to the wharf by strength of habit. He knew Westminster as well as he knew his mother's house.

A wherryman helped him into a boat. He landed in the bottom on his first attempt to sit on one of the narrow slats, but no harm done. His muscles were so loose they offered no resistance.

"Where to, Master?" the boatman asked.

"Twickleman." That didn't sound right. Francis giggled. "I mean Twittledom."

"Twickenham?"

"That's it!" Francis beamed at him. "Twittlebum. Mr. Bacon's house, if you know it."

"I know them all."

They rowed upstream into the darkness, following the yellow glow of the lantern dangling above the prow. The tide appeared to be coming in, and they soon passed the crowd of boats between Westminster and Chelsea. Francis closed his eyes to savor the cool, clean breeze, but he wasn't sleepy. The thrill of his achievement kept his heart pounding.

Proof — tangible proof — of corruption in Robert's court. It was a rare catch and one for which he would find many uses. He'd give it to Anthony first so one of his secretaries could make copies. The secretary could also add up the sums by month, by county, and by year. His Lord of Essex would be pleased to have those details to add weight to his negotiations.

He wasn't much worried about damaging his cousin's reputation. Robert would persuade everyone he'd known nothing about it. He always found a way out of trouble. That had been true since childhood.

Francis sighed happily. The gentle motion of the boat and the soft splashing of the oars in the water soon washed away the hectic noise of the tavern. He could feel the furrows smoothing from his brow. He closed his eyes, only for a moment. His head sagged, then his shoulders. Perhaps a little rest would do him good. He slid to the side of the bench and laid himself down along the humble plank. His feet, still planted on the bottom boards, kept him from sliding forward. He closed his eyes and sighed.

* * *

"We're here, Master."

A hand gripped Francis's shoulder and gave him a shake.

"What? Who?" He raised his head to take bleary stock of his situation. Somehow he'd slid to the bottom of the boat and curled himself into a ball. He struggled up to a sitting position but needed help to get back onto the bench.

Wherrymen were used to such things. It was a long way from Westminster to Twickenham, after all. If Francis were as wealthy as his cousin, he'd have a barge with a bed of pillows on a soft couch.

The boatman hoisted him onto the wharf. "Your house isn't far, Master. Can you get there on your own?"

"Certainly. Certainly." The vertical posture revived Francis's wits enough to find his purse and pay the man. He bade him a pleasant journey back downriver and turned his face toward home.

The beam-and-plaster house shone whitely in the silver starlight. It seemed half a mile away. He chanted the first lines of the *Aeneid* to encourage each foot to take another step. The meter seemed made for staggering up a long path. *"Arma virumque cano, Troiae qui primus ab oris."*

At last, he reached the door. He had to use both hands to press down the handle but managed to open it with one strong push. Then he tripped over the threshold and fell flat on his face.

"I sing of arms and the man," he remarked to the dusty floor. Then he giggled at the absurdity of it all.

He heard someone clucking his tongue in Spanish. Strong hands gripped his shoulder and hip, turning him face up. "*Ay mi,* Francisquito. Look at you! You are as drunk as an old soldier. What did I tell you? You make a most terrible spy."

"Not true." Francis dug into his pocket for the little notebook and held it high. "I won the day." The book was lifted from his hand. Antonio grunted dramatically.

Francis knew that sound. It meant he had impressed the old scoundrel. He grinned at the ceiling and laughed. Then his head rolled to one side and he fell sound asleep.

TWENTY

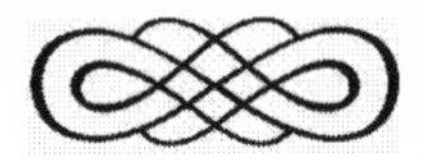

Tom unfolded the letter from Mr. Bacon and read it through. He gave a low whistle and finished dressing. Another item to discuss with Trumpet while they watched the children enjoy their morning airing in the garden. She'd invited him yesterday, and it seemed harmless enough. Stephen never rose this early.

Tom manfully refrained from playing with his son, resisting the winsome tot's efforts to engage him. William seemed to have inherited his true father's charm as well as his mother's persistence. Tom granted himself one light stroke of the boy's hair, then banished himself to the sidelines.

Trumpet kept her eyes on her sons as she talked, following their enthusiastic play. The nurse and William's favorite usher stayed close enough to swoop in if trouble loomed. She half turned her head to ask, "Did Mr. Bacon say which wards paid that monstrous king's fee? That was a breaking point for you. It might have been for someone else as well."

"Charles Midley did. The Leynhams don't seem to have paid any of the irregular fees. Mr. Bacon suspects Mr. Leynham and Mr. Strunk had an independent arrangement, thanks to their old friendship. But Dorothy doesn't need that motive, does she?"

"She has more than enough without it."

"Mr. Bacon only quoted one entry in full." Tom opened the letter again. "Here, where it mentions a payment from Leynham to Strunk 'for assistance in securing the wardship.' We know from Dorothy what that means, but as evidence, it's worthless. Leynham could argue that he merely offered a gift to encourage the attorney to recommend him as a guardian."

"We need those deeds." Trumpet laughed at William, who was trying to stand on his head. "She must have them in her possession. She seems so confident about her chances in court."

Tom longed to catch his son by his chubby ankles and walk him upside down around the path. The feeling overwhelmed him for a minute. When the usher went to perform that fatherly duty, he sighed. "Can't you search her room at the Antelope?"

"It won't be there. Too public. I think you should ask her about it this afternoon. They're bound to send you two out to stroll in the garden."

"I can't just ask her. What excuse would I give?"

"You don't need one." Trumpet's voice turned bitter. "Once this marriage takes place, what is hers will become yours. You can ask or do whatever you want."

"That's the part that makes no sense to me. Our Dorothy is no fool. According to you, the driving impetus of her life is gaining control of her own lands. Why would she turn right around and surrender them to me?"

"Good question." Trumpet clapped her hands as William completed a series of full turns, arms outstretched. "Maybe she plans to marry you, attach your lands to hers, then murder you and marry Charles."

Tom frowned at her. "That isn't funny."

"It wasn't meant to be, not really. Think about it. You're a barrister, a member of the Inns of Court. You'd be a big help in suing her uncle. After that, you'd only be in the way."

"No one could be that devious." Tom gave her a wry smile. "Except you. But I do thank you for the cheerful thought. It will be a great comfort to me this afternoon as I'm signing away my future."

* * *

"She's a lovely young lady." Lady Russell spoke in her most aristocratic voice. "Her father was a knight. Her grandfather as well. She's quite wealthy, with lands all across the south. She even has a pleasant manor in Kent near Greenwich. Handy to the Thames. You could be in Westminster in an hour or two. Isn't that what you want?"

Tom regarded his guardian wearily. "I said I would sign the contract. Don't expect me to celebrate."

She clucked her tongue as if he were a sulky child, which was grossly unfair. He knew that from an impartial viewpoint, Dorothy Leyhnam was a good match, even a very good match. But he'd spent enough time with the woman to take her measure. Her character provided a strong counterbalance to her assets.

In truth, neither mattered very much. Stephen, of all people, had driven that point home, turning the tide of Tom's resistance. "Marry the wench and get on with your life," he'd said, or near enough. Since there could be no getting on without the marriage, Tom had grudgingly surrendered.

The housekeeper appeared at the library door. "They're here, my lady."

Her Ladyship clapped her hands in excitement. She loved to win, and this had been a long battle. She granted Tom a joyous smile. "My heart swells to know that I will leave you well settled when we part."

They would do that this afternoon. Once Tom signed the marriage contract, he would dip his quill again and sign the agreement releasing him from the debt to his guardian. Mr. Bacon had helped with the language, but the terms were simple enough. When Tom contracted an approved marriage, Her Ladyship would forgive his debt.

Dorothy Leynham preceded her uncle Geoffrey into the spacious and well-appointed room. They both wore the eager expressions of commoners meeting a noblewoman in her private realm. Dorothy sent a conspiratorial smile toward Tom, then dropped her gaze in a show of maidenish modesty. Greetings were exchanged, followed by a few minutes of talk about the fineness of the weather so late in November and how the queen's restless shifting from Somerset to Whitehall and back again affected the traffic in Westminster.

Not that they weren't all gratified to have Her Majesty once again in their midst. The Leynhams seemed to have forgotten that they actually resided in Kent.

They'd dressed in teams. Tom and Lady Russell wore their customary black, accented by brilliant white ruffs. The Leynhams, by accident or design, had both chosen dark green costumes. Tan linings peeked through the slashes on the sleeves of Uncle Geoffrey's doublet. Dorothy's skirt displayed a forepart of spring green sprigged with pink roses.

Everyone but Tom had donned their best manners.

Excitement brought a glow to Dorothy's cheeks and a gleam to her hazel eyes. Her gown made the most of her lean figure. She might not be Tom's type — meaning she wasn't Trumpet — but she was a comely lass. He could perform his marital duty without a qualm when the time came and make sure she enjoyed the event as well.

She batted her lashes at him. "We've missed you at the White Bear, Mr. Clarady. You haven't come to the Antelope for several days either. Have you grown tired of our company so soon?" She offered him a girlish pout.

He hoped these coy gestures would disappear once they took up residence together.

"Yes," Leynham said. "I sent a letter to you at Gray's yesterday but never received a response. Are they having trouble finding you?"

His narrowed eyes revealed his suspicions. They wanted to know where Tom had been hiding. He caught Lady Russell's eye. She knew the stakes. Let her answer.

She rose to the challenge. "Tom's been resting. He's had such a trying time lately." She gave them the impenetrable smile of a countess who considered a subject closed. "I'm sure the young people would enjoy a few moments to talk privately. Mr. Leynham and I can review the contract without their help, I believe."

"Of course, my lady. We've been through the details so many times now, making sure both parties are considered equally. But it is wise to review the final copy. And I'm sure the happy couple have things to say to one another."

Leynham gave Tom a penetrating look. Did he, like Dorothy and Charles, assume Tom had killed the court officials? If so, then why, in the name of all that was holy, were they here? Surely he wouldn't knowingly marry his niece to a murderer.

And if he didn't believe it, why not? Tom was the obvious suspect, after all. Perhaps Uncle Geoffrey had private knowledge.

On the other hand, Tom had made a similar bargain with his doubts. Trumpet could be right. She often was. If so, coy mannerisms weren't the worst thing Tom would have to fend off from his future wife. He'd fire her cook and hire his own, first thing. He'd insist on separate bedchambers with locking doors. And he'd spend most nights at Gray's until he gave Dorothy a child and found Midley a wife.

Until then, he'd watch his back.

Dorothy moved dutifully toward the door. Tom heaved an audible sigh to remind Lady Russell he was present under duress and went to take his soon-to-be betrothed's hand. He tucked it into his elbow. "Let me show you the herb garden. It's pleasant in all seasons."

This garden, like the orchard, was surrounded by eight-foot walls of yellow brick mellowed by the autumn sun. They'd donned their cloaks against the chill, but the day was as fine as they had declared it earlier. A light breeze cooled their cheeks and set wisps of brown hair dancing around Dorothy's face.

Tom showed her a few features of interest, including an ancient rosemary trained up an arbor. It still bore a few purple blossoms. Dorothy ran her hands over the needles and lifted them to her nose. She sighed with pleasure and offered her hands to Tom.

Tom inhaled the wholesome fragrance and smiled at his new life partner. "Let's have lots of rosemary in our garden, shall we?"

She laughed, not girlishly. She cocked her head at him, then looked back toward the house. The walls blocked any view from the ground-floor windows. She took Tom's elbow and guided him to a bench, seating herself with her back to the house. "Sit with me, Thomas. May I call you Thomas?"

"Please do, Dorothy." Tom sat, wondering what the new game would be.

She gathered one of his hands into both of hers. She gazed at him, eyes roving across his face as if soaking up his masculine beauty.

He smiled. He couldn't help it. Everyone liked to be admired.

Then she blinked. Another sort of smile formed on her wide lips, neither maidenish nor coy. This was the smile of a woman with a plan. Tom had seen it often enough on Trumpet's lips and even Lady Russell's. The fine hairs rose on the back of his neck. That smile invariably heralded trouble for him.

"I have a confession to make, Thomas." Dorothy licked her lips. "And I must ask you to keep what I'm about to tell you a secret from both our guardians."

"I tell Her Ladyship as little as possible, as a general rule."

"A wise rule. I knew you were a wise man in spite of your foolish manner."

Tom frowned. He was rarely foolish and then only on purpose, to make people laugh or sneak up on someone.

"I am the one who proposed this match," Dorothy said. "Or rather, I begged my uncle to propose it to Her Ladyship. I convinced him I had fallen in love with you and would have no other."

"I see." So far, this confession was less than flattering.

"I needed something to distract Uncle Geoffrey, and a marriage contract is most absorbing. He and your guardian have been as busy as two bees for the past two weeks. It's been a relief to me, I must say. Not having him looming over me every minute of every day."

"What purpose does this distraction serve?"

Dorothy's eyes sparkled. She bit her lip and studied his face again. "It will be simplest if I lay out the whole scheme. I'll try to be brief. Will that suit you?"

"I'm all ears."

She giggled. "Well. First, you must know that I love Charles. I always have and always will. To be candid, I consider him mine, though he strayed from me for a while. He has agreed to marry me now though, provided I pay his and his mother's marriage fines."

Poor Charles! Caught in the same coils that had trapped Tom. And wasn't Dorothy the clever minx! She'd used the same lure to catch both fish.

Tom pointed at the house. "I'm sure you would be very happy together, apart from one small check. We're about to sign binding contracts in there. Or had you forgotten?"

"Of course not, silly. I have a plan, if you'll let me tell it. Charles gave me a ring to seal our bargain." She glanced over her shoulder, then drew a chain from beneath her partlet to exhibit a small golden ring. She tucked it back out of sight. "I gave him one too. We plan to trot them out when the time comes. It will be soon. I turned twenty-one yesterday."

"Congratulations."

"Thank you. I present my documents to the Court of Wards on Friday. That's why we're rushing through these negotiations here today. I begged my uncle to agree to everything to ensure there's no delay. But your guardian is every bit as eager to move swiftly."

"She's afraid I'll back out again and find another way to gain my livery."

"Is there another way?"

"I could borrow three hundred pounds if I knew someone with that much money. Or I could tangle her up in lawsuits if I put my mind to it. I could sue her for disparagement for that other marriage proposal. I wouldn't win, but it would take time and cost her money."

"Oh, I like the sound of that!" Dorothy squeezed his hand. "That's one of the reasons I chose you, apart from you being so handsome and well-spoken. Your comeliness made it plausible that I had given over Charles at last."

Another unflattering compliment. She had a knack for them. Tom considered her story so far. "An exchange of rings effects a betrothal. That contract we're about to sign will be invalid from the start."

"Precisely. Aren't you clever? But our guardians don't know it. You're being released from your fine in a separate document — if my uncle reported it correctly."

"Lady Russell and I sign that release immediately after signing the marriage contract." Tom grinned at the woman beside him. "Our contract takes immediate effect. I insisted on that. Too many things can happen between betrothal and marriage. You might fall in the river, for example. Not that I wish such a thing!"

She flapped a hand at that remote possibility. "I said you were clever. I knew it from the start."

"When do you two plan to make your revelation?"

She swatted him on the arm. "I love the words you use! You present your case in court next Tuesday, don't you? Prove you paid for all those beastly licenses and seals, along with the contract proving you've resolved your debt to your guardian?"

"That's right."

"Charles and I will stage a little performance on that same day. Don't be surprised if you catch us embracing in a dark corner of the Antelope or even the court. But do please act surprised, if you can."

"I shall rail at you, or rather, at him. How dare he steal my lady love?"

"That would be perfect. In case the secret betrothal doesn't convince anyone, I will repudiate this marriage. You and I will both be legally out of wardship by then, so the Court of Wards will have nothing to say about it. I'm hoping you'll be generous and not insist on payment of the penalty which your guardian included in the contract."

"It's a standard clause. But I wouldn't touch that money with a long-handled oar." Tom lifted his chin as if offended. Her plan was complicated but well mapped out. It could work. The shortness of the time between steps would help.

He bowed his head, extending his hands. "You are a genius, Mistress Leynham."

"Aren't I though?" She batted her lashes at him, girlish once more.

Tom scratched his bearded jaw. "I have another question for you. A separate matter."

"Oh?"

"You mentioned once upon a time that your uncle tricked you into wardship. He bought lands owing feudal duty between your father's death and the court's inquisition."

She cocked her head. "Did I tell you that?"

Now he couldn't remember. Too late. He'd have to brazen it out. "You must have."

"We did drink a little too much at that supper of yours. What do you want to know?"

"Out of professional interest as a barrister, I would like to have a look at those deeds. They must have been hastily drawn up. Possibly even antedated or otherwise altered. I know we're not really going to be married" — thank the merciful God in his heaven — "but if we were, I would be managing that part of your suit. Do you have those deeds in your possession?"

All the playfulness vanished from her face. She narrowed her eyes at him.

"I can help you." He summoned conviction to plead his case. "I want to help you. It'd be good practice for me, for one thing. If this plan succeeds, you'll have saved me three hundred pounds and given me my freedom. I owe you."

"True." She licked her lips, considering. "Of course I have them. I knew they must exist when I overheard my uncle and aunt discussing their trick shortly before we came to London. I searched his library when they went to collect Charles." She flashed a sly smile. "Uncle Geoffrey knows they're gone, which is causing him no end of worry. I'm not sure he credits me with having taken them, however. That's a trifle insulting, isn't it?"

"You play the ninny to perfection, when you want. It's an effective shield." He let her enjoy that compliment, then pounced. "Where are they?"

She fended him off with a laugh. "In a safe place." A slow cat's blink told him he could expect no better answer.

Tom pursed his lips, showing her a rueful dimple. She giggled but said nothing.

Where could those deeds be? Not at the Antelope. Too public, as Trumpet had said. Not on her person. Her pocket could be picked on the street, and then where would she be? She might have hidden them in her house in Kent, but that house was ruled by her aunt. No hiding place could ever be truly safe from the servants.

Did she already have legal counsel? She'd proven herself to be a masterful planner. She had probably engaged someone the day they arrived. Or, more likely, after a few mornings observing the courts. That was worth finding out. Another job for Trumpet.

"I do have one last request, Thomas." Dorothy took his hand again and met his eyes squarely. "I must beg you not to send any bottles of poisoned brandy or accost any officials in any way. At least not for a few weeks."

Tom's mouth opened, but astonishment had left him speechless. He closed it again.

She nodded, approving that response. "My plans are sound, you understand, but delicate. Another death too soon might overset them."

He couldn't argue with her without revealing knowledge he shouldn't have. She seemed sincere, but this woman could rival the best actors at the Theatre.

He surrendered to the moment. "I'll do my best, Mistress."

TWENTY-ONE

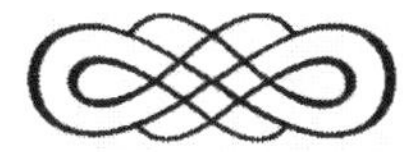

"We cannot follow them all at once, my lady," Catalina said. "We are two and they are three."

"True." Trumpet sat on the bed, pulling a man's stocking up over her knee. "And we should stay together. You never know what will happen." She straightened the top band and bent double to do the other one.

They had sneaked up to their room at the Antelope early this Thursday morning while most of the guests were either still snoring in their beds or breaking their fasts in their rooms. Trumpet had told the steward at Dorchester House that her aunt Lady Chadwick had requested her help reviewing her winter wardrobe. She should not be expected home before supper.

She had grown weary of this investigation. All they did was go around in circles. Tom did it literally, pacing around the house and gardens. You'd think erasing a three-hundred-pound debt would cheer a man up, but Dorothy's mad scheme had replaced that source of worry. He seemed set to spend the four days before his court date prowling restlessly through her house like a brainsick cat.

Trumpet wanted proof of something — anything — to remove Tom from the center of suspicion. Then he could go home, and her work would be done. For the first time since her marriage, she would be glad to turn her back on London and its troubles for the Christmas season.

She rose and pulled on her galligaskins, cut generously around the hips to cover her maternal figure. She tied the stockings to the canions, tucking the laces out of sight. She straightened up and heaved a sigh. "We'll start at the Court of Wards and see who we see. We can't lurk around here dressed as men."

Catalina watched her mistress with sympathetic eyes. "He won't marry her, my lady. Not if her plan succeeds."

"And that's the trouble, isn't it? That plan depends on meticulous timing. What if the court adjourns early, citing lack of an attorney? Neither Dorothy nor Tom will attain their livery. The betrothal between Dorothy and Charles could be annulled because both parties are considered infants in the eyes of the law."

"We are close to the end, my lady. All will be well. You will see."

Trumpet knew she was raising improbable obstacles. But her heart felt as if it had been stuffed with wet wool. She'd never been prone to melancholy, but she couldn't stop fretting. Things could go wrong. They often did. Then Tom would have to marry the woman. Either she would prove a devious witch who would torment him and sour his spirit or she would grow into an attentive, caring wife. Tom would learn to love her, and Trumpet would lose him.

She couldn't face it, even though she'd known this day would come. She could never be as cruel as Elizabeth Tudor, demanding that her admirers remain bachelors all their lives. She'd seen the way Tom looked at William, with pride, sorrow, and a kind of hunger. He needed children he could claim to balance out the pain of the one he couldn't.

Trumpet's best hope — and Tom's — was that Dorothy would be found guilty of two murders and hang. That was one sure way out of a marriage contract.

That thought cheered her up. She didn't hate Dorothy — they might be friends in different circumstances — but she wanted her out of Tom's life. If jealousy lay behind that wish, so be it. She wasn't ready to share him yet.

She pulled on her gray doublet — the most forgettable color — and turned around so Catalina could lace her up in back. Then they took turns gluing on their beards and moustaches. Catalina opened her box of charcoal pencils and added subtle touches to roughen their faces. Hats with wide brims and gray gloves completed their disguises.

They left the inn without meeting anyone they knew and joined the throng streaming toward Westminster. The crowd had flowed the other way yesterday as the queen returned to Somerset Place. Trumpet had been obliged to dress in a heavy, brocaded court gown complete with a yard-wide French farthingale and a foot-tall supportasse covered with sheer lace to walk beside her husband in the procession. What with donning the clothes, gathering at Whitehall, strolling at a snail's pace up the Strand, and doffing the clothes again, the day had been lost.

She and Catalina went first to the Court of Wards, peeking inside to see who was watching. No sign of Dorothy.

"She must be in Westminster Hall," Trumpet said. "But let's check Requests to be sure." No luck there either, though it took longer to be certain. The Court of Requests attracted a lot of women, both to press suits and to observe.

Outside, Trumpet spotted Charles idling in the old palace yard. He wore a dark blue suit with white linings, which suited his fair coloring. He leaned against the wall of the constabulary, which stood opposite the court, with the air of man waiting for a friend. Dorothy, perhaps, or Uncle Geoffrey. Who else did he know here besides Tom?

He glanced at her and Catalina as they passed without any sign of recognition.

"We are invisible," Catalina said with a touch of pride. She'd had to remake all of Trumpet's costumes after the birth of her second child.

They walked around to the front of Westminster Hall and entered. They blanched, as always, at the volume of noise filling that vast stone edifice. The wooden timbers of the hammerbeam roof and the rich clothing of the people crowded in front of each court soaked up some of the clamor, but the assault upon the ears took a moment to adjust.

The ears recovered more quickly than the nose, which suffered fresh insults every few yards. The smell of warm bodies and moist wool filled the whole hall and was soon forgotten, but some people seemed to bathe themselves in civet or lavender before leaving the house. One woman wore a dusty fragrance that made Trumpet sneeze until they'd walked past her.

They strolled about with the firm steps of substantial gentlemen, their hands clasped behind their backs. They paused now and then, cocking their heads as if straining to hear the voice of some barrister pleading a case. No one could hear anything from more than a few feet away, but that didn't stop onlookers from nodding their heads and commenting to one another as if they had full knowledge of the proceedings. Young men in the sleeveless gowns of law students clustered at the front, lips moving as they strove to commit key phrases to memory.

Trumpet smiled. She'd been one of them for a few glorious months. She didn't miss this part, though she appreciated what she had learned.

They finally found Dorothy standing with her maidservant behind the bar at Common Pleas. She could have tugged on the barrister's wide sleeve, if she'd wanted. She must have arrived soon after eight o'clock to garner such a choice position.

"She's in the perfect spot," Trumpet shouted into Catalina's ear. "She'll stay till eleven."

Catalina nodded. "What about the uncle? I do not see him."

"Nor I." Trumpet coughed at the strain of talking over the echoing throng. "Let's go outside."

They strolled back through the crowd and out into the yard. Trumpet's head felt lighter at once. Many people filled this space as well, but their clamor rose to the skies. A breeze flowed up from the wharf, blowing the smells of perfume and sweaty people away.

Trumpet considered their options. "Let's come back at eleven, when the courts adjourn, and try to catch Dorothy as she comes out."

"We will stand on both sides of the great door."

"That should do it. She's wearing green, which isn't too common."

"What shall we do until then, my lady?"

"Let's go back and check on Charles. After that, I don't know. We should try to find the uncle."

"I do not trust this uncle."

"Nor do I."

They walked back around and found Charles standing upright, staring avidly toward the entrance to the two lesser courts, Wards and Requests. A man dressed like a clerk in plain black robes with a flat cap had just come out bearing a small black satchel. He seemed absorbed in his own thoughts and didn't so much as glance back when Charles fell into step a few yards behind him.

"Aha!" Trumpet said to her co-conspirator. "Let's stalk the stalker."

They hung back a dozen feet or so, stopping now and then to point at features of interest on the buildings they passed. They stuck to Charles's trail but otherwise behaved like two gentlemen visiting the awesome seat of English government and making the most of the experience.

Charles strolled after the clerk, his longer legs easily keeping up with the clerk's steady pace. The peculiar train wended its way out the north Westminster gate, past a row of brick houses, and across King's Street to the house where the servants of the Court of Wards spent their days.

"Oho," Trumpet murmured. "Could this be another court official? What will he find on his desk, I wonder?"

Nothing, perhaps, since Tom wasn't there to throw a tantrum and provide cover for the murderer.

The clerk entered the building. Charles waited, standing in place, for a count of ten, then followed him inside.

"Shall we go in after him, my lady?" Catalina seemed doubtful.

Trumpet dithered. There couldn't be many people in there now that the attorney and principal clerk were gone. "Best not. But you skip around and watch the back door. I'll whistle if he comes out this way." She'd learned to whistle through her fingers from the blacksmith's son at Orford many years ago.

They didn't have to wait long. Charles came out the front door, walking down the street with a spring in his step. Trumpet stuck thumb and finger between her lips and shrilled the signal, keeping her eyes on the man in blue. When Catalina joined her, they hurried to catch up.

In a minute or two, they reached the sign of the White Bear. Charles went inside.

The two women crossed the street and pretended to watch the traffic. Trumpet saw Charles take a seat at a table by the front window, then turn to speak to the serving wench.

"We're through here," she told Catalina. "According to Tom, Charles spends most of the day at that table." Then she had an idea. "Let's go back to the clerk's house for a minute."

They went inside this time. Trumpet opened doors until she found a room with someone in it. "I beg your pardon. I'm looking for someone with the Court of Wards."

"Not many left." A grizzled man with spectacles on his nose pointed up. "Try the first floor."

So she did, brazenly opening doors, saying, "Pardon me," then closing the door again. At last, she found the man they'd been following. "Are you the Clerk of the Court of Wards?"

"I'm one of the auditors. We haven't a clerk at the moment."

"Auditor. I see. Well, sorry to disturb you." Trumpet closed the door. "I wonder what the auditor does," she whispered to Catalina.

"Mr. Tom will know."

Trumpet peered into the stairwell before descending. She caught the top of a tall black hat on the head of man whose general shape resembled Geoffrey Leynham. Placing a finger to her lips, she led the way down on tiptoe.

At the first landing, they paused. It was lucky they did because Uncle Geoffrey walked right under them to exit through the front door. He had a fat book cradled in one arm. When the door closed behind him, Trumpet said, "I want a look at that book."

Catalina chuckled. She knew her mistress well.

Their feet touched King's Street as the abbey bells boomed the hour. Many people stopped to count. Ten booms: ten o'clock. Plenty of time to follow Uncle Geoffrey and get back before the courts let out.

He strode up the street, out the court gate, and onto the Strand. As they passed Charing Cross, the crowds thinned and his stride lengthened. The women had to pick up their pace to keep him in sight. When their quarry turned left opposite Somerset Place, Trumpet knew where he was headed.

"He's going back to the Antelope to read that book, curse him." She puffed a little, out of breath. "We don't have to follow him."

"Thank you, my lady." Catalina's brow shone with sweat.

They could both use more exercise. "We'll ride every day in Dorset," Trumpet declared. "Ride in the morning, walk in the afternoon. And when we return to London, I'll hire a dancing master. A good intelligencer should be able to walk all day and still engage in a vigorous sword fight at the end of it."

"If you say so, my lady."

"We shouldn't be seen too much at the Antelope in these clothes anyway." Trumpet pictured the area in her mind. "The Crown and Anchor isn't far from the Temple Bar. Let's go there. We'll have a bite and a drink and then take a wherry back to Westminster."

Catalina sighed in relief. "Thank you, my lady."

They found a table in a dark corner. Trumpet toed off her shoes with a groan. They ordered cool beer and a plate of bread and cheese. Soon they lolled against the backs of their chairs, legs extended, wetting their parched throats and filling their empty stomachs. Beer was best when a person was thirsty, with the tang of hops and those refreshing little bubbles.

"I reckon we have half an hour," Trumpet warned. "We don't want to miss Dorothy."

"I hope she does something bad. She is the only one left." Catalina munched another square of the nutty cheese. "What is an auditor, my lady?"

"He counts things, I think. Revenues, fees, that sort of thing. He may also be the one who checks another man's figures. Can this be the right sum, he asks? Because you seem to be about five thousand pounds short today."

Catalina's wide mouth formed an O. "Is that possible?"

"Anything is possible in the Court of Wards. They practice every form of corruption known to man." Trumpet drained her cup. Should she have another one? No, they had more work to do, which meant more walking. She didn't want to be weighed down.

The bells at St. Dunstan-in-the-West tolled the half hour. "Time to go." Trumpet grunted as she stuffed each foot into its shoe.

They had only a short walk down to Temple Wharf. The breeze on the water revived them, the cool air sweetened by the scents rising from the gardens of the great houses on the north bank. They arrived at Westminster Hall with plenty of time to position themselves on either side of the great pointed arch at the entrance. Some folks were already slipping out, talking with animation about the cases they'd heard or bickering about where to have dinner.

Trumpet and Catalina watched the people with open interest. Why not? They weren't the only men waiting for friends here or hoping to snatch a moment of a busy barrister's time. Many men dressed in lawyer's gowns milled about the yard, glancing frequently toward the huge doors.

The abbey's mighty bells delivered eleven echoing booms. The trickle emerging from the hall became a stream. Then the stream became a flood.

Trumpet set her hands on her hips, leaning forward and shifting her gaze from the middle of the crowd to the edges, fearing to miss her quarry. She remembered to lift her gaze. Dorothy was taller than the average woman. And today she'd chosen a tallish, mannish, green hat with a yellow feather. Trumpet caught a glimpse of that feather and followed it down to the hat, the hair, and finally, the face.

Dorothy Leynham.

Trumpet gave a small "Ha!" of victory. She kept her eyes on that feather while the crowd bustled them both into the wider spaces of the yard. She felt Catalina come up alongside her. "Look, my lady. Is that not a barrister?"

A man with a long black robe over his somber black suit stepped toward Dorothy and offered her a nod, touching his round black cap. His wide sleeves bore two velvet stripes, dark against the glossy grogram of the robe.

"Yes, it is. Does he look familiar?"

"Not to me, my lady."

Trumpet thought he might but couldn't be sure without a closer look. "Let's see where they go."

They didn't go far. The Crown was an inn of superior quality, far enough off King's Street to allow its guests a little peace. Trumpet left Catalina outside and filed in behind a group of well-dressed men speaking in West Country accents. Dorothy and her counselor climbed the stairs to the first floor. Trumpet followed them up to another public room, less noisy than the one below. The smells of roasting brawn and savory sauces filled the air, making her stomach growl.

She used the group of West Countrymen, who couldn't seem to decide which way to go, to maneuver around where she could get a good look at Dorothy's barrister. Yes, she knew him. Philip Something. A shortish fellow with dark blond hair and a tightly pointed beard. Tom would know.

She jogged back down the stairs. Nothing else could be learned here, but proving that Dorothy had already obtained legal counsel had been high on her list. Trumpet would bet a week of cold sallets for supper that Philip Something had possession of those deeds. As a member of Gray's Inn, Mr. Bacon could probably think of a way to pressure him to testify about that improper transaction. Or Tom could wheedle it out of him over mugs of ale in the hall. Wasn't Philip Somebody one of his messmates? Perhaps Dorothy had heard his name from Tom.

They had to wait in a queue to stuff themselves into an overcrowded wherry, but at least their feet were spared another pounding. They staggered out at Temple Wharf and limped up Chancery Lane to Holborn and home — or what passed for home on this busy day.

"Shall we have dinner now, my lady?" Catalina asked hopefully.

"Soon. One more thing to do first."

Dorothy had once remarked that her uncle liked his dinner promptly at noon. She'd scoffed at his rigid habits. But regular habits were a gift for a spy.

She and Catalina walked slowly through the archway leading to the inner yard at the Antelope. They took turns gazing into the windows, searching for their man.

"There he is, my lady." Catalina tilted her head to point at a window upstairs in one of the semi-private dining rooms. Uncle Geoffrey sat tucking a large napkin into his ruff as he spoke to a serving man.

"Perfect!" Trumpet led the way into the tavern on the ground floor, searching for Dolly, who often assisted with her subterfuges. She promised the harried woman a shilling to let them into Mr. Leynham's room. "We only need a few minutes."

Dolly agreed. She'd known Trumpet since the girl had been a boy. She knew no harm would come to the guest, and that Trumpet wouldn't ask if it weren't important.

Uncle Geoffrey had left the hefty tome open on the table in his room. Catalina took up a position by the door, although what they would do if he chose to come back up was anyone's guess. They couldn't jump out a second-floor window, nor could they both squeeze under that bed.

Trumpet laid one flat hand on the open page as a placeholder, then flipped the book closed. The brown leather cover showed its age with cracks and yellow patches. The words "Court of Wards" still gleamed in gilt letters inside a frame with curlicues at the corners. The title page had been written by hand. "Records from the South and South-West, 1551 –."

She blinked at the page, marveling at its age and at the fact that this weighty volume held records for only a portion of England's counties. There must be at least thirty, all told, though she couldn't name them all.

She flipped through the pages, reading an entry here and there. They were records of sales of land — farms and manors for the most part. Each entry included the date, the year, the name of the property, the name of the seller, and the name of the buyer. Most of them contained a price, a fascinating and distracting figure. She could have bought a manor, complete with orchards, not far from her grandparents' hall in Devonshire for a mere five pounds back in 1559.

Each entry included a note about feudal duties. "Descent from the church" was a common phrase. Often a lord's name was given. Trumpet recognized some of the titles as long extinct. The Duke of Somerset, for example, had been executed for treason in King Edward's time. She doubted he had ever performed knight service for anyone, but his lands carried that debt forevermore.

She didn't need to read the whole book to understand why Uncle Geoffrey had lugged it here to study at length. He wanted another ward or two now that his were about to kick free of their traces. For that, he needed estates owing feudal duties. He'd been making a list. She noticed it as she laid the left half of the book back down on the table. He could bring that list with him to the quarterly assize courts in Kent. He and his wife could prompt gossip about landowners with grievous illnesses and young children. He could pick up a couple of juicy wardships for himself and sell the rest to the new attorney.

Dear Uncle Geoffrey was shopping for his next victims. If he couldn't find the perfect match, he could use his talents to trade a farm here and a farm there to build traps for the wards of his choice. Such a bother to have to wait until their fathers died.

Trumpet's stomach lurched. She'd had enough. All her suspects were presently enjoying well-cooked dinners. Now it was her turn.

"Let's go downstairs and find a table where Uncle Geoffrey can't see us. I want a big cup of wine. Maybe two. And an enormous plate of beef."

TWENTY-TWO

One potential witness had yet to be questioned by anyone: the northman, Gordon Shaftoe. Francis had been told by one and all that no one could talk to him thanks to his incomprehensible northern dialect. And yet there were other languages.

Any lad wealthy enough to fall into wardship must have had some education. True, some wardships were worth as little as twenty pounds per annum, but even those boys would have attended the local grammar school. He would have some Latin — the universal language.

Shaftoe had been present both times Tom lost his temper in the Court of Wards offices. The three investigators had agreed that the murderer had most likely witnessed those eruptions or learned about them soon after. Mr. Shaftoe apparently spent the bulk of his days napping in that quiet anteroom. He might not understand much of what he heard, but one assumed his eyes still functioned normally.

Francis walked through the brick house where the officials of Wards and Requests conducted their affairs — or had done. No ginger-haired youth snored in the corner today.

Francis had written Tom to ask where the northman might be lodging. Tom thought he might be at the Lamb and Flag, which had cheap beds, six to a chamber. Francis shuddered at the thought of returning to the scene of his recent humiliation. At this hour of the morning, however, Mr. Dickson would presumably be quilling away in his cubicle.

Even so, he surveyed the patrons seated near the windows as he approached the tavern and paused inside the door to probe the depths of the public room. The few patrons scattered about the long tables made the space look emptier. Those who worked in Westminster, as well as those who came to watch them, were still in court. He had not quite an hour before the floodgates opened.

He passed through two low-ceilinged rooms that stank of stale smoke but were mercifully free of the billowing stuff. He found Mr. Shaftoe at a small table in a side room. The young man rested a cheek on one fist, curling the other hand around a short mug. He might be posing for a portrait of a melancholy man in spite of his choleric complexion. Lines of sadness or boredom marred his freckled face.

Francis turned back to ask the barmaid for a large mug of best ale. Not for him. He would never touch another drop in this establishment. When she handed it to him, he returned to the small room and set the mug before the ginger-haired youth.

"Mr. Shaftoe?"

"Wee wants ta knaa?"

"I'm Francis Bacon. You don't know me, but I've been investigating the murder of Attorney Strunk."

"Strunk?" The bleakness in Shaftoe's eyes spoke volumes about the solitude imposed by his linguistic impediment.

Francis waved a hand to apologize. *"Latine loqueris?"*

"Etiam!" Light shone in the brown eyes.

"Ut ego sedens?"

Shaftoe gestured gladly at a three-legged stool.

Francis drew it closer to the table and sat. He pushed the tall mug toward the northman with a smile, receiving a broad one in return. He proceeded to explain his role in the recent tragedies, including his certainty that Tom had not committed either murder.

Shaftoe listened closely. At one point, he made a downward motion with one hand to ask Francis to slow down. He said he could read and write Latin better than speak and hear it. He'd only had one year at university, but he enjoyed the works of Cicero and Marcus Aurelius. He liked to write poetry too but had never showed it to anyone.

Francis called for writing materials. He and his witness shared the quill and paper, passing each across in a silent but active interrogation. It proved to be an excellent method, resulting in a record of both questions and answers.

Shaftoe was adamant that Tom had not bludgeoned Mr. Bowcer, at least not with that chair leg. He couldn't speak to the poisoning of Mr. Strunk. He never went there on Saturday, and he'd arrived too late on Monday to witness the discovery of the body.

However, he did have an observation to share about Bowcer's murder. He claimed Charles Midley had picked up the broken chair leg and stuffed it under his doublet. Everyone else had been so busy shouting they hadn't noticed. Shaftoe would swear to this before any judge in the land. He didn't like Midley, who had sneered at him on two occasions. He did like Clarady, who had once bought him a beer for no reason other than kindness.

Shaftoe's account was convincingly detailed. He said Clarady had dropped the chair leg as he came out of Bowcer's office. He'd stood there for a moment, head turning right and left as if expecting someone. Then he'd looked down at the pretty lady with green eyes and frowned, shaking his head. She reached for him, but he shook her off and ran down the corridor.

Shaftoe saw him collide with Charles Midley, grabbing him by both shoulders to keep from falling. Clarady could not have been holding anything in either hand at that moment.

Clarady ran off out of sight while Midley came on to join the group. Everyone had risen at that point, the better to wave their arms around, it had seemed. Midley stepped on the chair leg, then stooped to pick it up and slide it under his doublet. The clerk came out and spoke in a loud voice, and everyone sat down again. Midley bowed to the ladies and left.

The green-eyed girl and her maidservant left the same way Tom had gone. They seemed to be following him, but Shaftoe couldn't swear to that. The tall girl went into the office, though where she sat Shaftoe couldn't guess. She came out and left through the front door with her maidservant.

Bowcer came out next. He frowned at Shaftoe, who in truth had no business there. He simply had nowhere else to go. Then Bowcer turned around to lock his door and went down the corridor toward the back. The bells had not yet rung five o'clock, but they began tolling the hour as Shaftoe stepped onto King's Street.

The helpful northman filled two pages in a round, schoolboy hand. Francis read through the whole written conversation. He couldn't think of anything else to ask.

"Gratias." Then he had a better thought.

He took a fresh sheet of paper and wrote a note in Latin to Sir Avery. Gray's had a few members from Yorkshire who might be able to converse with this lonely young man until his guardian arrived. Richard Strunk ought to have thought of this first thing. Another strike against the grasping attorney. Tom would have, if he hadn't been so disordered by the Court of Wards's labyrinthine procedures. Another strike against the court.

He handed the note to Shaftoe. The lad grinned, though sudden tears shone in his eyes. *"Gratias."*

Francis folded up the testimony and tucked the pages into the front of his doublet. He rose, touched his hat, and left. As he crossed the threshold, he sent a brief prayer toward heaven that he never be obliged to enter that establishment again.

He directed his feet toward the courts. His original plan had been to catch Robert on his way out to make an appointment to discuss Strunk's book of bribes. Anthony's secretaries had made three copies. Francis would retain a copy for future reference, but he had decided the original ought to go to his cousin.

In which case, why wait? It seemed fitting to render this proof of corruption in the Court of Wards to its master on its very doorstep. He looked forward to watching Robert struggle to maintain his stoic expression while summing up the crimes committed by his father's appointee.

Should he tell Robert about Charles Midley? Francis found the northman's testimony convincing. Midley could only have one reason for picking up that chair leg and hiding it under his doublet: to follow Bowcer into that alley and batter him. Furthermore, once Midley extracted the leg from its point of origin, no one else could have obtained it. Crucially, Tom had not taken it with him when he ran away.

What a monster Midley was! As cool as deep water, pretending to be a hapless victim while keeping both eyes open for that stroke of luck. He couldn't have known Tom would fly into a rage in the attorney's office and choose choking on wine as a suitable punishment. Midley had heard those words and acted on them the next day. He must have had murder in mind already, his victims selected, and had been waiting for the right moment to act. He'd chosen Tom to hide behind because the distracted man had made himself available.

Would he try it again now that Tom had gone into hiding? Francis doubted it. On the other hand, what about that feodary in Kent? If Midley had killed him, he hadn't bothered to find someone else to blame. It may have been an accident — or an accident aided by a helping hand. Francis had learned that Hughes, the feodary, had fallen off a bridge. If Midley had pushed him, he might have been emboldened by the lack of response. That may have been the spark that had fanned the embers of his anger into action.

Robert should know about Midley since officials of his court might still be at risk. But Francis's first duty was to Sir Avery Fogg, the representative of Gray's, and therefore his client. Also, Francis's first personal concern was to relieve Tom of suspicion. Sir Avery could be counted on to recognize that priority. Robert could not. He would reserve Midley for another conversation and focus today on the crimes of the court officials.

Francis approached the gate that led into the series of yards around the smaller courts of Westminster, like Requests and Wards. Robert's coach stood waiting a few feet from the entrance. The elegant carriage had been designed to proclaim its owner from afar. The sides and roof had been painted a deep, rich blue. Small square windows, one in each door and two on either side, could be left open or shielded with blue curtains. Everything that could be gilded had been: window frames, edgings along roof and bottom, and frames set into the doors to augment the Cecil coat of arms painted thereon. The roof had been similarly decorated so that people gazing out of palace windows would know Sir Robert Cecil had arrived.

Francis could avoid the crush in the palace yard by waiting here. Robert would feel obliged to offer him a ride at least as far as Somerset Place, his most likely destination. They could talk in private while snailing through the traffic.

Robert appeared at the end of the yard, walking quickly with the short steps he'd trained himself to use. Striding emphasized the deformity of his twisted shoulders, regardless of the quality of his tailoring. His lips pursed as he noticed Francis. "I suppose you've brought the document you hinted at in that absurd note."

"Twenty pounds seemed a fair price to me. Dickson could've got more from the next attorney."

Robert puffed that away. "I paid him five, which is all you should have offered. He accepted it without demur."

"No doubt." The intended insult didn't dent Francis's good humor. He'd solved the crime — both crimes — though no one else knew it yet, and he'd brought home proof against his cousin's court. Small victories to some, but he would revel in them while he could.

"It's a little notebook kept by Richard Strunk. We should discuss the contents, but not out here on the street." He glanced at the stream of lawyers, clerks, litigants, and onlookers milling around, casting curious glances at the queen's advisor.

Robert's eyelids fluttered. "Very well. We can talk in the coach. I'm only going as far as Somerset Place, but my man can take you on to Temple Bar, if you like."

"I would appreciate that." Francis stood back to make way for the coachman, who had jumped down when he saw his master coming. His blue livery matched the coach, though his linings were white, not gold. A white plume bobbed above the wide brim of his short-crowned hat. He'd tilted the hat to shade his eyes from the glaring sun, though the rays shone behind him. He opened the door and let down the step.

Robert climbed in and seated himself on the seat facing forward. Francis took the opposite one. He never minded riding backward; in fact, he rather liked it. Robert drew the curtains closed at once, casting them into a soft blue shadow.

The coachman replaced the step and closed the door. He stood for a moment fiddling with the latch, then returned to his bench at the front. The coach rocked a little under his weight. He clucked the horses into motion, moving with exquisite care through the crowd.

Francis drew forth the notebook and handed it to his cousin. "This is in Strunk's hand."

Robert opened it and leafed through the pages, pausing here and there to read something more closely. After a minute or two, he closed the book, holding it in his lap. "What do you intend to do with this?"

"What I just did."

"I mean, will you give a copy to Lord Essex?"

"I haven't decided yet." Anthony would advise it, and His Lordship had asked him for this very thing, though he hadn't known it existed. But he didn't quite trust the earl to use the information with discretion. One needn't share everything with one's patron, not if it might do him more harm than good in the long run.

On the other hand, Francis had no obligation to share those concerns with Robert. Let him press the spies he paid to watch Anthony if he wanted an answer.

The coach turned tightly to the right. The pace picked up a little. King's Street was always crowded at this hour, mainly with other coaches and men on horses. People on foot clung to the sides of the road.

Francis had a keener question. "What do *you* intend to do with it?"

"What do you mean?"

Francis snorted. "I've handed you incontrovertible proof that the Attorney of the Court of Wards had been demanding and receiving bribes for years. Anthony's man added up the sums for last year. Strunk took in nearly three hundred pounds. I don't know how much of that he paid to his assistant — or his master."

Robert's eyes narrowed. "We do not receive payments from our officers."

Not once they've purchased the office, he should have said. Both Robert and his lord father gladly took bribes from guardians. In fact, no one could obtain a wardship without them. The wealthier the ward, the larger the bribe. Everyone knew how that worked.

The coach stopped, started, then stopped again. Horses on either side expressed their impatience in blustery breaths. They must be queuing up to pass through the court gate. Francis pulled the curtain back an inch to peek out. Clouds had begun to cover the sky, but the people hastening hither and yon still looked sweaty. He much preferred riding in this private, shaded refuge.

He caught sight of Tom striding back toward the heart of Westminster. How could that be? But no, this man wore a green and brown doublet with knee-length slops. Tom would never come to Westminster dressed so informally. Unless he'd sneaked out in disguise to do — what? Something no one had bothered to mention to Francis.

Ah, well. He'd hear about it later if that really was Tom. He'd only seen the man from the back.

He closed the curtain and gave his cousin a cool look. "I don't see how you can read those entries without feeling the need to act. They are proof of absolute villainy taking place right under your nose in an institution for which you are responsible."

Robert shrugged his fine eyebrows. "Strunk is dead. What would you have me do? Prosecute his corpse?"

Francis grimaced at the ugly image. "You could recruit auditors from outside Wards. New-made graduates from the universities, perhaps. Have them examine the books from top to bottom. I would have them search all the chambers first without warning. Strunk kept that book behind a portrait of the queen."

"Which one?" Robert smiled, though briefly. He shook his long head. "I won't cause more upheaval after these recent tragedies. It would look as though we blamed the victims for their deaths."

"They provoked the rage which drove the killer. I don't blame them in a narrow sense, but they played a role. They lit the brand that started the fire."

They both rocked sideways, Francis to his left, Robert to his right, as they rounded the curve at Charing Cross. Their progress should be smoother now, though still at a plodding pace. They weren't in any great rush, and one barely noticed the rocking at this speed. With the thick curtains and the constant movement, the coach made a wonderfully private chamber for a sensitive conversation. No one could hear them but the coachman, and he had been trained to discretion at Burghley House.

Robert's face took on the smug expression he wore far too often. "Some quieter response would be more appropriate. And perhaps we can find men less prone to temptation to fill the empty posts."

"Quieter," Francis echoed bitterly. "So no one can see what you're doing, which will, in fact, be nothing. If you ask any questions, people will hear about it. Rumors — half of them likely to be true — will run rife. Pamphlets will appear about dark doings in the Court of Wards. Your reputation and that of your father will be tarnished, to say the least."

"That has nothing to do with it."

"I think it does." Then a flash of insight struck his mind. He pointed a finger at his cousin. "That's it, isn't it?"

"Is what?" Robert snapped.

"The true reason you and your father have been obstructing my suit for the Attorney Generalship. You know that once in office, I would conduct an inquiry into practices in the Court of Wards. It's infamous. An inquiry is long overdue. You can't risk that level of scrutiny, can you? So you must keep me out at all costs."

"Oh, Frank! That is arrant nonsense." Now Robert pointed a finger. "Neither of us stands in your way. We never have. In fact, we see advantages to your being named."

Francis leaned against the padded seat and folded his arms across his chest. "Results do not support that assertion."

"Results." Robert fairly spat the word. "If you think Her Majesty follows my father's advice in every case, you are living in the land of dreams." He placed his hands on his thighs, tilting his head to regard Francis with a measuring look. "All right. I'll tell you the truth, if no one else will. Our queen will never appoint you to any position of real influence or income. You have only yourself to blame. You should never have spoken against that triple subsidy."

"Not that again! I apologized."

"No, you didn't. You said you were sorry if your actions caused offense. That's not the same thing as being sorry you did it. Everyone, including Her Majesty, understood you to mean what you in truth meant — that you were not sorry you spoke against it and would do so again."

Francis started to object, but Robert talked right over him. "I'm going to tell you what you need to hear, once and for all. You're not cooperative, Frank, not reliably so. You're not biddable. She can't count on you to conform to her wishes."

"I pride myself on that characteristic. I speak the truth as I understand it." Francis granted himself a smug smile. "And my understanding is usually quite sound."

Robert's eyelids fluttered. "Not in this matter. Her Majesty doesn't want truth. She wants compliance. She's a monarch. Loyalty always comes first. You thwarted her that day in Parliament in front of everyone. She'll never forgive you for it." He paused, then added, "In this case, she has the added pleasure of teaching Essex a lesson."

The coach stopped. "We're here," Robert said. Then it started moving again, turning hard to the right. "Why is he turning?"

Francis shrugged. He had sunk farther into his seat during Robert's lecture and had no interest in the movements of the coach. He knew in his heart that his cousin had it right. He had fatally offended his sovereign queen last year by arguing against the special tax she wanted to support the war against Spain. He'd thought it too great a burden for the common man and a dangerous precedent. Someone had to speak up.

He heaved a grievous sigh. Why did that someone always seem to be him?

"What in God's name is he doing?" Robert pulled aside a curtain to look out.

Francis drew his curtain back as well. All he could see was a high stone wall about four feet away. That couldn't be the front of the palace. There would be people walking past and guards in green-and-white livery. "Where are we?"

"I have no idea. There's only another wall on this side as well." Robert pushed his head out the window and shouted at the coachman. "Wilson! What are you doing?"

"Wilson isn't here today, Sir Robert. He came over a bit sick this morning, just after he drank the cup of beer I offered him." The coachman's high-pitched laugh sent a chill up Francis's spine.

He sat up straight. "Who is that?"

"How should I know? We have a hundred servants at Burghley House. I can't keep track of them all." Robert stuck his head back out the window. "Where are we?"

"Strand Lane, sir. Right alongside the palace."

"You can't take horses in here, you idiot! There's no place to turn around."

Strand Lane was a narrow passageway, about twelve feet wide, that sloped down to the river. It wasn't used for much. Its main purpose was to channel water between two great houses from the street to the river in times of heavy rain.

"Let's get out and walk. It will take him an hour to remedy this." Francis grasped the handle of the door and gave it a twist. It came off in his hand. He pushed on the door. It didn't budge. He tried the other door with the same result.

"He's done something to the latches and locked us in." He eyed the square windows doubtfully. "That would be a tight fit. Why in God's name did you make these windows so small?"

"Privacy, of course. I discuss confidential affairs of state in here, you know. Given my usual route, we're often stopped by traffic. Besides, I will not climb out a window, not here in full view of the palace." Robert banged on the front wall and shouted, "Coachman! Open these doors at once!"

The man only laughed. "That would ruin my plan, now wouldn't it?"

Plan? A shiver raised the fine hairs on Francis's neck. He had a sudden premonition of disaster. He stuck his head out the window and shouted, "Help! Help! He's locked us in!"

"Who are you shouting at?" Red spots flared in Robert's pale cheeks. He hated to be made ridiculous. That would be his first thought — not that a determined murderer had laid a trap for the master of the court he hated.

He pounded on the sides of the door. "Open this door at once, I say!"

"You're in no position to make demands, Sir Robert." The man clucked his tongue. They rolled a few feet farther down the lane, then came to an abrupt halt. The coach rocked as the man jumped down from his bench.

Both passengers stuck their heads out to watch with growing horror as the man unhitched both horses. He turned their heads back up toward the Strand and slapped each one on the rump with a soft, "Off you go."

Francis pulled his head in as the beasts trotted between the coach and the wall.

The two cousins traded grim looks. "What do we do now?" Robert asked, a thread of fear in his normally cool voice.

TWENTY-THREE

"It felt like I was signing my life away," Tom said.

Trumpet offered him a sympathetic frown. "It must have been awful." He'd been telling her about the meeting at Lady Russell's house on Tuesday. They and Catalina had come up to the green parlor to watch the clouds rolling in from the southwest. And to discuss various matters in private.

"If Dorothy's plan fails . . ." Tom shrugged, his eyes bleak. "At least I'll have that manor on the Thames near Greenwich to console me."

"Nonsense. There are ways to get out of a marriage contract. It might cost you, but you'll have control of your own rents by then."

"True." Tom brightened. His fits of melancholy passed off more quickly as he neared the end of his ordeal. "We've agreed to wait until June to marry. She could die of natural causes before then. Her parents succumbed to plague, after all."

"She could hang in the next month if I'm right about her." Trumpet bit her lip. She'd been worrying over a thorny question only Tom could answer. "She's a little bit like me, isn't she? In some ways, I mean. The planning, the determination . . ."

Tom laughed out loud. The merry sound melted her doubts away. He took both her hands and met her eyes.

"She is not like you at all. Yes, you are both superlative plotters, and yes, you each take a bold — one might say ruthless — approach to achieving your ends. But she uses people like tooth cloths, reaching for whatever's handy and tossing it aside when she's done. She doesn't care about anyone. You can see it in her eyes and hear it in her voice."

"Except for Charles."

"Including Charles. She said, 'He's mine,' as if she were speaking of a horse or a house. He's one of her possessions. I pity him for it. You, on the other hand, love everyone who comes under your care. Me, obviously, and thank you." He opened one of her hands and planted a kiss in the palm. "Your children, naturally. Stephen, in his own special way. Your father, in a more special way. Your Uncle Nat and Aunt Blanche. Francis Bacon. Anthony Bacon. Ben. Catalina. That stray black cat I've seen you feeding bits of sausage in the herb garden. Doubtless all the people back at your old castle."

Trumpet twisted her lips in a complicated frown, trying to stop the tears from flowing. Traitorous drops, they must be battled back.

In her heart, she knew he was right. She didn't think of herself as one of those loving, nurturing women, like the mother she barely remembered. But she would fight off armies of Turks to defend every person on Tom's list. And then make sure they had food and something hot to drink afterward.

She gazed up at him from under her lashes. He shot a quick glance at the door and dropped a kiss on her cheek. It felt like a renewal of spring.

She sighed. He looked into her eyes with desire darkening his own. He wrapped an arm around her waist, pulling her into his chest as he lowered his lips to hers. She rose onto her toes, trusting him to hold her steady, and coiled her arms around his neck. One hand stroked into his curls to cradle the back of his head as she surrendered herself to the kiss.

When they broke for breath, she blinked. A giddy smile slipped across her face. "I've missed that."

"Me too. I miss you, sweetling." He nuzzled her temple, the edge of her cheek, her ear.

A flash of desire jolted her back to the world. She pushed him away with both hands. "Stop." She took a few steps back. "We can't. We musn't."

He gaped at her as if he didn't know where they were. Then he shook himself. "No, we can't. Not here. Not like this." He took a breath and laughed a little. "I forgot about everything for a minute there."

"Me too."

"It felt good."

"Mmm."

And here came another problem. If Tom was feeling like his old self again, he must leave this house — the sooner, the better. First, because they'd owed Stephen a debt of honor for his protection. And second, because their lust for one another had been pent up for so long they'd be careless and get caught. They had a routine for sneaking Tom in from Gray's when Stephen went out to gamble and entertain his *amour*. Best to wait until that could be revived.

"Let's talk about Charles." Trumpet walked to the sideboard and poured two cups of wine. She kept her back to Tom as she stirred in water and sugar, waiting for her heartbeat to regain its normal rhythm. Then she turned and handed him a cup from arm's length.

"He's up to something," she said. "That or he's grown desperately bored." She told Tom about following Charles as he followed the auditor from court to chambers. "What does an auditor do?"

"He keeps the accounts. His record is the master of them all. There are two or three, I think, but I haven't met any of them. They stay in the background. They take in receipts from the other officers rather than dealing directly with wards and guardians."

"Then why would Charles follow one?"

"Perhaps he didn't know he was an auditor until he reached his office. He could've done like you — knock on the door, ask a stupid question, and leave."

"I suppose so. But he lurked at the door of the court all morning, as if waiting for someone. Another victim, perhaps?"

"That's a leap."

"I don't think so. He fits in every way. He knew about your threats, both times. He could have picked up the chair leg if you dropped it in the anteroom. He hates the court and everyone in it. You've said that's his favorite theme after a few drinks. He has good reason to hate them. Perhaps his plan is to destroy the court by killing everyone who works for it. In which case, that auditor could be next." Trumpet gasped. "Shouldn't we warn him?"

"Go ahead if you want. But Charles can't be the killer. At least, we can't prove him guilty. I mean, we mustn't. Because if we do, he'll hang, and I'll have to marry Dorothy."

"Oh, for the love of God, Tom! You will not have to —"

Noises rose up from the lane below. Tom cocked his head. "Did someone cry 'Help'?" He walked toward the window to look down. "What's a coach doing down there?"

Trumpet went to stand beside him. Catalina crowded in beside her. "A coach cannot go down there," the Spanish woman said. "Can it?"

"It cannot," Trumpet answered. "You can't turn around at the bottom. Besides, there's nothing at the end but the river. It's more of a sluice than a lane." She pointed at the roof of the coach. "Isn't that Sir Robert's coat of arms?"

A head poked out the window. "Help! Help! He's locked us in!"

"That's Mr. Bacon!" Tom pounded on the glass as if he could be heard fifteen feet below.

"He must climb out the window," Catalina said.

"Not likely," Tom said. "Neither one of them could manage anything that agile."

The coachman hopped off his bench and stuck something under one of the front wheels to hold the coach in place. When he straightened up, they got a good look at his face. "What ho!" Tom cried. "That's Charles Midley. What's he up to?"

Midley began to unhitch the horses. As he freed each one, he slapped it on the rump to send it trotting back toward the Strand. He turned to speak to the men inside.

"God's bollocks," Trumpet said. "He's going to roll that coach into the river. We've got to stop him." She met Tom's blue eyes for one long moment while they thought it through together. "You go after Charles. He mustn't get away with this. Catalina and I will roust out our boatmen. They might be able to push the coach onto the bank. Or at worst, fish those men out of the river."

"You'd better hurry," Tom said. "I doubt either of them can swim."

TWENTY-FOUR

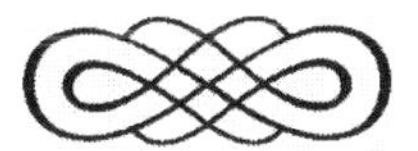

"We must get out of this coach." Francis tried to shove his upper body through the window in one door. The padded sleeves of his doublet caught on the trim. He wriggled, grunting, and made a little progress. Then the coachman loomed up in front of him.

He studied Francis as if encountering an odd type of bird. "I don't know you."

"I'm Francis Bacon. Who are you, and what do you think you're doing?"

"Ah! Thomas Clarady's master. I've heard a great deal about you. Tom was so sure you'd work out who killed that weasel Strunk. Alas, I'm afraid you failed." He placed his flat hand across Francis's face and pushed him back into the coach.

Francis fell awkwardly onto the bench.

"Who are you?" Robert's tone had turned petulant with fear.

"He's Charles Midley." Francis heaved himself upright. "Aren't you?"

"Good guess! Too late though." Midley spread his arms across the span of square windows and thrust his face toward Robert. "You don't really care who I am, do you? I'm just another of the hundred wards whose lives you've destroyed with your court. Well, now I'm returning that favor."

He banged a fist on the door, startling both of his victims. Then he turned away to kick something wood-like to one side. The coach began to roll.

Midley disappeared behind it. He gave a loud grunt, and the coach picked up speed. Not a lot, but enough to carry them down to the bottom of the lane. Here, as Francis remembered, it sloped steeply into the water.

"Brace yourself!" he cried, pressing his hands against opposite walls.

The coach rolled into the river. Cold water splashed into the open windows, but the well-crafted cabin bobbed up again, rising above the surface. The swift current pushed them sideways at first. The iron-clad rear wheels dragged behind, turning them gradually in the direction of the flow.

Francis and Robert gaped at one another. Robert's naked terror mirrored what Francis felt. They slid to opposite sides as if by mutual accord and shouted out the windows, "Help! Help! Save us!"

The initial splash had thrown half a foot of water onto the floor of the coach. Francis couldn't tell if more seeped through the boards. It couldn't be much. This elegant bauble had been masterfully crafted. The floor and sides were as tightly snugged together as a boat.

"We're floating." Robert showed a shaky smile. "If we could steer ourselves toward the bank, we might be all right." He looked about as if searching for an oar. The cabin held nothing but cushions and curtains, which would only drag them down as they became saturated.

"We're sinking," Francis said. "The axle is pulling us down. Wood floats, but iron sinks. The rate will depend on the relative proportions of the two substances."

Robert glared at him. "I may not have taken all knowledge to be my province, but I do know that much. What does your famous philosophy advise us to do?"

Francis gave him a sour look. His studies had yet to bear fruit of a practical nature. He surveyed the interior, hoping for something useful to appear. Nothing did. "We must escape before the windows go under. We'll never survive that flood. I doubt we can break through the roof, so these ridiculously small windows are our only hope."

Robert shot him a bitter look. "Then they will have to serve." He knelt on the bench facing sideways, grabbing at the window's edge as the coach rocked. More water splashed in on the other side.

"Careful!" Francis scolded. "Move gently. The more water inside, the faster we sink." He snatched off his hat and used it to bail out an inch or two. A futile gesture. Every movement caused the coach to rock, bringing in another splash. Now the icy water rose to his calves. He shivered. How long could they endure the cold?

Robert ignored him. He stuffed himself into the window up to his shoulders, wriggling vainly to squeeze through. "I'm stuck!" Panic raised his pitch.

Francis grabbed two fistfuls of his doublet and hauled him back in. "Take off your doublet." He started unhooking his too.

Robert bit his lip, scowling. "My shoulder," he whispered. A wet shirt would reveal his deformity to all the world, assuming they survived.

"Your life, Robert."

He shuddered and complied. This time he got most of his upper body out, then pulled back again. "I can't swim!"

"Bodies float, don't they?" Francis snapped. "You may have to abandon your purse."

"Yours is empty, I suppose."

Fear had not improved Robert's temperament. If only Francis had been pushed into the river with someone like Sir Walter Ralegh or Charles Blount. Both could doubtless swim like porpoises and tow the coach to safety with their teeth.

A voice shouted outside. "Hoi, Masters!" Something bumped against the front of the coach, making both men shriek. Their impromptu vessel turned slightly toward the bank.

Rescuers? Or Midley in a stolen boat, making sure they went under?

Francis struggled to untie his wet laces. He watched with amazement as Robert turned around on the bench and thrust his silk-stockinged legs out the window. He pushed himself along with his elbows until most of his lower half dangled outside.

Then he screamed. "Something's grabbing at me!"

"It's all right, my lord," another voice said. "Let us catch you." The Southwark accent was unmistakable.

"Wherrymen!" Francis nearly fainted with relief. Tears blurred his vision momentarily. He shivered as he finally wrestled out of his doublet and knelt on the bench. Feet first or head first?

"I'm stuck!" Robert cried again. His round hose had bunched up at the hips, blocking his progress.

Francis slid his feet back into the cold water. "What have you got in there?" He thrust a hand rudely into his cousin's hose and pulled out a thick wad of horsehair. Men stuffed their hose with such things to maintain that full melon shape. "God's bones, Robert, if I drown for this . . ."

"How was I to know a madman would push me into the river this morning?"

"If you'd done something about the corruption in the Court of Wards, this would never have happened."

"God's whiskers, Frank! Not now!"

He had a point. Francis dragged out another handful. Then he shouted, "Pull!" out the window of the door. Robert's body was drawn straight out, feet first. His hat fell off at the window's edge and his head dipped under the water, but only for a minute.

"Grab those legs!" "Haul, man!" "You got him!"

Francis waved a hand, but that wherry had already turned away. Would they leave him here to drown?

He sloshed through the rising water at the bottom of the coach to try the other window. He would dive out head first. His purse was empty, as it happened, and his long, unstuffed galligaskins would not impede his egress.

He couldn't swim either, but how hard could it be? Dogs did it with no training whatsoever. Even sheep could swim if necessary. He was a man and thus had a mind. He could choose to act like a beast when need demanded it.

He knelt on the bench and looked out. The wall of some great house rose above a strip of mud. The tide was going out. That explained why they kept moving downstream in spite of the rear wheels. The force of the outgoing tide must be stronger than the weight of the iron.

He scolded himself. Now was not the time for observation. He lowered his head and extended both arms out the window. Something pounded against the other side, pushing him closer to the bank. It also let in more water, which now rose to the bottom of the bench.

He couldn't wait for rescuers. They might not even know he was inside. "I'm coming out!" he shouted, hoping someone would hear him. Then he gathered himself, drew in a deep breath, and plunged into the river.

The cold drove precious air from his lungs. His hindquarters began to sink with the weight of his woolen clothes and leather shoes. He flailed his arms and legs, almost vertical in spite of the relentless pushing of the tide. He thought of the dogs and the sheep and tried to paddle with cupped hands.

It worked. His face broke free into the air. He gasped, then drew in a shuddering breath. Then he panted like the dog he strove to emulate, paddling his hands and feet for all he was worth to keep his head above water.

"Grab this, Master!" A long oar extended toward him. He gripped it with both hands and hung on as it was pulled toward a wherry. He squeezed his eyes shut against the water, not opening them until rough hands grabbed him under the armpits. The wherryman hauled him up to the gunwales, letting his upper body flop into the boat. Another hand gripped the seat of his slops and hauled his bottom half up and in.

Someone rolled him over. "You're safe now, Master."

"Thank you." Francis gazed at the homely face above him. He'd never seen a more beautiful sight. "And Robert?"

"The other lord? He's in another boat."

Francis exhaled the last of his fear and closed his eyes again. He made no attempt to rise. He doubted he had the strength. He would lie here until they took him wherever they wished. The wherryman would have to lift him out and lay him on the wharf. He would lie there until someone who knew him came along with a cart.

The wherryman resumed his seat in the bow. His oars splashed as the boat turned hard around. "We're taking you both to Dorchester Wharf. The lady's orders."

Trumpet. She must have been looking out the window. Francis smiled up at the cloudy sky. He was well and truly saved. He thought a prayer of thanks to his Creator. *Not done with me yet, my Lord.*

Then three new faces loomed into view — cheerful, pink-cheeked, young men's faces framed by lace-trimmed ruffs and velvet caps. *"Gaat het goed met je?"*

"Dat was spannend!"

Dutchmen. Visitors to the English capital, no doubt. Here to see the sights. They'd have a more exciting story to tell than they could ever have expected.

"Go away," Francis said in German, hoping they would understand it.

They laughed and patted his chest as if he were a great fish they'd landed and were eager to bring back to their inn.

Francis closed his eyes again. He could only hope that Robert had been rescued by a boat full of lawyers with cases in his court.

TWENTY-FIVE

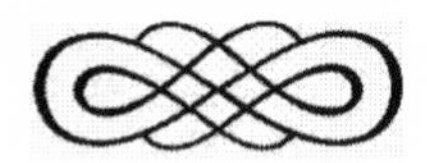

Tom pounded down the Strand, stretching his long legs where he could, twisting sideways through clots of people. He shouted, "Move! Make way!" as he ran, always keeping his eyes on that blur of blue and white ahead of him.

He could have caught Charles if he'd reached the street a minute earlier. The murdering knave had lingered at the top of Strand Lane to watch Sir Robert's costly gray mares trot fretfully down the road. They would soon find their way to Burghley House, which wasn't far.

Charles and Tom had clapped eyes on one another for one long moment, and then the race began. They were well-matched as opponents. Tom had the advantage in length of leg, but Charles was four years younger and had the lead. If his destination had been in doubt, Tom would have had no hope of catching him. But the man was most likely going back to the White Bear.

Where else could he go? He had no friends here.

The crowd grew thicker around the curve at Charing Cross. The best Tom could do was a fast walk, pushing people rudely out of his way and ignoring the curses they hurled at his back.

At last, they approached the sign of the White Bear. Tom lagged his quarry by half a dozen house fronts. He ducked into a doorway as Charles cast a glance over his shoulder before entering the inn. Tom tilted his hat brim down to shield his face in case someone he knew was sitting by the front windows. Then he ducked his head and strode briskly toward the door.

He crashed into the solid body of a man about his size in height and build. The man grabbed his shoulders.

"Beg pardon," Tom said.

"Watch where you're going, lad." The man had a West Country accent and a familiar voice.

Tom raised his head and looked into a pair of blue eyes exactly like his own, apart from the sprays of wrinkles around the corners. He reared back on one foot to take in the whole face — an oval face framed by blond curls and a ruddy beard, with a dimple in the left cheek.

"Dad?"

"Tom?" Captain Valentine Clarady's face broke into a broad grin. "My boy! I found you!"

"God's bones, Dad! You're alive!" Tears sprang into Tom's eyes. He let them fall, laughing and shaking his head. He wrapped his arms around his father's chest, sobbing and laughing. "You're alive. You're alive."

Valentine's arms circled Tom's body, hugging him tightly. "My boy, my boy." His voice sounded husky.

After a while, Tom sniffed and pulled back. "How? Where did you —"

"It's a long story." Valentine clapped his son on both shoulders as if testing to be sure he was real.

Tom could not take his eyes off that beloved face. More wrinkles, he judged, and as brown as old oak. He must have been at sea at least some of the past six years.

Then he remembered his mission. "I want to hear it. Every word. But right at this moment, we've a villain to catch. A murderer, Dad, who tried to put the noose around my neck. I chased him inside here, but he could go out a window once he's grabbed his stuff."

"What are we waiting for?" Valentine grinned.

Tom laughed for sheer joy, clasping his hands and raising his tear-filled eyes to heaven. His father was alive!

"He's fair," Tom said as they strode into the public room. "Round face, a few inches shorter than us. Wearing blue and white, though he might be changing clothes. Not five minutes ahead of me."

"I'll go up the front, Son. You find the back stairs. We'll search floor by floor."

They hugged again, then went their ways, each trusting the other to perform his part with diligence and skill. Tom cut through the kitchen, waving at the startled cooks, and found the narrow servants' stairs near the back door. He'd have to keep half an eye on these as he prowled the upper floors. Charles could use them to escape.

But where could he go? Travel cost money. He'd claimed utter poverty, but then he'd also claimed ignorance about that brandy. He could have a chest of silver coins under his bed, presently being poured into a leather pouch.

Tom walked on the balls of his feet, leather soles silent on the wood floor. He strained his ears for the sound of metal clinking or clothes rustling behind each door. At the back of the long building, he found one door not quite shut. He flung it open to find Charles sitting on the windowsill, one leg in and one leg out. He held a lumpy sack with the inside hand, doubtless filled with clothes.

Charles stared at him, mouth open, frozen on the sill.

Tom tilted his head back and shouted into the corridor. "Dad! I have him!" Then he took three quick strides across the room and caught Charles by the ruff. He dug in his hand to grip ruff, doublet, and shirt together and dragged his captive onto the floor. Charles kicked and turned. Tom ignored him. He pulled his knife from the scabbard at his back and set the blade under

Charles's ear. He lowered himself to one knee, supporting himself with a hand on Charles's back. The struggling stopped.

"You should thank me," Tom said, making conversation. "You can't jump out a window that way without breaking your ankle. You have to perch on the sill, turn full around, and then lower yourself as far you can by your hands. Then you let yourself drop, curling into a ball the moment your feet touch the ground. If you'd gone to university, you'd know that."

Charles's body tensed as if to make another attempt to get free. Tom put a little pressure on the knife, and the villain collapsed with a groan.

"My room was on the ground floor," he said. "But I was only there for a year. Leynham said it wasn't necessary and refused to cough up the fees."

"You could sue him for that if you weren't going to hang."

The captain burst into the room, taking in the situation with a proud smile. "Good work, Son."

"This is one of my jobs, as it happens."

"There's a story or two there, I reckon."

"More than a few." Tom drank in the sight of his long-lost father. He looked fit enough. He hadn't starved, wherever he'd been. "Were you in the Indies?" Charles kicked a little, so Tom pressed the knife a trifle harder. "Less of that now." The kicking stopped.

"Puerto Rico. But that's the end of the long story." Valentine pointed at Charles with his chin. "What do we do with this churl now that we have him?"

"Good question. I can't kneel like this much longer. I'm getting a cramp in my foot."

"Let's get him up." Valentine reached down to grab Charles under his arms. He hauled him to his feet in one mighty heave. There was nothing like the seafaring life to keep a man in trim. He studied the face before him with interest. "A murderer, you say?"

"I saw him try to drown Mr. Bacon and Sir Robert Cecil by rolling their coach into the river. Not half an hour ago."

Charles snarled at him. "You couldn't have seen anything. That lane was empty."

Tom caught his father's eyes, and they shared a rich chuckle.

Valentine said, "Not what you'd call a wily rascal, is he?" He tilted his head for Tom to take one arm while he gripped the other.

Charles pressed his lips together, too late. He looked from one Clarady to the other, turning his head from side to side as if doubting his own eyes.

Tom did the honors. "Allow me to introduce my father, Captain Valentine Clarady, presumed dead for the past six years and returned by some as-yet-unexplained miracle. Dad, this is Charles Midley, a fellow ward of the queen. You'll have heard about that from Mother, I imagine."

"I have, though I could scarce believe it. She's well and sends her love, by the way. I went home first." As was right and proper. And on the way, if he'd been sailing from the west.

"We're all well now." Tom looked around the small room. It held a rumpled bed, a backed stool, and a small table with a bowl and pitcher. Charles's clothes chest stood open, its contents scattered all around. A smaller chest lay open and empty on the bed. Tom had been right about the cache of coins. He saw no rope nor anything like it, and the bedposts were too short to be useful anyway.

"My room is bigger than this," Valentine said. "And I've a proper bed with curtains. Let's grab a few pairs of this fellow's stockings. They'll do for tying him up, as long as we don't leave him alone."

"We'll lash him to the mast and order some dinner. I'll send off a few notes while we're waiting for the food. I want the sheriff to come collect this whoreson knave. And I think I know where Mr. Bacon can be found."

They hustled their captive up the main staircase. They met a maid coming down. Valentine stopped her with a grin. "Look who I found."

She clapped her hands. "Your son! Mercy, Captain, he's the very spit of you."

"We'll take dinner in my room today, Jane. A full spread with two bottles of your best wine. We're hungry, and we have a lot to talk about." He cast a look at the scowling captive. "Just the two of us. This one will be fasting, the better to ponder his sins."

She turned to go. Tom laid a hand on her shoulder. "I'll need a writing desk straightaway."

He and his father stiff-walked Charles to a fine large chamber overlooking the busy street. This one held a large bed with four stout posts supporting a tester and red curtains. It offered a round table with three chairs, among other amenities.

Tom and his father wrestled Charles onto the bed with his back to a post and his legs outstretched. They pulled his arms behind him and bound them with stockings. Being knitted of fine yarn, they stretched into long ropes and would be impossible to break. Charles spluttered and complained until Tom threatened to stuff a dirty stocking in his mouth.

He glared down at his former friend. "I had some sympathy for you, Midley. I understand the rage and the frustration. God knows I do! But you used me, hiding behind me. All the while pretending to be my friend. I can't forgive you for that."

Valentine had been listening, his face growing darker with every word. "You know, we could've had a rougher time getting him under control. No one would think twice about a few knocks here and there." He curled a fist where Charles could see it.

Tom gave it some thought. It would feel good to pound Charles's smooth, round face, but only for a minute. It would feel better to hand him over to the sheriff and think about what awaited him in Newgate. "Not worth it."

Jane came in with a writing desk and set it on the table. Another wench followed her with a green bottle and two clay cups. Valentine gave them a bit of Clarady charm in thanks. They'd be well tipped later. He poured two cups of wine and handed one to Tom. He raised his in a toast. "To my beautiful, brilliant boy!"

"To my beloved father, home again, thanks be to God!" They drank, then Tom sat down and opened the desk. "Forgive me, but I have to get these notes off now. Someone must come collect this churl."

He also couldn't be certain Mr. Bacon and Sir Robert had survived. He had great confidence in Trumpet, but a coach wouldn't stay above water for long. With a strong tide and a tardy boatman, things could go wrong in a hurry.

He sat down and opened the desk, pulling out paper, inkpot, and quill. He used his knife to pare the quill into the shape he preferred, then dipped it in the ink. He addressed the first note to Sheriff Hanton, bidding him to hasten down to Westminster to arrest the man who had murdered the Court of Wards officials. He paused for a moment, composing a brief explanation in his head.

His father patted him on the shoulder, then went to sit on the edge of the bed to talk to Charles. "That's my boy." He tilted his head to point at Tom. "He works that quill like a true master of his craft. You can't see him, but it's a joy to watch."

Tom grinned down at his paper, wiping a tear from his eye with his knuckle.

"What's your story, boy? What name did Tom give you — Charles?"

"Charles Midley."

"What'd you do, then? My son calls you a murderer. Who'd you murder?"

Charles didn't answer.

Tom looked over his shoulder. "Two officials of the Court of Wards. They were demanding fat bribes on top of the exorbitant regular fees. I lost my temper a couple of times, and that churl took advantage of it."

"That's low." Valentine curled his lip at Charles. "Low and dirty. I suppose you think you're a witty one, keeping an eye out, acting in the nick. Like a rat on the prowl for that prize crumb of cheese. I'm not saying there aren't men who need killing. I can think of a French corsair whose life won't be worth a cut farthing when I catch up with him. But a man owns his deeds, or what is he? No better than that rat."

Charles spoke at last. No one could resist the pull of Captain Valentine for long. "You have no idea what they did to me and my mother."

"Why don't you tell me, then?"

Charles spat out his story. Tom, having heard it more than once, went back to his letter. He advised the sheriff to stop by Dorchester House and inquire after Sir Robert Cecil on his way down to Westminster. He folded the note, wrote the sheriff's name across the front, and set it aside. He'd need a candle to seal it.

Valentine said, "You were wrongly treated. I can see that. But execution isn't ours to deliver. If it were, the Spanish would be short a few grandees and there'd be no governor at the prison in San Juan."

Tom turned full around. "Is that where you've been all these years?"

"Most of 'em. That's the middle of the long story."

"Can't wait to hear it. I just have one more letter."

"Write, write. I'll give this cowardly cur something to chew on while he waits for the noose."

Tom took another moment to revel in the sight of his father's face, then turned around and pulled out a fresh sheet of paper.

Behind him, Valentine made good on his promise. "I doubt Newgate is any better than La Fortaleza. You'll want coin, or things will go bad for you. I had a ponderous great pearl, like the one my son's wearing. Brought that back from the farthest reaches of the Orient, I did. Bought me a clean room on the top floor and three meals a day for five years. 'Course, everything costs more in London, don't it? Your best hope is friends who care enough to stick around."

"Dorothy will take care of me," Charles said.

"Who's Dorothy?"

"A girl. A rich one. She loves me. She would never abandon me." Charles sounded so certain that Tom couldn't help but put another oar in.

"I wouldn't be so sure. That's a woman who takes care of herself first and foremost. I'm betrothed to her, Dad, as it happens."

"Without my consent? Never."

Tom snapped his fingers. "I hadn't reached that thought yet. But I'm free, aren't I? Your coming home puts me on the windy side. That contract was signed by my guardian, but since my father's alive, the whole wardship is void. Therefore I have no guardian, and that contract has no legal force."

Valentine grinned at Charles, pointing a thumb at Tom. "He's a barrister now. Did you know that? His mother and I are so proud." He shook his head at their captive, disgust written plain on his face. "You're not much younger than him, and look at you. Tied up like a goat on the foredeck waiting for the slaughter. You've done nothing with yourself, by your own account, but store up grudges and murder a couple of pasty clerks in the sneakiest way. You're a scurvy wretch is what you are. I wouldn't have you on my ship. Your big mistake was trying to throw the blame onto my son. Don't you know he's the wiliest intelligencer in England?"

Tom had to laugh. He set down his quill, walked to the bed, and kissed his father on the cheek. "That's down to you, Dad. I think about you every day. I ask myself, 'Is this what my father wanted? What would he think of it?'"

Valentine clutched his hand. "You're a grown man, Tom. Ready to choose your own path. I can see it in the way you hold yourself. You act like a man who knows who he is and where he's going in the world."

Did he? It didn't feel that way, especially not these past few weeks. But it must be in there somewhere, or his father wouldn't be able to see it.

Jane came in to spread a cloth on the table, shifting the writing instruments to each side as she smoothed it out. Tom asked her for a lit candle, and she left. He went back to the table.

The next note went to Trumpet, whom he addressed as Lady Dorchester in case anyone else happened to see it.

Did you get them? Are they hurt? I'm assuming they're safe until I hear otherwise. You'll never believe this, but my father is here. He's alive! I found him at the Bear, which is where we caught Charles. We're here now, about to have dinner. Not Charles, he's tied to the bed. I've written to the sheriff. I told him to stop by Dor. House on the way here. All is well. Better than well, if Mr. Bacon survived his dunking. My father is alive!

Thomas Clarady from the White Bear, Westminster, this 27th of November, 1594.

He folded it and wrote, *Lady Dorchester, Dorchester House, the Strand,* on the front.

"Lady Dorchester?" Valentine had ambled back to the table. "Stephen's mother?"

"His wife. Didn't Mother tell you? Stephen's the eighth earl now. We're friends again, on a new footing. Her Ladyship and I were talking in an upstairs parlor when we saw that knave roll the coach down the lane."

"Talking, were you?" Valentine's voice held a note of fatherly skepticism that sent Tom reeling back to the last time they'd last spoken. They'd been standing on the docks east of the bridge, waiting for a boat to take the captain down the river to his ship at Gravesend. Valentine had caught wind of Tom and Trumpet's special friendship and warned him to put an end to it.

The words still echoed in Tom's mind. *The nobility, they're not like you and me. Touch her at your peril. One whisper of scandal and all we've built for you goes crashing onto the rocks.*

They hadn't crashed yet, though they'd come close. "Talking, Dad. She was my hostess. I spent a week in her house under Stephen's protection, hiding from the sheriff." He told his father about the last two weeks, although he didn't explain his extraordinary fear of jail.

Valentine took a different lesson from the tale. "Lucky thing, finding the old earl up to his eyeballs in debt back then. Who could've known that match would 'scape you from hanging one day?"

"You always had a keen eye for a bargain."

Jane came in with a pair of candles. Charles twisted his head around to plead with her. "You must help me, Jane. These men are deranged. You know me. I've been here two months. Bring Alfred up from the tavern and a couple of grooms. Save me!"

Jane bit her lip as she studied the situation. A kindhearted lass, though none too quick. At last, she said, "It's true I've known you nigh on two months. And I've known the captain scarce two days. But I trust him, and I don't trust you, and not just because he gives me better tips. Besides, it's not my job to meddle in the affairs of our patrons." She set a hand on her hip and tilted up her round chin.

Tom used one of the candles to soften the yellow wax provided by the inn. He pressed the seal his sister had given him into the wax, leaving the impression of a tiny anchor with wavy lines to represent the sea. He drew a flower on the front to mark it for the delivery boy.

He handed the letters to the maidservant and started to reach for his purse when he had a better thought.

"That varlet has a purse full of silver, I'll wager. Search his pockets, will you, Dad?"

Valentine did as he asked, being none too gentle about it. He found a large leather pouch, which he emptied onto the table in a jangling of silver and copper coins. Tom picked out a big one and handed it to Jane. "This is for you." While she gasped her thanks, he found a few smaller ones and poured them into her other hand. "And these are to send these letters out with the fastest boys you can find. The plain one goes to the Guildhall in the city, but the one with the flower goes to Dorchester House on the Strand next to the palace. Make sure it gets there as quick as can be."

"Yes, sir, Mr. Clarady. I know just the boy." And off she went.

Tom clapped his hands together and rubbed them with satisfaction. This day had turned out to be the best day ever. "I'm hungry." He grinned at his father.

Valentine had been counting the coins back into the pouch. "He's got a good two pounds six here, not counting the farthings."

"What should we do with it?"

Valentine scratched the beard along his jaw. It was darker than Tom's and an inch longer, but otherwise so much the same. "No point in giving it back. They'll just take it away from him at the jail. We'll pay the inn first. He can treat me to my bed and board since he put us to the trouble of catching him. We'll spend the rest on a feast at that place you lawyers like once we get your Mr. Bacon back."

"Sounds good to me."

Jane returned with two young men bearing large trays of plates and covered bowls. The aroma of fried whitefish and spiced apples made Tom's stomach growl. He sat down and inspected each dish with his nose. "It could be an hour before the sheriff gets here. Plenty of time for a good meal and a long story."

He dished up whitefish, conger in souse, and green pottage. He filled their cups to the brim. They satisfied their first hunger, then Tom took a break, leaning back in his chair. "Last I heard, the *Susannah* blew up in the harbor at Dieppe with you aboard. How'd you get from there to Puerto Rico?"

"I went aboard to see that all was ready. Alone, thank God. The scurviest scoundrel on the seven seas threw a bag over my head and smuggled me onto his ship. Then he lit a long fuse to fire the gunpowder in my hold and slipped away through the smoke."

"Does this scoundrel have a name?"

Valentine nodded. "Jacques Le Bon, French corsair and long-standing thorn in my side." He proceeded to tell a wild tale of kidnapping and deceit.

Le Bon had a crafty scheme to take advantage of the confusion following the defeat of King Philip's armada back in 1588. News wouldn't reach Madrid for weeks, though they'd know who to blame when it came: Sir Francis Drake, England's greatest admiral. Philip would pay a fortune to any man who captured El Draco.

Le Bon had no intention of working that hard. Reasoning that one fair-haired Englishman looked much like another, he kidnapped his old rival Valentine Clarady and sold him at auction in Bilbao.

He'd fetched a steep price, Valentine reported with pride.

Tom laughed. "You look nothing like Drake."

Valentine spread his hands in a wide Spanish shrug. "They didn't know that."

Empty dishes were replaced with full ones. The second course included salmon baked with vinegar and onions. Roast tench and florentine custard rounded out the feast.

The tale continued. Valentine changed hands a time or two, then finally managed to smuggle himself onto a ship about to set sail. Unfortunately, he'd been misinformed. Instead of going east to France, this ship sailed west all the way to the New World.

The Spanish captain sold Valentine to the governor of Puerto Rico, assuring him he could sell the captive on to the next ill-informed grandee for a tidy profit. The governor tried for five years with no takers. By then, Francis Drake had returned to the New World to sack more Spanish ports. Captain Clarady had lost his value.

The servants returned with the sweet course and a letter from Dorchester House. Valentine filled two plates with gingered bread, sugared almonds, and blackberry tarts while Tom slit the seal and unfolded the note.

He held the half-open page under his nose the way he always did with letters from Trumpet. The scent often told him where she'd written it and what she'd been doing. Civet meant she'd been dressing for court. Rosemary said she'd been out in the garden. Milk and lavender spoke of the nursery. This one smelled of lemon and beeswax. She'd written it in the library.

He caught himself and startled a bit. Just a bit, but his father noticed and quirked his lips. Tom cleared his throat and read the note aloud.

"Mr. Bacon and Sir Robert are unharmed, if soaked through and boiling mad. Mr. Bacon can prove Midley is the killer with testimony from the northman, who speaks and writes Latin, as it turns out. His notes were drenched, but he can elicit the testimony again. The northman is most willing. He dislikes Charles and remembers you buying him a beer once for no reason. Sir Robert will light a fire under the sheriff's tail, never fear."

Tom turned half around. "Did you hear that, Charles? You shouldn't have been so stingy. If you'd bought the man a drink or two, he might not be so eager to see you dance the hempen jig." Tom gave his father a sheepish grin. "I should've thought to speak to the poor fellow in Latin. Further proof of how distracted I've been."

"My boy speaks Latin," Valentine said to no one. "That's the mark of an educated man. I've picked up a fair bit of Spanish over the years. Can't see it doing me any good, but you never know. Dame Fortune likes to have her fun, as they say."

Tom turned back to the table. He eyed the plate of dulcets before him, girding himself for another bout. He picked up a bit of gingered bread and asked his father, "How did you escape? That fort in San Juan is said to be unbreakable."

"Cards. I used to play with the governor every Saturday afternoon. In the end, he owed me so much money he had nothing left to bet but my freedom. I swabbed the decks of a Spanish supply ship all the way to Saint Jean de Luz, where friends cleaned me up and brought me the rest of the way home."

Tom shook his head in wonder. "Whoever said Dame Fortune has no sense of humor should have a look at your life. I'm glad you're alive and glad you're home. You couldn't have come at a better time. I could've caught this murdering knave without you, most like, but I'd have been obliged to marry a woman I don't love nor even trust." He tilted his head toward Charles. "The famous Dorothy, who claims to love that scurvy rat. We shall see if she does — but from a safe distance." He raised a cup. "Here's to freedom, for the both of us!"

Valentine echoed the words and drank deeply. Then he put down his cup and set his elbows on the table, folding his hands together. "So, me boyo. Tell me more about this Lady Dorchester."

TWENTY-SIX

3 January 1595, Gray's Inn Hall

Francis Bacon sat at the top of the darkened hall below the dais. He'd pushed his chair back toward the wall so he could watch both the performance — a masque of his own devising — and the audience.

He'd worried about the reception his masque would receive. A week ago, Gray's had hosted another Grand Night, inviting so many people the hall was filled to bursting. Noble guests thronged the dais until there was no room for the performers. Half the audience left in a huff. Those who remained were too disgruntled to enjoy the comedy that came next, written by a newcomer named Shakespeare and performed by the Lord Chamberlain's Men. The whole disastrous event had been dubbed the Night of Errors, a joke based on the title and thus a compliment of sorts for the author. Francis had thought the play rather clever, if one enjoyed physical foolery and endless punning.

Tonight, for a mercy, everything had gone smoothly. The hall was full, but not overly so. No outside players had been hired to complicate the program. Nearly the whole Privy Council had chosen to attend: Lord Burghley and Sir Robert, Lord Buckhurst, Lord Heneage, Lord Essex, Lord Howard, and Lord Keeper Puckering. Many had brought their wives. Many other lords and ladies adorned the festivities as well. The yellow light shining from sconces and hanging candle-branches reflected from their glossy silk garments and pricked bright sparks from the jewels on their hats and breasts.

Best of all, they loved his masque. They laughed and clapped in all the right places. Francis basked in their enjoyment, even while knowing their favor wouldn't last.

A year ago — no, two years — Francis would have been thrilled by the mere presence of these great lords and ladies. His cup would have overflowed at their approval of his work. He would have thought, *Ah, these are friends.* Connections, at least. Allies. They recognized his worth. They appreciated his contributions. They would help him rise when opportunities appeared. In those days, such opportunities were always just around the corner.

He had believed in them with all his heart. A position in government worthy of his merits and his father's name would come to him. He was young, if somewhat past the thirty-year mark. He could wait.

But thirty-three could no longer be considered young. He had spent the past year and a half being batted back and forth in a contest between Queen Elizabeth and Lord Essex. He should have known how it would end. He *had* known, if he were honest. But he could never have refused his lord's excited plan. Now he could neither win nor leave the game.

They'd worn him out, those mighty two. He'd used up favors, humbled himself, and raised a mountain of debt to maintain the appearance of a man worthy of a high position. He'd sent gifts to every legal-minded courtier with access to the queen. He'd brought himself and Anthony to the brink of ruin, and all for naught.

Tom may have been right in his stubborn refusal to take on debt to achieve his goals. He'd passed the bar by his own efforts. No one, not even Francis, had expected him to hold on so long. He'd had offers from lords like Ralegh and Robert Cecil to seek his fortune in their service. He'd turned them down, honoring his father's memory by staying the course.

He could never have guessed his father would come home, voiding the wardship and canceling that onerous marriage contract. Several days passed before Tom realized his father's return took him a step backward as well. Lady Russell and Captain Clarady had hammered out an agreement that would triple Tom's allowance while gradually returning control of the estate to the captain. Tom was reduced to a mere heir, not a landowner. Even so, Francis hoped for a bounty in the form of fifty or sixty pounds in thanks for the support he'd provided over the years.

Dorothy had attained her livery. She'd filed suit against her uncle in the Court of Requests the very next day. Through her lawyer, Philip Littlebury, she had obtained funds to lease a house in Chelsea, where she intended to live until she had bankrupted her uncle. Leynham had scurried back to Kent with his tail between his legs, no doubt to scour his house for something he could present in his defense.

Francis doubted he would succeed. Ah, well. The man had brought this trouble upon himself, as had those greedy officials in the Court of Wards. No lessons had been learned there, of course. Business would proceed as usual when Hilary term began.

Midley had been hanged on the fifteenth of December. The wheels of justice moved slowly, as a rule, but this time the defendant had attempted to drown the most indispensable man in the realm. Testimony from Sir Robert Cecil tended to speed things up. No evidence was considered, or asked for, in regard to the murders of

Richard Strunk and Ralph Bowcer, though their names were added to the list of Midley's crimes.

Strunk's book of bribes had sunk to the bottom of the Thames — Robert's copy anyway. He acted as if he'd never seen or even heard of it. Francis and Anthony agreed that no good could come from stirring that pot and buried their copies under their beds. Francis burned the record of Graysians who had been forced to pay blackmail.

After much discussion with worldly-wise Antonio Pérez, Francis had finally acknowledged that Robert had spoken the truth about his prospects with the queen. Her Majesty regarded him as a useful tool, but she didn't trust him. He had made a fatal error in placing conscience before loyalty. That, she could never forgive.

He would do it again — he would always put conscience first — and she knew it. That bridge to a position of influence had been burned.

He still had many skills. He had a deep knowledge of history and literature as well as fluency in several languages. He could write better than most. She wanted him nearby, ready to serve in the humble roles she granted him. She would not allow him to retire from the court to a scholarly life in Twickenham or Cambridge. He could not rise. He could not leave. For his one unavoidable sin, she had trapped him in a form of earthly limbo.

Francis let his gaze wander over the faces of the great ones nodding and smiling at his masque. He had learned something important through this long ordeal. He could not rely on those councilors, these cousins, or this queen. None of them would offer him the helping hand he needed. Nor could he achieve his lofty aims on his own.

For the first time in his life, he had no plan, no animating dream to draw him forward. He could feel the emptiness of that loss in his bones.

He sighed and sipped some of the delicious hollock they'd served that night. This too would pass. Time's wheel would turn. Most of the great ones here tonight would be gone by the century's end, taken by old age.

The tide would turn one day not too far off, bringing young James Stuart down from Scotland. Francis intended to be ready for him.

HISTORICAL NOTES

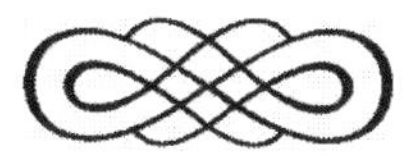

You can find maps of the places we go in this series at my website on a page called "Maps for the Francis Bacon mystery series:" www.annacastle.com/francis-bacon-series/maps-for-the-francis-bacon-series. Some are downloadable, and some are links to maps I don't have rights to, including a delightful interactive map of Elizabethan London.

First, I must thank John Lynch for giving me a few authentic bits of Yorkshire dialect for my lonely Northman. Only another author could grasp so quickly what I wanted: a few choice tidbits to tickle my reader's ears. Most of us don't remember the days when dialects of English could be impenetrable to those from far enough away, but in Bacon's day, it was very much a consideration. John publishes historical fiction under the name R. J. Lynch, including the lively, eighteenth-century James Blakiston series.

In what must be a first for this series, I made up everyone in this book except the regular cast:

Francis Bacon.
Anthony Bacon.
Sir Robert Cecil.
Lady Elizabeth Russell.
Robert Devereux, Earl of Essex.

The Court of Wards, however, was absolutely real, notoriously corrupt, and loathed by everyone. If anything, I understated its perfidy. I.d have . to write a multi-generational saga to fully tell that tale. There is one excellent non-fiction book to fill in the gaps, if you're interested: *The Queen's Wards: Wardship and Marriage under Elizabeth I* by Joel Hurstfeld. (1958, London: Longman's.) I highly recommend it. Your librarian can probably order it for you through interlibrary loan. It's the only scholarly book on this subject, which affected so many Tudor families. It's engagingly written and stuffed full of astounding anecdotes.

For example, did you know that the Earl of Southampton had to pay Lord Burghley five thousand pounds to escape a marriage to Burghley's granddaughter, Elizabeth Vere? We can imagine how much that rankled. It makes my wards seem almost lucky by comparison.

Indeed, it's well to remember, as we head into the tumultuous final years of Elizabeth's reign, that Burghley was Master of the Court of Wards for most of that reign. He appointed himself as guardian to the noblest young orphans. The earls of Oxford, Surrey, Rutland, Southampton, and Essex all fell under his care. The latter three grew up together, dining at the same table and being tutored in the same classroom as crookbacked little Robert Cecil. Those men knew each other intimately from childhood. Their rivalries, and their loyalties, were always more than political.

Francis must have visited that house too from time to time, while his father lived in York House across the street. That's another thing that can be hard to remember: how small the world was, in some ways.

ABOUT THE AUTHOR

Anna Castle holds an eclectic set of degrees: BA in the Classics, MS in Computer Science, and a Ph.D. in Linguistics. She has had a correspondingly eclectic series of careers: waitressing, software engineering, grammar-writing, a short stint as an associate professor, and managing a digital archive. Historical fiction combines her lifelong love of stories and learning. She physically resides in Austin, Texas, but mentally counts herself a queen of infinite space.

BOOKS BY ANNA CASTLE

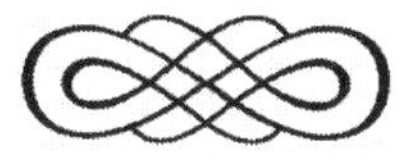

Keep up with all my books and short stories with my newsletter: www.annacastle.com

The Francis Bacon Series

Book 1, Murder by Misrule.

Francis Bacon must catch a killer to regain the queen's favor. He recruits Thomas Clarady to chase witnesses from Whitehall to the London streets. Everyone has something up his pinked and padded sleeve. Even Bacon is at a loss — and in danger — until he sees through the disguises of the season of Misrule.

Book 2, Death by Disputation.

Thomas Clarady is recruited to spy on the increasingly rebellious Puritans at Cambridge University. Francis Bacon is his spymaster; his tutor in both tradecraft and religious politics. Their commission gets off to a deadly start when Tom finds his chief informant hanging from the roof beams. Now he must catch a murderer as well as a seditioner. His first suspect is volatile poet Christopher Marlowe, who keeps turning up in the wrong places.

Dogged by unreliable assistants, chased by three lusty women, and harangued daily by the exacting Bacon, Tom risks his very soul to catch the villains and win his reward.

Book 3, The Widow's Guild.

London, 1588: Someone is turning Catholics into widows, taking advantage of armada fever to mask the crimes. Francis Bacon is charged with identifying the murderer by the Andromache Society, a widows' guild led by his formidable aunt. He must free his friends from the Tower, track an exotic poison, and untangle multiple crimes to determine if the motive is patriotism, greed, lunacy — or all three.

Book 4, Publish and Perish.

It's 1589 and England is embroiled in a furious pamphlet war between an impudent Puritan and London's wittiest poets. When two writers are murdered, Francis Bacon is tasked with ending the tumult once and for all. But can he and his assistants stop the strangler without stepping on any very important toes?

Book 5, Let Slip the Dogs

It's 1591, Midsummer at Richmond Palace, and love is in the air — along with the usual political courtships and covert alliances. Secret trysts, daring dalliances, and a pair of pedigreed hounds keep Francis Bacon and his gallant team busy while trying to catch one devilishly daring murderer.

Book 6, The Spymaster's Brother

Anthony Bacon is home from France. An invalid, his gouty legs never hinder his agile mind. He's built the most valuable intelligence service in Europe. Now the Bacon brothers are ready to offer it to the wealthiest patron.

Then Francis finds the body of a man who's been spreading dangerous rumors about Anthony. Clues point to his private secretary. Can they sort through the lies before disaster strikes?

Book 7, Now and Then Stab

London, 1593. An anonymous ballad calls for violence. The mayor offers 100 crowns for the author's name. Thomas Clarady wants that money and drags Francis Bacon in to help.

Then the authorities turn on two popular playmakers. One is tortured. Another is killed in a brawl. The official story seems plausible, but Tom doesn't buy it. He refuses stop digging, uncovering a plot best left buried.

Bacon and his team hazard their lives to find the truth. Whether justice can be obtained is another matter.

The Professor & Mrs. Moriarty Series

Book 1, Moriarty Meets His Match

Professor James Moriarty has one desire left in his shattered life: to stop the man who ruined him from harming anyone else. Then he meets amber-eyed Angelina and his world turns upside down. Stalked by the implacable Sherlock Holmes, he's tangled in a web of murder and deceit. He'll have to lose himself to save his life and win the woman he loves.

Book 2, Moriarty Takes His Medicine

Professor and Mrs. Moriarty help Sherlock Holmes investigate a case he can't pursue alone: a doctor who may be committing murders for hire, ridding husbands and sons of their fussy, wealthy wives and mothers. When Angelina defies James to enter the lion's den, he must abandon his scruples and race the clock to save her — and himself.

Book 3, Moriarty Brings Down the House

An old friend brings a strange problem to Professor and Mrs. Moriarty: either his theater is haunted or someone's trying to ruin him. The pranks grow deadlier, claiming the first victim; then someone sets Sherlock Holmes on their trail. The Moriartys must stop the deadly pranks threatening a West End Christmas play before someone they love is killed.

Book 4, Moriarty Lifts the Veil

Professor and Mrs. Moriarty each take on a small case to fill the time before their next play opens. They place a bet on who will finish first. James will find out if three old soldiers have been cheated of their discharge pay. Angelina must find a missing servant, presumed to have been poached. But as they start asking questions, things take a dark turn. They uncover corruption at the heart of a circle of Army officers. A man is murdered, a friend is blamed, and Sherlock Holmes is sent to catch him. The Moriartys must use all their courage and ingenuity to save their friend, stop the loathsome crimes, and put the killer behind bars.

The Cunning Woman Series

Book 1, The Case of the Spotted Tailof

Welcome to Ayreford in 1591, where cats can talk and fairies are real.

Jane Moone leaves her thriving practice as a cunning woman in London to return to Ayreford to care for her aging father Amias. She's scarcely settled in when her only client's husband is murdered. The tailor is found in his workshop covered in red spots with a bottle of tonic from Moone's apothecary. When her father is arrested, she joins a handsome barrister to figure out what really happened. He doesn't see the magical beings all around them, but Jane does. With help from a talking cat, a frog-like fairy, and a hedge witch, she puts the pieces together to free her father and put the real villain behind bars.

Book 2: The Case of the Tangled Maypole

It's May Day, a time of joy, but Jane Moone must investigate a sorrowful death. The gossiping daughter of local cunning man, Roger Quirk, is found strangled in a tangle of maypole ribbons. Suspects abound. Puritans wanted to stop the festivities. Quirk wanted to stop his daughter's mouth. Someone among his patients might have a secret worth killing to suppress. And the angry fairy who protects Quirk shadows Jane's every step. Jane has to peel back the glamors and risk her life to bring the killer to justice.

Book 3: The Case of the Miscast Curse

Jane Moone is hired to identify the witch who cursed a sheep. But her client has already decided who did it — the hedge witch who happens to be Jane's father's sweetheart. Could Dorcas do such a thing? Or is there another old witch begging at kitchen doors and flinging curses right and left. Some are harmless, others are truly dangerous.

Jane and her father, a powerful wizard, must peer into the heart of a near-fatal curse and find the wandering witch before an innocent dies.